LOVERS AT WAR

Also by Elizabeth Warne

Ragtime Girl
Wild Silk
An Impossible Dream
Kissing Cousins

LOVERS AT WAR

Elizabeth Warne

WEST LOTHIAN DISTRCT COUNCIL
DEPARTMENT OF LIBRARIES

HEADLINE

Copyright © 1994 Eileen Jackson

The right of Eileen Jackson to be identified as the Author of the Work has been asserted by her in accordance with the Copyright, Designs and Patents Act 1988.

First published in 1994 by
HEADLINE BOOK PUBLISHING

10 9 8 7 6 5 4 3 2 1

All rights reserved. No part of this publication may be reproduced, stored in a retrieval system or transmitted, in any form or by any means without the prior written permission of the publisher, nor be otherwise circulated in any form of binding or cover other than that in which it is published and without a similar condition being imposed on the subsequent purchaser.

All characters in this publication are fictitious and any resemblance to real persons, living or dead is purely coincidental.

British Library Cataloguing in Publication Data

Warne, Elizabeth
Lovers at War
I. Title
823.914 [F]

ISBN 0-7472-1034-9

Phototypeset by Intype, London
Printed and bound in Great Britain by
Mackays of Chatham PLC, Chatham, Kent

HEADLINE BOOK PUBLISHING
A division of Hodder Headline PLC
338 Euston Road,
London NW1 3BH

To the gallant citizens of Bristol who fought – and sometimes gave their lives – and won the battle of the Home Front during World War Two.

Chapter One

Visitors always sent Mrs Penrose into a state of deep anxiety, even when they were family. Especially when they were family, thought Sid, rubbing vigorously at a small brass bowl.

'Mind you do those bowls till you can see your face in them,' her mother called from the kitchen. 'Don't leave Brasso in the patterns.'

'Yes, Mum.' Sid continued to rub, though she never could see the point of seeing her face in a brass bowl when every room in the house boasted at least one looking-glass; the curves of the bowl distorted her features anyway.

This afternoon would witness the Saturday ritual.

Family would arrive to tea. Not all of them, which was just as well, thought Sid, contemplating the number of their relatives who lived in and around Bristol. The semi-detached villa on Warmley Hill wasn't large enough to take them, though it was astonishing how many managed to cram into the rooms when it was Mum's turn to do Christmas.

'What are you up to?' called Mum. 'Why do you take so long?'

The question was rhetorical. Sid always took too long when dusting because her mind was apt to stray to more interesting things. Today she was remembering the young window-cleaner who winked at her through the plate-glass windows of Madame Rita's hairdressing salon where she worked. Then memories of a far more worrying kind intruded. That scene in the salon . . .

'Sorry,' she said to her mother, her automatic reaction to a reprimand.

She finished cleaning the brass fire-irons and candlesticks, polishing the furniture and the floorboards surrounding the square of carpet with copious amounts of beeswax, and had a last look round. Everything gleamed. She took the dusters to the kitchen to be washed.

The same routine had to be gone through every Saturday morning, even if the best room hadn't been used at all through the week. It would never do for any of Mum's sisters to catch her out with a speck of dust. They were all married to shopkeepers who made good money, even in these days of depression and unemployment, and they prided themselves on their spotless homes. Mum was the eldest of Grandma Lacey's family, and insisted that the others visit her for Saturday tea rather than the other way about.

That afternoon, four of Mum's sisters arrived to gossip comfortably while their children played noisy games in the garden, having first been instructed not to go near the vegetables. This stricture was issued every Saturday, and always after they had gone Dad grumbled, swearing that one of the little devils had squashed something he had been cherishing. His vegetable-growing was really an indulgence, since he owned and ran a thriving greengrocer's shop.

Sid was detailed to serve tea. It had long been recognised that she, at seventeen, the eldest daughter and not given to going anywhere much, should be her mother's helpmeet. Father's too, if it came to that, she being the one who warmed his slippers and made sure his pipe was ready on the shelf by his tobacco jar along with a box of matches. He was entitled to relax after his week's work. Penrose the Greengrocer gave fair weight and always sold off bruised stuff more cheaply on Saturday nights, a concession deeply appreciated by those who were struggling with poverty. Little official assistance was given them, and there were still large numbers of families whose children were ill-clothed and poorly shod – or had no shoes at all – and who were, ultimate evil, underfed. Mr and Mrs Penrose were compassionate as far as their limited imaginations allowed, and they gave pennies to collections for the needy, though they couldn't resist a comment or two.

'Their mothers could feed them on bone broth. That wouldn't cost much. And mending their clothes wouldn't hurt them,' Mrs Penrose grumbled. 'They don't seem to care how they look.'

'The men could find work if they went far enough to look for it,' said Mr Penrose. He had never really recovered from the shock of the General Strike of 1926 and was thereafter suspicious of those he considered below him in class. Sid had been only seven at the time, but could still remember that the house had rung with his indignant protests.

Sid felt that their reasoning was flawed, but still she liked to see Mum bustling contentedly about her comfortable house and Dad, well fed, with his feet on the kitchen fender, shirt-sleeves rolled up, newspaper in his large, rough hands, smoke drifting from his pipe. She wished she could understand the way his mind worked. One of the uncles said he played his cards close to his chest; certainly she had never known him to express affection, though his attitude towards his family was benevolent, if distant. The only way she could express her love was to be of service to him: when she was little she had earned a penny a week polishing his ankle-high boots. That job had now devolved on Raymond, the only boy, and at eleven the youngest in the family. He didn't enjoy it, and sometimes his eldest sister helped him out.

Sid had once been labelled the tomboy of the family; though she couldn't remember this. After Raymond's birth she had been expected to help with the new baby, mostly by amusing her younger sisters Audrey and Irene. She had been only six years old, but could remember her pride in being depended upon.

'Sid!' called Mum from the best room, 'where's that hot water and the milk we asked for?'

'Perhaps she's had to milk a cow,' suggested Aunty Ella in her raucous voice. The others laughed immoderately. The joke was old and unfunny, but when the sisters got together they laughed a lot. There were four of them here today, five if you included Mum, though Aunties Joan and Bea left most of the talking to the others.

Sid carried the tray into the living room. 'Sorry,' she mumbled.

'Have you fed the kiddies yet?' demanded Mum.

'Not yet.'

'I suppose you were day-dreaming again,' said Ella. The sisters appeared to find this hilarious and thus encouraged, Ella went on, 'What do you dream about, Sid? A nice chap, I suppose.'

Sid resisted the temptation to answer back. She placed the tray carefully on the glass-topped coffee table, Mum's latest acquisition.

'Go on, tell us,' urged Aunty Joan in not unkindly tones, 'what do you dream about?'

'She spends so much time on her own I shouldn't have thought she had any dreams left,' said Aunty Maud.

There was more laughter, though Mum looked displeased. She saw her sister's comments as criticism of herself. Sid reacted stonily. If she gave way to her feelings and told them to shut up and leave her alone she would never hear the last of it. And Dad wouldn't like it. He would gaze at her, looking surprised and melancholy. She hated that look, and she would certainly receive it if he learned of the trouble she was in at work.

She checked to see that there were enough iced cakes on the orange and white plate supported by a silver stem, then slid from the room. The kitchen walls were thin, and she could hear every word the sisters said, except when they lowered their voices to discuss some extra juicy piece of gossip.

'She doesn't say much,' she heard Ella say. 'What does she do with her spare time? Seventeen and she's like a forty-year-old.' Ella had a waspish tongue, generated by the air of disapproval with which she was sometimes viewed, because once she had deviated and gone to walk in Staple Hill main road one Sunday night and met her future husband. No one had anything against Jack except the fact that he refused to live in Kingswood and Ella had settled in Staple Hill and had to get a Bence's bus over to Kingswood every day. The family car was idle while her husband was in the shop, but none of the sisters had ever driven a car; none of them had even considered the possibility.

'Remember the days when we walked up and down Regent Street on a Sunday night pretending we never noticed the boys?' Maud asked.

'That seems a long time ago,' sighed Ella. 'Nineteen-twenty was the first time I clicked with a boy. I was just fifteen and thought I was the cat's pyjamas in my new dress. Our mum ran it up on her treadle. It was ever so pretty.'

'She's been a good mum,' murmured the others.

Ella was still uncharacteristically dreamy. 'I had a cream straw hat with a pink and white bow and the dress was pink and white stripes and showed my ankles.'

'Gave you the dazzles to look at it,' said Maud.

'Her ankles or the stripes?' asked Bea.

Ignoring them, perhaps not hearing, Ella went on. 'Really pretty it was, with a wide white collar.' She giggled. 'Underneath I had my first broderie-anglaise bodice and artificial silk bloomers with elastic and lace below the knees.'

The sisters shrieked with mirth.

Joan said, 'I remember trying to cut a pair of mine down when the fashion for skirts was up over the knees; the silk shot into a thousand runs. Mum was furious. She said I should have run stitches round the legs before I used the scissors.'

'Those were happy days,' Bea said. 'Innocent days. A kiss and a cuddle was all we allowed our boyfriends, even when we were close to being married. I wonder what the girls get up to now?'

Mum, who was the only sister to have children old enough to go out alone in the evenings, took this as more personal criticism, and said sharply, 'My girls don't get up to anything, I'll thank you to know.'

Bea hastened to placate her sister. 'Of course not, my love, I know they've been brought up too well. But some girls . . .'

Sid could almost see the three dots at the end of her aunt's sentence. All the sisters devoured the inexpensive women's magazines and enjoyed the stories of heroines virtuous until ruined by callous men, and thoroughly subscribed to their ultimate punishment. Years ago, unknown to Mum, Sid had read some herself, her eyes bulging at the hinted awfulness of the fate of some of the characters. She hadn't understood anything really, except that having a baby without a husband was the absolute, supreme awfulness. She'd no idea as to why girls gave birth at all, leave alone in so reluctant and ruinous a way. Even now she had only a sketchy notion of sex.

At the age of thirteen, she had discovered the public library and begun borrowing books and revelling in more sophisticated fiction, though nothing had enlarged her knowledge of bodily functions.

Mum thought so much reading was a waste of time. 'You'll wear your eyes out,' she grumbled, 'then you'll have to wear glasses and you'll never get a husband.' She would sigh despairingly.

'I don't think our Sid would know what to do with a boy,' said Mum to her sisters. She sounded quite mournful, though Sid was sure that if she took to going out at nights she would be missed round the house. There were plenty of small tasks to perform in the evenings: mending for instance, though, 'She's that cack-handed she can hardly hold a needle,' Mum often complained.

This was true. Sid was happier helping Dad in the long, narrow garden.

'It's funny how she's so different from the girls,' said Maud.

'The girls' were Audrey and Irene, the pretty ones.

'Sure she's our Eric's?' Ella said.

'Ella!' exclaimed Mum, 'what a thing to say!' but she knew her sister wasn't serious and she laughed with the others.

'Well, she's not like anyone I've seen in our family,' said Maud. 'A beanpole with a face like the back end of a bus.'

'It's not that bad,' protested Mum, without conviction.

Sid resented her aunt's denigrating statement. She knew she wasn't good-looking, but that window-cleaner seemed to like her looks. Of course, she couldn't be sure if his smiles and occasional winks were significant and, in any case, a window-cleaner would not be considered a good catch for a greengrocer's daughter. On the other hand, thought Sid, they might be glad to know she could attract anyone in trousers.

Maud said: 'She reminds me of that sister of Mum's who died quite young. She's on that early photo.'

'I remember,' said Joan. 'She does look like her. What was her name?'

It seemed no one could remember, and the great-aunt with no looks who had had a short term of existence was relegated once more to oblivion.

'Has anyone heard from Jess lately?' asked Bea. Sid listened avidly. The subject of Aunty Jess was raised most weeks and fascinated her. Jess had escaped from the maternal web and married a man from the other side of Bristol, a Clifton man with a good gown shop. She might as well be on the other side of the country as far as the sisters and their mother were concerned. They seldom shopped in town and then only in Castle Street and Wine Street. Jess had become practically a foreigner.

Sid sat in the kitchen, enjoying the emptiness for a moment before she called the children in. She watched them through the window for a few minutes as they played and shrieked, healthy kids with rosy faces, dressed in warm clothes and strong shoes. When she called them they burst through the back door with the energy of an express train and automatically Sid reached for a cloth to wipe their noses. Spring hadn't quite arrived, and the air was chilly, and when it was chilly the children got runny noses. Sid accepted this as a fact, just as she accepted the fact that her fourteen-year-old sisters, Audrey and Irene, had pretty names to match their pretty faces and she had acquired a name to match her plain face. Sidonia, she was really called. Mum had seen it on a tombstone somewhere, but as her first child had grown up it had become clear she didn't suit its air of rarity and romanticism, so everyone called her Sid now. Dad had begun it when she was quite young. She had been standing on a stool, leaning perilously over the fire, peering at herself in the mirror above the mantelpiece when he had growled, 'Stop staring at yourself. You've got no looks to speak of and you're as bony as a boy.'

Dad's word was believed implicitly, so if he said she had no looks it must be true. Audrey and Irene had been born within eleven months of each other (a fact which had caused some sly amusement in the family) when Sid was three. Both girls were fair-haired, white-skinned, with pretty mouths and bright blue eyes. Their figures were nicely rounded with breasts as developed at fourteen as Sid's at seventeen. They were an acceptable height for a girl, too, five feet three inches; not like Sid, who had reached five feet seven and was still growing.

If she stood straight Mum would sigh and mutter something about 'beanpoles'. If she tried to hide her height she was grumbled at for being round-shouldered. As if her sisters hadn't blessings enough, their hair was naturally wavy and curly, while Sid's was darkish brown and nearly straight. Her skin was olive, almost sallow, and her mouth wide, while her eyes seemed to have no true colour at all, looking pale green one day, pale blue the next, and sometimes a kind of brown. Her nose was nothing to write home about either. An ugly duckling, that's what she was, with no possibility of turning into a swan. At fourteen she had been sent to work for Madame Rita, and had spent three years sweeping up hair-cuttings, handing pins and curlers to the qualified assistants and their apprentices, making the tea and washing the towels. Her own hair was apt to get greasy, and was held back by a ribbon to keep it well out of sight. When she had been working for Madame Rita for a few months, her employer, getting quite desperate as she saw the child she had employed growing into a thin, unattractive female who was no advertisement for the salon, had persuaded her to have her hair Marcel-waved, but the rigid waves had made her face look even more bony. Then Madame Rita had permed it, and the frizzy, tangled curls which rioted over her head had been a nightmare to them both until they grew out. It was decided to forget the subject of Sid's hair, and once more she wore it pinned well back. However, she was good-natured, and it gave her real pleasure to watch the local women being beautified by the fashionable Marcel waves and little sausage curls; she was fascinated by those who entered curtained cubicles as brunettes or grey-heads and emerged as blondes, the most desired colour these days. Mutton dressed as lamb, Mum called them. Dyeing your hair was the sin of vanity. Sid knew that the result was achieved by peroxide and eye-watering ammonia, because she was the one who stood patiently handing the chemicals to the seniors. She always listened avidly to the instructions given the two apprentices, and had learned the theory of hairdressing if not the practice.

'When Marcel-waving, place the groove of the curling tongs underneath the hair,' said Madame Rita, who was actually Mrs Edith Shelton 'If you get it the wrong way round you'll get crimping and the client will be furious. The hair must be curled layer by layer until the final wave is deep enough to hold a sixpence. That's perfection, and that's what I want in my establishment – perfection.'

The clients thought they were lucky to have Madame Rita's salon, where even a manicurist came twice a week to tend to the richer clients. They were sure she could have attracted the rich in Park Street or Queen Street, but she had an ailing husband and an elderly mother who lived a few minutes walk away in Charlton Road and she liked to be near them through the day.

The children were shouting at Sid and tugging her skirt. At any minute Mum would come bustling out, annoyed by the racket.

'Come on, our Sid,' shouted Aunty Joan's eldest boy, 'we want our cakes.'

'Sorry.' Sid reached for the big cake tin and dispensed fairy cakes with different coloured icing. The children always quarrelled over them, though they all tasted the same because the colours were simply that, just colours, not flavours. After snatching at the cakes they raced outside, and Sid sat down again with a cup of tea, then jumped up as she heard her name called from the living room.

'Come in here,' said Mum. Sid obeyed reluctantly. She knew that tone of voice. 'Your aunties want to know if there's been any news about Mrs Wade's girl.'

Sid hated it when they pumped her for gossip heard during her work. Mrs Wade was a client whose daughter had been discovered to be pregnant and sent away somewhere. It was odd how the clients talked, sometimes to each other as if the assistants didn't exist or had no ears; sometimes to the girls themselves, apparently assuming that what they heard was treated with a confidentiality equal to a priest's.

'She's gone away,' she said.

'It's true then, is it?' Maud lowered her voice. 'She's expecting?'

'She may be.'

'May be! Either you are expecting or you aren't. Where's she gone?'

'I don't know.'

'You never know anything,' complained Maud.

'More like she won't tell anything,' said Mum. 'She's so secretive.'

Ella said, 'I knew that fellow she's been walking out with would let her down. He's no good and she's a hussy, so she deserves what she's got.' She glared at Sid. 'You're a deep one. It's always the deepest ones that are worst.'

'What's that supposed to mean?' demanded Mum, her face reddening.

Sid hated it when they fell into one of their skirmishes. 'She could be expecting, I suppose,' she said in an effort to placate them.

Then Mum looked cross. 'Answer your aunties properly, can't you?' She looked despairingly at the others. 'You see what I have to put up with? She *never* tells me anything.'

'I do, Mum.'

'Don't argue with your mother,' said Maud. She had a way of looking a person up and down and making them feel guilty of something.

'Sorry.'

'You're always sorry,' snapped Mum.

'Are the girls at work?' asked Joan, anxious to avoid a dispute. It was a rhetorical question. All knew that Audrey and Irene were apprenticed to a large drapery shop in St George and worked on Saturdays.

'They won't be home till later tonight. They're going to have tea with a friend,' Mum said, her tone making it quite clear that Irene and Audrey had her approval. They had friends. Respectable friends. In the plural. Sid had one, Angie, a girl she had gone to school with whose mother had never married her father, though the whole of Kingswood knew who he was reputed to be and that he had a respectable wife and several children.

'And I suppose Raymond's out playing football,' said Joan.

'He is,' agreed Mum. 'It's a match for his school,' she added proudly, 'and Eric's gone with him.'

'What? Who's minding the shop!'

'Eric got old George in.'

'George used to have a barrow in Old Market, didn't he?' said Ella.

Mum frowned at her acerbic tone. 'He's good with the customers. You'd never know he'd been on a barrow.'

'He's helped out before, hasn't he?' said Joan.

'Yes, and he's trustworthy.'

'But the Rovers are playing at home!' said Ella. 'If Eric can take time off, why didn't he go there?'

'Raymond wanted his Dad to see if he's improving.'

'What a good father he is,' said Bea. 'Not many would give up so much to watch a boys' match. I suppose Eric will be taking him into the business in a couple of years.'

Mum said carefully, 'He may, he may not. As you know, he got a scholarship to the grammar school.' Mrs Penrose tried not to sound proud.

'So did Sid,' reminded Maud. 'But you sent her to the secondary school and she left there early.'

'Boys are different,' said Mum.

There were murmurs of agreement. Boys had to earn a living all their lives. Girls got married.

'His headmistress says he's very clever,' said Mum. 'He might even go to university one day.'

Her sisters stared at her. This was a case of getting above herself if ever they'd heard one.

'He'd have to be brilliant to do that,' said Bea, in a tone which expressed her doubt.

'He's clever enough,' said Mum, 'and we can afford to keep him idle.'

'Is he staying on at school to be idle?' asked Bea.

'It was just an expression,' said Mum, keeping her annoyance in check. 'I meant he won't be earning. Of course, he'll be studying.'

'Studying what?' asked Ella.

'He's very fond of sums,' said Mum.

'Sums?' said Ella. 'Then he'd be good in the shop with his father.'

'Well, nothing's settled,' said Mum.

'Will he want to come into the business after all that education?' asked Bea.

'I don't know. We'll have to wait and see.' Mum was getting flustered.

'He'll be like a fish out of water among all those snobby gentlemen's sons,' said Ella. Sometimes, talking to Ella was like being pierced repeatedly by a pin.

'My son's a perfect gentleman!' said Mum hotly. 'He opens doors for me and stands up for a lady when we go in a bus or tram!'

'You know what I mean,' said Ella. 'You'll have to buy uniform, cricket bats, pay for all sorts of things, even books, I shouldn't wonder.'

'We can afford it,' snapped Mum. It seemed as if the tea party was heading irrevocably for one of the uncomfortable spats which occurred from time to time, after which the sisters sometimes divided into factions. It had been known for half the family not to speak to the other half for a couple of weeks.

'Empty the slop-basin, Sid,' commanded Mum frostily.

Sid, who hated the complications caused by rows, deliberately spilt some of the slops over the tablecloth.

'Clumsy!' cried Mum. 'We'll have to get the cloth off and soak it in cold water. Help me move the tea things.'

Argument forgotten, her general instruction was quickly obeyed by her sisters, and Sid rolled up the cloth to take to the kitchen.

'What have you got to say to your mother?' demanded Maud.

'Sorry,' mumbled Sid.

'Take the teapot out and refill it and fetch in those biscuits,' said Mum.

As she left the room, Ella said, 'She's a sulky one. I can't think where she gets it from. You're certainly not like that, Sarah, and our Mum's always cheerful.'

Sid, pleased that she had averted a quarrel, swilled the tablecloth beneath the cold-water tap and put it into a basin to soak. Then she added a fresh spoonful of tea to the pot, poured boiling water over it and stirred, emptied what was left in the slop-basin, and returned to the best room with a tray holding the tea and a plate of biscuits.

'Shortbread biscuits,' said Joan, 'my favourite. Did you make them, Sid? You're lucky to have a daughter who can cook, Sarah. My Lily's twelve, and last time she tried to make cakes they were as heavy as lead and didn't taste much better. In the end I chucked them out to the hens and they weren't too fussy about them, either.'

There was a burst of laughter and Joan said, 'I thought Mum would be here today.'

Sometimes Grandma Lacey, a widow, graced their tea party, leaving the only unmarried sister, Mattie, in charge of her draper's shop.

'She couldn't manage it. She's had a cold.'

'She's much better,' said Bea, 'but she's afraid of going out in the cold.'

The women's eyes went automatically to the mantelpiece where photographs crowded, charting the progress of Grandma Lacey and her daughters. They fascinated Sid. It seemed that Gran had always been plump. She had been quite an advanced Victorian woman, taking to photography with an unusual enthusiasm; each of eight frames displayed a baby cradled in her arms, wrapped in a large white shawl. Grandpa, a stout, proud figure in a waistcoat with a watch-chain across it stood behind her chair, looking down at his latest production with the satisfaction of a man whose virility could never be questioned. All the babies were as plump as butter, and looked so similar that when Sid had asked Mum which of the babies had died young, Mum couldn't pick it out. Other photographs showed them taken at various stages, standing in rows, still plump, dressed in white frocks and hats, with long white socks and shiny black shoes. Their wedding pictures proved that they had all begun married life with ample flesh which had clung and expanded. They were still very well rounded, while Grandma was definitely fat.

It was taken for granted that the sisters would visit their mother at least once during the day. Sid was quite fond of Grandma Lacey, though her grandmother had never taken to her. Sid was fascinated by her assumption of authority in all matters. She was like a spider who had spun a web sticky enough to hold her offspring close and, through them, her sons-in-law. Her only son had died young, and she seemed to consider it the duty of her daughters' husbands to assuage some of her loss by being available and useful. Jess's husband, who remained independently aloof, was held in scant favour, though reluctantly respected for his superior style of business and his high income.

The following morning, Eric Penrose called to his daughter, 'Come on, Sid, let's see how the garden is today.'

She followed her father. He wore old, thick trousers, and heavy black gardening boots. She had on an outgrown mac from which her narrow wrists stuck out, and wellington boots that kept none of the chill away from her feet. Dad struck the soil with his spade. 'Still too hard to plant. I wish spring would arrive. Come on, we'll do some pricking out.'

The greenhouse was kept comparatively warm by a smelly paraffin stove which threw diamond-shaped lights on to the green painted roof panels and made Sid feel sick if she stayed there too long. The place was almost too small for them both at the same time, but she treasured these moments with her father. As they carefully dug out the tiny seedlings and potted them, her devotion swelled and blossomed and she wished with all her heart that she had the words to tell him how she felt.

Audrey and Irene sometimes called him 'Pop'. They used to sprawl on his knees, their chubby arms round his neck. Dad called them 'pusscats' and slipped them pennies for sweets. They no longer sprawled on him, but he often slipped them a threepenny bit which secretly they spent on Woolworth's make-up. Since fashion dictated only a slightly curvaceous shape, they dieted; Mum had stopped trying to make them eat more when they explained that the store refused to employ anyone in the fashion department whom the buyer considered overweight.

Sid was half nervous of her father's casual nearness in the greenhouse, half revelling in her ability to help him. When they had finished they went down the garden to the rhubarb patch, and Dad lifted one of the pottery drainpipes he used for forcing.

'Look at that,' he said happily, 'lovely! All young and pink. It'll cook in minutes. That'll make your Mum's eyes shine and we'll have rhubarb tart for our dinner.'

'Ow be, Eric?' said a neighbour, walking along the narrow bumpy lane which led to the backs of the terraced houses.

'How be, Bill?' answered Dad.

It was the stock question and the stock answer; no one ever assumed that a full explanation of the state of mind or health of either man was of interest. Men lived such different lives from women, mused Sid. Her mother and aunts echoed the behaviour of the salon customers as they gossiped and laughed, tore characters apart, envied, sympathised, loathed. No one was immune, no woman's bodily ailment too private to discuss, no childbed too horrific to dissect. Men kept themselves aloof. She supposed they must talk in the pub and the trams on the way to the football ground, but they were uncommunicative in the family setting.

'Dreaming again,' said Dad, 'I've been trying to hand you this rhubarb for the last five minutes.'

An exaggeration, but Sid apologised.

'Yes, well,' said Dad, 'It's all right saying sorry all the time, but it would be better if you paid attention to what was happening round you. I wonder you don't harm Madame Rita's customers. Hairdressing places can be dangerous.'

Dad laughed to show it was a bit of a joke, but his words sent a shiver over Sid. She had been trying to put it out of her mind, but on Friday an apprentice and a trained assistant had been away with heavy colds. Madame Rita, hard pushed, was setting a client's hair for an important occasion, and Sid had been given the task of using the curling tongs on a lady who simply wanted her well-permed hair groomed for the evening.

'After all this time you should have learnt enough to manage a simple job like that, muttered Madame Rita. 'You've heard my instructions so often you ought to know exactly what to do. Just remember, the most important thing is that you don't burn Mrs Keevil. You ought to be able to do it right after all these years.'

Mrs Keevil was known as 'a tartar', fussing the girls when they worked, and grumbling if she was kept waiting for a second. Sid had approached her with a smile of confidence she didn't feel. Mrs Keevil had frowned at the substitution, but she had been in a hurry, and had submitted to Sid's hands. Almost inevitably, as Sid had dreamed of being a fully-fledged hairdresser, she had burnt the tip of the client's ear. Madame Rita had practically had to grovel as she applied a soothing balm and gave her personal attention to the rest of the hair-do – without charge. As if that wasn't bad enough, the client on whom Madame Rita had been working had become thoroughly incensed at the delay, and Madame Rita had had to lower her price for her too.

After they had left, Madame Rita had torn into Sid. 'How can you be so stupid? I might have expected it from a fourteen-year-old apprentice, but you're – how old now? – my God, seventeen – and I can't trust you to do the simplest thing. I can't see you ever being a proper hairdresser.'

Sid's face had reddened to a beetroot shade as she writhed beneath Madame Rita's words, while the other girls pretended not to hear. Sid knew they would tease her next week.

Saturday had been Sid's weekend off. She had offered to work to replace the sick apprentice, promising to give all her care and devotion to the task, but had been angrily refused.

'I can do without your kind of help,' snapped Madame Rita. As Sid turned away, ashamed, she thought her employer had muttered, 'For good.'

She wondered what would happen if she were dismissed? No one in the family, in the entire history of the family, as far as she knew, had ever been sacked. It would be a disgrace; presumably she wouldn't be given a reference. Dad couldn't give her work even if he wanted to. His only full-time employee was a boy who packed up orders and delivered them on a bicycle with a huge basket at the front. She could do that, she supposed, but then the boy would be unjustly out of a job, and anyway, who ever heard of a young woman on a delivery bike? Her uncles similarly employed boys, while retired friends filled the breach if extra help was needed. Their wives occasionally stepped in, but it was accepted that no respectable married woman above a certain class ever went out to work on a permanent basis. Their lives were circumscribed. In their youth they attended school, obtained small, unimportant jobs, and concentrated on acquiring a husband, running a home and giving birth.

Sid had decided that such a mapped-out future was unlikely to be hers. Without looks, grace or charm, what would become of her? She would probably end up like some of the withered, nervous spinsters one saw behind small shop counters, or, more likely, struggling on inadequate wages as cleaners. It wasn't as if the idea of an early marriage, home and babies held any appeal for her; she had always dreamed of doing something different and exciting, but she wondered if she was abnormal. She hoped not. Certainly the flirtatious window-cleaner gave her a thrill. She didn't find him particularly attractive, but even if a girl wasn't eager to tie herself down, she liked to be asked. If she was sacked she would lose touch with him! Last week he had gone a little further and offered her a bar of chocolate. She had been too embarrassed to accept it, but she thought he might try again. Maybe, given time, he would ask her out. Roy Hendy was younger than her and certainly no oil painting with his strong features and unruly hair, but he was male.

After Sunday lunch, Dad brought the car to the front door. Raymond had cleaned the exterior, man's work, and Mum the interior, woman's work, and it was shining bright and ready for the obligatory Sunday afternoon run. The whole family got into the car. The younger members were a little squashed in the back, but that didn't stop Mum from enjoying the envious stares of their next-door neighbours who couldn't afford a car. She watched them as Mr Jowett and the eldest boy climbed on the three-wheeler motor-cycle and Mrs Jowett and her two small daughters got into the sidecar, a manoeuvre impossible to perform with distinction. Mum had once caught a glimpse of knee-length pink knickers which had filled her with a satisfied horror. She always stepped on the running board of the car, seated herself and swung both legs into place firmly clamped together. As the years passed and she had grown plumper, this manoeuvre had become more difficult, and she had even suggested that they might consider buying a bigger car than their Ford 'Y' saloon.

Dad answered. 'That won't happen for a long while yet. It wasn't all that easy to save for this one, and we've only had it a year. I'd have to go into debt to get a bigger one.'

Raymond had said, 'Some people buy things on hire purchase.'

His parents were indignant.

'I can't think where you got the idea that we would ever want something we couldn't afford to pay for,' Mum had snapped. 'We've never been in debt and never will be. We always pay the rents of the house and shop at the right time. And we've got some put by for emergencies, haven't we, Dad?'

'Yes,' agreed Dad, deciding that everything necessary had been said by his wife.

Raymond had subsided, abashed.

Today, however, Mum managed to enter the Ford perfectly and nodded graciously to Mrs Jowett who gave a small wave. Dad took a familiar road to Pucklechurch, and then drove through Mangotsfield, Downend and Staple Hill, where they passed Aunty Ella's house. Dad always drove carefully, very near the centre of the road, an irritation to young men and girls in faster cars as they zoomed their way about, car hoods let down. The young men wore caps firmly planted on their Brylcreemed heads, the girls sported colourful berets, their bright chiffon scarves streaming back in the wind. Dad was impervious to hooting horns and cries of annoyance, though Raymond, Sid and the girls curled up in embarrassment.

'One day I'll be in a car like that,' murmured Audrey.

'So will I,' agreed Irene.

'Bet I'll be there before you,' said Audrey.

'You won't, I'm older than you.'

This reminder reduced Audrey to speechless fury. The girls looked alike and were of a similar height, and were often mistaken by strangers for twins. Irene tried to be assertive, but ended by deferring to her younger sister. Sid thought it was as if Irene had left some of her strength of will inside Mum's womb, which had been so quickly occupied by her sister. Audrey had absorbed Irene's lost attributes, acquiring the same beauty, but aggression enough for two.

Dad stopped the car outside Grandma Lacey's house. 'We've been beaten to it, as usual,' said Dad, 'there's Ella and Joan's cars.'

All the families' material possessions were referred to as if owned by the womenfolk, a tribute to Grandma who reigned in matriarchal splendour.

'Jack and Gordon are a bit mean with their petrol,' said Mum in tones of deep satisfaction, firmly attributing failures to the men. 'We always take longer drives than them.'

'What about the others?' asked Raymond mischievously. 'Do they take longer drives than us?'

'No,' snapped Mum, 'they set off later. My dishes are always washed and put away before theirs.'

The front entrance to Grandma Lacey's thriving draper's shop was guarded at night and on Sundays by a locked gate. Dad rang the outside bell. The door was opened by Ella.

'How's Mum?' asked Mrs Penrose.

'Much better,' said Ella. 'Our Joan's here.'

'I can see that for myself,' said Sarah, glancing back at her sisters' cars.

Sid held her breath. The sisters often became belligerent when they were with Grandma Lacey, each one competing for the attention and approval of their mother, as if they were still children. Sid had often wondered what their husbands thought of this slavery to their mother-in-law's wants, but she had never heard Dad complain, and presumably the others didn't either. Of course, there was William Venner, Aunty Jess's husband. It was claimed that he deliberately kept her away from the family gatherings. 'Toffee-nosed' was what they called him, though Sid liked him. Jess was nice, too, but it was true she seldom visited her mother and sisters.

She sniffed deeply as she walked through the shop. She could almost taste the familiar scents of new cloth and furniture polish, sizing in the pillow-slips, mothballs among the blankets. The drawn window-blinds made it dark, but she part-saw, part-visualised the brown linoleum, the shining oak counter, the dozens of drawers containing everything from stiffening material, corset steels, pins and large rolls of elastic to artificial silk flowers and decorative ribbons.

Grandma Lacey was dressed in her Sunday best, a heavy, black shiny dress, her abundant grey hair pulled back in a smooth bun and skewered with a long, pearl-headed pin. On her ample bosom was a cameo brooch which moved up and down with her breathing, like a boat on a sea swell, Sid always thought. She was a handsome woman who had never used make-up, and frowned on those who did, even in these modern times. All she ever did to improve her looks was put a dab of rice flour on a shiny nose. Sid could dimly remember her grandfather, though there were popular stories in the family of Grandma's intense grief at his loss, whispers which told of her hysteria and her loudly expressed desire to follow him to his grave. Sid found this fascinating, if incredible. She couldn't imagine Grandma Lacey flinging herself about in an access of grief or wanting to die. She was cared for devotedly by Aunt Mattie, who worked in the shop, cleaned the house, shared the cooking and, as far as anyone knew, had no boyfriend. It was assumed now that she was unlikely ever to attract one. It was an arrangement which suited them all; Mattie too, Sid supposed. She was in the kitchen preparing tea, and Sid went out to see if she could help.

'Yes, please,' said Mattie. 'Lay up the trolley with plates and things. I've made sandwiches and cakes.' As Mattie made sandwiches and cakes every Sunday, this caused Sid no surprise. What always did surprise her when she saw her youngest aunt was that no man came courting her. Of course she was quite old, over thirty in fact, but she had been a beauty, and was still daintily pretty, with a cloud of fair hair only tinged with silver.

The other family members arrived, and the level of noise rose in Grandma's parlour. The children were supplied with food and ordered outside to play in the paved yard bounded by high walls.

Sid wheeled in the tea-trolley and placed it before Grandma. 'I've had a nasty few days,' she was saying. 'The doctor called it a cold, but he didn't know how I suffered. Men! They never understand women, even doctors. I had pains everywhere, but they've gone now.'

'What do you think it was?' asked Gordon.

Joan gave him an angry glance. 'What a thing to ask a lady!'

'It's all right as it happens,' said Grandma. 'It was rheumatism. I've got to expect it at my age. I'm probably not long for this world anyway.'

There was the chorus of protests she expected and accepted complacently; Sid wondered what she would say if someone agreed with her. Not that she believed the statement about her being not long for this world any more than anyone else, including Grandma, who sat firmly in her armchair, her knees slightly apart, her back straight, her hands deft as she handed out teacups. She looked as solid as Kingswood clock tower, and as enduring.

After tea, Sid helped Mattie wash up. The men drifted to the small best room where Ella's husband, Douglas, sat at the piano and began to bash out a medley of popular tunes. He played rather badly, and Sid could picture him, his thick fingers plonking on the keys, a cigarette dangling from his lower lip, his eyes half closed against drifting smoke. She wondered if he fancied himself as a night-club entertainer. They assumed just such a pose in films.

She realised that Mattie had been speaking and said, 'Sorry, I was miles away.'

Mattie didn't respond with a reproach as the others would. 'I know, love. What were you dreaming of?'

'Nothing much.'

'I wouldn't laugh at you, you know.'

Sid did know. Mattie treated her as an adult.

'How old are you now?' she asked Sid.

'Seventeen, going on eighteen.'

'That can be a lovely age,' sighed Mattie.

'Was it lovely for you?'

'Some of it.' Mattie became brisk as she poured the water away and refilled the bowl to swill out the tea-towels. 'Do you have a boyfriend yet?'

'Not really.'

'Is that a yes or a no?' asked Mattie with a smile.

'There's a chap who quite likes me. I think.'

'You're not sure?'

'No.'

'You'll have to make encouraging noises.'

'I wouldn't know how.'

'Smile at him, speak to him if the opportunity arises. Who is he?'

The question startled Sid and she blurted out, 'Only the window-cleaner at work.'

'No occupation is demeaning to an honest man, and window-cleaning can be a lucrative occupation if it's done well.'

'He does it well,' said Sid eagerly. 'The windows shine and reflect like a still pond when he's finished.'

'Have you ever told him so?'

'No, how could I? I mean, it sounds so daft.'

'Not to a window-cleaner,' said Mattie firmly, 'especially one who admires you. Next Sunday I expect to hear that you've established friendly relations.'

'Don't count on it.' Sid hung the last cup on a hook.

Mattie took the tea-towel from her and plunged it into the soapy water. 'I most certainly shall.'

'You don't understand.'

'I understand broken hopes all too well,' said Mattie, so quick and quietly that Sid wasn't sure she'd heard the words correctly, but when she asked for a repetition, Mattie shook her head. 'If you like the fellow and believe he likes you, make an effort. Men can be as shy as girls, you know.'

'Can they?' This was an entirely new concept.

'Of course. But how can you be expected to know about the behaviour of young men when you've lived your whole life enclosed in this family? It's like an octopus. I believe its tentacles are provided with strong suckers which never let go.'

Sid remembered something about Mattie. 'You went to the grammar school, didn't you?'

'Yes, not for long. I had hoped . . . but there, it isn't any use to look back.'

'Did you want to go on with your education?'

'Yes, but I knew I couldn't.'

'I knew they'd never let me go to a grammar school.'

Mattie sighed again. 'No. It's such a pity.'

'Why didn't you stay on?'

Mattie hung the tea-towels over a clothes-horse. 'I'll hang them outside in the morning.' No respectable woman would hang out washing on a Sunday. 'The family always thought your grandpa was indulgent in allowing me to go to the grammar school. Then he began ailing, and both of them needed my help so I had to take time off. He died soon after, and any dream I had of returning to school was gone.'

'How old were you?'

'Nearly fifteen. I've been here ever since.'

'Here. All those years. What a terrible shame. You might have met some nice man if . . .' Sid stopped, red with shame. How could she hurt Mattie's feelings like that?

Mattie seated herself in a kitchen chair and motioned Sid to the opposite one. 'I've been wondering for quite a while whether I should have a talk with you. This isn't really the time or place, but I can't bear to watch what they're doing to you.'

'What . . .'

'Hush now, and let me speak before we're interrupted. I did meet a nice young man. He proposed but I felt I had to turn him down. I was so sure that your grandmother couldn't do without me. I believe now I was wrong. Mum was a very strong woman – still is – and anyway she could have afforded outside help. I want to be sure you don't make the same mistake. All your life you've been called an ugly duckling, but you're not. You could make yourself attractive. I'm surprised that your employer hasn't seen the possibilities.'

'She did try doing my hair. It was awful both times.'

'Was that the time you appeared with iron waves followed by frizzed-up curls?'

'Yes. Fancy remembering. That was ages ago. What do you think I should do?' Then Sid remembered the events of last Friday. 'I have an awful feeling...' She got no further before the children came racketing into the kitchen demanding more food. After that it was time to leave. Mattie followed her up the gloomy passage leading to the shop. 'We'll have a longer talk another time, Sid.'

Sid nodded.

Chapter Two

It had rained heavily in the night, and when Sid arrived at the salon she found Roy Hendy busy on the windows, cleaning the muddy water splashed up by passing cars. Madame Rita, the perfectionist, always engaged him for extra work when she thought it necessary. An apprentice looked round when Sid entered. 'Hurry up! You know Madame Rita likes us here early, especially you.'

Sid felt a flash of anger that a younger girl should be so bossy, though she didn't make the mistake of assuming that her presence was missed because of her importance. She was expected to clean the salon thoroughly before it opened, even when she had cleaned it last thing at night. In fact, Madame Rita was as pernickety as Mum. She saw that on Saturday it had received only a sketchy wipe over from the apprentice, and she hurried to get dusters and mop. They would open in half an hour at nine on the dot.

Madame Rita walked out of her office. 'I expected you ten minutes ago, Miss Penrose.'

'Sorry,' said Sid automatically.

'If a salon is dirty, clients won't patronise it,' Madame Rita said. 'And why should they? A clean establishment is what I want and what I intend to have.'

Sid washed and polished until everything sparkled. When she glanced at the windows, Roy Hendy was watching her, his hair sticking up in spikes, his cheeky smile lighting up his face. He even winked. It gave Sid a nice, warm feeling.

In spite of the incident with the curling tongs, Madame Rita was behaving exactly as she always did on a Monday morning. Sid began to feel more confident, her nerves gradually easing. Roy folded his ladders and stacked them on top of his hand-barrow, waited for his payment, then touched his cap and left. Sid was sorry to see him go. The first clients arrived. Madame Rita was the only hairdresser for miles around who opened on a Monday morning, which was why the assistants were given time off on Saturdays.

Sid worked diligently until there was a lull and Madame Rita said, 'Come into my office, Miss Penrose, I have something I wish to say to you.'

The other girls looked at Sid, excitement in their eyes. It wasn't that they enjoyed seeing someone in trouble, not exactly, but anything that relieved the grind of work and gave them a new topic for gossip was welcome.

Sid followed her employer into the cubby-hole she called her office.

'I think you know what I'm about to say, Miss Penrose.'

Sid couldn't answer for the sudden dryness in her throat.

'It's no good adopting a sullen attitude . . .'

'I'm not,' gasped Sid, 'honestly . . .'

'How long have you worked here? Over three years? Well, you can't remain any longer without a *proper* position. I had hoped that you could acquire the skills needed by an expert of the art of coiffure, but I can see no possibility of it. That dreadful affair of last Saturday!' She placed a hand over her heart. 'I still haven't recovered. I have no alternative but to let you go.'

'Let me go?'

'To release you. To allow you to look for a position which suits your talents better.'

'But I'm happy here, Madam Rita. I don't mind if I have to keep doing the cleaning work and helping the girls. I'm good at that.'

'So you should be by now! No, it won't do. The job is unsuitable for someone of your age. I shall take on a junior.'

'You'll get someone straight from school,' burst out Sid, 'and won't need to pay her as much. Not that I get a big wage!' She wished instantly that she'd kept a still tongue. She had made her position worse, if that were possible.

Madame Rita frowned. 'What impertinence! What kind of wage would you expect to receive? The tasks you perform can be done by a child. I cannot imagine now why I have kept you so long.'

'I'm sorry, I'm dreadfully sorry. I didn't mean to be impertinent, but I must have a job. Please reconsider your decision, Madame Rita, I'll do anything . . .'

'I'm sorry, Miss Penrose, I have engaged someone—'

'Already? Before you sacked me?'

' —who will begin tomorrow. A junior apprentice whose mother has been asking for a place for her daughter. In future I shall not consider employing someone simply for odd jobs—' As Sid tried to protest further she held up her hand for silence ' —and if I ever change my mind I shall engage a fourteen- or fifteen-year-old who will be better fitted for the more mundane tasks around my salon.'

As Sid stood red-faced and finally silenced, Madame Rita thought what an unprepossessing girl she was. Tall, gawky, slightly round-shouldered, no idea how to make the best of herself. She handed her an envelope. 'In here is a week's wage. I am not obliged to give it to you after what you did. You should have been sacked on the spot. I have also included a reference, though in all honesty I couldn't find a lot to say in your favour. If you want my advice, Miss Penrose, you will look for a place as a domestic. I believe I've heard you say you help a lot at home, so it will suit you better.'

Sid fetched her hat and coat. She wanted to slink out through the back door, but forced herself to walk through the salon which was full again. The girls looked at her then away quickly, suddenly embarrassed by her sombre face.

Sid said as boldly as she could, 'It's goodbye then, but I'll see you from time to time. I might even,' she added in a defiant burst, 'come here to get my hair done.'

She knew no one believed her. Outside, she walked fast for a few moments, then stopped. Where could she go? Home was unthinkable. Mum would have a fit when she told her what had happened. She must find a job, but didn't know how. Mum had taken her to Madame Rita when she left school. She knew there was a labour exchange somewhere in Kingswood, and a passer-by told her its address, but before she had gone many steps she was hailed by a loud voice.

Turning, she confronted Mrs Keevil, who grimaced and touched a gloved finger to the tip of her ear. 'It's still painful. My husband said I should sue for damages.'

Sid went cold. If that happened, would it be possible for Madame Rita to pass on such a claim to her parents? She wanted to walk on, but felt mesmerised by horror. 'I hope you won't,' she said.

'You shouldn't have been allowed to touch the tongs.'

'I know, but it won't ever happen again. I've been sacked.'

Mrs Keevil looked pleased. 'And a good thing too.'

Sid started to walk away on shaking legs, but was brought back by Mrs Keevil who said, 'I suppose you'll need another place.'

She turned. 'I'm on my way to look for one.'

'How about working for me?'

'What?'

'I want a parlourmaid. You're tall enough and skinny enough to fit the uniform. My last maid died – she was elderly.'

'A parlourmaid? For you?'

'You want work, don't you? I need a maid.'

'But I know nothing about the job of parlourmaid.'

'You could learn. It's only housework. Even you can do that. I've seen you sweeping up in the salon.'

Sid felt a flash of anger. All her life people had denigrated her, ridiculed her. She swallowed angry words. 'I dare say I could,' she said, her need for a job outweighing any other consideration. 'I was quick at school.'

'Were you, indeed?' Mrs Keevil sounded disbelieving. 'Domestic crafts, I suppose?'

'Not only that. Writing and arithmetic and things like that.'

'Much good it's done you so far.'

'You're very kind, but I don't think I want to be a maid. I'd much prefer to be a shop assistant.'

'You've already proved you're not much good at dealing with the public.'

'A shop would be different.'

'I see. Well, I suppose I'll just have to see my solicitor. In fact, I'll go now while the burn is still quite bad. I visited my doctor this morning and he was shocked.'

Sid stared at her. She was always over-dressed, wore too much make-up, and her heels were so high they almost tipped her forward.

She was unkind and vulgar and she had the power to drag her into a courtroom and demand money. The idea was unthinkable. It would devastate Mum and Dad. 'If I come to work for you will you forget about the burn?'

'I can't forget it. Not for a long time. It throbbed so dreadfully last night my husband wanted to call the doctor out there and then. I shall always have a scar, but if you were under my roof, working for me . . .' Mrs Keevil allowed her words to dwindle.

'I didn't know it was such a bad injury.'

'Oh, didn't you? Well, it was and it was all your fault.'

'If I work for you could I live at home?'

'Certainly not. You'd share a room with Cook.' She waited for a reply, then said, 'I can't stand here all day. Will you take the position or not?'

It was a job and better than going home to tell her family about her disgrace. 'All right, I will.'

'Aren't you going to thank me?' asked Mrs Keevil sharply.

'Thank you.'

'Perhaps I'm doing the wrong thing. Perhaps it would be better for me to visit my solicitor as I intended to do.'

'No, please don't do that. I'm just a bit shocked. I didn't expect the sack and I certainly didn't know I'd be offered a job by you. Not after what I did.'

'So you have some shame, after all.' Mrs Keevil glanced at her watch. It had a gold wristband encrusted with diamonds. She handed Sid a card. 'This is my address. Go to it and show the card to Cook who will instruct you in your duties.'

'What about collecting my things?'

'You can fetch them from home later.'

She walked away without a backward glance, and Sid stood in the street, looking down at the piece of white pasteboard embellished with Mrs Keevil's name and address in fancy calligraphy.

The front door was opened by a fat, bad-tempered looking woman in a chintz dress and a white apron, down which she had recently spilt something. She snapped, 'Yes. What can I do for you?'

Sid held out the card and said, 'I've come to be the parlourmaid.'

The woman looked her up and down. 'Are you experienced?'

'I help a lot at home.'

The woman sighed. 'I see. Well, you're better than nothing. I can't keep answering the door in the middle of work. When you rang the bell I tried to hurry and tipped a bowl of eggs and cream down my front. All wasted, and I'll have to do a bit of fiddling or her ladyship would stop it out of my wages as soon as look at me, except she's afraid I'd leave, and good cooks can always get a job, but she'll make a huge fuss. Mean as dirt, she is. Well, come in, do, don't stand there gawping all day.'

Sid followed the cook to the basement which was paved with large, flat stones and displayed nothing in the way of comfort except a rag rug and a rather battered rocking-chair near a small range. Sid, miserable at the general air of unfriendliness, had been on the point of saying she couldn't possibly stay, but the homely rocking-chair reminded her that if she didn't she would have to face the prospect of explaining to her parents she'd been sacked.

'There's a uniform up in the attic room. You'll share the room with me. Two prints for morning and two black dresses for afternoon and evening. You'd normally have to supply your own, but the last maid died. She don't seem to have had any relations, so all her stuff's still here.'

'I'll have to wear a dead person's clothes?'

'She was a nice woman and they've all been washed and ironed. It's not unusual to pass things on.'

'Do we have to work all day and the evening as well?'

'We get some time off, but the hours are long.' Cook had begun to beat a fresh bowl of eggs and cream but stopped. 'You said you help at home. Have you ever been a maid?'

'No. I'm sorry. I was in a hairdresser's.'

'Is that all? Lord! That woman! I suppose she expects me to train you as well as everything else.'

'I'm sorry.'

'You should be. And don't keep apologising,' she added confusingly.

'Are there any other servants?'

'No fear. It's you and me, my girl, and there's a terrible lot to be done. Ma'am, as she likes to be called, like the queen, entertains a lot, and everything's got to be just so. She'll grumble if a fork's not straight on the table.'

'Can I run and tell Mum what's happened? I go home for dinner and it's nearly time. She'll worry.'

'Make it quick then. I could do with your help. She's got a party on tonight. And here we call it lunch, not dinner.'

'You're ten minutes before your usual time. Why are you home early?' demanded Mum. 'You're not ill, are you?'

'No. Mum, I'm ever so sorry but Madame Rita . . . Well, last Friday some of the girls were away ill and she let me use the curling tongs and I did something really silly. I burnt a lady's ear and Madame Rita sacked me.'

Mum sat down heavily. 'You did what? Oh, I don't know why I should be surprised. How could you be so clumsy? Trust you to mess up a chance like that. Heaven knows why you're so cack-handed. I don't suppose she gave you a reference?'

'Yes, though probably not much of one.'

'Where is it?'

Sid handed her mother the unsealed envelope. Mum read the words and handed it to Sid who read: 'Miss Penrose is honest and hard-working.'

'That's all!' Sid cried angrily. 'After all the years I worked there?'

'You can hardly blame her. I don't know how you'll get another job.'

'I've already got one.'

Sid was quite pleased to see that she had taken a good deal of the wind from Mum's sails. 'Where?'

'With Mrs Keevil. She's the one I burnt.'

Mum was astonished. 'You've been offered a job by the woman you burnt? She must be very forgiving. What's the job?'

'Parlourmaid.'

'What! I won't have you going out as a servant. We must get you something better. Perhaps an office job would suit you. At least you couldn't burn someone.'

'If I don't go to her she may get cross and make trouble over the burn.'

'What kind of trouble?'

'I'm not sure. She mentioned her solicitor. She was very angry.'

'Her solicitor! It would be in all the newspapers! And you never said a thing about it all weekend.'

'I thought it had blown over.'

'I can't think what your aunties will say when they hear that you've gone out as a domestic. And as for your Grandma Lacey... No one in our family has been reduced to that. Still, I suppose they won't be surprised. They know you're not much good at anything.'

Sid asked, 'Will you miss me?'

'What? I suppose so. You'll have to come round on your time off and give me a hand.'

Sid gathered up her few possessions and packed them in one of the holiday cases.

This time she took notice of the exterior of her new mistress's house. The garden was suffering from the effects of a cold wind, but everything was planted in orderly rows. There was a small circle of lawn on either side of the path and, in the exact centre of each, a well-pruned rose-bush. The woodwork of the house was painted bottle green, and the brass door-knocker gleamed. A future job for her, she supposed. Cook let her in. 'She's back,' she whispered. 'She wants to see you. In there.' She pointed to a door and disappeared down the stairs.

'There you are,' said Mrs Keevil. 'Cook told me where you'd gone. I suppose your mother was pleased you were coming here. There aren't many women who'd give a job to someone who'd injured them. What did she say?'

'She's pleased I've got work,' said Sid, somewhat mendaciously.

Mrs Keevil sniffed. 'Is that all? Take your case downstairs and ask Cook to show you where to change into your uniform. I'm holding a dinner party for some very important people tonight. Later, Cook will give you a list of your duties.'

Cook was grilling fish for Mrs Keevil's lunch. 'We'll have something ourselves in a minute. Go on beating that butter and sugar. You can do that, can't you?

'Yes, I like cooking.'

'That'll be useful just as long as you remember that I'm the cook

24

here. Hang your hat and coat in the corner cupboard for now. She wants castle puddings for tonight. She would. It means fussing with ten little dishes. That's right, keep beating. I can't put the flour and baking powder in yet. After lunch you can prepare vegetables. They're over there on the draining-board. I'll serve the fish. She'll be cross if you go up in your ordinary clothes. There's fruit for dessert. Then we'll eat and I'll show you where our room is so you can change. She expects the trolley to be laid up for tea by three o'clock, though no one ever visits until four – she makes rules and expects everyone to abide by them – and there's all the dishes to wash, some from breakfast. I haven't had time. Fancy having eight people for dinner in a house this size tonight. Eight! Her husband's an assistant bank manager and she's got ambitions for him. His boss is one of the guests. He's retiring next year and she wants his job for her husband.'

'He's got an important position, hasn't he?'

'Not bad I suppose,' said the cook grudgingly. She put four pieces of toast under the grill. 'I'll say this for her: the house has got all the modern conveniences. She probably likes to boast of them to her friends.' She turned the toast over, ladled butter on to it, and added a pile of grated cheese. The rich mix bubbled, wafting a delicious aroma into the kitchen.

After lunch, Cook led the way into the hall and up the stairs. She whispered, 'She's got ears like a lynx, so be careful. When I was younger I worked in a real gentlemen's house, and dinner parties could mean dozens, but there was an enormous kitchen and a huge staff to get through the work. Even then, we had an awful lot to do.' She stopped for breath and sighed. 'They were good days, but they're past for me. I never got to be head cook. I left when I was twenty-five to get married. Me and my Andy were happy, though we never had kids. Wanted them, but nothing happened. When he died I was nearly fifty. He was ill a long time and I didn't have much money left. There's not so much work in gentlemen's houses nowadays. There isn't the money. Lots of them have only half a dozen servants.'

She paused again on a half landing, panting. 'There's no back stairway here, the house isn't big enough. It riles her to have to let us use the same stairs as her. We're forbidden to go to our room if there's guests, and we have to use the outside lavatory. I don't mind that. She's had proper plumbing put in and it's convenient, though its cold in winter.'

They had begun climbing again, and her speech was punctuated by gasps for air. They reached the first landing. 'Four bedrooms here which you'll have to clean in the mornings as well as the bathroom and everything else.'

'Does anyone else live here? Do they have any children?'

'Don't make me laugh. Having a baby might spoil her figure. Life's not fair. There's me and my husband wanted kids and couldn't, while she ... You'll have to keep downstairs clean as well, though Ma'am occasionally picks up a duster and feather mop herself. Of course, in a real gent's house you'd have proper set tasks.'

'She said you'd give me a list of my duties.'

'I will that. A long list. You'll be general dogsbody, working from half-past six till half-past eight, later if there's guests, an hour and a half off about two o'clock. No time to do anything much for yourself.' Cook pushed open the door which led to a flight of uncarpeted stairs, at the top of which were two more doors. She climbed the steeper stairs, now really fighting for breath. 'These stairs are cruel. I don't come up here more than I've got to. That's the lumber room and this is our room.'

Sid was unexpectedly pleased with her future bedroom, even though it would be shared with a stranger.

Cook said, 'It's a better room than some I've known. Of course, she didn't do it to make us happy. She wanted a new bedroom suite and what she wants she gets. She could have sold this stuff but she thinks that's beneath her. She likes her friends to think she's got money to spare. She boasted for months about giving her servants new furniture. Of course it wasn't new really. Is it better that you've got at home?'

'Not better, but just as good.'

'Are your parents well off, then?'

'I don't know. No one ever grumbles about money.'

'What does your father do?'

'He's Penrose the greengrocer. Perhaps you've heard of him.'

Cooked looked at her with new respect. 'Heard of him? I certainly have. I get all our stuff from there. You can trust him to give good weight and not hide bruised fruit at the bottom of the bag.'

Sid was immensely pleased. 'My dad's a good man.'

'That he is. Now change into a black dress and apron for afternoon and I'll go down and make us a nice cup of tea. Bring the frilled cap with you and I'll show you how to wear it.'

The clothes were, as Cook had said, clean and crisp with starch; they fitted her quite well. She tied a frilly apron round her waist and took one of the caps downstairs.

'Sit down,' said Cook. 'I can't reach your head properly if you stand. My goodness, but you're a beanpole and no mistake. Taller than the last one. You fix the cap with hairpins. I'll lend you some of mine for now. There, you look nice. Just like a real parlourmaid.'

'Aren't I a real parlourmaid?'

'No. You're what's known as a house parlourmaid, but *she* won't tell you that. It's a double job. Come on, let's have a cup of tea and a slice of cake.'

The tea was hot and strong and the cake delicious. Sid said so and Cook smiled. 'One of my finest Madeiras, though I say it as shouldn't.'

'Won't *she* be cross at our eating it?' asked Sid, falling at once into the disrespectful way of alluding to her employer.

'We've got to eat, same as every other body. She dare not grumble too much. She's afraid I might leave and you can't get girls into the kitchen when they can get better paid jobs in factories *and* regular hours. I'm not the best, I've seen *them* cook in my time, but I'm good and I'm all she's got. I always make two of everything. One for them and one for us. After all, there's two of them and two of us, so why not?'

Sid couldn't think of an answer to such a piece of logic. 'What's your name?' she asked. 'Or do I just call you Cook?'

'I'm Mrs Dingle. What's your first name?'

'Sid.'

'What?'

'It's short for Sidonia.'

'That doesn't sound like a name for a Christian.'

'I think it must be all right because Mum saw it on a tombstone.'

'Well, I never heard the like before.'

'I looked it up once in a book of names in the library. It's given to girls born about the date of the Feast of the Winding Sheet, but I don't know what that means.'

'Neither do I. Sidonia! Good gracious! Well, she won't call you that and she won't call you Sid either.

'She knows I'm called Sid from being in the hairdresser's.'

'She still won't have it. Can't you think of a more ordinary name?'

'What kind of ordinary name?'

'Well, like Mollie or Jenny or something?'

'Would Sarah do? It's my mum's name and my middle name.'

'I reckon so.'

That evening Sid was kept busy, hurrying up and down the basement steps with loaded trays, serving food to the guests. She concentrated so hard on not dropping anything and trying to remember all Mrs Dingle's instructions that Mrs Keevil had to speak more than once to gain her attention. She smiled apologetically at her guests. 'A new girl. I shall begin her training tomorrow.' She spoke as if Sid weren't there, exactly as the clients at Madame Rita's.

So did the guests. 'Do you have much servant trouble?' asked one.

'No,' answered Mrs Keevil. 'My last maid stayed until she died. We gave her a decent funeral.'

When Sid relayed this to Mrs Dingle she snorted. 'Gave her a funeral indeed! Poor old Grace left enough money in an envelope for her funeral expenses. That was all she did leave, poor soul.'

'What did she die of?'

'Overwork, I shouldn't wonder. Well, to be fair, she was well over sixty. She stayed because she'd nowhere else to go and upstairs wasn't going to get rid of a woman who didn't care if she had time off or not.'

'Didn't she have any friends?'

'One. A woman older than her. They used to meet sometimes.'

Sid wondered about Grace. Would she end up like her? Working all her life and only one friend? The way her career had gone so far it seemed frighteningly possible.

She settled into her new life more quickly than she had expected to. Mum had always been strict about manners at home, and although Mrs Keevil was exacting, she was no worse than Mum. She began to enjoy the rituals of table-laying, didn't mind the rough work, and was delighted to discover the modern tools, including a vacuum cleaner with a special attachment which reached all the way to the ceiling, and a washing machine. No one in her family had a vacuum cleaner or a washing machine. And she was young and resilient and had always been strong. On two occasions her employer reproved her for singing at her work. Mrs Dingle was pleased with her, too. Sid had a light hand with pastry and never minded extra work when the cook was busy or tired.

One day, when Mrs Keevil was out, Mrs Dingle sat by the kitchen range with a cup of tea and a plate of home-made biscuits while Sid made apple pies, a task she particularly enjoyed. She loved the sweet-sour smell of cooking apples, the texture of flour and fat as she crumbled it between her fingers; she revelled in the moment she took the pie from the oven, steaming with the spicy scent of clove, the pastry nicely browned. 'You've been here three weeks, Sarah,' said Mrs Dingle, 'and you've never got out once except to see your family – and you work when you get there.'

'Is it three weeks? I hadn't realised.'

'Haven't you got a boyfriend?'

Sid continued to rub the flour and fat. 'Not at present.'

'Did you have a quarrel?'

When Sid didn't reply, Mrs Dingle took a bite of biscuit and mumbled through the crumbs, 'I suppose you quarrelled. What was it over? Did he want you to do something you shouldn't? Men are awful, aren't they? Even my husband – and he was a good chapel man – used to try it on, but I said it was marriage or nothing. He respected me for that. He told me so after we were married. Isn't that typical? But he was a good soul and I miss him, so I do.'

Sid hoped that the long speech had made Mrs Dingle forget her original questions. It hadn't.

'So why did you quarrel?'

'We didn't. I mean, I've never had a boyfriend.' The shame was out and she waited for the cook's astonishment and ridicule.

'Why ever not?'

'Boys have never taken to me. They go for my sisters. They're pretty.'

Mrs Dingle gave her a considering stare. 'So are you. At least, you would be if you stopped straining your hair back and used a bit of powder and lipstick. You've got lovely eyes, too.'

Sid stopped work to stare at her. 'Lovely eyes? They're no proper colour. My hair's like floss silk and won't take a permanent wave, and my nose has a bump in it and I'm thin . . . Men like girls with a bit of flesh, or so I've read.'

'Well, what a speech. I'm not surprised about your hair not taking to a perm, but it could be made nice.'

'It's greasy,' said Sid, carefully cutting the pastry edges from the first pie, then flaking and fluting the edge of the crust.

'Use lemon when you rinse it. That'll help. We've got half a dozen lemons in the pantry. She wants lemon meringue pie. You can have one.'

'Won't she miss it? Will it really take the grease from my hair?'

'She'll not notice the loss of one lemon.' She stood up and looked at the two pies. 'They look a real treat. I'll take over now. I shouldn't let you work in the kitchen as well as all the other things you do, but you're so good at cooking and I enjoy your company so much. It's a pleasure having you here.'

'Is it?' No one had ever said such a thing to her before.

'Don't sound so surprised. I bet your family miss you at home.'

Sid scraped the flour and fat from her fingers as she considered. 'They don't say so.'

'Well, maybe not, people don't always say what they think.'

'Dad does. He says I'm ugly.' The words had burst forth spontaneously and Sid realised she was going to weep. As the tears forced themselves beneath her lids she hurried out of the kitchen, grabbing a dustpan and brush as she went. 'I've just remembered something I should have done,' she managed to gasp. She arrived in the hall wishing she wasn't there. Mrs Keevil was only a few yards away in her sitting room with the wireless playing. 'When somebody thinks you're wonderful,' sang the crooner. No one has ever thought I'm wonderful, thought Sid. Why should they? What had she ever done that was wonderful? She knelt on the hall rug, brush and pan at the ready in case Mrs Keevil caught her. She wanted to hide herself away somewhere and let her tears flow because she had been born without looks or talent, but there wasn't anywhere in this house unless she chased all the way up to the attic, and someone would be sure to want her back downstairs as soon as she got there. Tears dropped on to the pale rug and made little dark spots. She rubbed at them with her handkerchief. Then she heard footsteps in the sitting room. She wiped her eyes and blew her nose, trying to despise herself for her self-pity and regain control over herself.

'What on earth . . .?' began Mrs Keevil.

'I remembered some dust. Sorry, ma'am.'

'So you should be. You should have finished your cleaning ages ago. And you know I forbid the use of a dustpan and brush unless absolutely necessary. It merely raises dust and then it settles back on the furniture. And why aren't you in your black uniform.? You know I have friends coming to tea.'

'Yes, ma'am. Sorry, ma'am.'

'Look at me when I speak to you.'

'Sorry, ma'am.' Sid found her handkerchief and blew her nose, dabbing surreptitiously at her eyes.

'Have you been crying?' Mrs Keevil sounded as if she'd caught her desecrating a church stained-glass window.

'Bit of dust in my eye,' mumbled Sid.

Her employer frowned. 'I wonder if you'll do after all. Go and change. But take the dustpan and brush down to the kitchen first. The idea. Anyone might have called.'

Mrs Dingle heard of the encounter, her plump cheeks creased in a broad grin. 'She's a caution, isn't she? No one would dare call without being invited. Wait a minute, love. Were you really crying?'

Sid nodded.

The cook contemplated her for a moment. 'All right, run along and get into your black. I'm a nosy parker.'

'No, you're not, you're kind.' Feeling the tears threatening again, Sid fled upstairs. She stared at herself from all angles in the dressing-table mirrors. Could she look pretty? She saw only the bump on her nose, her lank hair, her sallow complexion which had grown more sallow now that she spent so much time in a basement kitchen. She gazed into her eyes, trying to imagine Cary Grant or William Powell doing the same. What man would ever look into them in love-sick torment when he could have his pick of stars like Marlene Dietrich or Jean Harlow? Or girls who did their best to resemble them. Like Audrey and Irene? Today her eyes looked paler than ever, more grey than blue. Heavens! that was the front-door bell. Mrs Dingle would have to labour up the stairs to answer it.

She bathed her face, changed, and hurried to the kitchen where the tea-trolley waited. 'Ma'am's put out because you didn't answer the door,' muttered Mrs Dingle, 'but she won't say anything in front of her guests.' The two women lifted the trolley up the stairs and Sid wheeled it into the lounge on the dot of four-fifteen, placing it in front of Mrs Keevil. The lounge was the most elaborately furnished room in the house, kept warm by a large and recently installed bronze-finish gas fire, of which Mrs Keevil was inordinately proud. She was telling her visitors what a mess the builders made. 'My dears, there was dust everywhere. It got into one's teeth and made one's eyes sore. It took hours for my staff to get everything clean again, but it was well worth it. Gas is so fast and clean.'

Her visitors murmured appreciatively and stretched out their hands to the glow as if to reinforce their approval. Sid already knew the story. Mrs Dingle had related it to her. 'The staff she talks about was me. Grace wasn't well enough to help. She tried, but the dust made her cough badly. I wouldn't be surprised,' she added darkly, 'if it hadn't helped cause her death.'

'Oh, surely not!' Sid was shocked.

'Well,' conceded the cook, 'maybe it didn't. She'd had a bad cough for a long time. But it could have.'

Mrs Keevil had been busy with the tweezers again, and her brows were the merest dark-pencilled line, her lashes stiffly black with mascara, her hair rigidly waved, the ends set in tiny curls, her face made up with foundation cream, powder, rouge and lipstick. Sid knew exactly what she used because for the first time in her life she'd had the opportunity to see a modern woman's dressing table. She'd felt guilty but couldn't resist examining all the bottles and jars when she was supposed to be cleaning. Today her employer wore an afternoon gown with short sleeves. The fashionable hem almost touched her ankles, and the material was thin, which was why the fire was turned on full. Round her neck was a chain and locket which a short while ago Sid would have assumed was gold but now knew to be gilt. She had discovered also that her employer's watchstrap had no real value.

'Gold and diamonds?' Mrs Dingle had laughed. 'It's all costume jewellery.' She was scornful, but Sid secretly thought it was very useful to ladies who couldn't afford the real thing. One of the visitors, presumably used to chilly houses, wore a wool coat and skirt with a jumper and looked hot.

'That will be all, Sarah,' said Mrs Keevil in her most affected tones. 'Return in five minutes to refill the hot-water jug.'

'Yes, ma'am.' Sid felt unexpectedly light-hearted. As she skipped back down to the basement she sang, 'When somebody thinks you're wonderful . . .' In the kitchen Mrs Dingle was dressing a chicken for dinner. She looked up. 'You sound happy.'

'I think I am.'

From that day Sid began actually to enjoy her job with the Keevils. She used lemon juice on her hair and found it became glossy without grease. She made a note of the stuff with which Mrs Keevil preserved her complexion, and visited Woolworth's on an afternoon off, from where she bought some Pond's cream, Rachel powder and a pink lipstick. When she first made up her face she used far too much. She grinned at her reflection: she looked like a clown. She washed her face and began again, using minute amounts. She still felt rather like a painted doll, but she didn't look like one, and quickly became accustomed to using make-up with skill. Mrs Dingle, who said she had learned a lot about make-up from the ladies' maids she had known, advised her to buy a slightly darker shade of powder to disguise the bump on her nose. It actually worked, and after all it wasn't such a big bump. She bought mascara and touched her lashes, and discovered that they were long and curled at the ends. Why had she never realised that before? She attempted to pluck her brows, but the pain brought tears to her eyes. 'Good job,' said Mrs Dingle, 'you don't want to look like *her*. She's like a Dutch doll.'

Sid's Sunday half-day arrived. It began at twelve, and she prepared herself carefully to go home. For the first time she dared to wear make-up. Her hair shone smoothly, and Mrs Dingle had used curling tongs to turn up the ends. She'd acquired a pretty scarf and a tiny hat which tip-tilted over one eye. She wore a necklace of glass beads, cheap but dainty. What would Dad say about her looks now? With her new-found confidence she hung her coat in the hall and walked into the kitchen where the family was assembled for their midday meal.

Audrey and Irene stared at her, open-mouthed. Her mother said she liked her hat, but it was Dad's approval Sid needed. He laid his paper down with great deliberation. 'Sid. What on earth have you been doing to yourself? All that muck on your face doesn't suit you. I suppose you're trying to look like a film star, eh? Shouldn't bother. You never will.' He laughed and, as if he had broken a spell, the others laughed too. Sid felt like a circus clown again with painted face, wide mouth, silly hat and all.

'It's modern,' she muttered.

'Take off your hat and we'll eat,' said Mum.

'When ladies visit Mrs Keevil for lunch or tea they keep their hats on.'

'Lunch or tea,' mimicked Raymond.

'Well, here we take our hats off in the house,' said Dad. 'What's this we've got? Pork? And lots of lovely crackling. Good.'

Sid went with the family on the Sunday drive, and ended up as usual in Grandma's house, having removed her make-up. She quickly escaped to the kitchen.

'What a pretty hat,' said Aunty Mattie.

'Oh, do you like it? I'm glad.'

Mattie gave her a searching look, but said only, 'How are you getting on in your job?'

'Much better than I expected. I'm learning a lot.'

'Good. You look well.' There was time for no more before Grandma was demanding something.

Sid returned to Mrs Keevil's at eight o'clock. She picked up a tea-towel and began wiping the dishes which Mrs Dingle was washing. 'Good lord, girl, fancy coming back early.' She peered at Sid's face. 'Something's upset you. What happened? You've rubbed your make-up off. Come on, you can tell your Aunty Dingle.'

'Dad didn't like it.'

Mrs Dingle frowned, began to say something, stopped, then said, 'Men can be awful stick-in-the-mud over their womenfolk. I think it's their clumsy way of protecting them. They visit a theatre or picture-house, fall for some painted hussy, then go home and yell at their wives and daughters for using a dab of powder and paint. There's a rhyme about that. "Little dabs of powder, little dabs of paint, make a girl's complexion, look like what it ain't."'

Sid laughed and said ruefully, 'I suppose that's what Dad thinks. He likes his women to look natural.'

'Good gracious me, that wouldn't do at all. Men soon get used to make-up.' Mrs Dingle chuckled. 'Many a man goes to bed with his lovely young bride and wakes up to find a quite ordinary girl lying beside him.'

'Doesn't that make him feel cheated?'

'Of course not. It makes him feel much better. There she is all rumpled and tousled after the night before. He's been feeling like a beast for assaulting the dainty young woman he married, then all of a sudden he finds she's just an ordinary girl and he loves her more than ever.'

Sid felt herself blushing at Mrs Dingle's outspokenness, but said only, 'Why bother to put make-up on at all then?'

'You have to catch a man first, and girls need all the help they can get.'

They finished the dishes and sat down in front of the range with cups of cocoa. The chair Sid had been allotted was an odd shape and not especially comfortable, but she didn't mind.

'I've hardly seen Mr Keevil,' said Sid. 'He looks quite handsome.'

'I suppose he is.'

'His little moustache is just like a film star's and he's very strict. I suppose he has to be if he works in a bank. Not that Dad isn't smart when he goes out anywhere special.'

'You think the world of your dad, don't you?'

'Yes. He's good and kind.'

'I'd love to have had a daughter just like you,' said Mrs Dingle.

Sid was too overcome to reply.

'I can't understand any woman not wanting babies like her upstairs,' said Mrs Dingle.

'Perhaps she can't have any.'

'More like she stops them.'

'Stops them?'

'You don't know much about that sort of thing, do you?'

'Not much. Nothing really.'

'I thought so. I've got something for you here. *Dr Davis's Little Book for Married Ladies*. Read it and you'll understand a great deal.'

'But it's for married ladies.'

'It should be read by any young woman out in the world.'

Sid took the booklet and slipped it into her pocket, then the servants' bell rang and Cook got up.

'Let me answer it for you.'

'You can't in those clothes. Besides, if you let her see you working during your time off, she might decide to cut it down.'

While Mrs Dingle was gone, Sid skimmed through the little book. It was small but comprehensive, and she became so absorbed she didn't notice her return. The cook smiled before she fetched a fresh bottle of sherry from the pantry to take upstairs. She reseated herself opposite Sid, who finished reading and looked up in a daze.

'I never knew any of the stuff in here. Mum never told me a thing. There's no need for anyone to have a baby unless it's planned. It must be a boon for married women to know these things. I'm sure a lot of them don't.'

'It's a good idea for single women, too.'

'Single women? But no good woman would ever do... you know...'

But Mrs Dingle only said mysteriously, 'Who knows when temptation will come her way?'

Sid began to use make-up again. She even wore it when she was working, but only discreet touches of powder and lipstick so that Mrs Keevil didn't object.

Early one morning she was on her hands and knees polishing the linoleum in the hall, when Mr Keevil stopped on his way out to the bank. She had served his breakfast and had been ordered to carry up a tray later to Mrs Keevil, who felt a trifle indisposed.

He put on his overcoat and trilby hat and picked up his gloves and umbrella. 'My, but you're giving that floor a jolly good shine. Be careful not to polish under the rug. We don't want any accidents, eh?'

'No, sir.' Sid sat back on her heels to reply. She waited, but he seemed to have no more to say, so she bent once more to her task. As he passed her he leaned over and pinched her bottom. It was a sharp nip and stung, and was so unexpected that the front door had closed behind him before she realised exactly what had happened. 'The cheek of it,' she said aloud.

She told Mrs Dingle who said, 'Good heavens, who'd have believed it? I wonder what else he gets up to? I thought his wife had him tied well and truly to her apron strings.'

'It seems she hasn't.'

'Obviously not. I suppose he's not been tempted by the maid before.'

'I'll take care not to be in the hall again when he's going to work.'

'No,' agreed the cook fervently. 'If she got a whiff of anything like that she'd throw you out immediately.'

When Sid thought of getting the sack for the second time she felt quite ill. She'd really make sure she kept well out of Mr Keevil's way. Was this the kind of thing that happened if you wore make-up? Perhaps she'd better not do so any more in this house.

She said as much to Mrs Dingle, who was indignant. 'A girl's allowed to make the best of herself without some lecherous man thinking he can take advantage. You go on the way you've begun, my dear, and if he tries anything else, make it clear to him that his attentions aren't welcome. Of course, he might only have been overtaken by an impulse. Men are like that. Probably nothing else will happen. He's more than likely sweating at work wondering if you'll complain to his wife.'

Sid shuddered. 'What an awful idea.' She looked at the kitchen clock. 'Ma'am wants her breakfast now. I don't know how I can look her in the face after what's happened.'

'I shouldn't try. She's a sight in her cold-cream and curlers.'

Sid laughed. 'I should know. I take up their morning tea.'

Sid placed the breakfast tray carefully on the bed-table and suddenly wanted to laugh. Mrs Keevil truly did look 'a sight' with her greasy face and the steel curlers which peeped out from beneath a pink boudoir cap. When she got married she'd never look like that in bed. She was on her way downstairs when she stopped. *When* I get married, she had thought, not *if*. 'God moves in a mysterious way,' she said aloud, recalling the phrase from Sunday school. Had she been destined to come here to meet Mrs Dingle and learn more about life? If that were the case, she must have been destined to burn Mrs Keevil's ear. Life took some funny turns. She smiled broadly all the way to the kitchen.

Chapter Three

Sid wanted to see her family, even though they still managed to make her feel less than adequate. If Mum didn't find something to criticise, Dad managed it. And if they failed, Audrey or Irene got their spoke in. Raymond was at an age when he hardly noticed outward appearances; he had his own problems, coping with incessant admonitions to wash behind his ears or get the tidemark off his neck and do his homework before playing football.

Dad finally gave up grumbling about her make-up. The girls didn't mention it at all, having decided it was in their interests to keep quiet because Sid might snitch on them and tell Mum and Dad that she had once come across them giggling in an alleyway near home, putting on make-up themselves, but her father could never leave her absolutely alone, and it seemed as if he thought up different ways of teasing her.

'You know those tomato plants I let you pot,' he said one day. 'They've all withered. I can't think what you did to them.' She could never please him, but he still held up his face for the kiss which was obligatory when any of his family left or arrived.

Sid had always given Mum three-quarters of the six shillings she had earned at the hairdresser's. Now she made seven-and-sixpence a week, and had automatically offered some of it to Mum who had said indignantly, 'You don't cost me a penny now, and Dad brings in plenty enough.' Sid had been delighted. Now she was able to buy nice things for herself. She learned gradually what was in fashion. Mrs Keevil took several women's magazines which were more expensive than Mum's and, as she made a point of leaving them out on her coffee table for visitors to admire, it wasn't difficult for Sid to pause in her cleaning and read snatches, usually before her mistress got up. She learned that a society woman had bet that for under two pounds she could dress herself from head to foot, jewellery included, plus buy ten de Reszke cigarettes, and sit at her elegant ease in the foyer of the Ritz Hotel. She had won her bet right down to panties and shoes, partly by using the ever-obliging Woolworth's, who supplied an imitation pearl necklace and pearl earrings for threepence each. Sid discovered in herself a sensual enjoyment of clothes, of silky underwear, of dainty shoes, of pretty little hats of the latest style, and of bead necklaces and scent. Her first purchase of the latter was a mistake, and she didn't blame Mum when she complained of the overpowering 'stink'. Scent, she realised, was not something to economise on, and she saved for a bottle of Yardley's Lavender. Her ability to give presents was also a delight for her. She took home matching blouses for the girls, who sometimes liked to dress the same, increasing the belief in strangers that they were twins; Raymond usually got chocolates. Mum wasn't easy. She had never worn anything but the plainest of clothes, and at Christmas and on birthdays her family usually gave her stuff for the house which she said she wanted. Sid preferred to give her something personal, and although Mum grumbled at the waste of money when presented with a little blue and gold enamelled butterfly brooch, she wore it often. Dad appreciated the occasional gift of tobacco, though he usually found some flaw which meant he could grumble about her 'waste of money'. 'This stuff's been in the shop too long', or, 'I'm sure they've changed the tobacco mix. It's different from the last lot.' Fortunately, as time passed, Sid found her family losing some of its power to distress her, and her confidence in herself began to grow.

She was happy to discover that Roy Hendy cleaned Mrs Keevil's windows too, and they had an opportunity to talk. He, like other tradesmen, was obliged to use the back door. This helped their acquaintanceship along. Mrs Dingle paid him from the housekeeping purse, and when she saw the looks he gave Sid, invited him in for cups of tea. He was well mannered, wiping his feet carefully and removing his cap before he entered. He might be a year younger than Sid, but he seemed mature for his age and he was certainly taller. Also, though she could scarcely believe it, he did seem attracted to her. Mrs Dingle always pressed him to stay a little longer, and one day she made an excuse and left the pair together. Both were embarrassed. Roy fidgeted with his cap and Sid got up to wipe imaginary finger marks from a cupboard door. Then their eyes met and they laughed at their absurdity. From that day their friendship grew, and when he asked Sid to go to the pictures with him, she accepted.

Their trip to the Regent picture house in Kingswood was a delight to her. She was comfortable with Roy. Sitting in the smoky dark watching the screen, she was absorbed in the delights of the double feature, but towards the end her thoughts wandered as she realised that she was here on her first date and she had no idea what would be expected of her. Would he walk her home? Would he try to kiss her? Did she want him to? The immediate reply was no. The idea made her nervous.

After leaving the cinema they discussed the film as Roy escorted her to Warmley Hill. They had quite an argument about this, because he lived in Staple Hill which meant he'd have to get the last bus or walk all the way home. But he was insistent that a man didn't take a girl out then leave her to find her own way back. A man, he called himself, and it didn't seem incongruous.

When she held out her hand to say goodnight, he took it and held it and she had to stop herself from trembling. Then he lifted her hand to his mouth and pressed his warm lips to its back before he said, 'Thank you, Sid. That was lovely. Perhaps you'll come out with me again.'

She was too breathless to speak and her assent came out as a gasp, but he seemed satisfied, smiled and left. She watched him walk away, glad he hadn't tried to kiss her lips, but fancy kissing her hand like that! He must have a lot of romance in him. She went into the kitchen where Mrs Dingle was seated by the fire, a wireless playing softly.

'You look as if you've lost sixpence and found half a crown.'

'Mmm.' Sid, still smiling, sat down staring dreamily into the fire.

'Oh, dear, you've got it bad. Did you have a good time?'

'Yes, lovely.'

'Did he bring you home?'

'Oh, yes.'

'Did he kiss you?'

Sid's face coloured. 'Sort of.'

'What's that supposed to mean? A kiss is a kiss.'

'On the back of my hand. As if I was a princess and him a prince.'

'Did he?' Mrs Dingle chuckled. 'A really romantic young man. Who'd have thought it of a window-cleaner?'

'That doesn't make him any less imaginative.'

'I suppose not. And he's a lad with initiative in these days of unemployment. Here, sit down and have a cuppa. Was the film good?'

'Yes, it was heavenly. Claudette Colbert is so lovely and she can be funny, too.'

'What about Clark Gable? He was in it, wasn't he?'

'He's . . . he's the most handsome, wonderful man . . .' Sid sighed.

Mrs Dingle laughed and shook her head. 'Remember he's only a film star on a screen and not for the likes of us. Roy is a real man.'

Mrs Keevil almost never praised, but Sid had to admire someone who brought such order to her life. During her years with Madame Rita, she had seemed for ever in a muddle, trying to obey two or three at once, never to be found where she was expected to be. She had taken it for granted that she was clumsy and rather foolish. Now she discovered that when she had a set task and was allowed the correct length of time, she could perform it creditably. Except for sewing. Work at it as she might, she was clusmy with her needle, and it was lucky that Mrs Dingle was able to do the odd repairs to the household linen.

Of course there had to be a flaw, and Sid found Mr Keevil's behaviour difficult to stomach. He had at first fulfilled her image of a bank clerk, a trim figure, medium height, who went to work in a dark suit and a bowler hat, carrying an umbrella whatever the weather, arriving home at the same time every evening. Not that she had ever been inside a bank. Dad brought his Saturday takings home and banked them on Monday. As they grew up, the children had been instructed never to reveal this secret to a soul for fear of a burglary. To think of such vast sums of money, perhaps twenty or thirty pounds, secreted in the house for two whole nights had added spice to their perception of life. Mr Keevil never worked in the garden. There was an odd-job man who did that, and decorating was always undertaken by professionals, so after changing into his leisure clothes – a lighter suit but still with a collar and tie – he was able to read his evening newspaper, eat his dinner in a leisurely fashion, then read a book or perhaps play some music on the gramophone or listen to a talk on the wireless. Mrs Keevil was fond of dance music, which she played when her husband was out of the house. It surprised Sid to realise that her employer most enjoyed her favourites, Josh Raven and his Melody Men and the Kissing Cousins.

'To look at our bosses from the outside,' said Mrs Dingle, 'you'd think he was henpecked, but sometimes I wonder. He can be as stubborn as a mule.' Happily for their servants, the Keevils were often out to dinner, though the number of dinner parties they gave almost made up for the extra leisure time in the kitchen.

When Mr Keevil didn't repeat the pinch that had so overcome Sid, she decided it had been a momentary lapse. But no sooner had the characters of her employers established themselves in her mind than she realised that Mr Keevil was simply waiting for any repercussions. She tried to avoid him but it was difficult, especially when his wife wasn't at home, and his fingers were for ever busy pinching or stroking her.

'I do wish you wouldn't, sir,' she pleaded desperately.

'Wouldn't what?' he asked once, coolly.

'Touch me.'

'Touch you? Really, Sarah, I brush against you and you call it touching? I fear you have a salacious mind.'

Later, when she made a stronger protest, he said, 'Don't be such a prig, Sarah, you know you enjoy my admiration.'

'No, I don't, sir!'

'You wear make-up, dress in attractive clothes on your days off. I've seen you with lipstick and a cheeky hat, black shoes with heels, dark silk stockings. Why do you wear such stuff if it isn't to be noticed?'

'You must have had a good look at me.'

'I did. I like my staff to look smart.'

'And that's why I wear make-up and nice clothes. To look smart.'

'Rubbish! All you girls are the same. You doll yourselves up to attract a man, then get indignant when he responds to your come-hither look.'

'Come-hither look? I don't know what you mean!'

For answer he had taken a step nearer and slid his arm round her waist. 'A trim little waist, Sarah. I like a girl with a nice figure.'

'You've got no right . . .'

Her indignant response was cut short by hearing Mrs Keevil's key in the front door, earlier than had been expected. Mr Keevil sprang back as if he'd been stuck with a pin while she, red-faced, continued to lay the table.

The fright didn't make him give up. When Sid appealed to Mrs Dingle for advice, she was sympathetic but realistic. 'There are too many men like him. You just have to learn how to cope with them.'

'I'm sure my Dad doesn't behave like that.'

'There are a few good ones.'

Then one day Mr Keevil cornered Sid when she was cleaning a

guest bedroom. She knew he had gone back to bed after breakfast, because his wife had told the servants that he wasn't well and to be sure he had everything he needed while she was at the hairdresser's. Sid was singing softly as she polished a bedside cabinet, deciding that one day she would own a beautiful bedroom of her very own, with a suite of matched furniture as nice as this. She was just thinking of the soft furnishings she would choose when, with a shock, she realised she was no longer alone. Mr Keevil was there, still in pyjamas, wearing his slippers and a dressing gown loosely tied.

He closed the door and leaned on it, staring at her. 'You're much too attractive to be a maid,' he said softly.

'No, I'm not.'

'You shouldn't frown like that. Surely you don't dislike being told you are attractive.'

'I don't like flattery.' She picked up the polish and dusters. Her heart was thudding. 'I must get on with my work.'

'You mean you think you aren't attractive? You are, you know. You shouldn't be here by rights.'

'Mrs Keevil told me to clean the bedrooms after I'd finished downstairs.'

He smiled. 'You know what I mean. You're worthy of a better situation in life.'

'Oh? What do you think I should be?'

He took a step towards her and she realised that she had fallen into a conversational trap.'

'A mannequin at the very least,' he said. 'Perhaps a film star.'

His answer was so absurd that Sid laughed.

He smiled broadly. 'There, I knew you were a sport.'

'No, I'm not.' She tried to stay calm. Perhaps if she humoured him she could get out of this with some dignity and still save his face. It wouldn't do to have her employer's husband resenting her. 'You've had your joke, sir, now please let me pass. I have my work to do.'

He took another step forward. 'We all have work to do. Fortunately, I cannot attend to mine today as I have a sore throat.'

'Fortunately?'

'Indeed, yes, for it enables me to be near you and take that kiss I've always wanted.'

'Don't be silly!' she snapped.

She regretted it instantly when he coloured angrily. 'Silly, am I? If you're not careful I could get you sacked. How would you like that, my girl? It's happened once to you, hasn't it? Your family is quite respectable in spite of their inferior class . . .'

'Don't insult my family!' she cried. 'What do you know about them anyway?'

'I know that a man of any degree in life wouldn't send his daughter out to skivvy. Did you know your whole family use my bank? I know every detail of their financial lives.'

'If I tell them what you're really like they'd put their money somewhere else.'

'But you aren't going to tell them, are you?'

'Don't you be too sure.'

'What would they say? Would they believe you? Do you imagine that they'd countenance such an upheaval in their businesses just because a silly girl provoked her employer into kissing her?'

Put like that, it seemed improbable. Sid couldn't imagine herself telling her parents about this anyway. She'd be too embarrassed.

'You see,' he said softly, 'I'm right. This is all a game to you.'

'I don't play this kind of game! Oh, please let me out.'

'You want to kiss me really, don't you? I've seen the way you look at me.'

'No, sir, I don't look at you in any way! I'd rather not see you at all. Let me out! Now! I'll scream if you don't.'

'There's no one to hear. Mrs Dingle's safe enough in the basement . . .'

'And *your wife* is out,' said Sid.

'Ah, my wife.' He took another step towards her. 'My wife. Do you like working for her? Does she get on your nerves with her incessant orders? I don't mind telling you, she gets on mine. She will play that dreadful modern dance music. Ghastly!'

'She's nice enough to me, and she uses make-up, too,' said Sid desperately, 'and she wears the latest fashions. I even saw her in a dress without a back to it when you went out the other night. Do you think she's like that because she wants all the men to kiss her?'

'Of course not.'

'Why not? You say I do. And she looks after you properly and keeps a nice house and you get good meals.'

'There is more to life than that. Do you know she wants me to buy a motor-car?'

'No, sir.'

Sid's hope that changing the tone of the conversation had eased her situation wilted as he took another step towards her.

'Yes, she wants me to take up driving. She harps on the subject at great length. I'm surprised you haven't heard her.'

'I don't listen to things that aren't my business, sir.'

'Admirable girl. But surely you can't help overhearing a few things. She's trying to push me in my job, too, when I'm really comfortable as I am. And she's a cold woman. A man needs a bit of comfort in bed, but she seldom gives it to me.'

Sid was horrified. Never could she have imagined that a man would speak to her of his intimate relationship with his wife. 'Don't! Please, don't. I don't want to hear.'

She had moved further and further back as he approached, and her legs were pressed up tight against the bed.

He moved swiftly and she tried to dodge round the bed, but he was too close. He held her shoulders in hands which proved surprisingly strong for a sedentary man. Then he pulled her to him and wrapped his arms about her so tightly that it was difficult to breath.

'You're choking me,' she gasped. It was as much as she could say before he slid a hand into her hair, gripped it painfully, and pressed his mouth to hers. His lips were hot and moist and clinging. It was like being kissed by a piece of wet rubber. He stopped for breath and she gasped a protest before he kissed her again. This time he inserted his tongue right into her mouth. She had never conceived of such a thing. It was horrible, revolting. She began to struggle, gagging and gasping; then, in a desperate attempt to free herself, bit down hard. He flung her away with such force that she sprawled on the bed.

'You bitch!' he cried incoherently as blood oozed from his mouth. 'You . . . you . . .!' He hurried away and Sid heard him go into the bathroom and begin running the tap. She fled downstairs to the kitchen.

Mrs Dingle looked up from her pastry-making. 'Why, whatever's up, Sarah?'

'Him! That horrible man! Ugh!'

'Horrible man? You don't mean . . .?'

'Mr Keevil. He caught me upstairs and kept kissing me. It was dreadful. He stuck his tongue right into my mouth.'

'The nasty little toad. Who would have believed he'd go so far? But of course, there's been only me and Grace for years. He wouldn't want us.'

Sid was at the kitchen sink, rinsing her mouth in cold water. She said through cleansing bubbles, 'If that's what kissing is like I wouldn't go far to find it. But no decent man would kiss like that.'

'Come and sit down and have a cup of tea.'

'I'm supposed to finish the bedrooms before she gets back. She'll go everywhere and look for dust.'

'You can have a cup of tea. It'll be good for shock. Then you can take over the work here – it's quite a simple lunch – grilled whiting, potato croquettes and cold beetroot. Mash the potatoes for me. Make them really creamy and don't forget to add a sprinkling of parsley. And she wants a butter sauce – I've shown you how to make that. I'll finish the bedrooms, they can't need much doing.' She grinned. 'I doubt if I'll be in any danger. In fact, I don't think you'll be again if you've given him a sore tongue.' She grimaced. 'Ouch! When you think how a mouth ulcer hurts . . .'

'Shouldn't I have done it? What if I've really injured him?'

'You did the right thing. The beast!'

'What will happen next? I'll always be afraid of him.'

'He's probably more afraid of you now.'

Sid smiled reluctantly. 'What sort of fellow would kiss that way?'

Mrs Dingle said, 'It's known as French kissing, and lots of men take great pleasure from it.'

'Ugh! What woman could?'

'A large number. One day you might.'

'Never!'

'When you find the right man you will.'

'No.'

Mr Keevil got up for dinner, which Sid served, noting with satisfaction that he didn't once catch her eye.

41

'What's the matter with you?' demanded his wife. 'You've hardly touched your food and I ordered fruit salad and cream with plenty of pineapple, just the way you like it.'

'Sorry, dear,' he said, his tone so meek that Sid could almost wonder if the scene upstairs had happened at all. 'I have a painful ulcer.'

'Well, that's the thanks I get for going to such trouble.' Sid wondered what trouble she had been to. Mrs Dingle had done the shopping and cooked the chops, she had opened tins of fruit, and the milkman had brought the cream. 'It's most inconvenient,' went on Mrs Keevil. 'Cream doesn't keep.'

'I'm sorry, dear,' he said meekly.

'Perhaps Cook will find another use for it. Sarah, how many times do I have to tell you which side to remove the plates?'

'Sorry, ma'am.' The reprimand helped Sid to keep a straight face, knowing that Mrs Dingle would ladle out the cream generously into their night-time drinks, making the cocoa rich.

'I dare say she can use it up in scones and cakes. If I had a refrigerator I wouldn't need to worry. We've discussed if often enough.'

'Yes, dear, I see the need. We will look into the matter.'

'We certainly will!'

Mrs Keevil tackled her fruit salad so angrily that juice dripped on to her blouse and made her temper even worse. 'You had better put gentian violet on the ulcer when you retire.'

Sid turned to the sideboard for the cheese and biscuits and allowed herself a smile. Gentian violet was bright purple and stained for ages.

'You know I can't go to the bank with gentian violet on my tongue,' Mr Keevil said. 'What would the customers think?'

'Then you'll just have to put up with it until it heals. Will you take cheddar or stilton?'

'Neither, thank you.'

Mrs Keevil sighed heavily. 'I go to immense pains to select the food you like and you refuse it!'

'The cheese is sharp. It would hurt my tongue.'

Downstairs, over the dishes, Sid relayed the conversation to Mrs Dingle. They were laughing when the bell rang.

'What do they want now?' wondered the cook. 'You've done all your work, haven't you?'

'Yes, but she's in a mood to find something to grumble about.'

'Well, try to put up with it as best you can, then we'll have a lovely creamy cup of cocoa.'

Mrs Keevil was truly angry. Sid had entered the sitting room in a philosophical frame of mind, expecting the usual exaggerated reprimand for a minor misdemeanour; afterwards she would feel better and that would be the end of it. This time, though, she knew at once that something was different. Her employer was alone in the room and there was real scorn in her eyes. Her cheeks were too painted to be pale, but there was a whiteness round her lips.

She wasted no time. 'Pack your bags and leave my house.'

'What?'

'I made myself perfectly clear. I want you out of my house.'
'But why?'
Her employer's face reddened. 'You know why. Do you want me to voice your shame?'
'What shame?'
'You are without a trace of decent feeling.'
'I don't know what you're talking about,' cried Sid. 'You can't expect me to go without telling me what I'm supposed to have done.'
Mrs Keevil stared at her for a moment, then turned her back and began to finger ornaments on the mantelshelf. She said, still with her back to Sid, 'My husband has told me everything. How you entered his bedroom when he was dozing, how you knelt on the bed and kissed him, how you unbuttoned yourself to tempt him.'
'*What?*'
Mrs Keevil continued. 'I've heard of servants who stoop to that kind of thing to get favours or even money, but I believed I could trust you because you come from a respectable family. What will they say about this?'
'It isn't true!'
Mrs Keevil swung round, her face now so suffused with colour it showed through her make-up. 'Has this kind of thing happened before? Perhaps Madame Rita got rid of you for other reasons than the one she gave.'
'She did not. She sacked me because I burnt you. If you had been kind you would have forgiven me and asked her to keep me on.'
'Would I, indeed? So that you could burn other clients?'
'You were the only client I'd ever touched. I hoped it might help my career.'
'Your career!' Mrs Keevil laughed nastily. 'I can't think why I'm allowing you to stand there arguing with me. Get out!'
'I've done nothing. I swear I've done nothing.'
'Are you suggesting that my husband is lying to me?'
'Perhaps his illness made him delirious. He might have imagined I was with him. I wouldn't dream . . .'
'Be quiet. Mr Keevil has a sore throat, not a temperature; he was not dreaming.'
'How can you think I would behave so badly? I've given you no cause to decide I'm not respectable.'
'You're not exactly averse to the men, are you? You were seen at the Regent with the window-cleaner, and Mrs Jenner next door says she saw you kissing and canoodling before he left. At my back door, too.'
'She's telling lies! Roy didn't kiss me. Well, only . . .'
'Only what? No, don't take the trouble to answer. Be quiet! It doesn't matter to me how many times you were kissed,' said Mrs Keevil. 'I don't like that kind of thing going on outside my establishment. It never used to happen and I won't have it.'
'All right, I won't do it again, but please don't send me away. My family will be so upset.'
'I dare say they will. You aren't fit to work at a civilised job. I should

go into a factory if I were you. Now go! I'm tired of this argument. I want you out of my house tonight.'

'It isn't fair! Where is Mr Keevil? Let him tell me himself what I'm supposed to have done. In front of you.'

'The impertinence! He has gone early to bed. He feels quite dreadful and it's your fault. He's even developed an ulcerated tongue. He doesn't wish to see you again.'

'Oh, doesn't he? Have you asked to see his ulcer yet?'

'Of course not.'

'He tried to kiss me. He stuck his tongue in my mouth. I bit it.'

'You evil-minded girl!' Mrs Keevil cried.

'It's him who's evil-minded. He wanted me, he said, because you and he don't . . .' Sid stopped. She had no words to describe what Mr and Mrs Keevil didn't do. She couldn't have got any further anyway, because her employer had no difficulty in interpreting her meaning.

She went ashen with fury. 'Get out! Now!' Her voice was low; there was a quality in that and in her eyes which frightened Sid. She looked capable of violence. She walked from the room, angry tears welling.

Mrs Dingle was furious. 'I'll leave with you,' she declared.

'No, it's wonderful of you to feel for me, but you can't. This is your home.'

'Oh, Sid, I shall miss you something awful. She'll not find another one like you. She'll get some ugly, sour-faced creature. I've loved having you with me, so young and eager to learn.'

'She doesn't think like that. Oh, Mrs Dingle, Dad and Mum will be so angry. At least, Mum will. Dad will just look hurt and that's worse.'

'But you'll tell them what happened.'

'They'll never believe such a thing of a bank clerk.'

'If there's any problem I'll come round on my next afternoon off and talk to them.'

Sid hugged her. 'You're an angel, but I don't think you'd better. They'd call it interference, and I wouldn't want you upset.'

Both women went up to the attic, where Sid folded her possessions and placed them in her case. Her three new hats she put in a large brown-paper bag. She kissed Mrs Dingle. 'I must go. The sooner I get this over with the better. I'm dreading it.'

'She owes you some money. At least ask her for that.'

'I don't think I could. On second thoughts, I will. Why should she refuse to pay?'

Mrs Keevil was still in her sitting room. She looked up when Sid entered. 'You!' she said malevolently.

'Tomorrow is pay day. You owe me money,' said Sid as coolly as she could.

Mrs Keevil opened her mouth for an angry retort, then closed it. She went to her desk, drew out a small brown envelope and put in some money. 'I have stopped tenpence, the sum you would have been entitled to by tomorrow.' She paused. 'It's your stupidity that amazes me most. Fancy thinking I'd believe that my husband would touch you, gawky, stringy-looking thing that you are.'

Sid left without replying. Mrs Dingle had been lurking in the hall. 'I heard what she said,' she whispered. 'Don't listen to her, it isn't true. She's afraid there might be some truth in what you told her. Perhaps he's misbehaved before.'

Dad had gone for a pint with his pals, but Mum's explosion of wrath more than made up for his absence. 'Sacked? Again? Can't you do anything right? That's two jobs you've lost inside four months. I can't think what my family will say.'

'Is that all you care about? What my aunties will say?'

'There's Grandma Lacey, too.'

'Yes. She's sure to be nasty. She hates me.'

'Don't be silly. She doesn't think you're up to much, that's true, but hate. . . . But she'll not be surprised. And why should she be?'

'I told you what happened.'

'Men don't do things like that without reason. You must have encouraged him in some way, flirted with him or something.'

Sid gasped at the injustice. 'I didn't! I didn't!'

Audrey and Irene had heard the row and came downstairs. 'Ooh, what's our Sid done now?' asked Audrey.

Sid told them what had happened. 'And I didn't encourage him. I don't even like him. He looks like a . . . a weasel.'

The girls shrieked with mirth. 'Keevil the Weasel,' they shouted over and over.

'Shut up!' yelled Sid.

They did shut up, amazed that their quiet, unassuming sister should have bawled at them.

'Do you believe it was my fault?' she demanded of them.

'Don't know,' said Irene.

'Shouldn't think so,' said Audrey. 'After all, you're a bit weaselly yourself. Perhaps that's what attracted him. Like to like.'

'That's enough, girls,' said Mum, but she didn't sound cross with them.

Sid walked out of the room and upstairs to the bedroom she shared with her sisters. She dropped her case and slumped on the edge of her bed, her head in her hands. She felt crushed. No matter what she did she messed it up. She'd kept her job with Madame Rita for years, but only when she'd been doing the most menial tasks. Where could she go next?

She heard Dad call, as he always did, as he walked through the downstairs passage, 'I'm home.' And Mum would push the kettle over the hob, where it would sing as it came back to the boil for his tea. Happy, familiar sounds and actions which could never be the same for her again. Everything had changed. She heard the murmur of voices, then a shout of anger from Dad. Footsteps reached the bottom of the stairs. 'Sid, come down here at once.' He was waiting for her.

'Into the best room,' he commanded.

The best room was cold and shiny with polish. Dad closed the door behind him.

'So you've disgraced us again.' Sid stared at him. Dad hated scenes.

He must be really upset. 'Do you know what you've done? Everyone in Kingswood and Warmley will hear about it. The daughter of Mr Penrose, the greengrocer, told to leave her job twice! And for what? First for burning a valued client and then, when you were lucky enough to get taken on by the very woman you injured, trying to ... to ...' Dad spluttered. 'How could you do such a thing? Mr and Mrs Keevil are respectable people ...'

'*He* isn't,' cried Sid. 'You don't know what he's really like.'

'This has never happened before. It was only when you went to work there ...'

'There was only Mrs Dingle, who's elderly. Grace, who died, was old too.'

'Are you standing there telling me that he was so overcome by your ... your good looks that he ...' Again the sentence was finished in splutters. Mr Penrose couldn't bring himself to put such matters into words.

'He's been pinching me and touching me ever since I went there, and this last thing ... How can you believe I'd go into his bedroom and ...'

'Be quiet!'

'If you won't listen, you'll never know the truth.'

'Save your breath for looking for another job,' said Dad. 'You'll need a lot.' He walked out.

The evening meal was a nightmare. Mum had cooked one of Sid's favourite dishes, a steak and kidney pie, the meat tender and luscious beneath its golden pastry crust, floury potatoes, home-grown green peas, but Sid left much of it on her plate.

Mum cast annoyed glances at her but said nothing. She was still shaken by what had happened, and even more by the rare occurrence of seeing Dad fly into a temper. The girls whispered and giggled until told to be quiet, and Raymond ate steadily, seeming not to notice the terrible atmosphere. He went out to practise football as soon as he had finished his currant duff and custard. Audrey and Irene raced upstairs to get ready to go to the pictures, their laughter floating back as they climbed the stairs. Sid sat on, food like a lump of lead in her stomach.

Dad pushed back his chair. 'That was a splendid meal, Mother,' he said, just as he did every night, just as if nothing had happened, as if his eldest daughter was not miserable and anxious and scared of the future.

Sid helped with the dishes. She wanted to assure her mother of her innocence, but had no way of doing so. Nothing she said would reduce the enormity of her offence in their eyes. She couldn't sleep that night. Her stomach churned and gurgled; she was in acute discomfort, physically and mentally. In the end she crept downstairs and drank two cups of hot water, hoping they would settle her. She longed for tea but didn't dare. If Mum found out she would be indignant. Life here did not include tea in the early hours.

Sid answered newspaper advertisements and was sent out regularly by the Employment Exchange, but she still couldn't find a job. She longed for something different, a place where she could exercise the few talents she had. No business firm would take on a girl of her age who'd had no experience. They preferred either seasoned women or someone straight from school and, most damning of all, she had only the one reference, from Madame Rita, which was almost worse than no reference at all. She grew so desperate that in one office she tried to lie. 'My references got burned accidentally,' she said, her face the colour of fire. She knew the office manager didn't believe her. She went to shops, but there were more applicants than jobs; she was a long way down the queue behind smart young men and women who were confident and clever. She visited a servant bureau but didn't even get as far as an interview. All she was offered was rough work in houses which employed proper servants; she knew Mum and Dad would be enraged by that.

The aunties were having a wonderful time. 'Our Sarah' had got a bit above herself with her notions of grammar school and university. It was bad enough having Jess with her husband's posh shop, her son at boarding school and her own car to drive, without Sarah putting on airs. Not that they weren't sympathetic, but it was immensely satisfying to have such a juicy piece of gossip to chew on.

'Fancy,' said Ella, 'one of our family getting the sack twice. I don't believe it's ever happened before.'

'Not even once,' said Bea.

'Leave alone twice,' said Maud.

When they went on their usual visit after the Sunday drive, Grandma Lacey was scathing. 'It's a downright disgrace. I didn't know how to hold up my head when I heard. And,' she added darkly, glaring at Mr and Mrs Penrose, 'I had to hear of it from a neighbour.'

'I came to see you the very next day,' protested Mum. 'It wasn't my fault Mrs Keevil told everyone in the hairdresser's and someone passed it on.'

'That's all very well,' said Grandma, 'but I couldn't believe it. I even argued with the woman. Do you hear that?' she demanded of Sid. 'You've turned your grandmother into a liar.'

Sid muttered, 'Sorry,' and went into the kitchen where Mattie was preparing tea. She smiled at her niece.

'Come on, love, sit down. You can have a cuppa before we serve the others.'

'Thanks. You're very kind.'

'Kind be blowed. They're a dreadful lot, aren't they?'

She was smiling, and Sid gave an answering smile. 'It's my own fault.'

'No, it isn't. That Mr Keevil really did try his tricks on you, didn't he?'

'You believe me?'

'Of course I do. I can't think why they're all so mean to you.'

Sid took a sip of tea. 'It's because I'm plain. They don't think any man would want me!'

'What about Roy Hendy? He took you out, didn't he?'

'Yes. He said he'd ask again, but I haven't heard a word from him since I was sacked.'

'Does he know where you are?'

Sid stared at her. 'I don't know.'

'I don't suppose he does. How should he? Even if he dared ask, neither Madame Rita nor Mrs Keevil would tell him.'

Sid sat up. 'I hadn't thought of that.' She slumped again. 'That's that, then. I can hardly look for him and ask him for a date. He'd think I was cheap.'

'I doubt it. I expect he'd be flattered. Bump into him accidentally. You know his hours at two places. You only have to tell him quite casually that you're looking for another job. See what happens.'

'Nothing,' said Sid gloomily.

'Really, dear, you can be exasperating sometimes. Why do you think he asked you out? Why do you think Mr Keevil wanted you? Would they be interested in an unattractive girl?'

Grandma Lacey called, 'Where's that tea? Will you be all day out there?'

When they had taken in the laden trolley, Sid followed Mattie back to the kitchen.

Mattie said, 'Have you tried for a position with your Uncle Robert?'

'Who?'

'Your Aunt Jess's husband?'

'Oh, yes, of course. But they'd never take me on. I've looked in occasionally when I was in town. Aunt Jess is so elegant, and her sales-girls are all beautiful.'

'They're not any better than you. You should make the best of yourself. You looked so pretty with a little make-up and your sweet hat. You should wear what you like and let them moan if they want to.'

Sid decided she would visit Clifton. She stood outside Jess's shop. One window held three carefully chosen gowns, the other a coat, hat, gloves, handbag and shoes. A wide chiffon scarf was carefully draped over a stand. A dainty white silk blouse and a black skirt graced a sculptured model, and a pearl necklace and earrings nestled in the folds of the scarf. Costume jewellery, thought Sid. She had learned a lot from her time with Mrs Keevil, assisted by Woolworth's trinket counter.

Aunt Jess was kind. She took Sid into the office at the back of the shop. As they walked through the carpeted, discreetly quiet sales space, the sales-ladies, dressed in smart black, smiled at her as warmly as if she were a customer.

'You look peaky,' Jess said. 'Have you been unwell?'

Sid told Aunt Jess everything, and she listened, really listened, waiting until her niece had finished before saying, 'Some men are like that. They'll go for any woman. It wasn't your fault.'

'It wasn't, was it? I admit I tried to make myself look nice with make-up and used a drop of scent, but I can't think that encouraged him. I know I'm not pretty, not like your sales-ladies . . .'

'But they aren't pretty. They are elegant and they have style, a more precious commodity than mere prettiness.'

'I wish I had style then.'

'But you have, my dear, if only you didn't try to hide your true self. Not that you've had much chance to do anything else,' she finished with a sigh.

Sid drank in the comforting words. Both Aunt Mattie and Aunt Jess were on her side. She hadn't been really surprised when the gentle, unsophisticated, loving Mattie agreed with her, but Mum always said Aunt Jess was worldly.

'I've tried everywhere to find work, Aunt Jess. I just can't get a job, and I've only one reference which isn't very good. Could you give me employment? I'll do anything.'

'I'm sorry, my dear. I have two excellent maids who have been with me since I married. One of them was with your Uncle Robert's family for years before. And my sales-assistants are well trained and perfectly satisfactory. I also have an apprentice and a part-time clerk. Really, I have nothing for you to do.'

'Do you know anyone who could give me work? Things are getting bad at home.' Sid's voice defied her efforts to control it, and it broke a little.

Jess looked worried. 'I hate to see you so miserable.'

'I'm sorry.'

'I could bet you're always apologising to someone.'

Sid was taken aback. 'Yes, I suppose I am.'

'Well, don't. Unfortunately you are what your upbringing has made you. It's a pity you weren't a rebel, but it isn't in your nature. I remember when you were small. You were so dainty, so quick and intelligent.'

'Me?'

'Yes, you. If you'd been my daughter – and I wish you had been; I was only able to have one child – I would have given you all the encouragement you needed. I would have allowed you to pursue your education, instead of which you were thrust into a world for which you were quite unprepared.'

Sid was amazed. This was an awesomely different view of herself.

'However, it's a bit late now,' said Jess, 'and my memories aren't going to help. If I hear of anything I'll let you know.'

A letter from Aunt Jess arrived three days later, three days in which Sid had tramped round seeking work, three days in which her mother had berated her and her father directed sorrowful looks at her over the top of his newspaper.

'Dear Sidonia,' she read and Sid's heart gave a little jump at seeing her proper name. 'I have learned that a former customer of mine, an elderly lady, is very much in need of someone as a maid-companion. Her name is Mrs Cardell and she lives quite near you in a place called Greystone House. You may know it.'

Sid swallowed hard. She knew it. The local children called it Blackstone House because its once grey stones were black with age and soot. It was deep in woods which had become well-nigh impenetrable, and rhododrendon bushes crowded so near the drive that they would have impeded a vehicle if one ever called. Her shopping was done by an old man who looked at all children as if he hated them. Mrs Cardell was said by the children to be a witch so, they reasoned, he must be her assistant. The gates in the high crumbling perimeter wall were always closed, but boys couldn't resist the temptation to climb in to gather the abundant conkers. They came out with horror stories of the black house and the witch who lived there. Sid didn't really believe them, but on the other hand no one really knew. Once, when her sisters had dared her, she had gone a few yards into the grounds. The boys had arranged to wait for her, and when they leapt out at her with banshee shrieks and wails, she had raced away from their crazy laughter and had torn her dress climbing over the wall. Now she was being asked to go to the gates, to walk right down the drive between the dark, dank foliage, to go inside, to meet whatever was in there.

Again she went to see Aunt Jess, who laughed at her. 'Foolish rumours, dear. Maybe the place is run down, maybe the old fellow doesn't like children. Do they tease him?'

'The boys do,' admitted Sid. 'And some of the girls,' she added.

'I'm not surprised he glares. I'm sure you'd find things very different if you went after the job. I've not seen the place for years, but when I was a girl they held parties and balls there in the enormous drawing room. I used to creep through the woods and watch the people getting out of their carriages or cars – such noisy, smelly vehicles they were in those days – and listen to the music. The room was decorated with hundreds of flowers and brilliantly lit by masses of candles. Women who were dressed like princesses danced with handsome men.' She gave a little laugh. 'Memories. I suppose they were quite ordinary people really. Perhaps I was only seeing their clothes. They were so elegant. In fact, I think it might have been those gowns that set me off on my career. And Mrs Cardell was the loveliest of all. She was like a queen. Once, I was so fascinated I forgot to be cautious, and was caught by a footman. I was scared; my shrieks brought Mrs Cardell to the window. She beckoned us inside. I waited for a humiliating scolding in front of her guests, but she bent down and gave me a sweetmeat. It was pink and white and more luscious than I'd ever imagined a sweet could be. Far too pretty to eat. I kept it until it got sticky and melted all over my Sunday camisole. Mum was furious. I was smacked soundly but I didn't care. I've never forgotten the way Mrs Cardell looked. Now she's old and frail, but she was a real beauty.'

'What happened to her? Why is the house so horrible now?'

'The money ran out. Times were hard after the war. Then her husband died. It was all so sad. But I'm sure she'll be nice to you. People don't change all that much. At least, go and look at the job. I'll write a little note of introduction.'

Chapter Four

'Greystone House? As a servant? Again?' Mum was incredulous.

'It's a job,' said Sid, 'if I get it.'

'If you get it, indeed! The job with Keevils was bad enough, but that was in a small house as a parlourmaid. There you'll just be a skivvy in a rich house. Fancy letting the Labour Exchange think you'd want to go on working as a servant. Why didn't you tell them you wanted to be in an office or shop, not demean yourself by forever cleaning up other people's mess?'

'That's all I've ever done. And I didn't get it through the Labour Exchange. Aunty Jess suggested it.'

'Aunty Jess! When have you seen her? You didn't tell me. What made you go there? I hope you didn't tell her about Mr Keevil.'

'Yes, I did. Why shouldn't I?'

'I would have thought it would be obvious! You didn't need to tell her everything. Now she'll think you're a bad girl and our name will be mud.'

Anger possessed Sid. Her mother didn't believe her account of what had happened. She wanted to yell at her. She wanted to weep. But she wouldn't let them provoke her. She said, 'No, it won't, Mum. She's not like that at all. She was very kind and understanding. She didn't blame me at all.'

'Oh, didn't she? Anyway, what does she know about girls? She's only ever had one boy.'

'She was one herself once.'

'Cheeky answers will get you nowhere! One boy and he'll never work in her shop. She hardly ever sees him. She's always busy and they've sent him away. She's the only married woman in our family who goes out to work.'

'Aunty Mattie works full time.'

'You're determined to have the last word, aren't you? Aunt Mattie's case is different. She's in the family business. She doesn't have to go out.'

Mum was red-faced and furious and Sid saw no point in quarrelling so she said nothing more, but Mum hadn't finished. 'Going out as a *servant* to Greystone House,' she ranted. 'It's going from bad to worse! All right, I haven't forgotten why you say you left, but I still wonder about that. Mr Keevil's got a senior position in the bank. He's always been well respected, and I've never heard a word of complaint against him.'

Mum's unjust words broke Sid's resolution not to argue. 'You don't believe me! None of you believes me! What have I ever done to make you think I'd allow a man to be familiar with me and then tell awful lies about it?'

'I'd perhaps be more sure of the truth if you'd gone straight to Mrs Keevil the first time he tried something on.'

'A pinch! I thought if I just let it go he wouldn't do it again.'

'What nonsense! Any girl knows that if you let a man touch you once he'll think you're cheap. No wonder he cornered you in the bedroom.'

'That's not fair. I hated his nasty ways. I was afraid to tell Mrs Keevil because I thought she wouldn't believe me and I'd be out of work again. I didn't dream he'd tell her himself. Of course, he put all the blame on me and she wouldn't listen to me.'

'There's no need to shout.'

'Isn't there? *You* don't believe me, my own *mother*!'

'Can you blame me? Well, I suppose we must think ourselves lucky if you're offered a job at all. When are you going for your interview?'

'I have to telephone her. And I'm not going as a kitchen maid. Aunt Jess said "maid-companion". It might be quite nice.'

'Well, it's probably as good as you can expect after all that's happened.' Mum marched out of the kitchen, every line of her back expressing anger.

Sid stood in the telephone box. She had given the number to the operator and the bell at the other end went on and on ringing. 'Sorry, no reply,' came the operator's clipped voice.

'Oh, please give it a little longer. I'm calling an old lady. She might be slow.'

Just as she was about to give up, the telephone was answered and a man's voice said quaveringly, 'Hello?'

She pressed button 'A' and heard the coppers fall. 'Hello? I'm calling Mrs Cardell. Could I speak to her, please?'

'Who is it?'

'My name is Miss Penrose. I want to make an appointment to apply for the job.'

'What job?'

Sid's heart sank. Perhaps Aunt Jess had got it wrong. Perhaps the position had already been filled. In a corner of her mind she rather hoped it had. 'Doesn't she need a companion-maid any more?'

'She needs a lot of things. Wait a minute.'

The receiver was bumped on to a hard surface and Sid could hear the sound of retreating footsteps on bare boards. Whatever kind of rich place had bare boards? Aunt Jess's house was as heavily carpeted as the shop. After an age the receiver was picked up again. 'She says to come now.' Before Sid could utter a word, the man cut her off.

'Well?' demanded Mum when she returned.

'I've to go now. I'd better change into something nice.'

'You'd better look as plain as possible if you're looking for a servant's job.'

'That won't be difficult, will it?' snapped Sid, her nerves strained beyond endurance.

Mrs Penrose tutted, which irritated Sid still further. By the time she had put on a dark dress from which she removed the pink silk rose she had pinned to it, shrugged into last year's coat, which was too small and which she had been saving to replace, rammed her old, unbecoming felt hat on her head, she was really annoyed. Darn the old woman for making her dress like a frump! Drat Mrs Keevil! Blow Madame Rita! And damn Mr Keevil!

'Put gloves on,' ordered Mum. 'And mind you've got a clean handkerchief. I'm glad you haven't got any muck on your face. At least you look like a servant.'

Sid waited for a more encouraging message, but none came. She stalked out of the house and almost slammed the front door.

In her fury she nearly forgot where she was heading, but her bravado died when she arrived at the sagging gates of Greystone House. The untended trees hung low over the boundary wall, and branches crowded the rutted rive. The dark green rhododendron bushes, which struggled only too successfully for space, looked intimidating; walking between them was an eerie experience. Only the thought of going home and telling her family that she was still out of work kept her going.

She turned a bend. The house lay before her. Aunt Jess wouldn't have recognised it. She recalled it as being a solid, respectable mansion, the grey stones kept clean, with long gleaming windows and newly painted woodwork, but in fewer than thirty years the stones had blackened with soot, the windows were grimy, the paintwork on the frames and the doors was peeling, so that in places the original bare wood was uncovered. There seemed to be dozens of chimneys, but only one gave forth a drift of smoke. Every instinct told Sid to turn and run. She hesitated, then took hold of the tarnished brass door-knocker and banged. It made hardly a sound. She tried a little harder, then in panic really slammed the knocker so that its echoes rang inside.

Nothing happened for a while, then she heard the slow shuffle of feet. She waited breathlessly for what would be revealed. The door was opened by an old man who stood glaring at her from rheumy eyes. 'Yes? What do you want?'

'I'm Miss Penrose. I telephoned. Mrs Cardell asked me to call.'

'She did, did she?'

'Wasn't it you I spoke to?'

'What if it was?'

Sid stared at him, bewildered.

He said, 'I suppose you'll be after the job. You won't take it. We've had four women here already and they've run away.'

'Run away?'

'In a manner of speaking. One stayed for a night then packed her bag. Said it was spooky. The others said they weren't trained to be a nurse.'

'A nurse? Is she ill?'

'No, just old, like me.' He grinned, showing large gaps in his yellowing teeth.

'Who's been looking after Mrs Cardell until now?'

'A maid she'd had from infancy. She died. Heaven knows how old she was. We buried her five weeks ago. I've been doing everything for her, but it ain't a man's job to look after a female.'

'No,' said Sid. She waited then said, 'May I come in?'

'What? Oh, yes, I suppose you'd better. But you won't stay.'

The house amazed Sid. There were cobwebs everywhere, as thick with dust as the furniture. It was obvious that the place had not been properly cleaned in months, maybe years. She began to wonder if Mrs Cardell would be wearing a tattered wedding gown among the ruins of her wedding feast, like Miss Havisham in Dickens's *Great Expectations*. She followed the man; her footsteps echoed as his had done when she had phoned. The hall certainly did have bare wood but it was oak, wide oak planks which should have been beautiful but were scuffed and dirty. Some cobwebs were draped artistically like shawls between the arms of graceful statues; others hung from the gas-lamp brackets.

'Didn't her maid do any dusting?'

The old man grinned. 'Her! She had the rheumatism so bad she could hardly get out of bed some days. This place is damp.'

Sid had already noticed the dank smell which permeated the great house. She stared at the big, ancient furniture with its lovely lines. She had never imagined anything like this. She had certainly never seen anything like it; deep down a part of her revelled in the unkempt beauty. She followed the old man up the uncarpeted stairway between carved pilasters and balustrades, and waited while he knocked at a heavy door.

'Come in,' called a strong female voice which was at variance with what Sid was expecting. Her nervousness was sublimated in her eagerness to meet the enigmatic character who neglected all these possessions. When she walked into the bedroom, an elderly lady was reclining on a daybed near the fire which was stacked high with coal. She didn't look like a witch, not the kind Sid had read about in fairy-tales. Her figure was well rounded and she wore a pastel pink gown. Her white hair was drawn back into a soft bun, her pale face was lined, but her eyes were fierce as they raked Sid; her nervousness came crashing back.

'You are applying for the position of maid and companion?' she said. She didn't sound impressed.

'Yes, please.'

'You're not very old.'

'No, ma'am.'

'I'm not "ma'am". Save that for royalty. You address me as madam.'

'Yes, madam.'

'You want a job?'

'Yes please, madam.'

'Why here? The others who've come have been older women who can't find anything else, and they ran away or left almost before they began.'

'Your manservant told me so, madam.'

'His name is Brindle. Isaac Brindle.'

'Yes, madam.'
'He's been a good and faithful servant.'
'Yes, madam.'
'You don't say much.'
'No, madam.'
'Is that all you can say?'
'No, madam.'
'My God! I wonder if you'll suit me.'
'I hope so, madam.'
'I want a companion, not just a maid. Someone who can sit with me, read to me sometimes when my eyes ache. You can read, I suppose.'
'Yes, madam.'
'I want a good listener. Sometimes I like to ramble a bit. And I need someone to talk intelligently to me. Your vocabulary seems to be severely limited.'
'Does it, madam?'
Mrs Cardell sighed and the delicate lace at her throat fluttered. 'I suppose I shall have to offer you the position. You look strong enough to manage the housework.'
'There seems a great deal of it needing done, madam.'
'Does that bother you?'
'No, madam.'
'For pity's sake, if you must talk in monosyllables, you don't need to say "madam" every damned time.'
'I'm only obeying your order.'
Mrs Cardell almost smiled. 'Obedient, are you?'
'Yes.'
'Show me your references.'
'I've a letter here from my Aunty Jess. Mrs Jess Venner. She has a gown shop. It's named "Jessica Modes". She sold you gowns and things.'
'Oh, Mrs Venner. A most obliging person. So you are her niece.' She read the note and handed it back. 'She recommends you. Says you are quick and clever. You have other references?'
Sid held out the envelope containing Madame Rita's letter. Mrs Cardell read it. 'It's not very impressive, is it?' She picked up the other letter. 'Your aunt seems convinced you are worthy of a job. Can you cook?'
'Yes, madam.'
The old lady's eyes gleamed. 'Really? Cook? Are you trained?'
'Only by my mother, but she's marvellous, although I suppose our sort of food would be too plain for you.'
'Can you cook potatoes that come out of the saucepan floury and white and not sloppy? Can you take cabbage off the boil before it's dissolved into slime? Can you make light pastry? I dearly love pies. And what about cakes and puddings? I have a sweet tooth.'
'I can do all those easily, madam. But if I spend a lot of time in the kitchen and more time cleaning away the cobwebs and dust, I shan't have much time left to read to you, shall I?' The words had formed

logically in Sid's mind and came out quite naturally.

Mrs Cardell really did smile this time. 'So you can talk. If we suit one another we shall have to make up a time-table. Of course, the work is bound to be hard. That doesn't frighten you?'

'No, madam.'

Mrs Cardell picked up Madame Rita's scrappy letter again. 'This reference refers to a time some months back. Where have you been since then?'

'With a family called Keevil. I was house parlourmaid. But I haven't a reference from them.'

'Oh. Why not?'

Sid took a deep breath and spoke fast. 'Because she sacked me for trying to make love to her husband, only I didn't, he tried it on with me, he stuck his tongue into my mouth when she was out and I bit it and she believed him and not me and...' Mrs Cardell's severe countenance was softened as she laughed outright and held up a white hand. Sid's voice trailed off. Then she said, 'It's the truth, though I don't suppose you'll believe me. Nobody else does.'

'By nobody else, you mean...?'

'My family.'

'More fool them. I'm sure you are honest.'

Sid felt like kissing her. 'Two of my aunties don't think I was lying, but they're different from the others.'

Mrs Cardell's eyes lit up. 'I would definitely like you to work for me. I long to hear all about your aunties and the others. You do wish to work for me?'

'Yes please, madam.'

'When will you begin?'

'Today? I can soon fetch my things. I only live a step away.'

'Today?' Mrs Cardell looked at her watch. The strap was plain gold and Sid was sure that it really was gold and not just gilt like Mrs Keevil's. 'It wants three hours to dinner-time. Do you think you could make me something nice? Brindle's been a perfect lamb, but his cooking is frightful.'

'As long as the ingredients are in the kitchen.'

'Will you go and look before you fetch your things? If you don't have all you need you can shop before you return.'

'Excuse me, madam, but you haven't mentioned my wages.'

'Oh, yes. I'll give you ten shillings a week all found.' Mrs Cardell spoke as if she was doing Sid an immeasurably good turn, but Sid was determined not to be put down any more.

'I'll be responsible for several people's jobs,' pointed out Sid, 'cleaning, cooking, and being a companion to you.'

'Board and lodging are worth quite a large amount.'

'I think twelve and sixpence would be fairer.'

Mrs Cardell said nothing for a moment. 'All right, twelve and sixpence. It is more than I expect to pay an untrained chit of a girl, and I shall expect you to earn it. By the way, why are you known by a boy's name?'

'What?'

'Your aunt says you are generally called Sid.'

'It's short for Sidonia but everyone calls me Sid. Except Mrs Keevil. She called me Sarah. She said my name wasn't suitable for a servant.'

'It's a beautiful name. You will be Sidonia here.'

'Thank you, madam.' Sid felt pleased out of all proportion. She went downstairs, where Brindle was hovering in the hall making ineffectual dabs at the cobwebs with a filthy feather duster on a stick.

'Can you show me to the kitchen, please?' asked Sid.

'Has she engaged you?'

'Yes. She wants me to make her something nice for dinner.'

'Does she? Has she given you any money for the shopping?'

'Not yet. I don't know what she needs.'

'She's not all that willing to hand out money.'

'Well, she'll have to if she wants decent food.' In spite of the bizarre situation, Sid's confidence was growing. After all, what was she dealing with? Two old people who needed help.

Brindle grinned. 'Will you make enough food for me?'

'For all of us, as long as I have the ingredients.'

'This way.' Brindle led the way along a dark passage in which were several closed doors. He gestured at them as they hurried by. 'Large drawing room, dining room, Mrs Cardell's sitting room – it's quite small – study, library.' He pushed open a door which was lined with green baize on the other side. Sid was fascinated. She had read about green baize doors. As they walked along a narrow passage she began to feel as if she was actually in a novel. She wouldn't be surprised if Count Dracula suddenly appeared among the cobwebs... She stopped this thought abruptly, taking a firm hold on her imagination as she thought of the dark nights she would have to face in this grim place.

'Where do you sleep?' she asked.

'Up in the attic. That's where we servants always slept. Of course, there's only me up there now. The stairs are awful steep.'

'Why don't you take another room. There seem to be plenty.'

'Me take one of the family rooms?' Brindle sounded shocked. He lapsed back into his grumbling mood. 'She'd give me what-for if I dared presume like that. You'd better watch your step, miss, if you want to keep your job.'

'My name's Sidonia Penrose, and you don't have to call me miss. I'm just another servant like you.'

'What a funny name!' He pushed open another door and Sid found herself at the head of a flight of stone steps. At the bottom was yet another door, behind which lay a huge kitchen. The house was built on two levels, and the back windows overlooked the vegetable garden. She looked round. It appeared to her that the whole of her parents' home could be fitted in. A vast fire-heated range was built into one wall, and alongside it another, smaller one. She wondered how anyone coped with them. She walked into the centre and gazed round at the dozens of pots and pans hanging from hooks, copper and brass, all tarnished and green, metal utensils, a dresser full of china as thick with dust as everything else.

Brindle opened a cupboard door. 'There's a few plates and things in there that we've been using. All that other stuff was for the days they had guests. The cutlery's in this drawer. Of course, she's got cases of silver stuff. It's still in the butler's pantry, that's that door over there. All of it needs cleaning. The housekeeper's room is through the door on the other side.'

'Where's the sink?'

'Over by the window.'

Little light penetrated the grimy glass. The stone sink was shallow and wide, with an open drain-hole from which an unpleasant smell emanated.

'All the other cooks used it,' said Brindle, sensing her dismay.

Sid hardly heard him. She had caught sight of an ordinary cooker. 'That's a gas stove.'

'I've been using it,' said Brindle.

'It works? Thank goodness.'

She became aware that she was shivering. In this stone-flagged cavern of a kitchen, the cold was insidiously penetrating.

'In the old days,' said Brindle, 'the ranges were always hot and the kitchen was lovely and cosy.'

'Well, I can't see myself ever using them. They're big enough to cook a banquet if you needed one. Isn't there a smaller fireplace to get the place warm?'

'I suppose we could get the one in the small range going. She won't buy enough coal to feed the big one.'

Sid examined the gas oven. It was thick with grease, much of it burned in. The inside was draped with cobwebs and thick with mice droppings. She grimaced and began a slow tour of the kitchen. There were droppings everywhere. Nothing here would be fit to use before it had received a thorough cleansing, and she couldn't possibly manage it before dinner.

'Here's the pantry,' said Brindle. 'Down the passage is the game larder and the cold-store. There's nothing in them any more.'

There wasn't much in the pantry. A bag of flour and one of sugar, both spilling their contents where rodents had nibbled; a lump of unappetising fat – margarine or butter, it was impossible to tell without tasting; a bottle of vinegar and a jar of salt; a few ancient-looking vegetables and some rusty cans. The tea was mercifully clean, stored in a tin caddy from which most of the original decoration had worn away. The remains of a bottle of milk which had been delivered that morning stood beside it.

'Is this all?' she asked.

'Yes. Well, what do you expect? I can't do everything.'

'I'm not blaming you. Doesn't she have any cats? At least they'd keep the mice away.'

'We used to have some. Don't know where they went.'

Probably somewhere warm with food provided, thought Sid. 'What were you going to give her tonight?'

'I was planning on opening a tin of baked beans.'

'Would that have satisfied her? She gave me the impression that she's fond of her food.'

'She is that. As good a trencherman as I've yet to see, but I can't cook. I forget things and they burn and when I don't they never seem to taste right. Anyway, t'ain't man's work, cooking!'

Sid went back upstairs.

'Well?' demanded Mrs Cardell.

'I've been to the kitchen. The place isn't fit to use.'

'Why not?'

'Because it's filthy.'

'Brindle doesn't grumble.'

'Well, I can't use it. And I'll need to buy clean food. The mice have been busy.'

'Can you provide something tasty to eat?'

'I can, but I'll need money.'

Mrs Cardell frowned. 'How much?'

'I'll let you know when I've made a list.'

'What do you want for tonight?'

'I can't cook for you tonight. It's a wonder to me you haven't been ill eating food from such a place!'

'It hasn't bothered us before.'

'When did you last see it?' asked Sid. The tasks ahead had made her forget her subservience. In fact, she realised, she had been talking to her new employer as if she was an equal, and had been answered in the same fashion.

'What a stupid question,' Mrs Cardell snapped. 'I haven't been in the kitchen for years. I must have been quite young.'

'Well, I've just come from it and it isn't fit to cook pig-swill in.'

'What do you intend to do?' Mrs Cardell sounded sulky and Sid wanted to laugh.

'I intend to clean the kitchen before I cook. I'll start as soon as possible.'

'Can you make me a pudding tonight? I adore pies with apples or rhubarb or cherries: anything, really.'

'No, I'm sorry, there won't be time. We can have fish and chips. I know a good shop.'

'Fish and chips? Cooked in a shop? I've never eaten such a thing.'

'Then you've been missing a treat.'

'I thought you said your mother was a good cook.'

'Even good cooks sometimes send out for food when they're spring-cleaning.'

Mrs Cardell stared at a painting on the opposite wall. It depicted Greystone House, its stones gleaming in a setting sun, a carriage waiting at the front door from which a man and woman in elegant Edwardian dress were emerging. She sighed and looked back at Sid.

'Very well. How much money do you need for our dinner?'

'One-and-six for fish and chips for the three of us, and a shilling for bread and butter.'

'All the shops will be closed this evening,' said Mrs Cardell suspiciously.

'Not the fish and chip shop – and there's a little corner shop too which stays open all hours,' said Sid. 'Their stuff's a bit dearer, but you pay for the convenience.'

'None of the other women I've employed complained like this.' Mrs Cardell still sounded quite sulky.

'But they didn't stay, did they?'

The old lady took a purse from her pocket and extracted a half-crown which Sid put into her pocket. 'I'm not a wealthy woman, you know.'

'I'll be thrifty. Home cooking is cheaper, and as soon as the kitchen is fit to use, that's what you'll get. Oh, by the way, do you take sugar in your tea? If you do I'll need to buy some.'

Mrs Cardell looked as if she might have more arguments, but she said nothing and opened her purse, extracting a further sixpence. 'Are you going home to fetch your things?'

'Yes. Do you have a vacuum cleaner?'

'Certainly not! They are for lazy women.'

'Or women who have a great deal to do, madam.'

'No servant of ours ever asked for one.'

'I dare say that was when you had a lot of help. They are very popular now, and a boon to busy mothers. That's what the advertisements say.'

'I'm not a busy mother and neither are you.'

'No, madam.'

Sid left, resolving that one day she would get Mrs Cardell to buy some household aids. She realised that she was actually looking forward to the challenge.

Her mother was eager to know what the old house was like and what the owner had said. Sid, keen to get back and begin a task which was beginning to look like a crusade, told her in as few words as possible.

'Mice everywhere? That's disgusting! Fancy letting a place get into that state. It's not healthy. You could catch something. And cobwebs? Such filth. Who'd have thought it in a civilised house?'

Sid packed her few belongings and was back at Greystone House within an hour. She then discovered what she should have checked, that there was very little soap, that the scrubbing brushes lacked many of their bristles, and that the only hot water came from heating it on the gas stove.

'How does the mistress have a bath?' she asked Brindle.

'There's a geyser in her bathroom next door to her bedroom. There's a couple more in guest bathrooms. They were the latest thing when they had them put in. I suppose they're old-fashioned nowadays.'

'People still use them. You'll have to show me where I can bathe.'

'I just have a good wash myself.'

'I shall want to bathe,' said Sid firmly. 'Could you light the fire in the small range, please?'

She began on the smaller kitchen table, scrubbing until it reached the white wood colour which was originally intended. The pantry shelves were next, and finally the gas stove. It defied her attempts to remove the muck, and she added to her growing shopping list a good oven cleanser. She washed and polished trays and some of the good dishes, and removed the tarnish from a selection of silver cutlery using a cleanser from a small can supplied by Brindle. He had several times come to the kitchen to see what she was doing, and she wondered what he was working on.

He explained that he was digging a patch of vegetable garden ready to plant out some greens. 'I got something else to show you,' he said confidentially on his latest visit to the kitchen. He lit a candle and led her to a small door which he unlocked with an enormous iron key. There was a flight of stone steps. 'The cellar,' he hissed significantly. 'It goes down really deep.'

She drew back. It looked eerie.

'Nothing to fear,' he said. 'It's where we keep the wine. Upstairs dearly loves wine with her food, but she wouldn't let me show the other women where it was because she said they'd steal it and some of it's valuable.'

Sid was mystified. How could wine be valuable? It was something people bought at Christmas, then threw away the bottles and waited until the next family occasion important enough to warrant drink, but she was gratified by Brindle's trust in her.

She was amazed by the cellars. They ran one into the other through archways and were lined with racks.

'They all used to be full,' he said. 'That was in the old days.' He sighed. 'Now there's not much left.'

In one of the arched cellars they found bottles of wine, many of them dust-covered. 'They're supposed to be like that,' Brindle explained, 'so don't think to come down here with your duster.' He reached out for a bottle. 'This is a fine Moselle. It goes with fish. It has to be served cold but it won't get warm in the kitchen the way it is now. She's likely to grumble if I open it, but she deserves something to get over having to eat shop-cooked food. Mind you, I like fish and chips myself.'

'I didn't know you had different wines for different food. You'll have to teach me about that.'

'I'll teach you, if that's what you really want.' He looked pleased. 'In the old days servants were properly trained. I was head footman once and expected to be butler, that's how I know about wine. But it never happened. The money went and that was that.'

Dinner was at seven-thirty. At seven Sid slipped out and returned with the food. She had already laid up Mrs Cardell's tray with a white table-napkin, silver cutlery, a pepper-pot, a small glass and silver dish containing salt and a tiny spoon, and a dainty cut-glass carafe of vinegar. Brindle had shown her the linen cupboards upstairs, huge places lined with shelves filled with every conceivable type of household linen, and all of it clean. She had taken a bundle of table napkins, using one for a cloth while Brindle opened the wine and wrapped it in another. He added a glass to the tray.

'It doesn't shine much,' said Sid.

'It's old lead glass. It's supposed to look like that. I don't hold with the modern crystal stuff.'

Sid had put the food in the range oven; and when she opened the door, the succulent smell wafted out, mixed with the scent of hot newspaper. She dished out a portion, covered the hot plate with a silver lid, and climbed the two flights of stairs to reach Mrs Cardell's bedroom.

Mrs Cardell inspected the tray incredulously. 'The old rogue! He's opened a bottle without my permission.' But she looked pleased. 'Put it on the small table. I shall sit there.'

Sid poured the wine as she had been instructed, and Mrs Cardell tasted it. 'Perfect.' She lifted the silver cover without enthusiasm, but her eyes brightened. 'It looks quite good.'

'It is good. Eat it up.'

'I'm going to. I don't need instructions from a servant.'

Sid's brows went up, but she didn't resent her employer's sudden change of attitude. The future looked like being interesting. She would learn as much as she could about high life, and perhaps Mrs Cardell would get to know something about conditions on the other side.

When she fetched the tray she saw that every scrap had been eaten. She bent over to take the tray and the old lady asked plaintively, 'Is there a pudding?'

'Not tonight, I'm afraid.'

Mrs Cardell sighed. 'Leave the wine. And thank you, Sidonia, for the civilised way you served my meal.'

Sid felt almost unreasonably pleased. Following Brindle, she climbed the stairs with her luggage, and was shown into an attic bedroom which contained a narrow bed with a lumpy mattress and some decrepit furniture. It smelt very damp. She slid her hand over the mattress. 'I can't sleep on this,' she said. 'It's almost wet.'

'I got no instructions to show you to any other room. This is where the maids sleep.'

'I'm not surprised no one will stay.'

'You'll stay, won't you?' Brindle sounded anxious.

'Yes, but not if I have to use this room.'

'Best go and speak to madam about it.'

Sid tackled Mrs Cardell, who gave permission for her to sleep in the nanny's room in the nursery suite. On first sight this seemed little better than the attics – it too was suffused with the penetrating cold which seemed to build up in unused rooms – but there was a large fireplace, and Sid hauled up wood and coal, made a good fire, protected it with the large nursery guard, and lay the mattress in front of it. Then she returned to her employer.

'I hope you're suited,' said Mrs Cardell in a derisive tone. Sid ignored it.

'I shall have to buy quite a number of things before I can do my work properly.'

Mrs Cardell received this news with a frown, and by the time Sid had come to the end of her list, she was annoyed. 'You'll bankrupt me,' she complained.

'The whole doesn't come to more than three pounds. I haven't listed any luxuries . . .'

'Bananas and apples. Fruit isn't a necessity.'

'They are good for you,' said Sid firmly, 'and I've included cooking apples, don't forget.'

Mrs Cardell's eyes brightened. 'We grow our own. We used to store them in long rows and Cook bottled and preserved ever so many. No one's been able to tend the trees, so I suppose those days are gone.'

'Not necessarily,' said Sid, 'but at the moment the pantry is empty apart from what's left of the rolls. We'll have them for breakfast, but when I've bought bacon and eggs, I'll cook you something more substantial.'

Mrs Cardell's planned protests were lost in her contemplation of such delicacies, but she said only, 'I shall be going to bed soon. Please return at nine o'clock.'

Brindle helped put the things in the pantry. He still looked surly and spoke in short grunts, but Sid had the feeling that he was quite pleased with the way things were going. She washed the few dishes and, with Brindle's help, carried in scuttles of coal and kindling and fed the range fire which Brindle said could be kept in all night by using the dampers properly. She could leave pans of water on the hob ready for tomorrow.

'There must be a hot water system,' she said. 'There are radiators in the house.'

'There's a boiler in the cellar. I suppose all the flues will be clogged up, even if we could use it.'

'You mean, we need the sweep?'

'I do all the sweeping needed round here, but she won't want to buy extra fuel.'

'You're a man of many talents.' He gave her a suspicious look, but promised to sweep the flues, mumbling that it would do no good.

'I'll need some large pans for water.'

Brindle said, 'No need. If you open that damper in the small range, it cuts down the oven and heats water in a big boiler. That's it on the end with a tap.'

'That's wonderful!'

'Glad you're pleased.' Brindle's expression remained lugubrious, but he lingered, warming his hands over the fire and accepting Sid's invitation to sit a while and drink a cup of tea.

At nine o'clock Sid returned to Mrs Cardell and helped her undress. Her underwear was all made of fine white cotton with touches of lace. Her corsets were the old-fashioned type which needed to be laced. 'I shall need you in the morning to lace them up again,' she said. When she was in bed, Sid made up the fire which Brindle had lit.

'Where's the fireguard?' she asked.

'Am I a child to need a fireguard?' demanded Mrs Cardell crossly.

'No, madam. But it would be safer.'

'Nonsense. I've lived here for most of my life and never needed such a thing.'

'I'll go shopping first thing tomorrow,' said Sid. 'Could you give me some money, please?'

Mrs Cardell reached into her purse and drew out three pounds. 'That's what you want, isn't it?'

'I've decided I'll need more. I won't have time to shop every day, and I have to buy scouring powder, brushes, polish and stuff.'

'How much more?'

'I'm not really sure. If you give me five pounds I'll bring you any change.'

'Five pounds! That's more than a week's wages.'

'It's certainly a lot more than mine.'

Mrs Cardell frowned, but she brought out two more notes and Sid put them in her apron pocket.

'Is there anything else you need, madam?'

'Just light my candle. I like to read a little at night. You may turn off the gas as you go.'

As Sid reached the door, Mrs Cardell said, 'Sidonia, I think you and I will do very well together. Provided you don't waste my money.'

'I hope so, madam.'

'Does she live in her bedroom?' Sid asked Brindle as they shared a bedtime cup of tea. She wished she had remembered to buy cocoa. It was such a comfort at the end of the day.

'No,' said Brindle. 'She was feeling out of sorts today. At least, that's what she said. I think she's bored. Usually she spends most of her time in her little sitting room.'

Brindle said he'd lock up. Sid went up to the nursery, warm and cosy now, made up her bed and soon fell asleep.

On her way to the shops early next morning, Sid met her friend, Angie Wright.

'Hello, stranger,' said Angie.

'I'm sorry I haven't seen you,' said Sid. 'I've been terribly busy lately.'

'So I heard'

'What have you heard?'

'Some daft story of you trying to get off with a bank manager.'

'How did it get around? And it was an assistant bank manager and I didn't try to get off with him.'

'That's what I thought. Neither of us are oil paintings. Our looks don't exactly drive men to distraction.'

Sid laughed and explained what had happened. 'Now I'm working in Greystone House.'

Angie's small brown eyes opened wide. 'With the old witch?'

'She's not. She's really very nice. At least, I don't know much about her yet, but I'm sure she is.'

Angie said wistfully, 'I don't suppose there's a job for me there?'

'Are you out of work?'

'They've been cutting staff at the factory. I was one of the unlucky ones. I've been to the Labour Exchange and tried for ever so many places, but I never seem to get chosen.'

'I don't think Mrs Cardell wants to employ anyone else, but I have a feeling she may have to. You'll be first if I'm allowed to hire anyone.'

She ended her trip with a visit to her father's shop, where there was the usual beautifully arranged autumn display of fruits and flowers. Dad was quite an artist in his way. He greeted her with his shopkeeper's smile which faded when he saw who it was. 'What are you doing here?'

'I've come to buy the greengrocery for Mrs Cardell.'

'Oh, your new boss.'

'Yes, and you'll have to treat me with respect now I'm a housekeeper.'

'Is that what you are?'

'That and a dozen other things. I must get back as soon as possible. I've been out for ages.'

Dad looked at her loaded bags. Then another customer entered and he turned his attention to her. Sid waited until the woman had left and said gently, 'My money is as good as hers, Dad, and maybe better.'

He was startled. 'What can I do for you?'

By the time Sid reached Greystone House her knees were almost buckling at the weight she carried.

Brindle greeted her sourly. 'She's been wanting you for more than an hour. You'd best go straight up.'

Sid washed her hands, combed her hair, and went into Mrs Cardell's bedroom.

'Where have you been?' The old lady was querulous.

'Shopping for food. You'll get your pudding tonight.' Sid almost added, 'if you are good', but remembered herself in time.

'What will it be?'

'I haven't quite decided. In fact, I haven't had time to unpack the bags.'

'Help me dress. I wish to go down.'

'Yes, madam.'

Dressed in a rustling dark blue gown, a necklace and earrings, Mrs Cardell moved down the stairway, leaning on Sid's arm. In the doorway of the small sitting room she stopped. 'There's no fire. And it's dusty. How dare you bring me to a room like this. Why haven't you attended to it?'

'I haven't had time, madam; and in any case, I didn't know you would come downstairs today.'

'Brindle could have done it.'

'It didn't occur to me to ask him.'

'He's made me a fire these last few weeks. I feel the cold. He should have thought of it.'

'Would you like me to fetch him, madam?'

'I hope you don't mean to be cheeky.'

'No, madam.'

Mrs Cardell sighed. 'I can't sit here. The days are getting cooler.'

'Do you want to go back to your room, madam?'

'I suppose so. No, wait, I'll come down to the kitchen with you. It's always lovely and warm there. Do you know, Sidonia, I haven't visited it since I was introduced as a bride, but I remember the heat and the baking smells.'

Sid helped her down the stone steps and pushed open the baize door. Mrs Cardell took a step inside then stopped, staring round. 'What's happened here? It's all so . . . dreary, so uncared for. Oh, dear, it isn't at all the way I remember it.'

'No, madam.'

Brindle was polishing the silver, a newspaper spread on the large table.

'You should be doing that in the butler's pantry!' exclaimed Mrs Cardell.

Brindle had jumped to his feet. 'Yes, madam.' He began to gather up the things but Sid said, 'Must he go there? I haven't had time to clean it yet, and besides, it's too cold for him.'

The old lady looked sadly at him. 'You're getting old, Brindle, like me. Our bones need a good fire.'

'There's one over there, madam,' said Brindle, still standing, hesitating over whether to obey his employer or stay where it was warm and relatively cosy. 'I lit it last night and it's going a treat.'

'Thank you. I'll accept the offer. Do sit down, Brindle, and finish the silver.' She sat by the fire, a pensive look on her face, and Sid hurried away with a housemaid's box to tackle the small sitting room. It wasn't small by Sid's standards and, as she cleaned, the perfection of the proportions and its beauty took her breath away. The wallpaper and furnishings had faded from their first glory, but the soft, blurred hues were restful. The curtains striped in green and cream could, she noted, do with cleaning. She'd tackle that sometime. The polished wood floor needed attention too, and something had been trodden into the plain wool carpet. The room wasn't very dusty, having been cleaned lately, if indifferently. She enjoyed lighting the fire, and enthusiastically rubbed the steel grate to a silver shine. She polished surfaces which were easily seen, resolving to come back and give the place a proper going over as soon as she had time. She treated everything with instinctive care, loving the rich brown, almost red wood, taking a particular delight in a small display cabinet with a mirrored interior, showing every aspect of the pieces of porcelain it contained.

She returned to the kitchen and found Mrs Cardell enjoying a cup of tea with Brindle. 'The room is ready for you, madam.'

'Thank you, Sidonia.' In her sitting room she looked round.

'I haven't finished yet, madam,' said Sid anxiously. 'I've just done the parts that show.'

Mrs Cardell smiled. 'A girl with initiative.'

'I'll tackle the rest as soon as possible.'

Mrs Cardell sat in an easy chair and held out her hands to the fire which was burning well. 'How lovely to see the grate looking as it should.'

'Thank you, madam.'

'Thank you, Sidonia.'

'Do you have everything you want? Will I need to read to you, because there are so many things needing doing?'

The old lady smiled. 'I won't take you from your many tasks, which I hope include making a nice lunch.'

Sid served her first lunch in the small sitting room, having declared the dining room far too dirty and cold for use. She waited anxiously for Mrs Cardell to say something. Her employer couldn't know that it was the first time she had ever coped with a whole meal on her own. She had learned something about cooking from Mum and more from Mrs Dingle, but much of it just by watching.

Mrs Cardell spooned up her pea soup appreciatively. This was one of Mum's recipes and could be quickly prepared; the ham-bone Sid had used had lots more goodness in it. 'A truly splendid soup,' Mrs Cardell declared. Her eyes gleamed at the sight of cauliflower cheese. She had finished it by the time Sid returned. 'How lovely! Bread and butter pudding! I haven't tasted it since I was in the schoolroom. What a splendid idea. With sultanas! Delicious.' At the end of the meal she leaned back and sighed. 'I'm very glad indeed that I asked you to work for me.'

'Thank you, madam.'

'Have you eaten?'

'Not yet, madam.'

'What will you have?'

'The same as you, madam.'

'And why not?'

'I'll bring your coffee.'

'Thank you, Sidonia.'

Sid saw her employer settled in her easy chair with coffee at her elbow, then she and Brindle tucked into their own meal. He ate as greedily as Mrs Cardell. 'Haven't had a blow-out like this in an age,' he said. 'You're a real good cook, Sid.'

Sid spent the remainder of the day scrubbing and cleaning the kitchen until it sparkled, but made sure she served up tea with home-made scones and shortbread biscuits and a dinner of three courses. By the time she went to bed she was more exhausted than she could remember. She barely had time to wonder if she could keep this up before she fell asleep.

Chapter Five

The time passed for Sid in a welter of cleaning and cooking, during which she scarcely had time to think about herself. Roy Hendy discovered her whereabouts.

He told her, 'I asked Raymond. I was watching the local lads play football and complimented him on his game. He's good. I asked casually where you were, but he said he didn't know.'

'You should have asked him a question about football. He could have answered that.'

'That wouldn't have told me where you'd gone though. Then I met your next-door neighbour, Mrs Jowett. I cleaned her windows when she was unwell. I asked her.'

'You didn't! Mum would be furious. They're rivals. If one gets new curtains the other follows suit. Dad dug up a small patch in the front lawn to make a flower-bed and the next day Mr Jowett was out digging his.'

Roy grinned. 'There are plenty like that.'

Sidonia laughed. 'At the moment, Mum's definitely up on Mrs Jowett because we've got a car and they've only got a motor-bike and sidecar. How did you ask? Did you tell her anything?'

'I didn't need to. I said I was asking people for introductions to get more work – actually that's true, I do it all the time – and had heard that Miss Penrose worked in a big house near by. She smiled and said it was true that next-door's daughter was employed in Greystone House and she might be able to ask her mistress, though probably she'd never get that near her because she was only a skivvy and had hardly been able to get a job herself.'

'Oh dear, poor Mum.'

On her next visit home Mum was furious. 'I've had that woman next door crowing over me because a window-cleaner wanted to know where you were. She calls you a skivvy. The cheek of it! Why I had to have a daughter without self-respect, I'll never know. So now you've taken up with him?'

'We're friends.'

'Not friendly enough it seems to give him your new address. Is he courting you?'

'What a question!'

'It's one that any mother has the right to ask.'

'I suppose you have. No, I don't think he's courting me.'

'A girl always knows that kind of thing.'

'He likes me, I like him. That's all.'

'Well, I don't know. In my day a man courted a girl, they walked out together, got engaged, then married. I don't think much of modern ways.'

'I don't know why you're so down on him. He's perfectly respectable.'

'Did I say he wasn't?'

'No, but you're trying to get me to tell you that I've made decisions when Roy's only an ordinary friend.'

'There's no ordinary friendship between men and women. Men are always after what they can get.'

'You didn't say that when I told you about Mr Keevil. You didn't believe me.'

Mum went red and ignored the remark. 'I hoped my daughter would look higher for a husband.'

'Mum! There's no question—'

'You've been seen out together.'

'We went to the pictures.'

'Did he pay for you?'

'Yes. He wouldn't let me spend a penny when I was with him.'

'Men don't go looking for girls and pay for their pleasures just for friendship. Mark my words, he's after something.'

'He is not. He enjoys my company.'

'Huh! That's what you choose to think.' The unvoiced implication was clear. What man would come looking for friendship with Sid? Sid, the plain one? Sid, the gawky servant? By 'something', Mum meant 'body-intimacy'. That's what she called love-making; though it was only very occasionally that she referred to it, and then only to her sisters.

'Which of my aunties saw us?' asked Sid.

'How do you know it was an aunty?'

'It's always an aunty, or a cousin, or—'

'All right, it was Aunty Maud.'

'I might have known. I suppose she said unkind things about me.'

'No she didn't. I wouldn't let her.'

'But she tried.'

'It's not for you to criticise your elders.'

Sid controlled her indignation. She felt betrayed and hurt and was surprised by a sudden desire to weep.

Roy took her out occasionally. She was genuinely too busy to see much of him, but he was tenacious and seemed content just to be with her. He always wanted a goodnight kiss, and the chaste brush of his lips didn't offend her.

One evening they saw *The Amateur Gentleman*. Afterwards they strolled back to Greystone House. It was a balmy summer evening, and from every garden they passed floated the sweet scents of flowers. 'I read the book,' said Sid. 'I love those old Regency dresses. Wouldn't it be wonderful if girls could wear them now? They're so romantic.'

'But you always look neat and so attractive. You've got the thin figure for today's fashions, and I admire your pretty little hats.'

She was pleased. 'Do you honestly mean that?'

'Would I say it if I didn't?'

'No, you're an honest man, Roy. Women's magazines always tell girls to choose honest men.' She smiled teasingly at him.

'Do you find that amusing?'

'No, but it isn't very romantic.'

'I didn't think you were that sort. I had no idea you cared for such a soft notion.'

'Don't you believe in romance?'

'Do you?'

'I asked first.'

After a moment he said, 'I suppose it depends what you mean by romance. Sometimes I think that going to the pictures makes women expect far too much of a man. Life is more down-to-earth.'

'Don't I know it!'

On previous dates, Roy had seen her to the gates. Now he walked her right to the back door. He looked up at the old house. 'Windows need doing badly.'

She felt a flash of suspicion. Did he see her only to get the job cleaning the windows? No, she couldn't believe that. If he wanted it he could ask to see Mrs Cardell. He wasn't timid.

'Everything here needs doing badly,' she said. 'I'm getting through the work as fast as I can.'

He looked her up and down. 'You've been getting thinner and you look tired.'

She was startled, then furious. 'Thanks very much. I thought you said you liked my looks.' She flounced off, but before she could open the door he grasped her. 'Don't get in a paddy about nothing.'

'Nothing! You said . . .' She stopped, unable to repeat his words. So, deep down, he thought she was skinny and unattractive, which was exactly what she was. In spite of his compliments, he didn't view her through a fond haze.

Roy's face softened. He pulled her close and she didn't try to resist. She badly needed comfort. She had to look up at him now. He was growing taller and his face had lost its boyishness. His nose, which had seemed so prominent when she'd first seen him, appeared to fit into the more manly features and give them added strength. His hair was longer and Brylcreemed into order.

'Well? Are you satisfied?'

'What?'

'You're giving me a very old-fashioned look. Are you satisfied with what you see?'

'Sorry I stared.'

'Did you like what you saw?'

She did. Very much. But a girl didn't say such things to a boy. Not unless they were engaged and perhaps not even then. 'You've grown taller.'

'And?' He was laughing at her and she didn't mind.
'And better looking.'
'And you've grown very attractive.'
'I thought you said I was skinny?'
'I put it badly. You are as slender as a willow and at one with its movements, graceful as it sways in the breeze. Your skin is like peaches and cream. Your hair is brown silk and your eyes are . . . what are your eyes, tonight? Blue, I think. Yes. blue, the colour of the summer sky.'
'You idiot!'
They laughed together.
'Have you swallowed a poetry book?' she asked him, smiling.
'No, though I like to read poetry. Sid, I think you're very pretty, more than pretty.'
The moment was immeasurably precious, and she pressed herself close to him. His arms tightened round her and he put his lips to hers, not in the almost brotherly way of previous dates, but clinging greedily. They moved on hers in a way which brought an instinctive response. Just before he drew back she felt his tongue slide through her parted lips and touch hers so lightly she could almost have imagined it. She found to her amazement that she didn't mind at all. In fact, the added intimacy was thrilling. Mrs Dingle had been quite right. Did this mean she was falling in love with Roy? She removed his arms and fled with a hurried, 'Goodnight.'

Sid found weariness to be the only real drawback to a job that was varied and fascinating. As she toiled to clean room after room, bringing out the particular quality of each, she began to absorb the beauty of old furniture, of perfect paintings, of glass and porcelain and silver. To think she had once believed this a witch's lair!
Mrs Cardell was no witch. True, she was sometimes a little difficult to please, even snappy, usually when Sid was a little late with her food.
'You know how I hate to be kept waiting,' she grumbled. 'You really must watch the clock.'
Sid was growing too fond of her to mind, and most of the time the old lady was keenly appreciative of her efforts to improve the place. And her love of good food was a joy. Sid had previously only been able to try her hand at a few dainties; here she could experiment as much as she liked. One day when she was tackling yet another kitchen cupboard, she found a pile of dusty cookery books. As she cleaned them of accumulated grime and the detritus of tiny creatures, and dried off the damp mould which had formed on the covers, she stopped to read bits, fascinated by some of the elaborate recipes, sometimes forgetting the time until she was reminded of it, usually by Brindle.
At first he had tried to help her in the house, but he was busy outside and Sid asked less and less of him. He seemed happy – well, she conceded, less grumpy – as he put out winter greens, plants grown from seeds, sowing more seeds, standing for hours in the greenhouse which, like everything else in this place, was large. As the nights drew in and it got colder, Sid worried about him when he came into the

kitchen, his narrow face and thin hands blue with cold. She always hurried to make him a hot drink, and encouraged him to remain there until he was warm.

At first he had argued. "'Tis best if I stay cold or I'll feel it worse when I go out again.' Then he had capitulated, basking in the warmth of Sid's kindness and the glow of the kitchen range. She saw that he was well bundled up with clothes, and ignored his mutterings about stupid fussy females. She was growing fond of him, too. Sometimes she felt quite motherly towards her two old charges, an idea which amused her. She intended to get the other range going; then the kitchen would be heavenly and she could plan ahead, make several dishes at once and gain more time for her other duties.

'There should be fires in every room,' she told Mrs Cardell on a particularly cool evening. Autumn was passing into winter, and on some mornings the ground was whitened by frost. 'It's cold enough already and can only get worse.'

Her employer frowned. 'That would cost a great deal.'

'We should get the boiler going and the radiators hot.'

'I dare say. Well, you couldn't cope with the boiler and Brindle certainly can't.' She said ruminatively, 'I remember there used to be a man, always with a black face and hands and filthy leather trousers and apron who appeared to me to live in the cellar. The housekeeper dealt with him. He was with us for years.'

'What happened to him?'

'I've no idea.' Mrs Cardell frowned. 'I suppose there may have been more than one man, but to me they always looked identical. It isn't easy to see someone properly through such grime. Why are we discussing the boilerman?'

'I was saying there should be heat in the radiators.'

'Brindle can't shift tons of fuel. He suffers from rheumatism.'

'Yes, I know, and he shouldn't be working out in the greenhouse without warmth. I can't think how the plants survive either.'

'I dare say he grows things that don't need heat.' Her eyes grew dreamy with memory. 'When I first came here we had exotic plants and flowers brought in for celebrations. I used to walk through the glasshouses sometimes during the cold months. Succession houses, the head gardener called them. He brought on fruit and vegetables and flowers so that we had delicious choices all year round. I loved the hot, steamy atmosphere. In mid-winter it was like a tropical jungle.'

'It's far from that now, and there's only one glasshouse.'

'I know. The others fell into decay. I sold the wood and glass.' Sid waited and Mrs Cardell said petulantly, 'I don't know how they are supposed to be heated.'

'I do. There's a big pottery pipe running right round. It carries water which should be fed from a stove near the entrance. Brindle told me that each glasshouse was heated separately because of needing different temperatures.'

'You think Brindle should have a fire in his glasshouse? Damn it, I'm not made of money!'

'If he has to spend another winter without warmth he may become too ill to work. Then where will you be? You'll never get anyone else to put up with it.'

'Oh, is that so? I thought lots of men were out of work.'

'They are, but you need an experienced gardener. Besides, he's been here so long.'

Mrs Cardell scowled, then said, 'Yes, he has. All right. See to it.'

'Thank you, madam. Another thing, I don't think his attic room is good for him either. There's no way of producing heat there. No grate, not even a plug for an electric fire.'

'I suppose you want him to join you in the nursery.'

'He could if he wished. There are three bedrooms as well as the sitting room.'

'Arrange things how you like!' said Mrs Cardell grumpily.

Sid said no more. Her employer's face was wearing one of her fiercest frowns. She pouted too, reminding Sid of a little girl. As she reached the door, the old lady said, 'I shall retire early. Will you read to me? I have a headache.'

Sid mentally consigned to limbo several tasks she had lined up.

She helped her employer to her bed and pulled up a chair.

'I have the book here,' Mrs Cardell said.

Sid read the title. '*Alice's Adventures in Wonderland.*' She riffled through the pages, stopping at the drawings. 'Isn't this a children's book?'

'I suppose so. But it's one of the few that adults can appreciate as well. It has always been a favourite with me and soothes me when I am nervous. Do you mean to tell me you have never read it? Oh dear, I tend to forget sometimes how limited a life you have lived. I suppose you've not had many books to read.'

She was in one of her crossest moods, and Sid refused to rise to it, even to explain that she had always been an avid reader. It wasn't her fault she had missed the occasional volume. She began to read. 'Alice was beginning to get very tired of sitting by her sister on the bank and having nothing to do . . .' Her thoughts went to the little girl on the drowsy river bank. It sounded wonderful. She pictured her lounging on the grass, warm, listening to the sounds of the river. She read on. '. . . a white rabbit with pink eyes which talked to itself – the well was deep . . .' The next thing she knew, Mrs Cardell was slapping her on the backs of her hands which lay idle on the book. Her head lolled forward. 'Wake up. The first time I've asked you to carry out a companion's recognised duties, you fall asleep. That simply will not do!'

Sid was still drowsy. 'I'm sorry, madam.'

'You usually are, aren't you, when you've committed some transgression? From what you've told me, you spend a lot of time being sorry.'

Sid stared at her employer. Her face was pink either with the heat from the fire or anger or both. She felt suddenly angry herself. 'I didn't mean to fall asleep. I'm tired. Very tired. I work from six in the morning, hours before you even wake up, and go on until I get to bed which is often very late. Last night I had five hours in bed. Brindle told me you used to employ dozens of servants. Now you seem to expect me to manage everything.' She stopped, appalled. This would earn her the sack. For the third time.

But the annoyance faded from Mrs Cardell's face and she leaned back on her pillows. 'I see. I see. Oh dear, how could I have been so thoughtless? It must stem from my pampered life. Now it is my turn to be sorry. I think in future you had better forget the unused rooms, Sidonia, and concentrate on the kitchen, the small sitting room and the occupied bedrooms.'

Sid calmed down too, thankful not to be packing her bags. 'I could do that, but I don't want to. This is such a lovely house. Its got the kind of things I've only ever seen in Bristol museum before, but I'm finding patches of damp on some of the rugs and carpets and a lot of the furniture has got a slightly blue tinge and feels quite wet. It seems an awful shame to let it all go to ruin.'

Mrs Cardell sighed. 'You are right. I must think about this. Find me an aspirin, please. They are over in the small drawer of my writing desk. Then you must go to bed.'

'Thank you, madam.'

Sid didn't go to bed, but she enjoyed sitting in the warm, quiet kitchen preparing vegetables for the following day and working out the menu. The mice had vanished, driven away by the two cats Brindle had acquired. They sat together on a rug by the range, one velvety black, the other bright gold, washing themselves and taking turns to lick each other. She had found the housekeeper's books, dank and smelly, needing urgent attention to save them. There was another treasure among them, a cookery book containing recipes written by several different hands. Brindle told her it had been compiled by cooks through the years. Sid found immense interest in reading the details of old menus. The variety of food and wine staggered her. The butler's pantry had yielded up more vast tomes containing the wages paid to each servant from the ladies' maids to the scullery girl. A whole new world was opening up to her. Now all the basement rooms were deliciously clean, the smell of mildew replaced by a fresh soapy scent, but she would have to stay vigilant to keep the house in good order. Soup bones simmered on the hob, and the gentle aroma of onions floated from the pan. Brindle had gone to bed. Not in the nursery. His look of horror when she suggested it had amused her. Perhaps he thought she had designs on him. But he had willingly moved his things down to the basement, where a couple of footmen had once slept, and where a tiny fireplace gave a welcome heat.

'Things are looking up,' he said as he went to bed. He was as subject to moods as his employer, and Sid wondered how they had fared when they had been alone together. She grinned at the pictures conjured up.

Two days later, Mrs Cardell said, 'Sidonia, I have decided that Greystone House is far too big for you to manage.'

Sid thought her heart would stop beating. Here it was again. Failure. She recognised its ugly face. Her fragile sense of belonging was about to be shattered once more.

'It isn't, madam, honestly. It's big, I know, but I don't mind hard work and I enjoy the cleaning and . . .'

'Sidonia!'

'Yes, madam?'

'Allow me to finish, if you please.'

'Yes, madam,' said Sid miserably.

'I am not a wealthy woman, but I do have funds. I have saved these past years and there are resources . . . I would like you to engage more staff. A woman who can come in daily and do the donkey work, a maid to help you, and a boy for the garden to give Brindle a hand.'

The abrupt uprising of Sid's spirits rendered her speechless.

'Have you nothing to say? You would be in charge, deferring to me, naturally, but I trust you to keep the house in good order. We might get a youth who could stoke the boiler. I must see about ordering fuel.'

'It's all in the housekeeper's book, madam,' said Sid eagerly. 'Everything. The names of the local coal merchant, and where you bought logs and how much was paid and everything.' She was almost incoherent. She would be in charge, a housekeeper in a grand house. The prospect was exhilarating.

'Have you anyone suitable in mind who could work as an extra maid?' asked Mrs Cardell.

'I've a friend who's out of a job. She's a hard worker.' Sid hadn't seen Angie for quite a while until the other day when she had met her in Regent Street looking even more down-trodden than usual.

'Is she trustworthy?' asked Mrs Cardell.

'Oh, yes.'

'Engage her then if you wish.'

'Would it be possible for her to sleep in, madam? Her mother doesn't treat her very well. She was never wanted.'

'Fancy not wanting one's own child. I can't imagine such a thing. Why was that?'

'Her mother doesn't know who her father is. She was never married.' Telling her employer of Angie's background was taking a chance, but sooner or later she would find out, and it could prove hard for Angie if it was later.

'Does it worry you that she's illegitimate?'

'No, madam.'

'What does your family say about her?'

'They think she isn't respectable, but she is.'

Mrs Cardell smiled. 'She may sleep in, if you wish. I assume she is near your age. It will do you good to have a companion.'

Sid thanked her and went downstairs. Mrs Cardell was such an odd mixture. Who would have thought she would suddenly decide that Sid would be happier with a friend near by? Her employer appeared to have no friends and no close family. She hadn't received a single visitor since Sid had begun working here, though there was the very occasional letter which, on Brindle's instructions, was taken to her mistress on a silver tray.

She took a couple of hours off that evening to go home. She couldn't wait to give her family the news. 'Mrs Cardell says I can employ Angie, poor thing, she's been out of work, and she can sleep in.'

Mrs Penrose stared at her. 'Angela Wright? That slut!'

'Mum, she isn't.'

'Her mother is.'

'I don't know much about her mother, but Angie is a nice girl.'

'Girls born in her way are never nice,' said Mum.

Dad, who had hardly bothered to put his paper down when he heard Sid's news said, 'It stands to reason they can't be. Bad blood.'

He raised his newspaper again.

'Angie can't help her mother's wrongdoing,' said Sid. 'Anyway, I'm going to ask her, and see if I can engage someone for the rough housework.' Sid raced through the exciting catalogue of her future plans. 'I shall be a housekeeper,' she finished exultantly.

Dad carefully folded his newspaper and put it down. 'I'm going out for my pint,' he said. 'I'm glad you've decided that you've got a decent job, Sid. I don't really see it that way. A servant is a servant. I've always been an employer like my father and his father before me. I'd never want to work for someone else.'

He walked out and almost took Sid's confidence with him. Almost, but not quite. He's self-centred, she thought. The idea startled her as much as if she'd had a sacrilegious thought about God.

'Your father's right,' said Mum.

'You worked before you were married.'

'Not in a menial place. I was apprenticed like Audrey and Irene to a high-class department store. But then you've always been the odd one out. Do you want a cup of tea before you go?'

Angie was delighted. A wide smile spread over her homely face, her small eyes glittered. 'Live in that big house with you? Oh, Sid!'

'You're not afraid of her? You used to be terrified even to look down the drive.'

'I know, but if you say it's all right, I believe you, and the thought of getting away from Mum is wonderful. It's not that I don't love her, don't think that, but you know how it is. Well, I don't suppose you do, being in a nice respectable family like yours, but I get awful lonely and nervous.'

Sid nodded. Angie would never understand that she felt like a misfit too in her own apparently cosy home. 'I'll expect you in the morning, shall I? The work's hard and Mrs Cardell can be quite crochety at times, and Brindle's bound to be suspicious of you at first.'

'I don't care! I don't care about anything if I can come and be near you.'

Sid felt guilty. 'Oh, Angie, all this time and I've never been to see you. I'm really sorry.'

'No need to be. You've had your hands full.'

Sid had no problem finding someone strong for the rough work. The Misses Weekley arrived in answer to an advertisement. Their appearance belied their name. The muscular, unmarried sisters had always gone out doing housework and washing, and their only ambition was to stay together. So many households could now afford only one servant that for the first time in their lives they were out of work. They lived nearby, which was another advantage, and Sid engaged them. She would worry later about explaining to Mrs Cardell how they had two cleaners instead of one.

The next morning, when she took her employer's breakfast to her in bed, she told her and waited for the explosion. No matter what Mrs Cardell said, she was determined to keep the sisters.

'You'll bankrupt me,' exclaimed Mrs Cardell. She surprised her by laughing. 'You take your position as housekeeper seriously, don't you?'

'Would you wish me to take it any other way?'

'Heavens, no.'

'You're not cross with me?'

'No. One is never cross with a good housekeeper or a splendid cook. One is far too afraid that they will hand in their notice, and you are fulfilling both functions at the moment. You will be doing the cooking in future, Sidonia?'

'I shall, but I'll teach Angie. She's a clever girl and learns quickly. She was in my class at school. Poor thing, she's never been appreciated. There's one more thing, madam.'

Mrs Cardell sighed. 'I know that tone of voice. You want something else.'

'A window-cleaner.'

'Surely one of the new staff can clean the windows.'

'Downstairs maybe, though they're very high, but upstairs needs a man with a long ladder and a head for heights. And the fanlights will mean he has to get on to the roof. You should have a young and strong man who's used to such things.'

'I see. May I take it that you know of just such a man?'

'I do. He's called Roy Hendy and he's building up his business. He's nice, too.'

'Why, Sidonia, I do believe he's a special friend of yours.'

'We've been to the pictures a few times.' Sid sternly suppressed the memory of Roy's kisses which were growing progressively more exciting.

'Very well. I leave it all to you. But he must be the last employee you engage. You had better learn how to keep the housekeeper's book. I shall want to inspect it every month. Remember, I'm not made of money.'

Sid paused at the doorway, made as if to speak, then opened the door.

'Come back here,' ordered Mrs Cardell. 'I cannot bear it when someone obviously has something they wish to say to me but walks off. What's got into your head now?'

Sid went slowly back to the bed. 'I couldn't help wondering why you haven't had enough servants for so long.'

'That's not your business.'

'I know, madam, that's why I decided not to speak.'

Mrs Cardell was silent for a moment. 'I think as each servant left or died I simply lost interest. I was widowed many years ago and life lost its savour. I didn't care much what happened to the house or me, and Brindle and I muddled along. I see now that I've been hard on him.'

'He's very fond of you, madam. He doesn't grumble.'

'It might have been better if he had. I have employed a few women, but they didn't stay and mostly got on my nerves with their plebeian outlook and small minds. You're different, Sidonia, thank God. Life is interesting once more.'

Sidonia went to bed that night, the last flames of the fire sending dancing lights over the battered furniture and the walls where some child had torn off strips of paper. I must do something about these rooms soon, she decided. She was in a state of joyful bewilderment. Joyful because for the first time she was wanted and appreciated by someone, bewildered as to why for so many years she had submitted to people who had treated her with such disdain. 'What a fool I've been,' she said aloud, then drifted into sleep.

She engaged a boy, Keith Bradley, to help Brindle, but finding someone to stoke the boiler proved more difficult. In the end she interviewed a large eighteen-year-old youth who was accompanied by his mother, Mrs Ford. 'He's a good lad,' she explained, 'though he doesn't think very fast. He'll work well. His name's Patrick.'

'Has he worked before?' asked Sid, reflecting that they spoke of Patrick as if he wasn't there. Did he mind? He was staring round at the kitchen.

'He's been fully employed every summer for the past four years as an assistant gardener in the parks. Winter, too, though on short time. He's awful slow on the uptake, but if you explain a couple of times what his duties are, he'll perform them properly.'

'I see. Will he want to return to the parks in the summer?'

'Not if you wish him to stay, madam. The foreman is hard on him. He isn't happy.'

'I see. I'm not madam,' said Sid. 'I'm the housekeeper.'

'He must learn to call you madam. He must have respect for you. That's if you take him. If he doesn't have respect for someone he can get very uppity. He annoyed the foreman.'

'Would you like to come and work here?' Sid asked Patrick, who had been staring at her.

'Yes.'

'Madam,' prompted his mother.

'Madam.'

'You'd spend a lot of time in the cellar with the boiler furnace.'

'I shall like that. I like being where it's warm. Furnaces are warm, aren't they?'

'And I shall need you to carry coal to the kitchen.'

'I don't mind. Madam.'

Sid engaged him, and Brindle found leather breeches and an apron discarded by a groom in the old stables. 'He'll be able to give you a hand in the garden when it's time to dig,' said Sid.

'That's as may be,' muttered Brindle.

Mrs Cardell was deeply upset when the association of the new King Edward the Eighth with Mrs Wallis Simpson was made public.

'A married woman who's already been divorced! And she'd have to get another divorce before she could marry His Majesty. In my day, king's mistresses knew their place and didn't flaunt themselves in public and try to grab the throne of Great Britain. Upstart person. She's no lady. She'll vanish into oblivion.'

But King Edward further aggrieved his many admirers by abdicating for the sake of his lover, and Mrs Cardell wore mourning on the day of his abdication announcement. Nine days later she changed into her best silk gown for the proclamation of his brother, the Duke of York, now King George the Sixth. When her outraged shock died down, she welcomed the enthronement of the new king. 'His wife is the Lady Elizabeth of Glamis and they have two little daughters. He has lived almost as a private gentleman until now,' she said, 'but he has answered his country's need with courage. His wife will do her duty, too. I believe we have a better man on the throne.'

In the Penrose household, the royal family was respected with almost holy reverence, and Mum was just as upset as Mrs Cardell by the scandal. Sid was too busy preparing for Christmas to pay much attention to outside events, and couldn't see anyway how the lives of such distant, important, wealthy people could matter much to someone like her. Roy brought her a Christmas tree on his handcart and helped put it up in the hall on Christmas Eve. Brindle fetched two large cartons of decorations from the attic, and Angie and the Misses Weekley hung the branches with shiny baubles, Angie teetering perilously on a ladder also supplied by Roy.

'I'll do the ones at the top,' he offered. 'I'm used to climbing.'

But Angie refused his offer of help. Sid winced to see her balancing on one leg to reach the ends of the branches while the two maiden ladies firmly grasped the base of the ladder, but Angie's eyes shone with childlike joy.

Brindle stayed a while to watch, accepting a glass of brandy, savouring it slowly. 'Best brandy this is,' he muttered. 'The master used to give us a decent wine and a bottle of brandy for the servants' Christmas dinner.' He looked significantly at Sid, who made a mental note to remind Mrs Cardell of her husband's past generosity.

Angie's happiness continued to sparkle almost as much as the baubles she was hanging. Good food, warm friendship and security had all conspired to give her health and pleasure; she looked quite pretty. Large logs burned in the fireplace in the hall, every room was warm and gleaming windows reflected the highly polished furniture. When Mrs Cardell came down on Christmas morning she stopped at the foot of the stairs and stared for so long that Sid got quite worried.

'It's all right, isn't it, madam?'

'It's just too beautiful. My dear, how on earth . . . so much . . .' She stopped, swallowing hard.

'Your sitting room is ready for you,' said Sid.

'Later, my dear. Angie, please bring me a chair. I'd like to stay here for a while. Sidonia, go upstairs and fetch out the parcels from my wardrobe. I'll add them to the others.'

Christmas Day passed swiftly for Sid. She seemed to be everywhere, working and supervising. The Misses Weekley came round to wish them all a happy Christmas, and received their presents of two lacy shawls with gratifying pleasure. They left a large box of chocolates to be shared and an indoor plant for Mrs Cardell, the pretty green and white pot tied with a scarlet ribbon. There were gifts for everyone under the tree. Sid opened hers from her employer and gasped at the glinting crystal necklace and earrings. Her present to Mrs Cardell was home-made sweets in a box which Angie had covered with green and red silk. Keith, the gardener's boy, and Patrick, the boilerman, chose to remain in Greystone House for Christmas, though Patrick could scarcely be persuaded to leave his beloved furnace even to eat. He finally arrived without his leather apron, his hands as clean as he could get them and his face washed, though Angie giggled at the tidemark of coaldust. Once at the table he put away food in amazing quantities and at great speed. Mrs Cardell had elected to eat dinner at the same time as the staff. 'It will be easier for you, Sidonia,' she said.

It seemed awful to Sid and Angie that she should eat alone, but she could hardly be expected to sit in the kitchen. Sid had supervised the laying of her lonely festive table, arranged a bowl of Christmas roses and lit the candles; Brindle had chosen the wines.

The crown of the feast, the pudding which Sid had made months ago, was declared to be the best ever. Brindle helped himself to the brandy and his ruddy face grew redder. He rose from the table and stumped to the door. 'I'm going to rest,' he announced. Then he returned, 'Thank you, Sid. I don't know when I've eaten better.

On the morning of Boxing Day, Roy called. 'Do you have time to walk with me?' he asked Sid.

She gave the request consideration. The food today was mostly cold, and Mrs Cardell had ordered her to take a rest, but she would prefer an outing with Roy. She checked with her employer who smiled benevolently. She was in her sitting room by a leaping fire, the box of home-made sweets open on a table beside her, along with a bottle of sherry from which she had just poured a liberal helping. 'These are delicious, Sid. Of course you may go out. It's sunny and blowy. Lovely walking weather.'

Roy and Sid walked until they had left the houses behind. The wind was quite strong, exhilarating, or maybe it was the sheer joy of success and being with Roy which made everything look wonderful. She peeped sideways at him to find he was looking at her. He pulled her to a stop and glanced quickly round. The only spectators were a cat sitting on the gatepost of a solitary cottage and a small grey donkey. 'Sid,' he murmured. His kiss was infinitely sweet as his tongue slid round her lips and into her mouth. Her response was instinctive and, as the kiss deepened, an urgent ache filled her body. It was thrilling in its intensity, yet half scaring, too. The ache became stronger and quickened into desire, and for the first time she understood why girls gave themselves to men. She pulled away.

Roy was flushed, his pupils were dark. 'Sid, you're wonderful.'

'I think we're going too far.'

'No, don't say that.'

'It isn't right to have such feelings . . . They're only for marriage.'

Roy laughed softly. 'No, they're not.'

'I don't approve of carrying on.'

'Carrying on! What an expression. You sound like your mother, or even your granny.'

'They're right in this.'

Roy sighed. 'I suppose so.' He slid his arm through hers. 'Isn't it time we were getting back if you're to serve tea to your old lady?'

'Angie said she'd do it.'

'Heavens, I hope she doesn't drop the teapot.'

'So do I. It's the Limoges and belonged to Mrs Cardell's mother. Oh, dear, perhaps I shouldn't have left her.'

'I was just teasing. I'm sure she'll be perfectly fine. She's come on a long way since living with you. She's not nearly as awkward. You're very good with her.'

'I see myself in her. So clumsy.'

Roy smiled. 'Maybe you were once. You certainly aren't now. I think you were bullied. It's wonderful to see how you've altered now you have a responsible job. Sid, you're such fun to be with.'

'And that's how you see me? As fun?'

'More than that,' he said gently, 'I feel much more than that for you. I think about you when I'm working. And after.' Sid waited for the words which might reveal deeper feelings. Did she want him to say he loved her? How would she respond? The problem didn't arise because he seemed to feel he had said enough for the time being, and for the rest of the walk they discussed films, books, and the window-cleaning business, which was doing well.

'I've engaged another fellow,' he said. 'It's a great feeling to be able to give a job to a man who's been out of work for ages. The thing about cleaning windows is that anyone can do it if they're willing to work hard and don't mind the weather.'

Back at Greystone House, he kissed her gently and they parted. When Sid walked into the kitchen, a beaming Angie was there with Patrick and Keith, all looking excited.

'Here's your present from Roy,' said Angie. 'He left it while you were upstairs getting your coat. He said to be careful not to drop it. It's big and very heavy.'

Sid tore off the wrapping paper. 'A wireless,' she breathed. She had always wanted a wireless. No one was allowed to touch Dad's. Raymond went every Saturday to change the accumulator.

'It's all ready to plug in,' said Angie. 'There's a place on the wall by the table. We've been waiting for you.' Keith put the plug into the wall and turned a dial and song-and-dance music filled the kitchen.

'It's Josh Raven's band with the Kissing Cousins,' exclaimed Angie. She bowed to Sid, 'May I have the pleasure?'

'Charmed, I'm sure,' said Sid, and they waltzed around the table cheered on by the others. Even Brindle poked his head round the door and a rare smile cracked his features.

'Did I hear music?' asked Mrs Cardell when Sid took in her dinner.

'I had a wireless for Christmas.'

'Did you, indeed? From your parents?'

'Oh, no, they gave me gloves and things. This was from our window-cleaner.'

'He's a nice young man.' Mrs Cardell looked a little anxious. 'You aren't thinking of getting married, are you?'

'Oh, no.'

'That's all right then. For me, I mean. Oh dear, I do sound selfish. I want you to meet a nice young man, but not quite yet.'

'I'm not ready to settle down.'

'Good. Does he feel the same? A wireless is quite an expensive present for a man to give a girl who's only a friend.'

That brought Sid up short. In the euphoria of Christmas fun, good food, Roy's disturbing, enjoyable kisses, her vigilance had been undermined. Of course Mrs Cardell was right, and the realisation that she would have to give the wireless back darkened the rest of the day.

Roy was incredulous. 'Take it back? I'll do no such thing. It's damned insulting of you to throw my gift in my face.'

'It's not like that, I really appreciate it, but it's not the kind of present a man gives to a girl unless . . .'

'Unless what?'

'You know what.' Oh, God, she was practically asking for a declaration of love.

Roy calmed down. 'Please, Sid, accept the wireless as a token of my esteem.'

She laughed unwillingly. 'You sound like the actor in *The Amateur Gentleman*.'

'Don't be daft, they didn't have wirelesses in those days . . .'

'I know that . . .'

'But nearly everyone has one now. Just think, you could have heard the Abdication speech and the Royal Proclamation if you'd had a wireless. And there are dozens of different broadcasts of all sorts.'

'I know. Oh, Roy . . .'

'Oh, Roy, what?'

'Nothing.' Sid was bursting with conflicting emotions but, to the great pleasure of the rest of the staff, the wireless remained where it was. And Sid couldn't help enjoying it as she sat in the kitchen at night, Angie knitting and sewing, crafts at which she was skilful, Sid studying the household books, while Keith lay on his stomach, his head in his hands, reading *Film Fun* and chuckling at the cartoon antics of Laurel and Hardy. Brindle made an occasional appearance and listened attentively, his ear cupped in his hand. Even Patrick was persuaded to leave the cellar where, when it was obvious that he would never consent to sleep anywhere else in the house, a room had been fitted out for him next to the boiler room. His only light came from a gas-lamp by his door, but he couldn't read anyway and he was happy. He sat staring at the wireless, smiling in his foolish way and tapping his foot to the rhythm.

'It's like a magic box,' he declared. 'My Mum hasn't got one.'

'Neither has mine,' said Angie. 'Not that it matters. She's never there.'

'Has your Mum got one, Keith?' asked Patrick.

'A little one. Not as posh as this.'

'Has your Mum got one, madam?' Patrick asked. Once latched on to a subject he worked at it.

'Yes, but she doesn't play it often.'

'Has Mrs Cardell got one?'

'Yes.'

'We've got one, haven't we, and we play ours every night, don't we?' said Patrick.

'I shall order the *Radio Times*,' said Sid.

When Keith had explained to Patrick that it was a magazine devoted entirely to wireless programmes he said, 'I can't read.'

'I'll read it to you,' Keith offered. 'And I'll read you some of my comic if you want.'

'I like it here,' said Patrick.

Chapter Six

Nineteen thirty-seven was proving a very wet year and, after a particularly heavy thunderstorm in July, the Misses Weekley reported a leaking roof.

'Water's coming in in three places,' said the elder sister, Nellie.

'There must be tiles off,' said the younger, Selina.

'Oh dear. That could be expensive. I'll speak to madam.'

Mrs Cardell was still asleep. She had had a restless night with pain in her chest, and Sid had stayed with her until the early hours.

'Shouldn't I call a doctor?' she had pleaded more than once.

Mrs Cardell shook her head. 'No need. I know what's wrong with me. My doctor told me a long time ago that my heart wasn't working as well as it might.'

Sid was horrified. 'But surely I should call him.'

'In the morning, my dear. I've used the medicine he advises and I can do no more.' Gradually her colour looked healthier and she said, 'I shall sleep now, and you must go to your bed. You'll be fit for nothing tomorrow.'

Sid lingered, agitated and worried. 'I didn't know you were ill. I've piled so much on to you, servants to pay and feed and fuel bills. I shouldn't have done it. I wish you'd warned me.'

'And miss some of the best months of my life? Stay for a moment longer, Sidonia. Sit here beside me. I'm not acutely ill, I just have to take care. Before you came I was in perpetual mourning, so miserable. After my husband died I just lost interest. Not having any children, or even any relatives I care about, it seemed pointless to go on. You have brought such pleasure to me, you and Angie and Keith and Patrick, and even the Misses Weekley. Funny souls, aren't they, but rather sweet? It's been such a delight to watch the way you've taught yourself housekeeping and discovered how to control the others, and remember, I'm so old that it really doesn't matter when I die.'

'It does to me,' said Sid fiercely.

'Dear girl. You are more than a servant.'

Sid lifted Mrs Cardell's hand and squeezed it. 'You mean a lot to me.'

'And will for many more years, I hope,' said Mrs Cardell briskly. 'Now, bed. That's an order.'

When her bell rang at ten o'clock in the morning, Sid took up her breakfast tray. The old lady was sitting up in bed looking quite pink and well. 'You see, Sid, it was just a false alarm. I wanted to be pampered.'

'You don't need to scare me just to get looked after,' scolded Sid. 'I've boiled an egg as lightly as you like it, and I've cut your toast into fingers.'

'Soldiers,' said Mrs Cardell, laughing. 'Just like Nanny used to make.'

'Now I'm going to telephone the doctor.'

Doctor Anderson reinforced what Mrs Cardell had said the night before. All the same, when Sid had to tell her about the new problem, she felt as mean as if she'd torn the tiles from the roof herself. 'I'm really sorry, but a leaking roof will soak into everything.'

Mrs Cardell took the news surprisingly calmly. 'This is a dreadful year for rain. We must do something. Would your young man know of a good roof-tiler?'

'He's not my young man and I'm sure he would.'

'If he's not your young man, why do you look so coy?'

'I do not!'

Mrs Cardell laughed. 'You don't now. Fierce would be a better word.'

'Sorry.' Sid laughed. 'It's true that Roy is a very good friend, but I don't want to tie myself to anyone just yet.'

'Very wise, my dear. On the other hand, it would be as well to stay friends with him. Decent men aren't easily come by.'

Roy offered to replace the missing tiles himself. He now had two men working full time, and had bought a car and trailer and taught Sid to drive.

He completed the job quickly and efficiently, but it transpired that water had been soaking unseen into the wooden floor of the attics possibly for years. The boards would have to be renewed, a job which required an experienced builder with more equipment than Roy could provide, and it would prove expensive.

Mrs Cardell nodded when Sid gave her this news. 'I see. I want you to telephone someone for me. Here is the number. Ask for Mr Harvey to visit me. He knows where I am. He's been before.'

Mr Harvey duly arrived, a small man with a bald head and a fussy manner. He wore a pin-striped suit. He remained closeted with Mrs Cardell in her room for half an hour, then left. Sid answered the bell and found her mistress sitting at her dressing-table with a jewel-box in front of her.

'Look at these, Sid. Mere trinkets really, yet they will buy us the security we need.'

'Are you going to sell them?'

'Mr Harvey is a jeweller. I've already given some to him. He has set a value which will pay for the new floors.'

Sid looked down at shining jewels. The only time she had seen anything like them was when she had peered into the windows of expensive jewellers' shops. There were rings, beautiful gold bracelets and chains, and necklaces of precious stones. 'It's such a shame to have to lose them,' she said.

'These are not the best ones. Mr Harvey knows that. He'd really like to get his hands on the important gems. There aren't many, and the settings are old-fashioned, but he'd soon change that. Bring me the leather case from my bureau drawer.' Sid did so, and Mrs Cardell drew out some velvet boxes which she opened with care. There were diamonds, rubies, emeralds, sapphires in elaborate settings, and a single strand of perfect pearls with matching eardrops.

'They must be worth a fortune,' breathed Sid.

'They are my insurance for my future. I have some money which comes to me from a trust fund, but it isn't enough nowadays to keep up Greystone House. A trickle of gems have gone Mr Harvey's way for years. He keeps buying the less valuable pieces in the hope that one day he'll get his hands on these.' She laughed. 'Put the boxes away.'

'Is this where they've always been kept?'

'No, my husband put them in the bank vault, though it seemed to me such a palaver getting them out when I wanted to wear them. He attended to that but I couldn't bother. I suppose I could have just left them since I never wear them, but I like to look at them sometimes. They bring back happy memories for me.'

'I could take them to the bank for you and fetch them.'

'Thank you, but I prefer to have them here.'

Mrs Cardell had flown abruptly into a petulant mood, and Sid stopped arguing. It wasn't her business.

The next day her mistress said, 'I've been looking at my jewellery again. Mr Harvey said they should be cleaned but I don't want the trouble and expense of sending them out. You could do them.'

'Me? I couldn't! I wouldn't dare! I know nothing about jewellery. What if I harmed them?'

'I'm not asking you to reset the damned things, just bring out the sparkle.'

'What's the point? You never wear them.'

'May I remind you, Sidonia, that you are my housekeeper and should obey me?'

'I don't think it's fair of you to expect this of me. It's a job for a specialist. Let me telephone Mr Harvey.'

'No, I want you to do them. I can't see what the problem is. My maid always dealt with them adequately. You're my companion. You should do them.'

'I'm also your cook-housekeeper,' said Sid crossly, 'but I'm not a jeweller.'

'How dare you speak to me like that!'

'I'm sorry.'

'You don't look it.'

'I don't feel it.'

The two women glared at one another across the inevitable barriers raised by the differences in their ages and backgrounds, then Mrs Cardell capitulated and said mildly, 'I'm sure there must be something in the housekeeper's book. Please, Sidonia.'

'Oh, all right, I'll see what I can find out.' At the door she paused. 'If I manage this to your satisfaction, will you think of storing them in a safer place?'

'Maybe. Where do you suggest?'

'How about under my bed?' Sid had meant it for a joke, but Mrs Cardell took it seriously. 'What a splendid idea. What burglar would search under a servant's bed for gems?'

Sid frowned as she hurried away. There was a recipe, in the housekeeper's book. 'Prepare clean soap-suds from fine toilet soap, dip any article of gold, silver, gilt or precious stones into this lye and dry by brushing with a brush of soft badger's hair, or fine sponge. Afterwards polish with a piece of fine cloth and lastly with a soft leather.' Sid undertook the task with immense trepidation, but it actually worked.

'They look a treat,' said a voice as she laid them out on clean tissue paper on the kitchen table to make sure they were completely dry.

'They do,' said Sid automatically, forgetting that the younger Miss Weekley was ill and the elder had stayed home to nurse her and that their place had been taken by Mrs Copley, a temporary woman whom Sid didn't much like.

'Have you finished your work?' she asked sharply.

'I have, missus, though it's too much for one.'

'I know, that's why I asked you just to give everything a quick dust over.'

She paid the woman who asked, 'Will you want me tomorrow?'

'No, thank you.' Sid made an immediate decision. She and Angie would manage until Nellie and Selina returned. The woman left, grumbling. 'Your gardener told me I'd have a few days, not just one.'

Sid returned the gems to her mistress, who was delighted. 'There, Sidonia, I told you it would be all right. I'll keep them with me today and tonight you can hide them in your room.'

'I was joking, madam. Don't you have a safe or something? In films there's always a wall-safe hidden behind a picture.'

'I dare say there is, but that's fiction and this is fact and I don't have one.'

Sid wrapped them in a linen cloth and stowed them in a box under her bed. She still slept in the nursery, and Angie had taken another of the rooms. Roy had added house decorating to his business, and had repapered the walls and renewed the paintwork at rock-bottom prices. His devotion to her never wavered, and she suspected him of doctoring the figures in her favour. She had chosen pale blue paper with tiny pink and green scattered roses, and Angie was knitting bedspreads to match. She was a fast worker, and had completed half the first one with wool bought with housekeeping money.

'When I've done ours I'm going to knit one for Patrick in all the colours I can get. He loves colours.'

'Does he? I didn't know. He prefers to live in such a drab place.'

'I know. He feels safe down there in the dark and dirt. He loves stoking the boiler. He's the only one who's pleased to be having a cool summer. I think he melts into the background so no one can hurt him. He's had a lot of hurt in his life, being jeered at and mocked at school. He never got past the second grade of the primary school, and he was such a great boy he was an easy target for mischievous children.'

Sid stared at Angie. 'I had no idea you were so good at diagnosis.'

Angie grinned. 'I'm not. I met his mother out one day, but I am learning a lot in Greystone House. About myself, as well as other things. Living with Mum was stifling.'

On her next visit home, Sid told her mother about Patrick and Angie.

'You'd best watch that girl,' said Mrs Penrose sourly. 'You don't want any goings-on.'

'Mum! Patrick? And Angie's not like that.'

'Bad blood will out. You've got a mentally defective man there, too.'

'Patrick is simple and harmless and Angie is quite clever. I wish you'd stop tarring her with the brush you use on her mother.'

'You do know how her mother makes her money?'

'Yes, she's on the streets. Angie doesn't like the way she lives, but her mother had the courage to hold on to her baby, so she's been crucified ever since. She couldn't get a job and did the only thing left. Why do people always pick on the woman? Why don't you get angry with the man who left her pregnant?'

Mum went red with anger. 'You've learned some fine things at Greystone House! You never heard them here. It must be a cesspool of gossip.'

'It's no such thing! It's all very respectable. Angie couldn't help knowing about her mum and she told me! And what's more she cried and said she'd always loved her even when she got drunk and beat her, which it seems she did a lot.'

'Disgusting! I wouldn't have that girl under my roof, nor the lunatic.'

Sid glared at her mother who got up and made up the fire, rattling the tongs in the coal-scuttle furiously. 'We'll not talk about those women again, thank you, and don't bring Angie here. Not ever. I don't want the girls contaminated.'

'How are Audrey and Irene?' asked Sid, controlling her temper.

Mum's face lit up as it always did when she thought of her darlings. 'Very well. They're almost through their apprenticeships, and have both been promised jobs. The manager is very pleased with them. And Raymond's doing ever so well at school. Dad and I are proud of them.'

Sid awoke and lay quietly, half dozing, half thinking about how much easier her life had become. Soon Angie would arrive with a cup of tea, a duty she insisted on performing. She was the first to rise in the morning, from choice. Except perhaps for Patrick. No one knew what time he went to bed or got up. He always seemed to be ready to stoke the furnace. Angie took him a cup of tea to the cellar, and called him when breakfast was cooked, a duty she had taken over.

Sid sat up abruptly as she heard Angie's feet pounding along the corridor. She burst into the nursery. 'Sid, get up, we've been robbed.'

'What?'

'It's true. We've had burglars in the night. The house is in a terrible mess.'

Sid threw on her dressing gown and dashed downstairs. A cursory glance told her that Angie was right. 'Telephone for the police,' she said. 'I must go to Mrs Cardell.'

Her employer was sitting up in bed, her old-fashioned lace nightcap awry. 'What on earth is going on? I can hear you running about.'

'Please try not to get agitated. We had intruders last night. Angie is calling the police.' As Mrs Cardell threw off the covers, Sid said, 'Surely there's no need for you to get up. Wait until we've cleared all the muddles.'

'Sidonia, you're not usually silly. How will the police know what has been stolen unless I tell them? And you must not touch a thing before they get here. Oh, I've just remembered. My jewels? Are they safe?'

'I forgot.' Sid ran to the nursery and was able to report that the burglars had overlooked the jewel-cases. In fact it appeared they had not been upstairs at all, which was a relief.

'There, you see,' said her mistress. 'If I'd had a safe it would probably have been broken open. If you've seen them behind pictures at the cinema, the thieves must have also, and I should have lost my precious gems.'

Sid smiled. Mrs Cardell was irrepressible. She helped her dress and gave her an arm downstairs. She wasn't quite as tough as she pretended, and Sid felt the slight tremor of her body.

The police had arrived. One waited in her sitting room for her while two others were looking around.

'I'm Inspector Kidd, madam. Sorry about this and sorry to have to ask you, but we need to know exactly what's been purloined.'

'Of course you do.'

'She's not even had a cup of tea yet,' said Sid.

The inspector looked her way with a keen glance, which made her glad she had nothing suspicious to hide.

'Miss Sidonia Penrose, my housekeeper,' said Mrs Cardell.

'Ah, then if Mrs Cardell can't remember everything, you will be able to, being as you're responsible for it.'

Sid felt her sway a little. 'She must sit down.'

'Of course,' agreed the inspector. 'Never let it be said that Inspector Kidd wasn't courteous to the ladies.'

Sid wasn't sure she cared for him. Mrs Cardell sat down and pulled her shawl around her shoulders. Angie had made a fire, but it wasn't yet burning properly.

'Dreadful weather we're having,' said the inspector.

'Indeed,' agreed Mrs Cardell. 'Sidonia, please fetch the folder from my writing desk. You see, Inspector, here is my insurance policy for all the valuable items in the house. Sidonia will show you round and check what has been taken. I shall remain here.'

Angie arrived with a tray containing tea and toast. 'I thought you'd best have this to go on with, madam.'

'How thoughtful of you, my dear. I shall be glad of it. See to it that everyone eats breakfast. There will be a lot of clearing up to be done when the police have finished.'

Sidonia took the list and led the inspector from room to room. Very little was missing. Ornaments here and there, a pair of vases, some porcelain statuettes of small value.

'Amateurs,' said Inspector Kidd contemptuously to Mrs Cardell. 'Probably some out-of-work louts who want to make an easy pound or two and don't know a thing about antiques. They were searching for money.'

'I could have told them they'd be unlucky there, Inspector.'

He laughed, enjoying the joke. She might be eccentric, the gentry often were, but he'd bet she had a fortune tucked away.

It took hours to tidy the house. Everyone pitched in. Except Patrick. He ate his meals with eyes wide open, fearful of the bad men who had come in the night to rob, listening to the excited chatter of the others, then disappearing into the cellar as swiftly as an owl fleeing from the sun.

By nightfall the house was spick and span once more, but it was uncomfortable to know that strangers had been in, fingering the contents, creeping about, deciding what to take and what to leave. The newspapers splashed the story on the front pages, and then the incident was closed. Nothing was recovered and Mrs Cardell accepted the modest insurance money with no signs of distress.

Two weeks later a large car came sweeping up the drive and stopped outside the front door. Three people got out and the chauffeur drove round to the stable-yard at the back. He knocked and came into the kitchen, removing his cap.

Sid was making pastry on the marble-topped table near the window. He said, 'Mrs Cardell's relations have come down from London on a visit. Will it be all right if I sit here?'

'Of course.' She looked at him, taking in the fact that he was attractive and well-spoken, and nodded. 'I'll make you a drink as soon as I'm through here.' She went on crumbling the fat into the flour, intent as always on producing her best, then Angie came rushing in carrying the housemaid's box. 'There's three ever such posh people arrived and one of them's a young lady with the most beautiful clothes with a black fur coat and pearl earrings and a wonderful hat and there's a nice-looking young man.' She realised they weren't alone. 'Begging your pardon, sir,' she said, blushing.

'Don't sir me, miss. I'm only Barton, the chauffeur.'

'Don't miss me,' responded Angie cheekily, 'I'm only Angie, the maid.'

Barton laughed. 'What sort of work do you do?'

'All sorts. House, parlour, kitchen. Like I said, an all-sorts maid.'

'In a house this size? Your mistress must work you very hard.'

'I don't mind. She's a love.'

Barton's brows rose. He really was a fine-looking man, thought Sid, and Angie's flushed face and her animation gave her an attraction of her own.

Barton said, 'I've never heard a down-trodden member of the serving class call their employer a love.'

'Well, you have now. And, if you don't mind my saying so, you don't sound at all like a chauffeur.'

'Then we are both different, because I would not call Mrs Prosser a love for all the gold in the Bank of England.'

'Who's Mrs Prosser?'

'A relative of your mistress: a cousin, I think.'

Sid put the pastry into the pie dishes.

'Where's the housekeeper?' Barton asked Angie. 'I suppose she's taking her ease in her parlour leaving you two girls to do all the work.'

'I am the housekeeper,' said Sid.

'But I thought you were the cook.'

'That, too,' said Sid evenly, filling the pie dish with chopped apple.

'Well, I've seen a few kitchens lately, but if this doesn't beat them all into a cocked hat. Do you mean to tell me you two do everything in this large house?'

'Of course we don't,' said Angie. 'We've got two women come in for the rough work, a gardener who was a head footman and can be again when he's needed, a garden boy and a stoker in the basement. And we could send out stuff to the laundry, but Sid and me don't mind doing it ourselves with a bit of help from the Misses Weekley.'

'Who?'

'Miss Nellie and Miss Selina Weekley, our cleaning ladies. They only come in pairs,' she added.

'Well, that's better, but it's still going it a bit to expect so much. Of course, things aren't what they used to be. My father—' he stopped.

'Yes?' Angie was expectant and Sid curious to hear what this unusual sounding chauffeur had to say.

'He – er – told me tales of houses with dozens of servants. Even then they had to work hard. Does your mistress entertain much?'

'No,' said Sid. 'Not very much. You ask a lot of questions.'

'I'm interested in people. I meant no offence.'

'None taken,' said Angie eagerly. Sid remained silent. Clearly Angie liked him. Sid wasn't sure of him. His cultured voice, his difference from other servants bothered her, though she admired his looks. Although his dark hair was cut short as befitted a chauffeur, it lay flat to his well-shaped head and his brown eyes were expressive. At the moment they showed humour, which annoyed her. She feared he might be amusing himself with Angie.

'Will your people be wanting beds?' she asked curtly.

'I reckon so. They said they'd be in Bristol for a few nights. Of course, they may go to a hotel.'

'Doesn't your wife mind you being away for days on end?' asked Angie.

The humour in his eyes deepened as he said gently, 'I have no wife. I have not yet met a girl I wanted to settle down with.'

'Oh, that's – um . . .' Angie's voice faded away and she blushed again. 'Who are the two younger visitors?' she asked.

'Mrs Prosser's grandchildren. They live with her.'

'Why don't they live with their parents?'

'That's enough, Angie,' said Sid sharply.

'I don't mind.' Barton smiled and again Sid felt a surge of annoyance. He was skilfully undermining her authority, and by doing so activating uncertainty which still possessed enough power to weaken her. 'Their parents died and left them money,' said Barton, 'but unfortunately they squandered it. Their grandmother pays them an allowance and they spend that as if money was nothing. Of course, you can't blame them—'

'Why not?' snapped Sid. 'The rest of us have to work hard for what we get. You do, don't you?'

'Yes, ma'am.' Barton composed his face and saluted her, and Sid found it difficult to maintain her indignation. He really was a charmer.

'I suppose money isn't anything to them,' said Angie. 'I don't suppose they've ever had to do a day's work in their lives.'

'No,' he agreed. 'I don't believe they have.'

The bell rang and Angie answered it. She returned quickly. 'They want three rooms prepared, and madam says could we find a room for Mr Barton?'

Sid glanced at the chauffeur. She had relented and, once the pies were in the oven, had made him a cup of tea and handed him a newspaper. He looked at her over the top, waiting for her reply, as if it mattered. If her employer had ordered a room for the chauffeur, she had no choice.

'Of course, that'll be no problem,' she said, and he let out a 'phew' of simulated relief and resumed his reading.

In her mind, she went over the guest rooms. They were all well aired and immaculate, and the linen cupboard was heated now so there was no problem with bedding. They'd be wanting lunch, she supposed, and dinner too. She would need to shop. She had meant to serve omelettes and a simple fruit salad with cream for lunch, but she decided that more would be needed now. She began preparations for a steamed pudding for dinner. The young woman might turn up her nose at such fattening stuff, but Mrs Cardell adored it. The lamb chops she'd intended for dinner would do for lunch, and she'd get a joint and some fish. There would be more vegetables to do as well. Presumably Mrs Cardell wouldn't mind handing over extra money to entertain relatives who had driven all the way from London to see her.

The three visitors went into Bristol for lunch, and Mrs Cardell frowned at Sid. 'Yes, I do see that you'll have to buy more food. I could wish them all in Jericho. The damned newspapers are so exasperating.'

'Newspapers?'

'The account of the robbery was picked up and published in London. My cousin Mrs Prosser saw it and decided to come down and investigate for herself.'

'I'm sure she meant to be kind.'

'No such thing. She knows I've no closer relative and she wanted to make sure that what she looks upon as her inheritance was reasonably safe. Pity she had to bring that pair of scroungers with her. Have you seen them?'

Sid was taken aback by this attack upon her employer's family. She had spent many hours with her mistress, reading to her, escorting her on walks round the garden, listening to her stories of her past life, and their relationship had developed into friendship; but it was still respectful on Sid's side, and this was strong stuff between a mistress and maid.

'No, I haven't,' she said gently, 'Angie let them in and I was baking.'

'And they've brought their chauffeur! That grandson of hers Mr Philip Prosser can drive, but I gather he refuses unless he's dodging around in his two-seater sports car. Miss Celia is also proficient behind the wheel. Mind you, it does seem an odd thing for women to drive motor-cars. I would have thought it required a mechanic.'

'Not really, madam. I can drive. Mr Hendy, the window-cleaner, taught me.'

'Really? Well, I dare say it's all right. I once tooled my own little carriage and pony, but there's so much more power in a car and it can be quite terrifying.' She drifted into memories. 'My late husband bought his first motor-car back in 1897, a dreadfully noisy thing that frightened the horses and any other creature unfortunate enough to meet it. Later we had others, less noisy but still alien to me. He used to laugh at me.' Her voice had grown husky and her eyes went to the photograph of a thin man with a large moustache who stared solemnly out of the frame. Sid knew it well, having dusted it often. 'He looks stern, doesn't he, Sidonia, but he could be such fun. And he was an honourable man. He need not have got involved in the war, but he insisted on doing something to help. He didn't care at all for the administrative job he was given and, as soon as he had the opportunity, he visited the front to see for himself what the men out there were suffering. They told me it was sheer bad luck that he should have been hit by a sniper's bullet.'

'I'm so sorry,' murmured Sid. This was the first time her mistress had said much about her husband, and Sid was touched. 'It must be a comfort to know that he and others like him put a stop to wars.'

'That's the worst part of it!' said Mrs Cardell angrily. 'They didn't. They gave their lives for what will prove to be the groundwork on which another war will be built.'

'Surely not!'

'Don't you read the papers, Sidonia?'

'I don't have much time. I know there are dictators and that Hitler keeps on demanding more territory. And there's the Spanish Civil War and other wars in other places, but it seems remote from us. I see horrible things on the newsreels at the pictures. I hate the thought of war. I can't believe that anyone feels differently, not in Britain.'

'I wish I could think you are right, but the way Europe was divided up after the last lot has been too bitter a pill for Germany to swallow. There's a genuine fear that Hitler will push and push until we have to fight.'

Mrs Cardell fell silent. Sid waited a while, then ventured, 'Will it be all right if I put Mr Barton in one of the bedrooms? The attics still haven't dried out properly.'

Mrs Cardell looked tired and sad. She said absently, 'Arrange things how you like, Sidonia. I know you'll do the right thing.'

Sid returned to her work, putting morbid thoughts of war behind her. Britain had enough problems with unemployment, without going out to fight other countries.

The visitors lost no time in putting her in her place. She appreciated properly for the first time the relationship which had developed between herself and Mrs Cardell. Mrs Prosser demanded what she wanted, and behaved as if the servants were automatons without eyes or ears. Mr Philip and Miss Celia were as bad.

Sid was taken shopping in style because Barton offered to drive her, otherwise she would have been left to struggle home with laden baskets. Even Mrs Cardell didn't comprehend the amount of food which had to be carried home.

'Shouldn't you be waiting for your employers' commands?' she asked.

'They've gone shopping. I'm to fetch them at five o'clock.'

'Won't they mind your using the car for me?'

'They needn't know. Mrs Prosser keeps her nose so high in the air she doesn't see much that goes on underneath, and Mr Philip and Miss Celia don't care.'

Sid bought the extra supplies they needed, including cream to serve with the pudding, and Barton accompanied her round the shops, carrying her shopping baskets. She had tried to refuse his offer, fearing it would make her look conspicuous; he had insisted in a way which seemed gentle, but which she realised later was implacable. At dinner that night she and Angie were both required to wait at the table. It was the first time they had seen the dining room in its formal beauty, and both were enchanted by the candlelight flickering over the silver dishes, the delicate porcelain which had been carefully washed and dried for the occasion, and the flowers in fluted vases, arranged by Brindle.

The guests could find nothing amiss with the food over which Sid had taken even more care than usual, and once her eye was caught by Mrs Cardell, who gave her a tiny smile.

'You have an excellent cook, Cousin Louisa,' said Mrs Prosser. 'It accounts for your increasing girth. When last I saw you I thought you far too thin. You may give Cook my compliments.'

'She has already received them. She is serving you now.'

Mrs Prosser looked offended. 'What an odd arrangement. I have never heard of such a thing.'

'My servants perform many tasks, Cousin Agnes. My needs are simple. I tend to live in my cosy little sitting room and not demand too much of them. Things have never been run more smoothly.'

Sid did her best to keep the satisfied expression from her face, but she caught the eye of Mr Philip and he smiled at her. He was quite nice looking, with his dark eyes and hair longer than she had ever seen on a man. A strand continually needed to be pushed from his eyes. She found herself smiling back at him.

'Serve Miss Celia, please, Sidonia,' said Mrs Cardell.

'Yes, madam.'

'Is your name really Sidonia?' asked Celia as she took a large helping of green peas. 'How very odd. Cousin Louisa,' she continued without pausing for an answer, 'why do you never come to London these days? The season this year was awfully jolly.'

'I had my season many years ago,' said Mrs Cardell mildly. 'At my age it holds few pleasures; I have no one to launch either.'

'That's true. What a pity. Grandmother enjoys all the frolic, don't you?'

Mrs Prosser smiled a little frostily. 'Some of the time.'

Celia giggled. 'I'm in her bad books, Cousin Louisa. At a ball I went off with a young man and permitted him to drive me home. Grandmother simply doesn't realise that times have changed since her day. Chaperons are no longer required.'

'While you are in my care you will do as I think fit,' said Mrs Prosser.

'Of course, darling.' Celia was unabashed. 'Have you nothing to say, Philip?' she demanded.

'I might if you allowed anyone to get a word in edgeways.'

'You're so rude to me. He's so rude to me, Cousin Louisa. Men are dreadful, aren't they?'

'I'm afraid my acquaintance was limited to one, and he was most courteous.'

Celia looked bored, and the conversation became general. As Sid served coffee later in the drawing room, Mrs Prosser asked, 'What made your mother bestow such an odd name on you?'

'She didn't think it was odd,' said Sid, doing her best to sound meek.

'I suppose not. Do any of your brothers and sisters have odd names? I assume there are a lot of you at home.'

The implication was that a girl of the serving class would come from a large family, their birth uncontrolled by any restraints. 'I have two sisters and a brother,' she said evenly.

Mrs Prosser waited until she saw that Sid was not going to volunteer further information. 'Louisa, have you any more of the brandy laid down by dear Hugh?'

Sid felt like thumping her. Mrs Cardell had deliberately not produced her best brandy. 'It's my comfort in my old age,' she always said. 'It's medicinal and who knows when it will be needed.' However, the rules of hospitality were too strong to be ignored, and Brindle brought up a bottle of the exquisite amber fluid. When Sid cleared the table, Philip had the bottle beside him and a full glass in his hand; when she went to remove the bottle he smiled and shook his head.

As she left the room she heard Mrs Prosser say, 'Now, my dear Louisa, tell us exactly what those dreadful burglars took.'

Sid went to the guest bedrooms to check that everything was in readiness, thanking heaven for the careful housekeepers before her who had enumerated in such detail all that was required. There were bottles of mineral water and glasses ready on the bedside tables, and covered plates of dainty sandwiches. The fires were burning well, the beds were turned down, and the gas-lamps needed only a pull on their chains to bring them up to full power.

Mrs Prosser didn't stay long. As soon as she discovered that only a few unimportant items had been lost and that they were well covered by insurance, she appeared to lose interest. Before she left she called Sid to her bedroom. 'I want to have a little talk to you. I don't suppose you realise it but the furniture, many of the ornaments and some of the pictures are of value. My cousin is too frail to attend to the house and has to place her reliance on servants, particularly her housekeeper.'

'Yes, madam,' said Sid, wondering what this was about.

'The furniture must be kept well polished, using only the best beeswax, the ornaments cleaned with the utmost care and washed with pure soap and clean water, and you must not use harsh abrasives on the silver.'

'Thank you, madam.'

Mrs Prosser looked sharply at her. 'I trust you will follow my instructions.'

'Mrs Cardell has already explained everything to me, and Mr Brindle, our gardener, was once the head footman; he takes care of the silver.'

'That is good. I paid a visit to the kitchen and the copper pans are not as bright as they should be.'

'Aren't they, madam?'

'No, they are not.'

'I expect it's because we no longer have a scullery maid. Angie and I can only do our best with a little outside help.'

'Just remember you owe complete loyalty to your employer and her possessions.'

'Yes, madam. I'm sorry I missed you when you came to the kitchen. I could have explained all this to you. When were you there? No one told me you'd visited.'

'What I do is hardly your concern. As it happens I popped down one night when everyone had retired. I felt it to be my duty to Mrs Cardell.'

Sid glowered and Mrs Prosser frowned. 'I don't suppose you've had a proper grounding in housekeeping. Times have changed.'

'Yes, madam.'

'You may go,' Mrs Prosser said irritably.

The staff were sorry to see Barton leave. Angie said, 'He's really nice, isn't he? I would have expected him to work in an office or somewhere like that.'

'Perhaps he's ready to do anything to keep out of the dole queue,' said Sid. 'He's not the only man having to take any work he can get.'

Celia and Philip decided to stay a few more days. They had friends in Bristol who had sent them invitations. Sid found herself with time-consuming extra duties, such as refurbishing and pressing Celia's dinner and dance dresses, while Brindle applied himself to the task of caring for Philip's clothes. He didn't seem to mind. Perhaps it brought back memories of the days when Greystone House was filled with young people making merry and he was roped in as valet.

Mr Philip and Miss Celia were out at a party, and Sid was waiting for them, sitting in the kitchen reading a book she had borrowed from Mrs Cardell. She was fascinated by the library. It wasn't a very big room, but was lined from floor to ceiling with books. She always sniffed happily at the leather aroma, dusted the volumes with loving care, and made sure that it was always ready for occupation. Mrs Cardell seldom used it, but an even temperature was maintained.

'Make use of it, Sidonia,' her employer had said, and she did. She had read all of Jane Austen's works, Virginia Woolf's, and George Eliot's who, she discovered, was not a man as she had always believed, but a highly gifted woman. She pored over an old copy of Mary Wollstonecraft's *A Vindication of the Rights of Woman*, and realised that women had for many years been feeling constrained by the conventions forced upon them. So she wasn't abnormal at all in wanting to live a life of her choosing. She felt her mind flowering and expanding.

She was so absorbed that she failed to hear the footsteps approaching the kitchen until the door opened and Philip Prosser said, 'Heavens, are you still up? It's gone midnight. I thought maids had to rise early.'

'I like to make sure that the house is properly secured before I go to bed. We've had one robbery. We don't want another.' She disliked the way the Prossers made free with the kitchen.

Philip smiled. 'You don't trust my sister and me to lock the doors?'

'I'm sure you would mean to, but you might forget on the very night it mattered most.'

'When more burglars, masked and carrying sacks marked "swag", might be creeping towards the house?'

She couldn't keep up her cool front. Philip Prosser had a way with him. 'Something like that. And I don't sit up every night. We usually retire quite early; Angie sometimes sees to the locks.'

'Angie being the plain maid who waits at table?'

'Not everyone thinks she's plain.'

'How nice of you to defend your co-worker. Perhaps I see her as plain beside you.'

Sid's eyes grew stormy. What a fool the man was if he thought he could flatter her in such a way.

Philip came nearer and she asked, 'What do you want?'

'What?'

'Why are you in the kitchen?'

'Oh, yes, I feel peckish.'

'Really? Aren't the sandwiches by your bed enough for you?'

'They are delicious, but I remembered the excellent roast you served at dinner and decided to help myself to a few cold cuts.'

'I'll do it for you.'

'Thanks awfully.'

Sid fetched the beef and slid a sharp knife through the succulent meat. Philip took the plate she handed him and sat down. 'Knife and fork, please,' he said.

With set lips she got him the utensils and he proceeded to eat, forking up large pieces, chewing vigorously and swallowing.

She couldn't resist being the efficient maid. 'Don't you need something with it? Bread, perhaps?'

'No, thanks. This is simply delicious.' He finished and wiped his hands on a napkin Sid handed him. When he remained seated she was nonplussed. This was her domain, so presumably she had the right to ask him to leave. But it was Mrs Cardell's house and he was a relative. She wished she knew what the etiquette was. Next time she saw Mrs Dingle she would ask. She'd seen nothing like this in the housekeeper's books. She was startled but relieved when he got up suddenly, a relief which vanished as he walked towards her and stopped, almost leaning over her.

'Do you know you have the most beautiful eyes?' he said.

She drew a sharp breath. So that was his game. He had decided to amuse himself with the maid. 'I think perhaps you've had too much to drink.'

He laughed softly. 'Does a man have to be drunk to appreciate a woman's looks?'

'No.'

'No, you would know that. How many men have those eyes tantalised? How many followers do you have?'

'Followers!' She knew what they were. They had definitely been mentioned in the housekeeper's books under the heading, 'Rules for Indoor Servants. No followers. If any maid should be detected bringing a young man on to the premises she will be instantly dismissed.'

'I think you're a little out of date,' she snapped. He frowned. Good. She was glad she could annoy him. Presumptuous upper-class philanderer.

'Out of date, am I? My grandmother doesn't allow followers.'

'She's an old lady and I suppose follows the old ways. Mrs Cardell is more modern in her outlook.'

'She's old, too.'

'Yes.'

'I hadn't thought about the subject before. It's quite fascinating. Do you bring your young men into the kitchen?'

Sid stood up and moved a couple of steps away from him. 'What I do is my business. I should like you to leave.'

'My naughty sister Celia left the party with a man I'd never seen before, and I feel it's my duty to see that she arrives home safely.'

'You can wait upstairs. What if she doesn't come home until morning? I've heard of breakfast being served at balls. You can't stay here all night.'

He pondered this, his brow furrowed. 'That's a poser! I can't think what I should do. Does it mean that you'll stay up all night if she does?'

'No. I need my rest. She'll have to ring the bell.'

He sighed and, in a good imitation of Mrs Prosser, said, 'All-night parties! Young women nowadays appear to have no sense of decorum.'

The laugh bubbled irresistibly out of her and he was delighted. 'I wasn't lying when I said you have beautiful eyes. You have, you know. And such smooth skin. I know society girls who spend pounds on face creams. They'd give a lot for a complexion like yours. What a pity you can't dress in clothes which would enhance your looks and set off your admirable figure.'

'I'd prefer it if you did not say things like that.'

'Would you? Would you honestly? Well, you are a strange girl.'

'I suppose all the others are flattered and fall at your feet.'

'No, I shouldn't care for that. Imagine one's feet covered by girls. I prefer them face to face. But they do tend to receive my compliments with gratification.'

'Fancy.'

'You're hard to impress, Sidonia.'

'Go away!'

He sighed. 'If you insist.'

He left. Celia arrived home at two o'clock, considerably affected by drink. As Philip had decided to forget her and go to bed, Sid helped her before turning in herself for a few hours' rest.

After that, Sid felt self-conscious in Philip's presence, and tried never to meet his eyes. She often failed in this as he always seemed to be watching her, ready with a smile which, for no good reason Sid could think of, seemed conspiratorial.

Mrs Cardell said one day, 'Are you well, Sidonia?'

'Perfectly, thank you, madam.'

'You're very quiet.'

'I dare say I'm tired.'

'I see. I suppose those graceless relatives of mine keep you far too busy. I do wish they'd go. How long have they stayed? Is it only a week? I find them most unsettling and Miss Celia . . .' She stopped, then said, 'Sidonia, I talk to you as I would to a friend. I discuss my relatives with you.'

'Yes, madam.'

'Don't be cool with me, please. I need you. I have no other confidante.'

'I keep the things you say to myself, madam.'

'I was sure of it. My eyes ache tonight. Could you find the time to read a little to me?'

'Of course,' said Sid.

Philip and Celia left soon after, and Sid assured herself she was glad to see the back of him.

Chapter Seven

A couple of weeks after the break-in, Brindle came hurrying into the kitchen clutching a copy of the *Evening Post*. 'Look at this, Sid! Another story about the burglary. Madam's going to be furious.'

On the front page there was a picture of Greystone House, a blurred photo of a much younger Mrs Cardell, and another clear one of Mrs Copley, the temporary charwoman. The caption read, 'THIEVES MISS JEWELS. See page 2'. The story described the burglary of Greystone House and how the thieves had taken little of value, entirely missing Mrs Cardell's collection of 'priceless gems'.

'Oh, lord!' cried Sid. She read on, 'Mrs Copley, a lady who was temporarily employed as a cleaner, told our reporter she had seen a large number of precious stones being cleaned by the housekeeper. "She keeps them in the house," Mrs Copley said when interviewed. "Madam was lucky the robbers didn't know that. She could have been murdered in her bed." ' Sid remembered the woman peering at her. If only she'd had the sense to hide the jewels. If only she'd cleaned them in the nursery. And she would have to show this to Mrs Cardell who was in bed recovering from one of her periodic attacks of chest pain, grumbling as usual about fussy doctors. There was no way to keep it from her. Someone would get in touch. And Mrs Prosser would be sure to find out and come to Bristol again, upsetting the household. She took the paper to her employer. 'There's a foolish account of the robbery in it,' she said lightly.

Mrs Cardell read the account and studied the photographs. 'Who is this woman?'

Sid explained.

Mrs Cardell showed surprisingly little reaction. 'What a tittle-tattling busybody. And what a nuisance that she happened to be on the premises when you were cleaning my jewellery. Damn! I suppose they'll have to go into the bank now or every thief in Bristol will be after them.' She looked at the paper again. ' "Murdered in her bed",' she read aloud. 'Rather melodramatic, but I might have put you at risk, Sidonia. That was thoughtless of me.'

'No, you were right. They didn't search under a servant's bed.'

'But you were not in the servants' attics. You sleep in the nursery suite.'

'It's even less likely that anything would have been hidden under a nursery bed.'

Mrs Cardell smiled. 'You are determined to see things in a favourable light. But I think you had better call for a taxi and I'll take them to the bank.'

'You mustn't think of it yet. The doctor said . . .'

'Doctors don't know everything. You will look after me. You always do.'

The jewels were safely stowed in the bank, and Mrs Cardell didn't go back to bed. In fact, the excitement seemed to spur her to better health. 'There are things I must do,' she said. 'I've been putting them off too long.' She sent for her lawyer and was closeted with him in her drawing room for a couple of hours, after which she looked pleased with herself.

On the following day, Philip Prosser came back. Angie was busy with Brindle in the empty game larder, checking over apples from the overgrown but still quite productive orchard, deciding which to store and which to use; so Sid answered the door. Her pleasure at the sight of him scared her. She wanted no complications in her life, and Philip could present a very tangled complication indeed if she wasn't careful.

'Come in,' she said formally.

'Thanks, I will.'

'May I take your hat and coat?'

'You may. Treat my hat carefully. It's new. Do you like it?'

Sid glanced at the soft brown felt. 'Very smart,' she said dispassionately.

'How are you, Sidonia?'

'Well, thank you, sir.'

He grinned. 'Come off it. None of your master-servant stuff with me. You're as happy to see me as I am to see you.'

'I'll tell Mrs Cardell you are here. Please wait in the library.'

'Where is it?'

'You were in there not long ago.'

'I know, but I've forgotten the way. Honestly!'

Sid opened the library door and he walked past her, then grabbed her and pulled her inside, kicking the door shut. She was taken off guard and tripped, and he caught her in his arms where he held her imprisoned before bringing his lips close to hers. 'I haven't been able to get you out of my mind. You're a witch, do you know that?'

'Don't talk nonsense!'

'I'm telling the truth.'

'Let me go!'

'Stop struggling. I want to kiss you.'

'No!'

'Oh, but I do. And you want to kiss me, don't you?'

'I do not!'

'Sidonia, darling, surely you were taught not to tell lies.'

His mouth touched hers gently and she gasped. 'Let me go, damn you!'

'Language.'

'Mr Prosser . . .'

'Philip . . .'

'Mr Prosser...'

'I won't obey you unless you call me Philip.'

'Philip, then...'

He still held her, and once again tried to kiss her. She twisted her head away and his hand went up to grip her hair. He tugged at it until she was forced to look at him, and again he touched her mouth with his. She kept her lips rigid. Her cap fluttered to the floor.

As soon as she could speak she said, 'You are a bully and I detest bullies.'

'I didn't hurt you,' he protested. 'I didn't pull hard enough for that.'

'Yes, you did, and furthermore you tell lies. You said you'd let me go if I called you by your name.'

'Oh, dear, I suppose I have completely blotted my copybook with you.'

'You haven't endeared yourself to me.'

'Forgive me, Sidonia, I know I was rough. I haven't been able to get you out of my mind.'

'I don't believe you. I'm sure you flirt with any girl you meet.'

'I do not!' He was indignant. 'They have to possess a certain charm, a measure of beauty.'

'Indeed! And which do I have?' She wished the words unsaid. She was only encouraging him.

'You have charm, even if you are a bit bossy sometimes. Beauty? Not conventional, but your eyes, as I said before, are lovely, and your complexion excellent. Your hair is nice, too.'

'How kind! You make me sound like a prize pooch.'

'Do I? Most girls enjoy compliments.'

'I'm not most girls. Now, please stand aside and let me out. I have work to do.'

'You're always so busy. All right, you can go if you give me one kiss, I promise not to touch you.'

'And we all know how you keep your promises.'

'Ouch! I asked for that.' He put his hands behind his back and leaned towards her, his lips pursed ridiculously. She wanted to kiss him. It horrified her but she had to acknowledge it. Her senses took over from her intelligence and she put her mouth closer and closer until it touched his. He slid his arms round her and this time the kiss was deep and hungry.

When they broke away he gasped, 'God, Sidonia, you're marvellous.' Again his mouth descended on hers and his hand moved over her shoulder and touched her breast. She could feel her nipple straining against her starched apron and sensation flooded her entire body. Then there were footsteps in the hall. 'That's Angie,' she said in panic.

She stepped back, smoothed her hair, and picked up her cap from the floor, pinning it in place.

'Sid? Where are you?' called Angie. 'I thought I heard the front-door bell.' Her footsteps tapped across the wide hall and she opened the front door then closed it. 'Sid?' she called again.

Sid stayed absolutely still. She should have emerged from the library when Angie had first called. She couldn't come out now. Philip might mischievously take it into his head to follow her. She didn't know how he would react. At the moment, she noted disapprovingly, he was convulsed with mirth.

'I think it's gone quiet now,' he whispered. 'What a pity we were interrupted just when . . . However, I'll be staying for a while and there will be many other opportunities for us.'

'I shall make sure you don't have another chance to get at me.'

'Why? You like my kisses.'

'Yes, and it simply won't do.'

'You sound exactly like my nanny.'

'If your nanny was here she'd sound exactly like me. Now go up to see your aunt.'

'*Exactly* like my nanny.' He grinned. 'Will you tell Angie?'

'Don't worry!' she said, and his laugh floated after her.

She went to the kitchen. 'There you are,' said Angie. 'I thought I heard the front-door bell.'

'You did. It was Mr Philip. I let him in and he's gone upstairs.'

'I came to look for you . . .'

'I can't think why.'

'Didn't you hear me calling?'

'I heard something. I was showing Mr Philip the way.'

'Couldn't he remember it?'

'Have you finished sorting the apples?'

'Not yet. I'm going to make Brindle some cocoa. He's cold.'

That Saturday evening, Sid prepared dinner and left Angie to cook it while she took her allotted time off. At home nothing had changed. Mum was in the kitchen hanging the newly washed dishcloths over the oven, the smell of tea-time kippers lingered in the air, and everything was spotlessly clean. Why should she have expected it would be different? Because Philip had kissed her and had changed her for ever? She knew now what it was like to want to be with a man, to yield her kisses to him. She knew she was foolish to think that way. He was from a different society, a man who would never look to the servant class for a companion. So why had she allowed a couple of kisses to send her spiralling into an uncontrollable longing for a man she didn't respect? How could a meeting of two mouths have given her a fiery need to be with him. She felt she was losing control.

'It's you,' said Mum.

'Yes. Where is everybody?'

'The girls are at the pictures. They're with a couple of boys. Nice lads. They were at school with them. I've asked them in for a cup of tea tomorrow.'

'What about the Sunday drive?'

'We'll just go straight to Gran's. The boys know they'll have to leave early.'

'They're so young,' said Sid, 'Audrey and Irene, I mean. Only fifteen. I didn't think you'd let them have boyfriends so soon.'

'They're not boyfriends,' said Mum sharply. 'They're just lads, and the girls have promised to stay together.'

'You were stricter with me.'

'You were the first. I had to be sure of what I was doing.' She changed the subject. 'I've been reading the newspapers. Fancy those burglars not finding the jewels. Fancy Mrs Cardell keeping them in the house. Where were they hidden?'

'Upstairs,' said Sid shortly.

'I hope you haven't come home in a sulky mood. You can't blame me if you're unhappy in that big house. I did my best for you.'

'I'm not unhappy. Mrs Cardell is a lovely lady. Where are Raymond and Dad?'

'Out in the greenhouse. Dad's trying to get Raymond to show an interest in growing things, but he's not been very successful so far. He thinks of nothing but football.'

'Dad encourages him to play.'

'As a recreation. As we tell him, when he gets married he'll need to know about gardening.'

'Is there a cup of tea in the pot?'

'Yes. Don't you want to help Dad? You used to enjoy it.'

'It's my evening off.'

'That needn't stop you making yourself useful.' Mum picked up a pile of darning. 'It's a pity you can't sew. Darning tries my eyes.'

'Can't the girls do it?'

'They haven't much time, what with their jobs and friends.'

Sid poured herself a cup of tea. It was strong and lukewarm and she didn't drink it. She wondered why she bothered to come home at all.

'How is Mrs Cardell?' asked Mum, cutting off a wool thread. 'I don't know how Raymond makes such big holes in his socks. I'll need to buy him some new ones.'

'She's bearing up.'

'What?'

'You asked after Mrs Cardell.'

'Oh, yes. It must have been a dreadful shock for her to have strangers rummaging among her things. I don't think I'd ever get over it. But folks like us don't get burgled that much. It's the rich ones in big houses that attract them.'

Sid refrained from attempting to explain her employer's position to Mum, who wouldn't have believed it; and in any case it wasn't her business. The thought startled her. Not so long ago everything about her life had been her parents' business. Now she felt allegiance to someone else. 'How are my aunties?' she asked.

'They're all right. And Grandma Lacey.' Mum's tone held disapproval. Sid should have asked after her grandmother's health before her aunts'. She looked at her mother, trying to see her as a stranger might. Mrs Penrose was sitting near the gas-lamp which hissed over her head, giving her extra light to see her sewing. She was absorbed in her task, performing services for her husband, children and home. Her forehead was a little more lined than one might have expected of a woman still in her forties, but her complexion, like that of her mother and sisters, was otherwise flawless, and her greying hair with its natural curl was pretty. She looked utterly content. Day succeeded day, each differentiated only by visits to or from the same people. Did she never feel rebellious? Had she ever?

'How are you, Mum?' she asked.

Mum looked up. 'I'm well. Can't you see I'm well? I dare say not. You've never been interested in the family, have you? Not really.'

'I have,' said Sid indignantly. 'I'm part of the family. I care about you.'

Mum said, 'I heard the greenhouse door close. Dad will be wanting tea.' She left her sewing to put on the kettle. Fresh tea for Dad. And no doubt fresh tea for the girls. But not for her. Sid gave herself a mental shake. Self-pity would get her nowhere and she had her own life to live now, a life near to her family in terms of distance, years from them in experience.

Dad greeted her with a nod. 'If I'd known you were here I'd have got you to help me. Our Raymond's useless.'

Raymond squirmed. 'I don't like gardening.'

Mum tutted. 'Wash your hands. The kettle's on. Would you like some cake?'

Sid shared the tea and ate a little cake.

'What's wrong with it?' demanded Mum. 'You used to love my cake.'

'I'm not hungry. I had dinner before I came out.' Actually she had nibbled a few bits and pieces while she was preparing the food, but she was too disturbed by conflicting emotions to feel like eating here.

'Dinner?' yelled Raymond. 'We had ours at dinner-time. We've just finished tea.'

'The gentry are different from us,' said Dad. As far as he was concerned, that closed the subject.

But Sid wasn't satisfied. Where once she would have held her tongue now she said, 'They're not really. They have the same feelings we do. They live in big houses but they can't use more than one room at a time any more than we can, and the expense of keeping the house up is shocking.'

Her family stared at her. 'Has the old lady made you her book-keeper?' asked Dad sarcastically.

'I'm the housekeeper and I have my own books and know what things cost.'

'You a housekeeper!' mocked Mum. 'That's a good one. I've never known you organise anything.'

'Perhaps I've never had the chance.'

'You had the chance of a good job with Madame Rita and you threw it away. Then there was Mrs Keevil.' Mum stopped, disconcerted, as she caught a warning in Sid's eyes.

'Does she tell you how much money she's got coming in?' asked Dad.

Sid wished she hadn't begun this. She was beginning to feel disloyal to Mrs Cardell. 'Of course not,' she said. She got up. 'I'll have to be getting back.'

'You've hardly got here,' said Mum. 'Are you off to see that window-cleaner?'

'Roy? No, I'm going home.'

Mum looked affronted. 'This is your home.'

Sid walked slowly the short distance to Greystone House, thinking about her visit to her family, trying to come to terms with the fact that she felt happier in Mrs Cardell's house than her own. She had the rest of the day off, but couldn't think what to do with her time. She was startled by a voice calling her name, then realised that someone had called her more than once.

Roy fell into step beside her. 'Dreaming?' he smiled. 'Are you free for a while? Can we go somewhere?'

'It's a bit late. The last programme will have begun at the pictures.'

'It's not too late for a drink.'

'In a public house?'

'Sure, why not? I won't take you into the bar. There are nice lounges for ladies.'

She didn't want a drink, and at this moment she didn't want Roy's company. In fact, she realised, she needed to get back to her own room where she could have peace to sort out the muddles in her mind; but Roy looked eager and she was fond of him. 'All right. A drink. But nothing strong.'

'I promise I won't slip strong drink into your lemonade and overpower you.'

'Idiot!'

The pub was brightly lit, warm and welcoming. Sid had never ventured inside one before and she liked the atmosphere of friendliness. She even liked the smell of wines and beer and tobacco. She sipped a glass of crême-de-menthe, which she had chosen because it was green and unlike any other drink she had seen. It was minty, too. Roy drank beer.

'I'm sorry I haven't been round lately, Sid.'

'Haven't you? I thought you cleaned the windows every week. I'm sure you do.'

For an instant he looked disconcerted, then responded to her joky manner. 'I meant in a personal capacity. Well, I can certainly tell you've missed me.'

'Sorry. I've been very busy.'

'Yes, I know you have. You've had the burglary to cope with. I suppose Mrs Cardell was really upset, and now there's that stupid story in the newspaper about her jewellery. Is it really priceless? When I started work there I imagined she was quite poor. Come down in the world, as the saying is. But now the house is spruced up and there are four women working there as well as Keith and Patrick and old Brindle.'

'She took the whole business remarkably well. The jewels aren't priceless, but they are costly, and if anyone asks they're in the bank. It's a nuisance because she used to enjoy looking at them and trying them on sometimes.'

'And what about you? Were you frightened?'

'At the thought of burglars? It's a creepy feeling, though they didn't touch anything of mine. They didn't even come upstairs. The police say they were amateurs, though Angie got nervous and slept with her light on for a few nights.'

'There's more petty crime these days. So many fellows are out of work and the younger ones get rebellious. I don't suppose they would have laid a finger on any of you. More likely to run like scared rabbits if you'd caught them. On the other hand they might have got frightened and hurt you. I don't like to think of you in danger, Sid. Do you know, I've had a good look at Greystone House. It could be broken into with a knife and fork. I've started a new line of business. Security. I employ a locksmith who tells people how to make their premises safe. He shows them different locks and bolts which they can buy and he can fit. I've spoken to the police about it and they've been very co-operative. Good security cuts down crime and saves them work.'

'Is there no end to your talents?'

He laughed. 'Another drink?'

Sid refused but Roy fetched himself a second beer.

'If your business enterprises are doing so well, why do you still clean windows yourself?' asked Sid.

'It gets me out of my office doing something energetic; besides, it helps me to see a certain girl I like very much.'

'Oh?'

'Don't "oh" me. You know I mean you.'

'You're a good friend, Roy.'

'I'd like to become more than a friend.'

Sid was startled. She wasn't ready to enter into a permanent relationship. Philip's image floated into her mind. He often crept there lately and wouldn't leave. 'I'm not ready for anything but friendship,' she said gently. 'I suppose your man would like to come round and check out the security at Greystone House?'

'It would be a good idea. If I come too will you show us round?'

'I might, though in the autumn there's so much to do to prepare for winter. We've had a good crop of apples and plums and I've been preserving and making jam and pickles as well as coping with the everyday work. And we've had visitors.'

'I know. I saw them in my humble capacity of window-cleaner. A grouchy-looking old woman, a good-looking sulky girl, and a fancy toff who looked as if a day's work would kill him.'

'That's no way to speak of my employer's esteemed relatives.'

'Do you like them?'

'Not really, though Mr Philip is friendly.'

Roy gave her a sharp glance. 'Don't tell me you've fallen for the toff.'

'Don't be silly. He's just another idle member of the upper classes who tread on the faces of us lesser mortals.'

Her jocular attempt failed to deceive Roy. 'You do like him, don't you?'

'Why do you keep on about him? I've told you . . .'

'There's something in your voice. I know you too well...'

'You don't know me at all really.'

'Whose fault is that?'

Sid moved to get up. 'I'm not going to stay here to quarrel with you. It's bad enough anywhere, but in a public house!'

'Sit down, please, Sid. I'm sorry. I've no right.'

'No, you haven't.'

'And we agree on the general toffishness of Mrs Cardell's family?'

'Mrs Prosser is starchy and I don't like Miss Celia, but Mr Philip isn't bad when you get to know him.'

Anger again flared in Roy's eyes. 'Men of that sort are no good to you, Sid, and you ask for nothing but trouble if you get mixed up with them. No matter how many working girls they flirt with, they never marry them. They always choose a blue-blooded woman with money. So don't go falling for him.'

Roy was really upset and worried, and Sid controlled her temper with an effort. 'Fall for Mr Philip? What an idea. As if I would. And you can't say the gentry are all the same. Look at Mrs Cardell. She's lovely.'

'If you did something really wrong or bad she'd turn on you,' said Roy darkly.

'I don't think so, though I should deserve it in those circumstances.'

'If she thought her nephew was interested in her housekeeper she'd soon have something to say.'

Sid's anger spilled over. 'If I did fall for Mr Philip, you wouldn't have the right to object.'

'I would object and I do have the right because I happen to care a lot about you.'

Sid wished she had followed her original intention to go to her room and think quietly. Roy was adding confusion to her already tangled thoughts. The more he said, the more annoyed she was getting. She said carefully, 'I won't make such a silly mistake as to care for a man so far above me.'

'He's not above you. No man is.'

'Then what's to stop me from accepting his advances?'

'Has he made any? He won't have marriage in mind. Just a quick fling he'll soon forget about.'

She regretted teasing him. He was flushed and looked desperately unhappy. 'I'm sorry,' she said, 'I shouldn't torment you. I know all men are supposed to be equal, but it's true people get on much better if they're from similar backgrounds.'

'You really got me going then, didn't you?' Roy still sounded cross but he was smiling in relief. 'It's just that I couldn't bear to see you hurt.'

He was deadly serious and she said tremulously, 'Roy, I do appreciate your friendship.'

'As I appreciate yours. Sid, won't you...'

They were interrupted by Mr Penrose's furious voice. 'What are you doing in here? They told me in the bar you were in the lounge, but

I didn't believe it. I told them, "No girl of mine would be in a public house".'

'But you came to check just the same,' said Sid as calmly as she could.

'And they were right and you've made me look a fool in front of my mates.'

'What exactly worries you, Dad? That I'm sitting here with a friend, or that you were proved wrong?'

He stared at her uncertainly. 'You shouldn't talk to your father like that.'

'And you shouldn't tell me off, certainly not in public. I'm eighteen, earning my own living, and have a perfect legal right to be here.'

'Legal right!' Dad lowered his voice and addressed Roy. 'It's your fault. Blooming window-cleaner. What do you think you're up to, bringing my girl into a public house? And what's that she's been drinking? Some made-up muck that'll turn her head.' Sid almost laughed. Here was Dad, who normally paid her the scantest attention, actually getting worked up because she was in a pub. 'I can't think what your aunties will say, or your Grandma Lacey. They're sure to find out. There'll be trouble. They'll blame Mum and me.'

Roy said, 'I'm sorry if you're upset, Mr Penrose, but I treat Sid with the greatest respect. She's only had the one drink and I'll see her safely home.'

'Dad,' said Sid urgently, 'people are looking at us.'

He glanced round at several who were regarding him with some amusement, went red and stalked out.

'Oh dear,' said Sid. 'The relations will really enjoy picking this one over.'

'Do you mind?' asked Roy anxiously.

'No, I don't. Gosh, I've developed into a rebel. Not so long ago I would have been terrified.'

'Do you visit your grandma much?'

'Hardly ever. She won't find that any great loss. She's never liked me. I miss Aunt Mattie, though.'

'Your family is weird. None of them values you and you're such a marvellous girl.'

His admiration was infinitely soothing. She wished she could fall in love with him. How much more simple her life would be.

The following day, Sid was astonished to find her mother being shown by Keith into the kitchen of Greystone House. She had reached the crucial point in the boiling of plum jam and dared not leave it.

'Sid,' said Keith, 'I saw your mum come up the drive.' He hurried back to the garden.

Angie was sitting at the table peeling pears. She jumped to her feet.

'Hello, Mum,' said Sid. 'Sorry I can't leave the jam.'

'Sit down, won't you?' asked Angie. 'I'll bring you a cup of coffee.'

'I'd rather have tea,' said Mum shortly, irritated at having to take second place to a pan of jam. She stared hard at Angie, the product of an illicit relationship. Angie, knowing exactly what Mrs Penrose was thinking, was so diffident she almost dropped the plate of home-made biscuits she offered.

Mum took one and bit into it. 'This is very nice,' she said. 'Did you make it, Sid?'

'No, those are Angie's. She's a brilliant cook.'

Mum was affronted, and finished the biscuit with a sour expression. She sipped her tea, looking round the kitchen and, as Sid stirred and fished out plum-stones, she was amused to see that she was impressed, even overawed, by the dimensions of the room and the utensils hanging on the walls, enormous both in number and size. She stared up at the bunches of herbs hanging to dry from ceiling hooks, over at the vast dresser where bowls of tomatoes, onions, apricots, damsons and apples waited their turn.

'Those tomatoes are past their best,' she said.

'We know that,' ventured Angie. 'I'm going to begin on making chutney with them as soon as I've finished doing the pears.'

'Well, get on with your work. If my daughter can ignore me to do hers, you can surely do the same. I'll be leaving soon anyway.'

Sid said, 'Leave the pears, Angie, and take over here. The jam is nearly ready. The next test spoonful should wrinkle as it cools. As soon as that happens, pull the pan off the heat and fill the jars. They're in the oven, so mind your fingers.'

Angie, glad to be doing something further away from Mrs Penrose, obeyed.

Sid sat by her mother. 'It's nice to see you, Mum.'

'This isn't a proper visit. In fact, I should be home making my own jam.' Sid waited, knowing the subject which was about to be tackled. 'Can't we go somewhere private?'

'I would rather not leave Angie. It's the first time she's seen jam made.'

'That doesn't surprise me. And I don't suppose,' nodding towards her, '*she'd* find anything wrong in being in a pub.' Sid frowned at her and she said quickly, 'Dad came home in a terrible state last night after seeing you.'

'Poor Dad. He needn't have got so worked up. I just had one small drink.'

'Some fancy green stuff,' he told me. 'The ladies in our family don't go into public houses.'

'I bet Aunt Jess does. At least, she probably uses hotels but it's the same thing really.'

'No, it isn't. Anyway, I don't know what Jess does, but it's got no bearing on the matter. I want you to promise me you won't do it again.'

'Sorry, Mum.'

'Well, that's something. And you'll not let the family down again?'

'I mean I'm sorry I can't promise.'

'What? Are you defying me?'

'I hope you don't think of it that way.'

'Well, I do.'

'I can't make a promise I know I won't keep. I enjoyed the atmosphere last night and can't see anything wrong with what I did.'

Mum stood up. 'You always were disobedient.'

Sid was angry. 'I was not! I obeyed you and Dad in everything. Between you, you ruled my whole life.' She knew she should stop. She saw from the corner of her eye that Angie had stopped work to stare at her open-mouthed, but the frustrations of years spilled over. 'I was put into a boring job, I worked for you at home, I was nursemaid to the girls from the age of three, I helped Dad in any way he asked. I've been the good, dutiful daughter, and I can't remember when you or Dad praised me and neither of you . . .' She stopped, horrified, not so much by her tirade but by the realisation that she was about to accuse her parents of not loving her. It wasn't something you yelled at your mother. Tears stung her eyes. Others arrived in the kitchen. Brindle and Keith wanted their mid-morning snack, and even Patrick's face, streaked with coal, was peering from the cellar door. She had been shouting. She was devastated by regret and shame and couldn't think how to extricate herself. Then the neglected pan of jam boiled over and a horrible burning stench filled the kitchen as the thick, sweet mixture ran over the stove.

Angie, her emotions already lacerated, burst into horrified tears. Sid ran over, grabbed a cloth and lifted the pan over to the wooden draining-board. 'Get the scourers and Vim, put gloves on or you'll burn your fingers, get as much as you can off before the heat hardens it. We'll let the fire die down tonight and clean it properly. For heaven's sake, Angie, stop crying.'

'I can't help it. I've probably ruined the jam. It'll be so thick you'll be able to cut it like jelly.'

'We can remedy that. It'll be something else for you to learn. Now get the scourers.'

Mum stood up. 'If this is a sample of how you do your housekeeping job, I don't think much of it.' She stalked out, having got in the last word, and Sid looked after her stiffly retreating back. She should go after her, call her back, say she didn't mean what she'd said; but she couldn't, because she had meant every word and saying them had loosened a hard knot of resentment inside her.

'She's in a right old temper,' said Brindle.

'Cor I'm glad she's not my mother,' said Keith.

'Mind your manners,' snapped Brindle, boxing his ears.

'Ow! You spoke about her first.' He ducked as Brindle lashed out at him again.

'I'm an old man. I've got privileges.'

'Hope I don't have to wait to be as old as you before I can speak my mind,' muttered Keith. Fortunately, Brindle was a little deaf and missed it, or Keith would have got no mid-morning break.

Angie still sniffed. 'Now I've caused bad feeling between you and your mum.'

'No, you haven't. It had nothing to do with you.'

Angie stared, then began to scour the top of the oven vigorously while Sid made drinks for them all.

Sid sat alone in the kitchen. The jam had been saved, the pears bottled and pickles made, and she and Angie had found it very satisfying to carry the jars to the larder. The kitchen was shining clean and all traces of jam removed from the hob. Angie had taken Patrick to see a Tarzan film. He loved them. After each one he could be heard carolling out an imitation of the Lord of the Jungle's cry of triumph. The first time it had been disconcerting, and both girls had raced down to the cellar, believing him to be ill.

'Me Tarzan,' he had said simply, grinning, and they had waited until they were back in the kitchen to give way to their mirth.

Sid was reading a copy of *Punch* magazine. Mrs Cardell passed them on to her; she enjoyed the humour. Her attention was caught more and more by the cartoons depicting Adolph Hitler and Benito Mussolini, with captions referring to their lust for power. Could Mrs Cardell possibly be right? Surely not. Surely there couldn't be another war after the last horror. But there were cartoons about men enlisting, too. She reassured herself that their enthusiasm could be put down to the shortage of jobs, but the facts together made her feel uneasy.

She heard footsteps, knew whose they were, and didn't turn round until Philip said softly, 'I was hoping I'd find you alone. Where is everybody?'

'Out.'

'Good.'

Sid put the *Punch* on the table. 'What do you want? You shouldn't be here.'

He picked up the magazine and flicked over the pages. 'It'll be war, as sure as fate,' he said.

'Surely you wouldn't want to fight?'

'If England called, I suppose I'd do my duty.'

'Don't you know what went on in the last war? The terrible killing and wounding? And where did it get us?'

'It wouldn't be like that. Things are very different now. For a start most of it would be fought in the air. Some on the sea, of course, but they won't have huge armies of men marching about and digging themselves into trenches. And if you get wounded, medicine is far more advanced. It might be quite a lark.'

'Not such a lark if you ended up dead! Though I suppose you'd be an officer giving orders to the lower ranks. They'd be the cannon-fodder, not you.'

He glared at her. 'What do you take me for?'

'I don't take you at all. I know nothing about you.'

With a swift change of mood he laughed. 'Yes, you do. You know that I like you. A lot.' He drew up a kitchen chair and sat as close to her as he could get. 'How cosy this is.'

'I'm glad you think so.'

'I'm glad you're glad.'

'Haven't you anything to do?'

'Like what?'

'You could play Bezique with your cousin. She enjoys a game. We often play.'

'She's got a bit of a pain in her chest.'

Sid started up. 'What? Where is she? I must go to her. She should have rung.'

'Stop panicking and sit down. She's as happy as a sandboy in her little sitting room, listening to music on the wireless. She'll call when she wants you. You know how she hates people to fuss over her.'

'Did you try to fuss over her?'

'Naturally. I fetched her a glass of brandy and didn't leave her until she ordered me to go away and sit somewhere else. She suggested the library, but I think this is much better. Unless you come to the library with me. There's a good fire and a deep, comfortable couch.'

Sid wished she could sew or knit. At times like these she didn't know what to do with her hands. She laid them demurely in her lap.

'You can't fool me by trying to look like a Madonna. I know what a passionate nature you have.'

Colour flooded her face and neck. 'You know no such thing.'

'I can't forget your kiss. I came down hoping for another.'

'Well, you won't get it.'

From the cellar there was a sound of something falling. 'Damn,' said Philip, 'is that black-faced gorilla you call a stoker likely to come up?'

'He's out. It'll be one of the cats after a mouse.'

'I thought he shrank from the light of day.'

'He loves going to the pictures. Angie takes him.'

'Oho! Do I scent a blossoming romance?'

'Don't be a fool,' she said shortly. 'He's only got half his wits. Angie is one of the kindest girls I've ever known.'

'Where are the intrepid gardeners?'

'Brindle's gone to see his latest grandchild, and Keith is visiting his family.'

'And the redoubtable charladies only come by the day. We are *alone*. Alone in the warm kitchen while the house slumbers above us.'

'Good lord, what film have you seen lately?'

'Not a film, a book. The hero guarded the heroine through many dangers and storms until she realised what a splendid fellow he was and fell into his arms. Right on the last page, too. It was most tantalising.'

'I wouldn't have thought romances were exactly your cup of tea.'

'They aren't.'

'Well, you didn't find a book like that here.'

'Yes, I did. One of the charladies dropped it from her pocket and I picked it up. It's from a library.'

'You should have handed it straight back. She'll be terribly worried.'

'Will she? I'll give it to her first thing tomorrow morning.'

'You should go round to her house now.'

'I don't always do what I should.'

'It seems to me you never do.'

'Wrong. I came here to save my dear old grandmother the journey, to see if Cousin Louisa was upset by the newspaper story. And I only returned to town on my last visit because I'd promised to take my sister to a ball. I didn't want to leave and I might as well have stayed here. She'd made a date with another of her conquests, and spent the entire evening dancing with him. Or other men while he glowered at them . . . Didn't you miss me?'

She had, and it had taken all her powers of control not to inquire after him from Mrs Cardell. 'Why on earth should I notice if you're here or not?'

'Now come, Sidonia, darling, you must have seen that my bed was not used and that there were no sandwiches required or water by my bedside. And what about meals?'

She had answered thoughtlessly, and by doing so had presented him with a weapon. Damn! 'Of course I knew you had gone somewhere, but it meant nothing to me.'

He clapped a hand to his brow. 'The pity of it. I am undone.'

'Did you read that in the library book?'

'No. I made it up. Just for you.'

'You are a fool.'

'You're not really angry with me, are you?'

She looked him in the face, ready to say something scathing enough to send him away, but her tongue wouldn't move. His eyes held hers and their expression excited her. She swayed a little towards him.

'Sidonia,' he murmured. He got up and pulled her to her feet. She knew he was going to kiss her and she wanted it. His lips held hers, moved to her eyes, her nose and back to her mouth. Her tongue responded to his and the ache of unfamiliar need coursed through her.

'Darling, darling Sidonia. May I come to you tonight?'

His question startled her. She broke away and stared at him, wide-eyed. 'Come to me? What do you mean?'

'You know what I mean. I adore you. I want to make love to you. Let me love you. Let me love you tonight.'

She was confused by her reactions. She wanted to believe that he had fallen in love with her. It was like all the fairy-stories she had ever read, stories in which a girl would be wooed and won by a prince in a matter of hours, moments even. But they were not in a story-book. This was reality. 'It's impossible.'

'No, it isn't. Don't you know how I want you? Surely you must have known from our first meeting. I did. Darling Sidonia, let me stay with you tonight.'

'I sleep in the nursery wing,' she said stupidly. 'Angie is there, too.'

His arms went round her again and she felt the strong beating of his heart. 'Then come to me. My room is right away from Cousin Louisa. No one will know.'

His mention of Mrs Cardell startled her. 'I wish you'd never come here!' she cried.

He smiled at her tenderly, 'Because you are afraid of yourself, aren't you? You want me, don't you? As much as I want you? Don't be afraid, my darling. I would never do anything to hurt you. But I must love you, I must. I can't get you off my mind. I came back because of you.'

'Leaving the young ladies of London sad, I suppose.' Her attempt at flippancy fell flat. 'Philip . . .'

'My name sounds so sweet on your lips.'

Clinging to her resolve, Sid said, 'What you suggest is out of the question. I'll never give myself to a man before I'm married. It's wrong.'

He pulled off her cap and kissed her ear, mumbling softly against it, his breath hot on her face, 'Nothing is wrong between two people who care for each other. Didn't you know that? You do, don't you? And you're a passionate woman. I sensed it.'

'How? I mean, I'm not passionate. I've never thought of such a thing.'

'A man always knows.'

Sid wanted time to think. He must be telling enormous lies. She didn't believe that he found her attractive. In spite of her contentment with life and the good eating, there was no rounded flesh on her, her nose still had a bump, she wasn't pretty like Celia or Audrey or Irene. A man like Philip could have his pick of London beauties. Yet he had returned and he sounded so sure, so convincing.

He shook her gently. 'Come back. What are you thinking?'

In her agitation she blurted, 'I don't believe you. I'm not the kind of woman who makes men . . .'

'Makes them what, darling?'

'Don't call me darling.'

'Makes men what?'

'I'm not pretty. I'm not particularly clever. I'm just your aunt's housekeeper, and as far as I can tell I'll never be anything else.' It hurt her to say these things, but they were true and she had to convince herself or she might begin believing him. 'Now go back upstairs and tomorrow you can return to London and forget me. As I shall forget you.'

'You won't, and I won't. My poor dear. You must have had a horrendous upbringing to have such a low opinion of yourself. Surely other men have shown an interest in you.'

'Yes,' she said. 'though one was horrible.'

'Do you think I am horrible?'

'Oh, no,' she said fervently.

'Do you care for me? Just a tiny bit?'

'Let me go.'

To her surprise he did and she instantly wanted his arms around her again. 'I'll not force myself where I'm not wanted, but I want you to know I truly do think you're marvellous.'

'It isn't enough.'

'You want more? You want me to tell you I love you? All right.' He slid his arms about her waist. 'I love you, Sidonia. I can't get you out of my mind. I love you most sincerely. I want your love. I do have it, don't I? You've got me completely enslaved.'

His language was overblown, she knew it, like the language in Mum's cheap magazines, but his dark eyes were luminous and tender. They were quite small, she realised, and he never opened them wide. His lower lip was full, his hair longer than most men's these days. He wasn't really handsome at all. Yet she wanted him. Desperately. She wanted him although he wasn't handsome. So he could just as easily want her. The realisation struck her. You didn't have to be a beauty, either male or female, to make someone love you. It was like the opening of a floodgate. She felt released from the inhibitions of the past. For most of her life she had been compared to her sisters to her detriment. Aunt Mattie had tried to tell her not to listen. Roy found her attractive. Even Mr Keevil . . . She smiled at Philip, a slow languorous smile. He gasped and grasped her, dragging her roughly to him. 'You're the biggest damned tease . . .'

'I don't mean to be.'

'You'll come to me tonight? Promise me?'

'I can't.'

'You can. You're an independent woman. You can do what you please.'

'Can I? I suppose so.' Another revelation.

'So you'll come to my room? You want to, don't you?'

'I don't know,' she lied.

'Come to me and find out. I would never try to force you. Wanting is half the battle.'

'Are we having a battle?'

'We will if you don't have the courage to follow your desires.'

'I'm not a coward.'

'I know that, my darling, just as I know so much about you. Promise me. Now!'

'I shall do no such thing.'

'You said you weren't afraid. I think you are. No one should fear love. It's the most wonderful thing in the world. I shall wait for you tonight.'

The bell from the small sitting room rang. Mrs Cardell was asking for Philip, demanding a game of cards. Sid spent the remainder of the evening in a dream which not even the noisy return of the others and Patrick's over-excitement could destroy.

She saw Mrs Cardell into bed, then read to her before settling her with a mild sedative.

'You're so good to me, Sidonia. What would I do without you?'

'You won't have to do without me.'

'Some man is sure to snap you up sooner or later.' She sighed. 'You mustn't let me get selfish.'

'I don't think you could.'

'I've mellowed. I think it's your influence.'

Sid laughed. 'You've not worried over things lately, that's all.'

'If I haven't worried it is because of your soothing presence. You look pretty tonight. Your eyes are shining. Has your window-cleaner been paying you compliments?'

Sid laughed again and Mrs Cardell took her hand. 'You're so good to me. So very good.' She talked a little more, mumbling incoherently as the sedative took effect and she drifted into sleep. Sid checked the fire, turned off the light and went to her room. She seemed to be living two lives at once: one on the surface where she followed her usual patterns like an automaton; the other a deep, sweet, thrilling existence where she was somebody else, a woman loved and desired.

Angie was asleep, snoring lightly. Sid would have liked to bathe but the plumbing was noisy and might wake her. She carried a large jug of hot water from the kitchen and poured it into a bowl by the nursery fire. She washed her entire body carefully, dried herself and used talcum powder and scent and brushed her hair to a glossy sheen, never once admitting even to herself that this was for anyone's benefit but her own. She slid her nightgown over her head and looked at herself in the cheval glass, wishing she had nightwear like Miss Celia's: satin or silk with lace. Her gown was plain cotton embroidered here and there by Angie with rosebuds. It would have to do. Do for what? For Philip to see?

She had been preparing herself like a bride going to her marriage bed, but she wasn't married and Philip was not for her. Yet he loved her and there had been more unlikely alliances. Who would have supposed that the king of Britain and the Empire would throw it all away as he had for love of a woman? And he had married her. Philip was telling her the truth. He was sincere and she had to believe him. And believing him she could allow her own tumultuous feelings to come to the surface.

Of course she wanted him. The fact that she had never been very close to a man couldn't blind her to her desire. She was the same as any innocent woman who found herself wanted for the first time, like any wife on her honeymoon. She tried to make one last stand against the ache which was tormenting her. She wasn't a wife and she'd always been told that a girl who permitted liberties would disgust a man and he'd never propose marriage. Then she reached for the dressing gown she had purchased since moving to Greystone House. It was of plain wool, as serviceable as her nightgown. She put it on and slid her feet into her slippers. She stood absolutely still for a moment. She had to make a decision which would affect her entire life. What decision? It had already been made.

Chapter Eight

Sid walked cautiously through her bedroom door into the day nursery where the fire still flickered. Angie always kept her door open, finding pleasure and reassurance in the friendly glow and the last, dancing flames. She seemed soundly asleep, but had a disconcerting habit of suddenly waking up and demanding to know what was happening. Sid stood motionless, watching the slight mound she made beneath her bedclothes, listening to her soft breathing. Angie said her catlike way of sleeping was a legacy from the days when she never knew who her mother had brought back to the house. 'Sometimes,' she had explained to Sid, remembering her years of misery, 'she'd have a rough boyfriend, "uncles", I had to call them. The older kids used to make fun of me and I didn't understand why, or why some of the uncles hurt her. I'd hear her cry out. It was dreadful.' She had paused. 'When I understood who the uncles really were, I was ashamed. Do you remember when I was thirteen and came to school with those awful bruises? My mother yelled so loud one night I rushed down. She was naked and a huge bully of a man was hitting her with his fists. I picked up a broomstick and landed it across his back with a terrible crack. He turned on me. I tried to defend myself but he got the broom and threw it in a corner, then my Mum picked it up and all naked and bleeding she began beating him with it. When he turned to fight her off I got a kitchen knife and stuck it in his back. Not far. I didn't want to swing for murder, but it stopped him. He left.'

Sid wondered why such memories should plague her now.

She moved at last, opened the door into the corridor and stepped through. As it closed behind her with a click, she put her ear to the keyhole, but there was no sound.

All the way to Philip's room she was assailed by a mixture of anticipation and terror. At his door she paused and took a deep breath as the enormity of what she was about to do struck her. Go back, a part of her mind warned, go back while you still have time. She took another step. She could have reached out and touched the doorhandle, but this was sheer madness which couldn't be justified, and she turned to hurry away. Then Philip's door opened. 'Sidonia, I knew you'd come to me, darling.' She fought an impulse to run as he reached out and grasped her hands. He looked overwhelmingly attractive in a dark silk dressing gown.

'Darling, darling Sidonia,' he murmured, 'I was sure you wouldn't let me down.'

'How could you possibly be sure?' she asked crossly, 'I didn't know myself.'

'You're here, aren't you?'

'I was just going back to my room.'

'Why were you here, then?'

When she didn't reply he bent and pushed his face into her neck, sniffing. 'What delicious perfume, my love. Lavender. Is it for me?'

'I always use it.'

'Not always. You usually smell of some wholesome kitchen scent – like baking, or herbs . . . Now do come in to the fire. It's draughty in the corridor.'

'How did you know I was here?'

'Maybe I heard you, maybe I just sensed your delicious presence. Come, my love, let's go in before someone sees you.'

'What if they do? I've done nothing wrong.'

'Of course you haven't, and I wouldn't dream of suggesting that you should, though if anyone should catch us like this who would believe it? We can just talk if that's all you want.'

Sid allowed him to lead her into his bedroom. She knew it well from the times she had cleaned it. It was one of the more masculine rooms, full of heavy, dark furniture with a tobacco-brown carpet and curtains. A sombre room, she had thought, but transformed now. He had piled the fire with coal which was burning strongly, and turned off the gaslight and lit candles. The room was suffused with his presence, the scent of his shaving soap and his cigarettes.

'Come and sit by the fire.'

She accompanied him to the low *chaise-longue* and they sat side by side. 'Isn't this cosy?' he said.

Cosy? It was the last word she would have used. Her senses were turbulent, her body giving out urgent and conflicting messages. She was nervous, wishing she had never begun this, while her senses clamoured for his love.

He turned her to face him and gasped, 'My dearest, you do want me, don't you? It's written in your eyes, your mouth. Oh, your delectable mouth.' He leaned towards her and she automatically put up her face for his kiss. His arms went round her, but he didn't hold her tight. He was giving her choices. She could go or stay. But now there was only one choice left for her. She responded to his kisses until he gasped and pulled her to her feet. His hand tugged at the cord of her dressing gown which slid down, leaving her in her nightgown. As far as covering went it concealed more flesh than the evening dresses worn by society women, but beneath it she was naked.

He began to tug it upwards and she trembled. He stopped at once. 'My darling, are you afraid?'

'No.' But her teeth were chattering.

'Cold?' He smiled into her eyes.

He let her gown slide down again and she stood there, still covered from head to toe with white cotton, wanting his hands on her flesh.

'Have you ever made love?' he asked.

'I've been kissed, that's all.'

'Sidonia! If you only knew how happy that makes me. Let me be the one to initiate you into the arts of love.'

'Arts?'

'Oh, yes, my sweet. There are dozens of ways we can please one another. Of course, we can't follow them all in one night, but...'

He took her by the hand and led her to the big bed where the covers were already pulled back. She saw wine and two glasses on his beside table.

She drew back. 'You *knew* I'd come, didn't you?' She was abruptly angry.

'No, darling, I didn't, but I hoped. If you hadn't I would have been horribly disappointed.'

She sat on the edge of his bed, not knowing how to proceed. He watched her for a moment, then knelt and began to kiss her ankles, her slender calves, her knees. He pushed aside her restricting gown, his mouth caressing more and more of her flesh until she had lost all fear and wanted only a release from such agonisingly, incredibly dear torment.

When he pulled her nightgown over her head she scarcely noticed, her whole self fiery with need. He lifted her legs to the bed and threw his dressing gown aside, revealing his own nakedness. She gasped at the sight of him. 'I didn't know...' she stammered.

He looked down at himself and smiled. 'I won't hurt you, my love.'

'No, but I didn't know...'

'My sweet, virginal love.'

He joined her on the bed and raised himself above her. She was more than ready, and he entered her with infinite control, giving her time to relax, minimising discomfort, until he was deep within her. Then he began to move, slowly, too slowly for her as a powerful tension built in her body. She tried to tell him how she felt, to beg him to give her release, but she was incoherent; she didn't know the right words for something which before this night had been a mystery to her.

'My love, my darling love,' he said, over and over as he increased his powerful thrusting, holding himself in check, waiting for her. There was no mistaking the moment when she experienced her burst of ecstasy. To her it was like a bud flowering to full bloom in an awesome second, the flight of a swallow, the crashing of thunder; yet more beautiful, more awesome than any of these. She felt him reach his own climax, and exulted in her power to bring him such joy before he sank upon her, gasping and sobbing for breath. Their skin was moist with perspiration. She felt they had merged into one being.

'My God, Sidonia,' he breathed. 'It's never been like that. What a woman! I love you, love you, love you.' He gently moved from her and lay beside her.

She raised herself on one elbow and stared down into his face in wonder. 'I love you, Philip. I had no idea what love could be like. To think we can share such marvellous moments for the rest of our lives.'

He reached out for his cigarettes. 'Smoke?'

'I don't, but I can learn. Oh, Philip, I can learn anything, everything from you, be anyone you want. I'll never let you down.'

'I know, my love. And I feel the same way about you. I don't know how I'll ever tear myself away.'

She felt as if he had punched her in the heart. 'You're leaving?'

He blew a stream of smoke into the air, where it caught the candlelight. 'Not yet, my darling, but of course I shall have to return to London some time.'

'Yes, of course. I wasn't thinking. You'll need to tell Mrs Prosser about me. Do you think she'll mind you marrying a servant?'

'You're no ordinary servant, Sidonia. Even your name...' He laughed and caught her hand and kissed its palm.

'You'll know how to put it to her, won't you, Philip? She's fond of you, isn't she?' She sighed. 'I shall miss you. I shan't feel properly alive until you come back.'

'Dearest Sidonia. You'll wait for me?'

'For ever, though I hope it won't be that long.' She gave a little laugh. 'When do you have to leave?'

'Not for a while. I couldn't possibly tear myself away from you yet.'

Sid returned to her room and climbed into bed. She was more exhausted than she had ever been, and happier. Her body tingled, vibrantly alive, desire satisfied yet lying dormant until the next time Philip would bring it to exquisite need. The little book given her by Mrs Dingle had stated the facts, but had given no inkling of the actual sensation of love. Mostly it had been concerned with preventing conception. Men took care of that side, wearing something that stopped babies. A protector, or sheath, or French letter it was called. There was protection for women, too. A rubber pessary which was sold in three sizes, small, medium or large. How did you know which would fit you? She smiled at the thought. One day she would be properly fitted by a doctor and Philip wouldn't need to bother, and married life would only produce babies when they were wanted. He could enjoy her whenever he chose, and they would discuss the question of children in a civilised way. She definitely wanted them. She hadn't been his first love, but she would be his last. He had been genuinely amazed at her ardent response. What a lover he was! How gentle, how perceptive, how incredibly tender, how fulfilling.

Eventually she slept and didn't wake up until Angie brought her tea. 'You're a sleepy-head today,' Angie smiled. 'I've been shaking you for ages.'

Sid drank her tea. When Angie had left she removed her nightdress, which was stained with the juices of love. She'd wash it herself. The Misses Weekley might be unmarried, but there was no guarantee that they wouldn't know about such matters. She wondered if either Nellie or Selina had been in a man's bed when they were young and their blood was hot. She couldn't imagine it, but there was no knowing.

She allowed Angie to serve Philip with breakfast, not trusting herself to see him so soon without betraying them. If she saw him now she would surely find the temptation to embrace him irresistible, but no one must know until they had told their families and put a proper announcement in the newspapers. She wondered if Mrs Cardell would mind a relative marrying her housekeeper?

Angie came into the kitchen. 'Mr Philip asked where you were.'

'Did he?' Sid busied herself with her scone mix.

'Yes, and when I told him you were too busy to serve, he . . .'

'He what?' Sid stopped and tried to conceal her anxiety.

'He didn't say anything for a minute, then he said he was glad you weren't ill.'

Sid wished she'd had the courage to serve him. Now he would think she regretted last night, when the truth was that she had only to think of him for her flesh to plead for his touch. She realised she had been kneading the scone dough like bread and it would probably be as heavy as lead. She threw it into the pail used for the few hens Brindle had decided to keep, and began again, concentrating on her work with difficulty.

Nellie and Selina Weekley plodded in and out of the kitchen with their polishes and mops, as dour as usual. Everyone came in for hot drinks midway through the morning. The day went on in its familiar patterns, but now everything was momentously different for Sid. She behaved normally but her mind was with her lover. She took the day's menu to Mrs Cardell, another recent innovation.

'Not that it's a new thing,' she had explained to Sid. 'In my girlhood home the housekeeper reported every morning to my mama, who approved of the menu, or changed it.'

'You never change anything,' pointed out Sid.

Mrs Cardell had laughed. 'I know, my dear. I'm always happy with what you choose, and you are so economical, never wasting a thing; but I like to see what you plan so I can look forward to my meals.'

This morning Sid realised she was being asked a question. 'Are you unwell, Sidonia?'

'Oh, no, madam, not at all. Why? Do I look unwell?'

'I don't know. Your eyes are so bright, your colour high, are you sure you're not running up a temperature?'

'Quite sure, madam. I think the good living here is making me almost too healthy.'

Mrs Cardell laughed. 'Impossible. No one can be too healthy. You know, my dear, my own health has improved since you took over Greystone House. Brindle looks a different man, too. How thankful I am you weren't put off by the cool reception we gave you.'

Sid took in what was being said, but still with only half a mind. She returned to the kitchen wishing even more that she had faced Philip this morning. She had no idea where he was and dared not ask. Stupid, really. It was a perfectly natural question. She needed to know how many to cook for.

At lunch-time she had still not seen him, but she prepared food for the dining room for two, and this time she did serve. He was there in his usual place, making a point of not looking at her. When she bent over him with the serving dishes, her nostrils picked up his male scent and she nearly dropped the cauliflower in white sauce into his lap. Surely he could risk one glance? Was he punishing her for not meeting him this morning? It turned out that he had breakfasted alone, while Mrs Cardell had had a tray in her room: they might have been able to speak freely. He tucked heartily into all the dishes and took a second helping of apricot mousse, though Sid was finding it difficult to eat today.

He looked at her suddenly. 'Did you cook the meal, Sidonia?'

'Yes, sir, with Angie's help. She's a good cook.'

'Sidonia is always ready to praise,' said Mrs Cardell fondly.

Philip said nothing more to her and Sid was annoyed. She wouldn't creep around him, wishing he would look lovingly at her while she revealed her need for him in all its nakedness. She instructed Angie to take the tray of coffee to Mrs Cardell's small sitting room while she began to wash up.

'Here, that's my job,' protested Angie.

'We'll change places today. I'll stay down here and later you can serve dinner. It'll be good for you, teach you more!'

Angie looked doubtful, but Sid was preoccupied and she didn't argue.

Sid discovered that Philip had indeed been punishing her for her neglect. After the kitchen was clean and tidy, she walked in the garden. The sun was almost set. The days were growing shorter as they crept inexorably towards winter; it was getting chilly, though the high wall still held some warmth in its shelter. She was staring at a clump of Michaelmas-daisies, not seeing them, seeing only Philip as he had appeared last night. Weak tears threatened to overwhelm her, then she heard his step behind her. She turned, ready to berate him for his coldness, but their voices blended.

'How did you like being frozen out?' he demanded angrily.

'How could you treat me so coldly?' she flashed.

'You began it, Sidonia. You've been avoiding me.'

They stared at one another for a moment, then he was close to her side, his hand brushing hers, not daring to embrace her where they might be seen.

'Brindle's still in the orchard,' he said. 'I had a scout round. There's a light in the greenhouse, too. The lad is there.'

'I know.'

'I'm amazed that they work such long hours. Most servants can't wait to get away.'

'Mrs Cardell makes us feel at home here.'

'I see. Why didn't you serve breakfast this morning?'

'I was afraid.'

'Afraid? You? After last night? I can't believe it.'

'It's true. I was afraid I wouldn't be able to stop myself from kissing you. Or something,' she finished.

'Especially the "or something", I hope.'

They laughed and the icy wall between them melted.

'You'll come to me tonight, my love?'
'Need you ask?'

For a week Sid felt she lived at a distance from everyone but Philip. She spent part of every night in his bed, and their love-making was as powerful and wonderful as the first time. Even better, Sid thought, as they grew to know each other and she cast off the last of her inhibitions. Over and over, during the tender, exciting moments before love-making, and again at the height of passion, he avowed his love for her as she did for him.

During the day she often caught Angie looking at her questioningly. She wanted to laugh and tell her the secret. She would be amazed when she discovered that her co-worker was going to marry her employer's cousin. Everyone would be amazed. Sid thought of telling them at home. She pictured Mum's mixture of bewilderment and elation as she took in the news, then relayed it to her mother and sisters. Sid could imagine her boasting. For the first time in her life she would beat Audrey and Irene. She wondered what they would say.

'Grandmother is demanding my return,' said Philip sadly one day.

He and Sid had met in the garden again. It was Sunday and she could have visited her family, but she couldn't bear to miss a single precious moment with him. Today it was dry but dull. Until that moment she hadn't noticed the weather, but even brilliant sunshine would have been clouded for her after such a remark. She controlled her dismay. She had vowed never to be a clinging type of female. 'That's perfectly natural,' she said. She even managed a smile.

Philip looked surprised. 'You don't mind?'

'Of course I do. I mind terribly, but Mrs Prosser is family; I mean, she's like a mother to you, isn't she?'

'Not quite.' Philip sounded bitter. 'My mother was a sweet, gentle creature. Grandmother has always been sour.'

'I'm sorry. Perhaps life hasn't been good to her.'

'You're a nice girl, Sidonia.'

'Am I?'

'You don't condemn.'

'How do you know that?'

'You work amicably with Angie. In fact, you got her the job here.'

'What do you know about Angie?'

'Only what I've heard from Brindle. Apparently he was disgusted when she arrived. He's over that now and admits that nice girls can sometimes come from humble, even bad, backgrounds. In fact, you yourself are proof of that.'

Her self-control was fragile and she flared up immediately. 'My background is perfectly respectable.'

'Of course it is, darling. Actually, I went to your father's shop one day and bought some apples. I liked him.'

'Did you? I'm glad.'

'As a matter of fact, I decided then to go to your home as well.'

'What?' Discovering that he had been so deliberately looking into her background gave Sid a sense of being dissected.

'You're angry with me. Please, don't be. It's perfectly natural for me to be curious about you. You already know about me, but all I've seen is that you are my cousin's housekeeper and companion.'

'Yes, I suppose so.' She wished he had asked her to take him to meet her relatives.

'They are fine, decent people,' he said.

She looked into his face, trying to read him. Fine, decent people! What did he mean? Good working-class decent? Would he cut them when they were married?

He made an effort to laugh lightly. 'You're staring at me, Sidonia. Are you cross with me?'

'Did you see my mother?'

'Is she of medium height, pretty hair, well built?'

'Yes.'

'Then I met her. She answered the door. I asked her if she would be interested in buying an encyclopaedia and she said, "No, thank you." She was determined, but polite.'

A silence fell between them which he eventually broke. 'I have a few shirts and things in the wash. Could they be made ready by tomorrow?'

'That can easily be arranged.'

'And you'll be with me tonight for a last wonderful time?'

'Last?'

'Last for now, I mean?'

'I don't know.' She wished she did not feel so angry. She wanted him to take happy memories with him. 'Yes, I'll be there,' she said quickly. 'It was a shock to be told you're leaving.'

'You knew it had to happen.'

'Of course. Will you tell your grandmother and sister about me as soon as you arrive?'

'Um, I don't think so. I'll see how the land lies. I must get Grandmother at a favourable moment. Celia will be scathing, I know, no matter what happens.'

'Do you think she'll learn to accept me as a sister-in-law?'

'We can only wait and see. Until tonight, my love.'

Sid stayed with Philip until five the next morning. They made love repeatedly, their imminent separation stimulating them to greater heights of desire and fulfilment. When Sid finally crept back to her room, exhausted and wanting only to rest, she found Angie awake.

'Where were you, Sid?' she called, sitting up in bed.

'I've been to the bathroom.'

'Are you unwell? I woke at four o'clock and got up to fetch a glass of water from the carafe. I didn't see you.'

'Is this some kind of inquisition?'

'Of course not.' Angie was hurt. 'I hoped everything was all right. I couldn't get back to sleep and I was worried. I looked in the bathroom and lavatories and you weren't in any of them.'

'We must have missed one another somehow. Oh, of course, I went down to the kitchen. I woke with a headache and wanted a cup of tea.'

'Did you have one?'

'Yes.'

'Speaking of tea, I should like some.' Angie swung her legs to the floor.

'At this hour? It's only just gone five.'

'Well, maybe I'll enjoy a cuppa in bed for once.'

Angie brought back a tray. She had laid it with two cups and saucers, a teapot, milk, sugar, and a plate of wafer-thin bread and butter. She put it on Sid's bedside table. 'We'll be gentry for an hour,' she said. 'Can I come in with you?'

Sid moved to make room and had to force down a piece of bread and butter. The very last thing she wanted was to eat and gossip with Angie. She would have to be up at seven and her body was clamouring for sleep.

Angie tried to be cheerful, but gave up in the end and removed herself and the tray. Sid heard her climb into her rather creaky bed. She felt mean at treating her so off-handedly, then she fell asleep. Angie didn't wake her until ten when she brought her more tea.

'Why didn't you call me?'

'I came up but you were sound asleep and looked quite pale. I thought, just this once . . .'

'Thanks,' said Sid briefly. 'Did you manage breakfast all right?'

'Madam only wanted a lightly boiled egg.'

'What about Mr Philip?'

'He wasn't there.'

Sid turned away to smile. He would have been tired, too.

'He's left,' said Angie.

Sid shot up in bed. 'Left? What do you mean?'

'Just that. I don't know when he went. Mrs Cardell just said he'd gone. She looked pretty fed up about it.'

Sid jumped out of bed and dressed rapidly. She knew Angie was staring at her curiously, but she had to know what had happened. How? She couldn't possibly ask Mrs Cardell. Yes, she could. She was housekeeper and had to know how many to cook for.

Mrs Cardell was in her small sitting room gazing into the fire, looking haggard.

Sid had entered quickly, her mind full of questions about Philip, but instead she asked gently, 'Are you ill, madam?'

'No.' The answer was abrupt, angry.

'I'm sorry,' stammered Sid.

'No, I am the one to be sorry. I shouldn't speak to you like that. It isn't your fault. To think I can't trust one of my own flesh and blood.'

Sid said nothing. She felt suddenly weak, awaiting a blow she couldn't endure.

When Mrs Cardell remained quiet and brooding, Sidonia asked mechanically, 'Are you sure you're not ill?'

'I don't feel one hundred per cent. I shall require a light lunch today. No rich pudding.'

'You must be ill!'

Mrs Cardell smiled weakly. 'Is that a diagnosis? No pudding, she must be ill? Stay with me a while. I need my companion today. Mr Philip . . .' She paused and rang the bell and, when Angie answered, asked her to bring coffee and two cups and saucers. She stared out of the window at the leaves which floated gently to the ground, not sensing the burning impatience and anxiety which filled Sid. 'Autumn,' she said. 'Soon winter will follow. Sidonia, I'm weary.'

Sid couldn't trust herself to answer. Her mind was a turmoil of questions she had no right to ask.

Angie placed the tray of coffee carefully on a small table by her mistress and left.

'Sit down, Sidonia. Pull a chair closer to the fire. Pour the coffee, please, for both of us.'

Sidonia poured. She forced herself to do everything carefully. She must concentrate. Her nerves were tender to the point of pain. Perhaps something had happened to Philip. There was the usual plate of biscuits, but neither woman touched them.

'Angie served breakfast this morning,' said Mrs Cardell, 'but of course you know that. I understand you were unwell during the night. Are you better?'

'Yes, madam. Angie should have called me earlier.'

'Not at all.'

This conversation about trivialities was driving Sid to a frenzy of anguish. She could wait no longer. 'Will Mr Philip be in for lunch, madam?'

'I expect a great deal of you, don't I? I dare say you have things in the kitchen you are longing to do, and I selfishly keep you here to talk to me. Don't you ever resent me? Don't you find it confusing to move between housekeeping and friendship?'

'I manage, madam.'

'Your voice sounds odd, so constrained. Sidonia, I would never wish to take advantage of you, though I fear I do.'

Sid wanted to drop on her knees and beg her employer to stop mouthing irrelevancies and speak of Philip. She sat, apparently demure, her cup and saucer in her hand. Mrs Cardell had fallen unbearably silent. Sid concentrated on the patterns on the china. Floral sprays on an ivory ground. It was good china but not the best. Mrs Dingle had told her about grand houses where they used porcelain costing more than a year's wages for an ordinary man. Porcelain for upstairs, earthenware for the kitchen and nursery.

When Mrs Cardell finally spoke, Sid jumped so violently she spilled coffee into her saucer. Mrs Cardell said, 'Mr Philip left very early this morning.'

'Left? I don't understand.'

'I should not expect you to. I certainly don't.'

'We still have some of his clothes in the wash,' Sid said stupidly, 'I have to sew a button on his shirt.' She had been looking forward to it. Even she could manage to sew a button, and it was a pleasant task to perform for the man she loved.

'I heard voices and a car at six this morning,' said Mrs Cardell. 'It must have been Mr Philip going off in a taxi.'

Sid was bewildered. He must have seen her out of his room and made immediate plans to leave. Why? She felt her brain would burst through her skull with the questions she wanted to ask.

Mrs Cardell said sadly, 'I trusted him as I would a son and he repaid me by stealing from me.'

'No!'

'I'm not surprised you are horrified.'

'What...' Sid had to moisten her lips. 'What...' She could get no further.

'What did he take? A brooch. My cameo, the one I usually wear at my throat. It's a good one and many years old. I dare say it will fetch a reasonable price. He also purloined my sapphire earrings and necklace, the ones I wore last night. They were lying on my dressing-table. He must have crept in on me while I slept.'

'But I don't understand. Are you sure? How could he have done such a thing? He'll never be able to come back here after this!'

'My dear girl, you sound more shocked than I. I'm sorry, but my own cousin is a thief. His grandmother told me she had missed money from her purse on more than one occasion at a time when Philip was the only possible suspect. She said she has forgiven him many times. I thought she might have made a mistake, but she hadn't.'

'I can't believe it.'

'Perhaps I should not have told you, though you would have missed the jewels. Besides, I look upon you as more than a servant. Of course, I would prefer you to keep this from the others.' Sid placed her cup and saucer on the table with infinite care. 'My dear, you're trembling. And no wonder. We've had a burglary, and now this: far worse than any burglary could ever be. My own cousin's grandson! To steal my belongings!' The old lady paused. 'Thank you for letting me talk to you. I don't know what I would do without you.'

'Thank you, madam, for trusting me. I'm sorry Mr Philip has let you down. I didn't think he was the sort to... I'm glad you are able to talk to me.' Sid removed the tray and walked downstairs on shaking limbs. Philip a thief. He was a thief. He couldn't return to Greystone House. Perhaps he'd send for her. Could she go on loving him? She needed desperately to be alone, to sort out her tumbling thoughts, to face her fears. But the kitchen was busy with the others drinking their tea or coffee or cocoa and plunging their hands into the biscuit tin and chattering excitedly.

'Sid, what's happened to Mr Philip? Did madam tell you?'

Sid looked woodenly at Angie, whose face was pink with excitement. 'Mr Brindle says he saw him go off in a taxi at six this morning. He didn't say anything about leaving yesterday, did he? We've still got some of his stuff.'

'It can be sent on,' said Sid mechanically. 'Without the shirt button.' The contemplation of this petty act of revenge unnerved her further. What a futile, ridiculous gesture in the face of such blatantly bad behaviour. Did this mean he had rejected her? She couldn't just assume that. How could he? He had told her she was the best lover he'd ever had. He'd told her he loved her. Of course, she would hear from him. He was weak, but that only meant he needed her more.

As time passed and Philip didn't write, Sid grew increasingly unhappy. When she missed her first monthly course, she was frightened but persuaded herself that it was because of worry. Mrs Dingle had told her that could sometimes happen. But when the second month passed, her fear overwhelmed her. She felt well except for a little nausea first thing in the morning, but although nothing showed outwardly, she knew she was carrying Philip's child. She cursed herself for a fool! She had fought for and won self-respect, a measure of independence, even of beauty. She had begun to feel pride in herself and her achievements, going to visit her family with her head high, using make-up skilfully, supervising a household of domestics with efficiency and success. And now she had been landed in the age-old, tragic dilemma of any woman who had trusted the wrong man. She felt used, soiled, and hellishly angry.

She often walked in the garden where she had enjoyed talks with Philip, and one day it occurred to her that he didn't know about the baby. What a fool she was! He had avoided contact with her until he saw his way clear to breaking the news of their love to his grandmother. Of course, that was it! He would rescue her. It was mean of him to steal from his aunt, but he hadn't taken much and she seemed to have forgotten. You didn't stop loving someone because they had weaknesses. With her by his side he would grow in strength. And he must have needed money badly. She must tell him her news very gently. It would be worrying for him if he was already financially embarrassed. She didn't place much hope in Mrs Prosser's help. It would be a struggle for them to live at first, but she was strong, she could work until the baby was born and soon get something after. People were not so interested in domestic work any more, and ladies were becoming quite desperate about the servant problem.

One night she waited until Angie was asleep and wrote to Philip in the quiet, dimly lit day nursery. She had obtained his address from Mrs Cardell's writing desk, an act she was ashamed of, but a necessary one. She needn't have waited until Angie slept, but she wanted to be totally alone to write such a vital letter.

She tried several ways, but in the end kept it simple.

'My dear Philip,' she wrote, crossed off 'my', put it back, tore up the sheet and began again.

Dear Philip,
  I'm sorry you went away without saying goodbye to me. Perhaps the thought of our parting was too painful. I have been hoping for a letter. I love you so much. I was prepared to wait but now something has happened which makes our contact urgent. I am expecting our child. I am happy to think I carry a part of you inside me, but I need you with me before I can break the news

to others. We could get married quite quickly and privately. Please come soon.

All my love, Sidonia.

She posted the letter with a heart full of hope, which eroded as day followed day without an answer. Christmas was upon them and she was as busy as always. She caught Angie giving her sideways puzzled glances sometimes. She knew she had grown quiet, not speaking unless she had to. Mrs Cardell noticed it, too.

She tackled her one day. 'Are you ill, Sidonia?'

'No, madam, I'm perfectly well.' What was coming next? Had she seen some sign? Her figure had barely altered, her waist was only a fraction bigger, her breasts a little swollen. Surely not enough to show.

'I'm glad to hear it. You don't seem your usual cheerful self.'

'I'm sorry, madam.' Sid resolved to force her worry to the back of her mind and look after those in her care. But it was so difficult. Everyone listened to the king's Christmas broadcast to the Empire, holding their breath as his stammer sometimes threatened to embarrass him. He succeeded beautifully and Mrs Cardell said, 'He's an example for every young man in Britain. We benefited in the end by the abdication of his brother.'

Sid had seen less of Roy. When he had taken her out she was abstracted, and her refusal to kiss him had annoyed him. She scarcely noticed his mood, while he went doggedly on hoping her coolness was temporary. He had helped again with the Christmas tree, and this year gave Sid a bottle of expensive perfume.

'I hope you like it,' he had said. 'It suits you, I think. Well,' he laughed, 'the name does anyway.'

She looked at the label, 'Country Beauty', and wondered for a moment if he was teasing her. To cover her awkwardness she unscrewed the fancy cap and sniffed. The scent was delicious.

'Thank you, Roy. I think it flatters me. The name, I mean.'

'I don't agree. You are beautiful to me.'

'Am I?'

'You are.' His voice was serious. 'Absolutely. Perhaps it's got something to do with your independence and a life you enjoy, but you've changed.'

Later Sid looked in the mirror. That infuriating bump on her nose was still noticeable but, in spite of her worry, her sallow complexion was tinged with a becoming pink and her hair was glossy. Her eyes looked enormous and the colour of jade.

For Sid the 1938 New Year celebrations fell as flat as Christmas had. The year ending had seen a Germany in which Adolf Hitler had decreed that unless Aryan German children were reared knowing only Nazi values they would be removed from their family homes, and in which he cemented his ties with other dictators.

Sid was more concerned with the fact that she received no cards from Philip. In fact, no one had heard from him since the time he left.

She decided that something had to be done. If he would not come to her she must go to him. She asked for a few days off and was granted them willingly. 'You deserve a change,' said Mrs Cardell.

Sid travelled to London. She had never been far from Bristol before, and was amazed when the train ran through mile after mile of London suburbs before it reached the station. The city streets seemed endless, their bustle loud and often incomprehensible, with foreign tongues on every side. She remembered that London was a cosmopolitan place, where even the cockney accents were difficult for her to follow. She bought a map and got her bearings, and decided to telephone Philip. She rang his number. A servant answered and asked her name.

'It's Miss Brown,' she said, deciding suddenly to keep her identity secret.

Philip's voice sounded so near she could hardly get the first words out. 'Hello, Philip, it's me. Sidonia.'

There was a silence. 'I was told a Miss . . . a mistake, obviously,' he said in unemotional tones which hurt. 'How pleasant to hear your voice. Are you telephoning from Greystone House?'

'No, I'm here, in London, not far from you.'

'What?' His loud exclamation hurt her eardrum.

'I said I'm quite close. I must talk to you.'

'What about?'

'Didn't you get my letter?'

'I got one, yes.'

'If you read it you must know why I have to see you.' Sid regretted her decision to phone him. She should have gone to his house. Or waited outside until she saw him. Now he was a disembodied voice on the end of a telephone line and couldn't seem to understand her.

'I told you about the – consequences. You know. About the way I am.'

'Yes. I was extremely puzzled.'

'Puzzled? Why?'

He made an exclamation of annoyance. 'I can't talk now.'

'Where can we meet?'

'Meet? Yes, I suppose we had better. I don't know where. In the National Art Gallery, perhaps. Trafalgar Square. Just inside. In an hour.'

Sid replaced the receiver, her heart racing. He had spoken to her almost like a stranger.

She found Trafalgar Square. She was early and sat for a while by the fountain, watching tourists feeding the birds. At any other time the laughter of children, the mixture of nationalities, the thrill of being in the capital city would have exhilarated her. Now she felt only a leaden fear.

When Philip arrived he looked exactly the same. She wanted to hold him tight, to tell him of her love, to hear him speak of his. She wanted to talk about the precious burden she carried and have him smile at the idea of approaching fatherhood.

The smile with which he greeted her held no pleasure. 'Sidonia, how well you look.' His voice echoed round the hall. 'This is no place to talk. Let's find a small gallery. We can sit and you can give me all your news.'

She followed him as he hurried up steps and past the rows of pictures, the tourists, the students who practised drawing. They arrived in a room of glass cases containing jewellery.

'I enjoy these,' said Philip. 'Such lovely stones.'

Sid flushed.

'Oh dear, I suppose you know I borrowed a few from my cousin.'

'Borrowed?'

'You sound condemning.'

'She was quite upset.'

'I know. It was awful of me, wasn't it, but I was on my beam ends. Not a spot of filthy lucre in sight.'

'You got my letter?'

'I've already told you I did.' He sounded petulant.

'So you know I'm to become a mother.'

'I do. Congratulations. What did you want to talk about?'

She stared at him. 'About our arrangements, of course. There's a baby on the way.'

'So you keep telling me. How can I help you? Is it money? Weddings are awfully expensive, aren't they? I suppose you'll soon be married to the baby's lucky father?'

She turned to stare at him, her eyes wide. 'That's why I'm here.'

'Really? I don't follow.'

'You know you are the baby's father.'

'Me?' He laughed lightly. 'Come on, Sidonia, darling, I wasn't born yesterday. I should be angry with you, but I'm not. I can see why you'd want to marry into a good family, but really, to try to trick me into it . . .'

'Trick you? You know I was . . . you know you were my first . . .' Sid's voice cracked.

'I'm not denying it and I told you how privileged I felt at being the one you chose to take the first bite of the cherry. But you were hot for me after that. You were insatiable.'

She gasped. He made it sound as if she had been at fault. 'So were you!'

'What man wouldn't be, given such an opportunity. But you had other men friends, and you would have needed someone after I left. A girl with an appetite like yours would soon have found another man to oblige them.'

An elderly cleric ambled into the room and seemed to take hours examining each case. 'Remarkable,' he murmured as he left.

Sid had gained a little composure, though her heart was still racing. 'Philip, tell me that this is your idea of a joke. Not a funny one, but still a joke.'

He looked at her, his face expressing incredulity. 'Of course not. I wouldn't dream of joking about anything so serious.'

She was silent, her mind unable to comprehend his reaction, her tongue stilled by terror.

'The baby is yours,' she managed to say at last.

'No, it isn't. It can't be. I was careful.'

'Something must have gone wrong. You are its father, you are, you are.'

He looked round nervously. 'Be quiet, for God's sake. Do you want everyone to hear?'

'I don't care. I'm not ashamed. Why should I be? I love you and you love me. At least, that's what I believed. I would never have let you touch me if I hadn't thought you loved me.'

He was reproachful. He actually sounded quite sad. 'Sidonia, my dear, we had an idyllic time together, but you must have known that the idea of marriage never seriously entered my mind. How could you expect a man of my class to marry a servant?'

His words were like knives in her heart. 'You said you loved me. You said it lots of times.'

'Of course I did. I still do in a way.'

'Then you admit...'

'Of course a man tells a woman he loves her when he's making love to her. What else would you have him do? Treat her with coldness? I did love you at the time. I'm very fond of you now. When you marry you must send me a piece of wedding cake and I'll rustle up a gift.' He added in a rueful, boyish tone, 'Though, to tell you the truth, I'm still pretty broke.'

'But what shall I do? Where can I go? You've got to help me. You can't possibly treat me like this. It's inhuman.'

'I've just said I haven't any money. Can't you understand? You were a delightful lover and, if I were wealthy, I'd gladly set you up somewhere and help you through this embarrassment; but it can't be done. Sorry and all that.'

Sid wanted to get up. She wanted to rend him with words, to claw his face with her nails, but her body refused to obey her mind. She felt as if she were turned to stone.

'Have you anything else you wish to say?' asked Philip. 'I can't stay much longer. I've a luncheon appointment I must keep. Grandmother has actually said I must work at something, and she's arranged for me to meet a jeweller. She thinks I could fill the post of his personal assistant.'

She rasped. 'I'm sure you'll do well. You know about jewels.'

He sighed. 'Now you're being mean to me again. I didn't get much for Cousin Louisa's things. They were very ordinary stones. And cameo brooches aren't worn these days.'

'Hers certainly isn't. At least, not by her,' said Sid.

'Old women! Always fussing about trivialities. The world belongs to the young. What does it matter that she can't wear some damned trinket? She never goes anywhere or receives guests. She can buy another one if she wants it.'

Arguing over Mrs Cardell's brooch was easier than talking about the baby. 'It had sentimental value for her and she's upset at losing it. Why didn't you ask her for money if you were so desperate?'

'She would have refused.'

'She's not well off herself any more.'

'I know that. She should sell and get a flat. Good God, Sidonia, you do your best for the old house, but it's run down. Grandmother keeps talking about the past when Aunt Louisa was wealthy, but the past bores me.' He glanced at his watch. 'I'll have to go.' She stared at him. 'Now don't look so tragic. Women have babies every day. Why not get married to your best boyfriend. The window-cleaner chap, isn't it?'

'Roy has never laid a finger on me, except for a kiss. Why should he take over your child?'

'If I were you I'd make sure he does more than kiss you as soon as possible. I'm sure he'll be a good, honourable window-cleaner and marry you.' He frowned. 'Damn it, Sidonia, I didn't want to leave you like this, but if you will keep arguing and quarrelling I've no choice.' He walked through the archway leading to the main galleries, and she heard his footsteps receding.

Chapter Nine

Sid travelled back to Bristol on an evening train, half numbed by the emotions which dominated her; fear, misery and anger all chased their way around her brain. She tried to control her thoughts, to face her situation, but she was overwhelmed by her sense of helplessness. She felt desperately vulnerable, as alone as if she were standing on a single rock in the middle of a rushing river. She had no idea which way to turn, no one in whom she could confide. The inescapable fact was that she was three months into a pregnancy which the man responsible refused to acknowledge.

When she had read about such situations in magazines, she had taken descriptions of girls' terrified responses with a touch of scepticism, feeling rather that those who landed themselves in such a predicament had been gullible. Fury bit into her. Damn him! Damn Philip Prosser to hell! She felt physically and emotionally exhausted. As the train wheels turned, their rhythmic refrain normally soothing, her mind went over and over the nights she had spent with him, trying to work out where she could possibly have misunderstood him. No, she hadn't imagined a thing. He had told her he loved her over and over. But today he had given her an explanation, a careless answer; it tore her apart to remember it.

When the train steamed into Bristol, she was still so churned up she wondered if she should take a room in a hotel until she had mastered herself. She had told the others she would be away for a short holiday; no one expected her back yet. She sat on a bench on the station, watching the trains and the hurrying crowds of people who seemed to have purpose in their lives. What would her future hold? She would lose her job. When Mrs Cardell discovered her state she could do no less than dismiss her. Of course, she'd ask who the father was; Sid resolved never to tell anyone. She'd give no one the chance to dig at her for expecting a man from a rich society family to stoop to marry her. Mrs Cardell might not be unkind, but she would be ashamed of Philip and feel betrayed by a woman she had trusted.

Sid thought of the coming child, wondering if she could possibly love a baby so unplanned, so massively inconvenient, unwanted. Yet already she felt protective towards it. That was simply a basic female instinct, she assured herself. Girls got rid of babies; she had learned that much, though she knew little about the realities. The future would hold many decisions. She decided to go to ground for a day or two until she could cope, but when she stood up, the station seemed to whirl about her, voices drifted away and she felt violently sick.

'Hey, look out, girl.' A woman's voice, loud enough to penetrate said, 'Sit down and tuck your head between your knees.' Sid obeyed and gradually felt less giddy, but still nauseous. 'That's the ticket,' said the woman. 'Here, have a drop of tea.'

Sid shook her head, but the woman poured some into her flask cup and held it up. Sid shook her head again, but the woman was aggressive in her determination to help, and held the cup to her lips, tipping it towards her, where it threatened to spill down her clothes. She took in a couple of mouthfuls and, surprisingly, it made her feel better. The woman said approvingly, 'That's a good girl. I'll have to go now. My train's in. Are you waiting for a train?'

'No, I'm on my way home.'

'Get there as quick as you can, dear. You look all in.'

It was growing late, Sid couldn't afford to pay hotel rates, and the thought of seeking inexpensive bed and breakfast daunted her. Wearily, she boarded a tram to Kingswood. Arriving at Greystone House she went in the back way, hoping to meet nobody. In the quiet kitchen she came upon Angie sitting by the fire, knitting a sleeveless pullover for Patrick, the wool leading from her capacious apron pocket.

She sprang to her feet. 'Sid! You're back already!'

'Why on earth are you up so late? You'll be worn out tomorrow.'

Angie said nervously, 'I just want to finish this bit. It's quite a complicated pattern to leave in the middle.' She held up the work and Sid stared at it. The knitting was indeed complicated and needed wools of more than one colour. She went on staring at it, trying to work out the pattern, but her eyes wouldn't focus properly.

Angie laid her knitting aside and came to her. 'You're not well. Here, give me your case.'

'I'm fine, really. I think I ate something that disagreed with me.'

'You should go to bed at once. Come on, I'll help you.'

Sid smiled. 'You're very kind.' She felt drained of strength. 'I'll go to bed at once.'

Angie saw her to the nursery suite and Sid undressed and climbed into bed. Too exhausted even to think, she quickly fell asleep. She was awakened by someone entering the room. The step was slow and heavy. Mrs Cardell. Sid opened her eyes. Her employer was standing there in her heavy wool dressing gown. Sid pulled herself up, though she found it ridiculously difficult. 'Angie tells me you are unwell.'

'Fancy disturbing you at this hour. I'm fine, really.'

'I was not asleep. That's nothing new, as well you know. I went to the kitchen for hot milk and Angie was just making up the fires for the night. I'm glad I saw her. Do you need a doctor, my dear?'

'No, of course not. I hope Angie hasn't been upsetting you.'

'She did quite right to tell me. She's worried. You look very pale. I think I shall call the doctor.'

'No!' A doctor was the last person she wanted to see. Mrs Cardell looked astonished. 'Sorry, madam. I shouldn't have yelled, but truly, I only need to rest.'

'Something you'd eaten, Angie said. I'm glad you came home to us. We'll take care of you.'

Sid wanted to weep. Home, Mrs Cardell said. She looked upon her housekeeper as part of her home. Sid hadn't realised how much Greystone House meant to her until she faced leaving it.

When her mistress had gone, Sid lay wakeful. Her head was beginning to ache badly. She hadn't eaten a thing for hours. Not since before she had seen Philip. How long ago was that? She climbed slowly out of bed, grateful to discover that the nausea had gone. After freshening up she sat by the nursery fire which Angie must have crept in and lit. Her headache was crushingly bad. Were headaches a part of pregnancy?

The door opened and Angie came in. 'Not in bed? I lit the fire. I thought it would be cosier. You looked quite grey; in fact you still look awful bad. Can I help?'

Sid smiled ruefully. 'I've a terrible headache.'

'When did you last eat?'

'Ages ago.'

Angie tutted and left, returning soon after with a pot of tea and a plate of scrambled eggs on toast, all served on the best kitchen china.

Sid realised that she was ravenously hungry. 'I'm really being pampered,' she said, immediately tucking into the food.

'You deserve it. We all depend on you. If it weren't for you I wouldn't have a job and neither would the others and Mrs Cardell would be lost without you. I never forget what you've done for me. Never.'

Her words scarcely registered as Sid wolfed down the food. After a second cup of tea her headache began mercifully to fade. She got up to look at the old alarm clock on the mantelpiece. Nearly midnight? Could it possibly still be the day she had been so cruelly rejected?

Angie looked approvingly at the empty plates. 'Good girl,' she said, sounding motherly.

'It was delicious, thanks. Angie, I've got muddled. What day is it?'

Angie laughed. 'The same day you went to London. You started off early. We were amazed to see you back so soon.'

'I'm amazed myself.' Sid's attempt at levity fell flat. 'How did you get on downstairs?'

'Everything ran fairly smoothly, but we missed your organisation. I never understood how much you did behind the scenes. You're so clever.'

'Thanks. Isn't it time you were in bed?'

'Yes, I was waiting to see if you needed anything.'

Again Sid felt helpless and weepy. Did pregnancy take away the power of resolution? She hoped not.

The following day found Sid feeling drained but a little better. She insisted on getting up and assuming her duties. Mrs Cardell complimented her on the way she had taught Angie to cook. 'She's not as good as you, and the lemon mousse turned out more like blancmange, but it was still edible.' They were in Mrs Cardell's favourite room. 'Sit down, Sidonia. Are you sure you are fit to be back at work? You look rather washed out.'

Sid felt suddenly irritated by the constant barrage of questions about her health. She knew she should feel grateful, but she didn't. 'I do wish you'd all stop fussing!' she cried.

Her employer stared at her. 'Sidonia . . .?'

'I'm sorry, madam, honestly I am, but I hate being fussed over. If you'll excuse me, I'll get back to the kitchen.'

'I don't excuse you. Remain seated. I should like you to read to me.'

Sid followed the words in the book with her voice, but most of her mind dwelt on the scene in the National Gallery. It played itself over and over again like a stuck gramophone record.

'You may stop now,' said Mrs Cardell. 'It is perfectly obvious that something has gone badly wrong for you. Perhaps I shouldn't pry, indeed, I know I shouldn't, but from things you've said I don't believe you can turn to your parents for advice. I've lived a long time. I would help you if I could.'

'Thank you, madam.'

'Remember, I'm here if you need me.'

'I will. May I go now?'

Mrs Cardell sighed. 'You may.'

Sid's life took on a new pattern. She went through the motions of living, feeling fortunate that the pregnancy didn't affect her physical state often. An occasional bout of nausea, tiredness sometimes, but that was all. Her body still hadn't changed shape much, so she only had to let her dress belts out a little. The problem lay in her mental state, the swings of mood which she found almost impossible to control. Roy repeatedly asked her to go out with him and couldn't understand why she refused. In the end she gave in, but refrained from all physical contact.

He was naturally puzzled and annoyed. 'You let me kiss you before,' he burst out one day.

She had been feeling unwell that day and snapped, 'Before what?'

'Before that damned Philip Prosser came on the scene.'

'How dare you!' His accurate strike unnerved her.

'Sorry,' he said, 'but you know the way I feel about you.'

'Do I?'

'Yes.'

'You haven't said much.'

'A man doesn't want to say much until he's sure of a good reception. You were getting fond of me and I intended to speak quite soon. Sid, I'm very fond of you indeed.'

She said nothing. She should stop him, but lethargy and a sense of inevitability took hold of her.

'One day I should like us to get engaged.'

She was repentant yet angry. Why had she allowed men to complicate her life? When she had struck out for independence she should have kept her goals strictly in view, then she wouldn't have had to put up with this dreadful torment.

'Have you nothing to say, Sid?'

'I'm honoured.'

'Are you being sarcastic?'

'Of course not.' Her vehemence convinced him. He couldn't know that it stemmed from the unworthy thought which had crossed her mind, the solution which Philip had suggested. If she led Roy on he would surely make love to her and she could tell him about the baby and let him think it was his and he would marry her. She dismissed it as unworthy. It was impractical, too. By the time she had accomplished such a plan she might be near her time. She wondered what he would do if she told him of her pregnancy now and asked him to marry her. It was out of the question. Even if he agreed, it would always lie between them. She said gently, 'You are a good man, Roy, and I like you a lot.'

'Are you sure? Philip Prosser . . .'

'If you mention his name to me again I shall scream.'

'There was something between you, wasn't there?'

She walked away fast and took the road back to Greystone House. When she finally looked behind he wasn't following her.

For a time after that Roy did his job and treated her like any other servant in a big house, only occasionally speaking briefly to her. She missed his friendship acutely, but the sooner he got over her the better for him. Then he began to ask her out again.

'I can't pretend I'm happy without you, Sid. I miss you terribly.'

She looked into his face. He was attractive, honourable, charming, and his eyes showed his deep sadness at the deterioration of his hopes. 'I'm sorry, Roy. I wish . . .'

'Don't say any more. I'm willing to wait.'

She didn't know whether to be glad or regretful.

When Sid passed her fifth month, her clothes began to strain at the seams. Her mother and aunts all remarked on her increasing weight, though her arms and legs remained slender and her face was, if anything, thinner. She caught Angie looking at her sometimes with troubled eyes.

Then Mrs Cardell sent for her. 'Sidonia, my dear, I think you really must see a doctor.'

'No, thank you.'

'You are putting on weight but not evenly. My dear, I know this is an awful thing to ask, but have you thought you might have some kind of growth? I'm sorry to sound so brutal, but taken in time these things can be cured. It might even be benign, but it must be cared for.'

Sid held on to the back of a chair. The time had come to confess, to say goodbye to her happy job, her hopes of advancing herself. 'I am not ill, madam. I know what's the matter with me. I'm expecting a baby.'

She didn't know what her mistress's reaction would be, and was surprised when Mrs Cardell took the news calmly. 'I feared as much. That's why I spoke.'

'You knew?'

'I guessed. Have you made plans to get married?'

Mrs Cardell's gentleness affected Sid far more than harshness would have done. She shook her head, unable to speak.

'Sit down, Sidonia. You look as if you're about to faint. Do you need a restorative?'

'No, thank you.'

'Won't the young man marry you? Is it the one who cleans our windows? You went out with him, didn't you?'

'It wasn't Roy.'

'Can you tell me the father's name? I might be able to help.'

'I'd rather not say, madam.'

Mrs Cardell stared at her for what seemed like a long time. 'You mean you will not say.'

'It's better if I don't.'

'I see. Have you made any plans at all?'

'Not yet.'

'The situation cannot be improved by your inaction. Do you intend to remain in Bristol to have the child?'

'I don't know what to do. It won't be possible to stay. My parents – my family – they'll all be angry and disgusted. I must go away.'

'Yes, I see. Of course.'

Sid waited. Here it comes. Dismissal and more disgrace. The fear of rejection never seemed quite to leave her. She had saved a little money, but not nearly enough to carry her through the next months. Where would she go? If her parents found out they would probably never acknowledge her existence again. Even Aunt Jess and Aunt Mattie would be ashamed of her. She was trembling now, and still Mrs Cardell didn't speak.

Then, haltingly, she said, 'You have been out very seldom since you came to work for me. As far as I can tell you have had only one boyfriend. I have met him a couple of times and I'm positive he would never let you down. There is one other man who has been available to you, one who has no scruples. It grieves me even to suggest it, but were you intimate with my young cousin?'

'Philip?' Sid gasped out the name irrepressibly. Not 'Mr' Philip.

'It is Philip. The damned scoundrel! It is outrageous! Outrageous!'

'I'll pack my bags,' said Sid wearily.

'Stay where you are, I am trying to think. In fact, I have been thinking for a couple of weeks now, ever since I was sure you were pregnant. I hoped it was not Philip, but . . .'

'I don't see how you could guess.'

'Don't you? I know him well. You're an innocent and not the first girl he has seduced. Mrs Prosser has dismissed two from her own house. There have probably been others.'

Sid closed her eyes. She should have known. He was so clever, so skilful in his approach, so experienced. She was only one of a line of girls whom he had soiled.

'What happened to the others?' she asked.

Mrs Cardell said, 'I don't know. I doubt if anyone even remembers their names. They may never have borne children, but we won't ever know. Do you want to keep your child? I shouldn't be surprised if you said no. Why should you love a baby foisted on to you by an unscrupulous man?'

'It wasn't like that. I loved him and thought he loved me. He said he did. I would never have given in to him if I'd believed otherwise.'

'No need to tell me that, my dear. I am sure of it. Have you tried to contact him?'

'I wrote and went to London . . .'

'The day you came home early feeling ill! I remember. I can guess at the way he received your news. It makes it all the more likely that you will wish the child to be adopted.'

'I can't see myself giving it up, but I can't think how to keep it.'

'No, the world can be harsh for women who don't conform, and for some reason it's made even harder for their innocent children.'

'I've heard there are special places where unmarried mothers can have their babies.'

'There are, but I would never allow someone I cared for to go to one. When I was younger I sat on various committees, one of which helped to run just such a place. The regime is unbelievably harsh, though even that is better than some cases I have heard of. There are girls living in asylums for the insane, classed as moral degenerates because they have borne a child out of wedlock.'

Sid closed her eyes, as if by doing so she could shut out the dreadful pictures conjured up.

Mrs Cardell said, 'Let us forget for a while that we're mistress and maid. Has Philip offered you any monetary help?'

'No. In fact, when I told him, he accused me of –' Sid choked on her words – 'of having had other men. He treated me as if I was a bad woman. He knows I fell in love with him.'

'Do you still love him?'

'No. I don't think I ever did. He's very clever.'

'It sounds like a typical story of seducer and seduced.'

'Do you think I was stupid?'

'No, my dear. I've heard the story many times, and most of the girls were innocent.' She paused, then said, 'Sidonia, I have an idea. Will you trust me?'

'Of course I'll trust you, but . . . please don't ask me to give up my child. Not until I've had it. I can make up my mind then.'

'Of course I won't. It must be your decision. For the present just carry on with your usual work, but avoid lifting weights.'

'You don't want me to leave?'

'Leave? Whatever gave you that idea? It would be like turning out my own . . . I am very fond of you. I would hate to lose you. Besides,' she added in low tones, 'if there were no other reasons, the child has been fathered by one of my own family.'

For the next few days, Sid felt happier than she had for a long time. Suddenly her body seemed lighter, her work easier. She felt a profound sense of relief, and the others were happy to welcome back the Sid they knew. She hadn't realised how oppressive her constant absorption in herself had been. There was laughter again in the kitchen.

Mrs Cardell sent for her. 'Sit down, Sidonia, and listen. If you disagree with what I am about to say, please tell me. I shall not be offended.' Sid clasped her hands nervously. 'I would like you to stay on here until your body thickens to a point where you will no longer be able to hide your condition. Fortunately, you are one of those girls who doesn't show much. I shall have some larger dresses made for you, which will help. Then I intend to develop several nervous symptoms, although I am perfectly well.'

'You shouldn't be subjected to this worry.'

'I'm angry with Philip and feel great sympathy for you, but I am not worried to a damaging extent. I am pleased to be able to return a little of the goodness you have shown me, though I wish it had been in some other way. As I was saying, I shall develop "nerves", and after a while I shall announce that I need a change of air. I shall say I am going somewhere bracing, and taking you along with me. That will seem perfectly natural. Angie is competent to take care of things at this end. She's a good girl. It was clever of you to realise that. We shall find a haven in a place in Scotland which I know well, and you shall have your baby there. You must wear a wedding ring, and I shall be with you to add countenance to you. I can be your aunt. Yes, that's the best relationship for our purpose. Your aunt.'

'Madam . . .'

'You'll have to learn to call me Aunt Louisa, not madam. How does the plan strike you?'

Sid had to speak through a lump in her throat. 'It sounds wonderful.' She had squeezed her fingers together until the tips turned white. 'If I go away, then decide to keep the child, how can I suddenly bring it here?'

'You can't return with it at once. That would certainly set off the gossips. I propose we leave it in a good nursery, or with a decent family. Later, it should be possible to introduce the child into Greystone House. I can't see my way clear there at present, but I'm sure everything will work out. You could help by telling people you are a little anxious about my health.'

'More lies,' sighed Sid.

'I'm afraid so, but not bad ones.'

Sid could only thank her.

She worked on until her pregnancy reached the sixth month. The new dresses were loose fitting, and her weight could be attributed to all the good food she was getting. She dropped hints frequently about her mistress's health, backed by Mrs Cardell, and when the visit to Scotland was announced, it caused little stir.

Angie was the only one who worried. 'You're leaving me in charge, madam? But I'm not a housekeeper. I'm not clever like Sid.'

'You're clever enough,' said Mrs Cardell. 'All you have to do is clean the place, oversee the others, and make sure everyone gets fed.'

'All?' Angie looked appalled. 'I don't know how to begin.'

'Yes, you do,' said Sid, who was sitting in on the interview. 'Just remember what I do and copy it.'

'Quite right,' said Mrs Cardell. 'The Misses Weekley will obey you, Brindle will go his own way as he always does, but he's thoroughly trustworthy and will control his assistant.'

'And Patrick adores you,' put in Sid, 'and will do anything you ask.'

Excitement began to build in Angie. 'I believe you're right. Perhaps I could manage all right as long as you're not away too long. Won't everyone be amazed to see me as a substitute housekeeper?'

'You must keep the books,' reminded Sid.

'I can do that. I'm good with figures.'

A week later, Sid and Mrs Cardell were installed in a small cottage on the west coast of Scotland, with a garden overlooking the sea. Arran was blue in the distance, and the bleak volcanic core, Ailsa Craig, loomed out of the water.

Sid gulped in the fresh cold air, stretching out her arms as if to encompass the beauty. 'It's wonderful.' She felt heavenly release after the prison of pretence.

'It is lovely,' said Mrs Cardell with satisfaction. 'When my husband was alive we came to Scotland for the shooting, and usually stayed a little while in this part of the country before returning home.'

Sid was to be called Mrs Brown. She wore a wedding ring, which was further proof of her mistress's exceptional kindness, being eighteen-carat gold. A woman came daily to clean and share the cooking, and Sid's duties were light. She walked almost daily on the wide stretches of beach nearby, or in the woods which sloped down to the sea. Sometimes she removed her shoes and stockings and paddled in the icy water. She should be miserable and apprehensive but she was not. Maybe she was cocooned, maybe pregnancy kept a woman placid, most likely she was happy because she was now so comfortable. She began to enjoy the swelling of her body and the way the baby kicked inside her. She didn't dwell on the way things could have been if she had been looking forward to the birth of a child who was welcomed by its father. Such thoughts were negative.

Mrs Cardell accompanied her on short walks. She was not strong, and Sid cared for her as best she could. In return her mistress watched over Sid's health. They couldn't do enough for each other, and their relationship altered from mistress and maid almost to mother and daughter. Mrs Cardell grew excited about the coming child, deploring the fact that convention made it necessary to hide it away. 'But not for ever if you want to keep it, Sidonia,' she declared fiercely. 'Not for long. I'll find a way.'

One day, as they strolled on the beach, she said, 'Have you considered the relationship of your child to me?'

'No. What exactly are you?'

'A cousin several times removed. I look forward to my new role. I had two babies of my own, but they both died soon after their birth. I shall enjoy yours.'

'I didn't know. I'm so sorry. You would have made such a wonderful mother.'

When Sid awoke one morning knowing that the child was on its way, she was driven by taxi to an expensive nursing home chosen by Mrs Cardell, her mistress holding tightly to her hand. Her labour was mercifully short and easy and she delivered her baby that evening. A girl.

Mrs Cardell came to visit. She sat holding the child in her arms, looking down on it with a tender, loving expression. 'What will you name her?'

'I thought, Amy. It's a nice name, don't you think?'

'I agree. Hello, little Amy.' She stuck her finger into the child's hand and the small fingers closed round it with surprising strength. 'One of my babies was a girl. I never really got over losing them. One doesn't, you know. Such sadness. My husband too was deeply grieved. This little one already has a place in my heart.'

Sid recovered fast. She and Mrs Cardell had already considered a couple of nurseries. They were well run, pleasant places but, inevitably, each baby had to share attention with others. They wanted the best for Amy, and they decided it would be better for her to live with a family they could trust. They met one in the McGregors. The husband was a fisherman and Mrs McGregor a born home-maker. They adored children and still missed their own four, who were grown and out in the world in good positions. They welcomed the idea of a child in the house again. So Sid and Mrs Cardell took the baby to Bill and Sheena McGregor, staying on a while to make sure she settled in. Sid wept the nights away, but in the mornings contrived to appear cheerful for Mrs Cardell's sake, until she saw that her mistress had been weeping too and they shed more tears together.

'It won't be for ever Sidonia. Maybe not for long.'

'She'll be such a long way away. I'll hardly ever see her.'

Mrs Cardell looked stricken. 'I hadn't given a thought to that. In my eagerness to find her a good home away from gossiping busybodies I picked a rather inaccessible place. Shall we change it?'

'No, I like the McGregors. One day I must take Amy from them. How will they feel?'

'They understand that this is a temporary arrangement.'

'Do they know the full circumstances?'

'They know that you were abandoned by a bad man.'

'And they didn't think I was immoral?'

'Not at all. Mrs McGregor tutted and said how glad she was that Amy had such a loving family. That made me so happy.'

Angie was delighted to welcome them back to Greystone House. 'You both look well, though Sid's lost weight. I suppose it's climbing all those Scottish hills. Thanks for the postcards. I've stuck them on the kitchen wall. I must go to Scotland one day and see it for myself.'

Sid settled back into her routine almost as if nothing had happened. At least, that's how it appeared to others, but she missed Amy terribly, far more than she had expected. Day and night, she ached with wanting her in her arms; it was as if she had a wound that would never heal. Often in the dark hours she wept for her daughter, then got up and paced the bedroom, alternately weeping and cursing Philip Prosser who had caused this anguish.

Mrs McGregor sent reports and precious photographs. These showed her child growing fast, and depicted her first smiles, her first tiny white tooth, her first short dress. Sid hid the letters and photos in her stocking drawer and devoured them daily.

Mrs McGregor wrote regularly and cheerfully. 'Amy is the sweetest child I ever knew. Even teething she hardly ever cries. When I go to get my messages I can leave her lying in her pram outside the shop and she'll coo and gurgle happily until I've finished. I put her under the old apple tree in the garden and she watches the leaves in the wind and the birds. She's a clever wee lass. And very pretty.'

Mrs Cardell begged to be permitted to pay the weekly sum for Amy to be cared for, but Sid insisted on sharing the expense. 'It's my duty to look after her,' she said.

Mrs Cardell read the letters and looked at the photographs with such a yearning smile one would have believed she was Amy's grandmother. Sid watched Angie knitting away in the kitchen, wishing wistfully that she could knit, though she'd have no valid excuse for making baby clothes. If Angie knew about Amy she would have overwhelmed her with knitted garments. Sid longed to talk frankly to her. Keeping Amy secret was agonisingly painful: she longed to shout to the world her pride in her lovely daughter.

Roy still cleaned the windows of the big house. His devotion had not altered, in spite of the fact that they hadn't been out together for many months. When she had sent postcards from Scotland to the others, she had simply included him in her messages. He was pleased at her return, and he renewed his invitations, but in the circumstances she decided she couldn't accept. He argued, but she was adamant. 'But I shan't give up hope, Sid, you'll see. One day you'll want me and I'll still be waiting.'

Sid just shook her head. She was no longer free, her loving duty lay with Amy. Perhaps she would never marry. The thought gave her a pang. She would be lonely and she would never have another child. Her loathing of Philip fed on her frustrations. When she felt ill with wanting Amy, Mrs Cardell thought of some excuse to get her out of the house long enough to go to Scotland and spend a few hours with her baby, but it wasn't often practical. The child didn't know her, of course, and though this heaped on the anguish, she was so open, so friendly and fearless, so welcoming of this big playmate who treated her lovingly, that Sid's pain was a little eased.

She had been so absorbed in the occurrences in her life, she had taken little notice of outside events. She also sent extra money to Mrs

McGregor for clothes and toys for Amy, spending as little as possible on herself, which meant that she stayed in Greystone House when the others went out. Eventually Mrs Cardell ordered her to go to the pictures for recreation.

'You are far too young to incarcerate yourself here. Yes, I know all the arguments. You save your money for Amy, you are unhappy much of the time. I understand all that, but you must take time for leisure. Such constant denial could make you depressed.'

'I'm sure it won't. I'm strong.'

'I am thinking less of your physical health than your mental state.'

'My *mental* state?'

'Don't get indignant with me, my girl. Women in the best of circumstances can suffer depression after childbed, and you are going through a dreadful time.'

Sid obeyed her, and went sometimes to a cinema where she actually enjoyed the films, though it was a shock to see on the newsreels that, while she had been immersed in her personal world, the rest of humanity seemed to have descended into turmoil, much of it caused by the German Chancellor, Adolf Hitler. There seemed to be a real fear of war coming to Britain. From then on she read the newspapers and listened to the news daily on the wireless, following events with a mind sharpened by the idea of possible danger to Amy. She couldn't really believe that Britain would fight again, and when she saw the evil bombs rained by the Spaniards upon their own countrymen, and the cruelty inflicted on China by the Japanese, she prayed that Britain would never have to cower beneath a hail of deadly bombs.

Sid was visiting her parents when the news of Mr Neville Chamberlain's successful visit to Herr Hitler was broadcast. He had arrived back in Britain, waving a piece of paper signed by Hitler and promising, 'I believe it is peace for our time.' The Sudetenland was to be sacrificed to the dictator's greed for power and land.

'He's a good man, that Mr Chamberlain,' said Mrs Penrose. 'He's saved us from war.'

'I never thought Great Britain would fight again,' said Mr Penrose. 'Why should we go out to die for other people anyway? We've done it once in the Great War, and look at Europe now, in a muddle again.' He then resumed his reading of his paper.

'You don't get any plumper,' said Mum, staring at Sid. 'You were a nice shape not long ago, but ever since you went with that old woman to Scotland you've looked skinny and quite haggard at times.'

'She was never meant to be a beauty,' said Dad from behind his paper.

Sid seethed with anger. Maybe if her father had given her some confidence she wouldn't have been so ready to fall into Philip's trap. She felt it to be an unworthy thought, but she was all too subject these days to retrograde musings. Mrs Cardell was absolutely right. Her mental state was not as strong as her physical.

'How is the old lady?' asked Mum.

'She's got a name. It's Mrs Cardell,' snapped Sid.

Mum looked astonished. 'Don't speak to me like that. I don't know what's come over you lately.'

She waited for an apology, but Sid didn't give her one. Why couldn't somebody apologise to her for once? Audrey and Irene burst in, noisy and voluble, prettier than ever. How old were they now? Irene must be nearly seventeen, and Audrey was sixteen. Sid looked at them properly for the first time for ages. Surely their hair was blonder: she suspected them of using peroxide to lighten it. Their faces were made up in the fashionable style, finished off with pillarbox-red lipstick.

'Hello, Sid. Remember, Mum, we're going out dancing tonight? Did you iron our frocks?'

'Of course I did,' said Mrs Penrose fondly, 'as if I'd forget.' She made tea for the girls and sandwiches, which she forced them to eat before they changed. 'You can't dance for hours on empty stomachs.'

'We wouldn't have to. They sell refreshments. No alcohol,' they chorused, 'we know. And watch out for the big bad men.'

'They've got a special boyfriend each now,' said Mum proudly. 'Good chaps with steady jobs.' Behind her back the girls made derisive faces at one another.

'Anyone I know?' asked Sid.

'Who? Our boyfriends?' said Irene.

'Shouldn't think so,' said Audrey. 'Girls your age are getting married and settling down with babies. Why aren't you?'

'Now then, that's enough,' chided Mum, but she was laughing. 'Sid's only . . . how old are you?'

'Twenty. Can't you remember?'

'I hadn't realised how time was passing. Don't you have anyone special in mind? What happened to your window-cleaner?'

'Where's Raymond?' asked Sid, biting off an angry retort.

'What? Oh, playing football. Practising, ready for the new season.'

Nobody noticed when Sid left, and she returned to Greystone House with a feeling of relief.

Germany marched into the Sudetenland, and the German-speaking minority welcomed the army of jack-booted, steel-helmeted soldiers carrying swastika banners. The country was part of Czechoslovakia, and the Czechs watched the annexation fearfully. Hitler ordered the evacuation of 'foreigners', stating that the Sudetenland was now a part of Germany and always would be, and promising that the region would be occupied by protective German troops. 'Never again shall this land be torn from the Reich', was his promise, and he thanked Almighty God for His blessing and told the people that this was the beginning of their march into the great German future.

Sid read of European Jews being cruelly treated by their fellow-countrymen simply because of their religion, and wondered what made people so wicked. A brief respite from tension was gained when a young actor named Orson Welles led the Americans to believe that they had been invaded by Martians. He had presented H. G. Wells's famous novel *The War of the Worlds* as a series of news flashes, and thousands had panicked.

Hitler's word counted for nothing, and he sent his army into Czechoslovakia, where the people tried to control their weeping. He announced that he had no further territorial claims in Europe. Everyone wanted desperately to believe him, but Mr Chamberlain declared in Parliament that Britain had pledged herself to go to Poland's aid if she were invaded. This seemed increasingly likely when Hitler smuggled arms into Danzig, a German city isolated by Poland on the Baltic, and when Poles began being arrested and sent to concentration camps. Members cheered at Chamberlain's resolute words and the people applauded him. After all, they told one another, they had Hitler's promise, so there was no real need to worry about war.

The issue of air-raid shelters to Londoners early in 1939, and the plans drawn up for the evacuation of children had led to plenty of grim jokes, but now Britain had to face the fearful possibility of war. Gas masks were issued, and in August it was thought advisable to begin evacuating children from danger areas.

Hitler broke his word and entered Poland. Mr Chamberlain gave him until 3 September 1939 to evacuate his troops; when he ignored the directive, Britain declared war. By now it came almost as a relief to many that the die was cast. Hitler must and would be stopped and the world would be at peace again. Britain was ready to fight, and the newsreels told the people about their wonderful weaponry, the amazing fighter planes, the preparedness of the country, reminding them that conscripts had been training since May. Britain was defiant.

Sid and Mrs Cardell talked long into the night about Amy. 'She should be all right where she is,' said Sid, 'but I miss her so terribly, and Bristol's reckoned to be pretty safe from bombing. I want her with me.'

'I think you're right. She's fifteen months old now. The wrench from the McGregors will upset her, but the sooner she gets to know her mother the better.'

'I can't let her call me mother.'

'No, but you can be an aunt. I shall announce that her parents were distantly related to me and have both been killed. A motor-car crash, I think. There have been lots of them since the black-out.'

Sid wrote to Mrs McGregor and went soon after to fetch her daughter.

'She's all ready for you,' said a tearful Mrs McGregor. 'Lucky thing my husband's at home from the fishing. He wouldn't have liked her to go without kissing her goodbye.'

Their obvious regret brought tears to Sid's eyes, too, as she thanked them.

'It's been a joy to have her here,' said Mrs McGregor. 'A real joy. I never saw a sweeter child.'

Amy, after a short hesitation, went to Sid, who held her in her arms, kissing her soft cheek.

The McGregors insisted on accompanying her to the station. They waved their farewells with assurances that they would welcome Amy back at any time, with or without her mother, and the journey to Bristol began.

Chapter Ten

It couldn't be expected that Amy would leave the only home she'd known and stay placid and unworried throughout the whole long journey. Mrs McGregor had provided food and drink, so that posed no problems, but when the child got tired and fractious, it was Mrs McGregor she wanted.

She threw her doll and her woolly dog to the floor, refusing to be comforted. 'Aunty Sheena,' she sobbed, 'Amy want Aunty Sheena.'

The words struck cold in Sid's heart as she rocked her daughter in her arms, loving her so deeply, yet alienated from her; her loathing of Philip Prosser fed on the havoc he had caused. In the end, Amy's cries quietened, she gave a sobbing yawn, and her eyes closed in sleep. Sid, thankful, held her close, her arms aching with the strain, but unwilling to disturb her. The other passengers, who had been viewing the sorry little scene, retired again behind their books, or closed their eyes and dozed.

One woman who had shown more interest asked. 'Is she yours?'

'No, I'm her aunt.' It gave Sid acute pain to mouth these first words of denial. She wasn't ashamed of anything she'd done. She had seen her sexual relationship with Philip as something beautiful, loving, to be cherished. He was the one who had demeaned it.

'She's leaving one aunt to go with another, then?'

Sid wanted to give the woman a dusty answer, but said politely, 'That's right.'

'Where are you taking her?'

'Bristol.'

'There now. I'd have thought she'd be better off in Scotland. It's bound to be safer there than the south.'

'No one really knows what will happen,' said Sid shortly. 'Bristol's reckoned to be all right.'

'But they've got the aircraft factory in Filton. I used to live there and I know.'

'We've been told there's to be no careless talk,' retorted Sid. 'Careless talk costs lives.'

The woman laughed. 'Do this lot look like spies?'

'I don't know how a spy is supposed to look.'

There were mutterings from the other passengers. They were crowded in the compartment because the train was full of servicemen. Every station was the same; men in khaki, territorials, soldiers on leave joining their regiments, and young men eager for the adventure of war.

The general order for conscription hadn't yet been given, but there were still more men than seats and they sat on their duffel bags in the corridors, playing cards, talking, sleeping, their heads lolling against walls and doors. When Amy woke and wanted the lavatory, Sid had to carry her, stepping over legs and arms and heads. The men were good-humoured, many excited at the prospect of a chance to get away from their humdrum jobs and lives.

Amy ate a hard-boiled-egg sandwich and drank milk, then joined Sid in staring through the window at the fields, exclaiming at the animals, waving at the men and women harvesting crops in the sun. The countryside looked so peaceful, it was impossible to imagine it under a hail of bombs, unthinkable to visualise an enemy army trampling down the crops. But there were many reminders that the war was real. Green areas were being ploughed under to grow food, trenches dug to shelter civilians. They caught bizarre sights of people practising their everyday tasks in gas masks.

The inquisitive woman left the train soon afterwards. A man peered out from behind his newspaper. 'Thank Gawd she's gone. Blinkin' nosy parker.' He grinned at Sid who smiled.

Amy settled surprisingly quickly into her new home. She wept for a few nights for her Aunty Sheena, but she couldn't resist all the love and attention given her by Mrs Cardell and the entire staff of Greystone House. Even Brindle wasn't grumpy with her, encouraging her to pick his precious autumn flowers to put in a vase in her bedroom, something no one else was permitted to do. She had been given the third room in the nursery suite, and Sid cared for her there, took her into her own bed and comforted her in the night if she was restless, brought her water to drink when she asked. Every task for Amy was performed in love and thanksgiving that she could have the child with her by day and night. She was filled with gratitude towards Mrs Cardell.

The war was being called 'phoney'. All that was happening on the home front was a so-far needless and seemingly random introduction of dozens of new laws and regulations which emerged from the newly formed Ministry of Information. People found them amusing or odd, sometimes sensible. Factory hooters were banned, except when being used to warn of air-raids or to sound the all-clear. Clattering football rattles were forbidden at matches because their future use was to warn of a gas attack, while handbells would announce safety.

Angie read the newspapers avidly. 'Do you know?' she asked Sid one day, 'that we could be prosecuted for having more than a week's supply of food in the house?'

'Fancy. How do they expect me to feed everyone here without reserve supplies?'

'Do you think the police will raid us?' asked Keith, his mind full of gangster films. 'If they find out about the pantry being full, would you go to prison, Sid, or would Mrs Cardell?'

'Don't be daft,' was Sid's short answer. She was wondering if she had enough cash to buy Amy a complete winter outfit in one go, or if she'd have to get it a bit at a time. She needed things for herself: a warm skirt, a couple of jumpers, and her coat was going thin at the elbows. Not that it mattered. Amy came first.

The preparations for a war which many now believed would never really develop went on. Eight thousand tuberculosis patients were sent home from sanatoria with instructions not to breathe over anyone, and their beds were made ready for air-raid casualties. Women, as well as men, had to practise crawling around on their stomachs to put out fires. The food for back-yard fowls was limited to twelve birds. It was all quite alarming at first, but as time went by and the fighting Allied troops neared the German border, it began to look as if the war would be over soon. When Anthony Eden, Secretary of State for War, launched a new service, the Local Defence Volunteers, an enthusiastic retired colonel headed a squad of men prepared 'to defend our beloved country in the event of invasion'. He was joined by indomitable old soldiers, some elderly men who had never seen a battle in their lives, and boys under the age of eighteen: all insisted that they were ready to lay down their lives for Britain. They were remorselessly drilled carrying anything which they could pretend was a gun, including wooden cut-outs, and caused more amusement than the members of the official Air-raid Precaution squad, men and women who went round checking blacked-out windows and yelling at any who showed a chink of light.

'Stupid lot,' sniffed Angie. 'Ordering us around like a lot of kids. And those others, marching up and down just as if they were in the real army, they look really daft.'

Keith watched them whenever possible. He didn't see them as a travesty of an army; he saw only men ready to fight. 'I'd join them,' he said, 'but I'll wait for my call-up and go where the real fighting is. I hope it won't be over before I get there.'

The staff accepted the story of the dead parents which Mrs Cardell had told them, and a great deal of kindly fuss was made of the 'poor little orphan'. Sid feared she'd become spoilt and unmanageable, but the child accepted the adulation and petting with aplomb, her sunny nature unchanged. To her, everyone in the house was either an aunt or an uncle, and Patrick ventured out of his cellar for quite long periods to give her piggy-back rides, lifting her high enough to pick a few remaining apples in the orchard. Amy had no fear of his black face and hands, and he had no care for the filthy marks he left on her clothes. Sid washed them herself, enjoying the task, delighting in the fact that her little daughter was loved by all.

'Patrick's making more work for you,' said Angie one day.

Sid was brought back abruptly from a life of her imagination, one in which she lived in a neat house with a husband returning every night to kiss his little girl and play with her before her bedtime. Not that he'd be coming home every night these days, what with ARP duties, or all the other things which those in reserved occupations or those ineligible for fighting were busy doing.

'Wake up, Sid,' Angie said. 'I'm trying to talk to you.'

'Sorry. What did you say? Something about work?'

'I said that Patrick is making you do more washing for Amy.'

'I don't mind. He's so sweet to her and she adores him.'

'You look tired. Hardly surprising when you were up half the night with her snuffling cold. Let me take over and you sit down for a minute.'

'No,' said Sid quite sharply. That wouldn't do. She must watch her step. The last thing she wanted was to irritate anyone over Amy. 'No, thank you, Angie. I like looking after the poor little mite.'

'The poor little mite has a whole army of adoring servants,' said Angie drily.

'I need a new coat,' said Mrs Cardell one night as Sid was helping her to bed.

Sid wondered why, since the wardrobe was stacked with clothes bought years ago and she still took the same size. It was true they weren't in the latest style, but that had never troubled her mistress before, and they were of excellent quality and beautifully tailored. And, furthermore, she had a fur coat and a fur cape. She was looking quite frail these days, with shadows beneath her eyes and a purplish tone to her lips; the thought passed briefly through her mind that Mrs Cardell might not have long to enjoy new clothes.

'Where were you thinking of buying your coat?' she asked.

'How about your Aunt Jess's gown shop? I used to patronise it. She and her husband are good buyers: nothing but the best for them. Smart, yet practical. I'm sure rationing will come in as it did during the last war. They must cut down the danger to merchant ships and the destroyers that guard them.'

Sid smiled. 'They'll not ration clothes, especially winter coats for elderly ladies!'

'Don't you be too sure.'

'They couldn't stop women from buying new clothes!'

'Maybe not, but I think we'll go to visit your aunt's shop as soon as I feel strong enough.'

Always alert where Mrs Cardell's health was concerned, Sid said, 'Shall I call the doctor?'

'No. He'll fuss and fume and I shan't obey him anyway.'

'Have you got plenty of your special medicine?'

'Yes, thank you, Nurse Penrose.'

Sid laughed. 'Mock me if you like, but someone has to take care of you.'

The old lady seized Sid's hand. 'Thank God I employed you. How could I have known what a blessing you'd be?'

'I've brought you worry, too.'

'I hope you are not referring to that exquisite little mite of a daughter of yours who, I need hardly remind you, is my distant cousin.'

'You've been so good to us.'

'No more than you deserve. I wish things could have turned out differently, but at least you'll be able to watch her grow up. I'm afraid there will be many others like Amy. During the last war there were many babies born who will never know their fathers, and some not even their mothers.'

'That would be unbearable. I'm so thankful and grateful to you.'

'We are good for each other, Sidonia. I shall telephone Mrs Venner and make an appointment. You must come with me, of course.'

Sid went home on a day when she knew the aunties would be visiting. They were in their usual places in the best room, teacups rattling, tongues wagging.

Sid heard them before she went in and when she appeared in the doorway they all stopped and stared at her.

'Thought you'd come and see us, then,' said Ella.

'About time you spared some thought for your family,' said Maud.

'Perhaps she's been away again. Have you been on holiday with your employer lately?' asked Joan in a more placatory tone. 'Scotland, last time, wasn't it? Has she got a house there?'

'No, she rented one,' said Sid.

'Well, has she rented one lately?' demanded Maud.

'Not lately. She's obeying the government and not travelling unless she must.'

Maud drew back her head, which gave the effect of her having two chins, both of them quivering with indignation. 'Is that meant to be a crack at me, just because I went to Weston for a week? The doctor said it would do me good. I had flu, though I don't suppose you knew or would care if you did.'

'I didn't know and I am sorry, and I don't think going to Weston is a crime.'

Maud was not pacified. 'She's getting cheeky,' she said accusingly to Mrs Penrose.

'Cheeky? I'm twenty-one,' said Sid, 'and I didn't mean to cheek you.'

'I should hope not. The doctor said he'd never seen a worse case of flu than mine . . .'

Tired of hearing about Maud's flu, Ella said aggressively, 'I suppose you think you're too grand for us now you work for the gentry.'

Maud laughed, 'How can she? She's only a servant.'

Mrs Penrose was torn between agreeing with her sisters and her dislike of hearing any of her family denigrated. 'You'd best bring another cup and saucer if you want tea,' she said shortly.

When Sid was out of the room, they didn't trouble to lower their voices. It had sometimes in the past seemed as if they wanted her to hear their comments. Today they definitely did.

'She looks as skinny as ever.' That was Ella. 'You'd think she'd get well fed, put on a bit of fat, in such a grand house. And when she went on holiday with old Mrs Cardell, she came back thinner than before.'

'That mightn't have been much of a rest,' said Mum. Sid was agreeably surprised to hear her making an excuse for her, even if it was only mild.

'I expect she might have had to work harder,' said Joan. 'Lots of the gentry are slow to spend their money. You should see some of the outstanding bills we've got for them.'

'Haven't we all?' said the others.

Sid brought her cup and saucer to the teapot and Mum poured for her. She took a slice of cake and sat down with her aunts, realising that this was the first time she had ever joined them in the tea-time ritual.

'How is Aunty Mattie?' she asked.

'Oh, you do remember her!' said Maud.

'Of course I do. I don't forget my family, but my job keeps me very busy. It's such a large house, and we don't have nearly as many servants as there used to be.'

'Aunty Mattie's well enough,' said Joan, 'though you don't notice her much. She's not got a lot of spirit.'

'I wouldn't say that now,' argued Maud. 'She's joined the Air-raid Precaution squad near the shop.'

This caused amusement. 'Fat lot of use she'd be in an air-raid,' laughed Ella. 'She'd dive under the nearest table.'

'How will she ever manage those funny stirrup-pumps that are supposed to put out fires?' asked Bea.

'How do you manage yours?' asked Sid.

They all looked at her as if she had made a rude suggestion. 'My Gordon looks after ours, thank you very much,' said Joan.

'So do our husbands,' chorused the others.

'What if your husbands are out? I suppose they've had to join something.'

'They all happen to be wardens. They patrol our own streets,' snapped Maud.

When the teapot and hot-water jug were empty, Mum bade Sid refill them. She obeyed. What did it matter if she was ordered about? She was no longer under her mother's thumb. She could escape now.

As she walked back in, Ella asked, 'What's all this we hear about a child in Greystone House?'

Sid clung to the pots of scalding liquid, placing them carefully before sitting down. The question had taken her completely by surprise.

'Is it true?' asked Maud. 'Has your employer taken in a girl? That's what I was told. Some say she's dressed in rich clothes? Is she an evacuee?'

'She's a relative of Mrs Cardell's,' said Sid quietly.

'Where are her parents? Gallivanting about in London, I suppose,' said Ella.

'Amy is an orphan.'

'Oh, well, I couldn't be expected to know that.' Ella puffed out her chest and sniffed.

'What happened to her mother and father?' asked Mum.

'Died in an accident in the black-out.' Sid got up suddenly. 'I'd best be leaving.' She couldn't continue to keep her voice steady under the barrage of questions.

'When are you going to visit your Grandma Lacey?' asked Joan. 'She often asks how you are.'

Sid doubted that. More likely her grandmother castigated her for a neglectful wretch. 'I'll try to get a Sunday afternoon off.'

'Make the effort,' said Mum.

Sid said her goodbyes and hurried out. She stood for a moment in the small, sooty patch of front garden, from where she could hear the laughter of her family. Her impulse was to go straight back to Amy, but Angie had been so proud to take charge while Mrs Cardell rested. These small daily decisions concerning her life and Amy's had to be made, and every one of them hurt. She had no visible rights as Amy's mother, no more rights than Angie or the Misses Weekley.

But she had to do something, so she wandered to Kingswood High Street to buy something for Amy. Her remaining toys and clothes had been sent on by the McGregors, but she was precociously quick, and Sid decided to get her a rag book of the alphabet.

Looking round the shops, a voice she knew hailed her. 'Hello, Sid.'

She turned to see Roy Hendy smiling at her. He was in army uniform.

'My, you do look smart,' she said.

'Thanks.'

'What are you doing these days? Apart from joining the army, that is? How's your business? I thought it was thriving. It must be a disappointment to leave it.'

'Can I take you for a cup of tea somewhere?'

Sid was feeling lonely, her nerves raw, and it was good to meet him and find him amicable. There was no reason why they couldn't just be friends. In a little café they drank tea and ate some rather dry cake.

'Food's deteriorating,' said Roy.

'Don't you know there's a war on?' smiled Sid. It was a phrase used thousands of times a day by millions of people as both a reproof and a shared joke.

'How have you been, Sid? You're looking well, though a bit tired.'

'Am I?'

'Are they working you too hard?'

'Not at all.'

'Will you enrol in one of the women's services?'

The question surprised her. She had been so wrapped up in her child she hadn't considered the possibility of having to leave her.

'Don't look so shocked. If that worries you, why not volunteer for munitions? That's a reserved occupation: you could probably stay in Bristol. There's the Filton factory and lots of small engineering works nearer the centre of town, all turned over to war-work.'

'A factory?' It had no appeal for her at all. It would be noisy, dirty, wearying and, worst of all, it would take her away from Amy for many hours of the week. But it would enable her to live with her daughter.

'I don't know how good I'd be in a factory. I'm not all that clever with my hands.'

'I don't think that's going to matter if you're building aircraft.'

'What?'

'Not by yourself, of course. There will be others to help.'

She laughed. 'I'll go to the Labour Exchange. I suppose you men think all women ought to stay behind and do the dirty jobs while you go away and collect all the glamour.'

'You bet! Sid, you look better when you laugh. You looked as if you had the cares of the world on your shoulders.'

'Have you packed your business in for the duration?'

'No fear. I've got some trustworthy older men to run it. It'll be there when I get back. If I get back.'

'Oh, don't say such things. We'll soon beat Hitler. Everybody says so.'

'I don't know about that. It's going to be a hard fight.' His voice held the same frisson of excitement as Keith's, and suddenly she was afraid for him. 'You do care about me. Just a little bit, don't you, Sid?'

'You're one of my very best friends,' she smiled.

He began to say something, but stopped and returned her smile.

Food rationing was introduced, which seemed to bring the war nearer to home. The newsreels showed fighting at sea. Denmark and Norway were invaded, then Holland was occupied by Germany on the grounds that they were to be protected against attack from the British. Belgium surrendered, leaving the British Army facing the enemy alone. Mr Winston Churchill took over as prime minister; his splendid oratory gave heart to all who heard him. They were gratified too by the king and queen, who tried hard to understand and share the inconveniences and hardships suffered by their people.

'They say that food is rationed the same as ours in Buckingham Palace,' said Angie.

Keith snorted. 'Huh! I bet they've got more stuff than us.'

'No they haven't,' argued Angie. 'It says here – '

Brindle spoke up. He did it so seldom that everybody listened. 'They won't be stuck with ordinary rations. They'll have venison and other game, and plenty of fish from their estates.'

'I suppose so.' Angie looked disappointed. 'I still think they're wonderful to stay in London. Who knows what's going to happen there . . .'

The king's special Christmas message was memorable, his quotation related and written everywhere. 'I said to the man who stood at the Gate of the Year: "Give me a light that I may tread safely into the unknown." And he replied, "Go out into the darkness and put your hand into the hand of God. That shall be to you better than light, and safer than a known way." '

On hearing the words, many women and not a few men wiped away surreptitious tears. Angie wept openly, her tears running down her cheeks and plopping on to the head of Amy, who sat on her knee, nursing an enormous teddy bear sent by the McGregors for Christmas.

'We're lucky to have such a king,' said Brindle.

Christmas had been as happy as they could make it and, inevitably, it had centred round Amy. Sid's gift had been a tricycle, and she had already mastered the pedals, though she needed a push to send it round and round the garden, a task happily undertaken by various members of the household. Mrs Cardell had watched the spectacle from her window, laughing until she was breathless.

She had written to the Army and Navy Stores in London for gifts for everyone, and they had all received two sets of new underwear in softest wool. 'Wars are always cold,' she had stated firmly. The men's parcels also contained socks, the women's silk and lisle stockings for everyday, and a smaller package with two pairs of fully-fashioned stockings of the softest silk.

They were speechless with pleasure. 'Silk,' breathed Angie. 'I've never bought any, never thought to own any. They cost so much. At least two-and-eleven a pair. I'll never dare wear them they're so fine.'

Sid said, 'I saw the catalogue. She bought us five-and-elevenpenny pairs.'

Angie's eyes opened wide in disbelief and she put the stockings back in their Christmas paper, as if just to look might damage them.

Mrs Cardell gave Amy a fully-dressed baby doll with eyes which opened and closed and a voice which said 'Mama'. It was christened Lola, and Amy adored it. Keith fastened a new basket on her tricycle for the doll and teddy bear.

Amy addressed Mrs Cardell as Aunt Louisa and gave her several rather damp kisses when she thanked her for her gift.

Sid didn't forget the McGregors, and sent them a photograph of Amy in a frame, for which she received immediate thanks.

After Amy was put to bed, Sid read stories to her until she slept. usually she was quick to slide into sleep after an ever-active day, but tonight she was still buoyed up by excitement and needed time to simmer down. Back in the kitchen, the radio played dance music. 'It's Josh Raven and his Melody Men,' said Angie, who was a great fan. 'The Kissing Cousins are going to sing. It's a special Christmas broadcast. Aren't they good to give up their holiday to cheer us up – and they're American, too, and needn't be here at all?'

Keith said, 'No, they're not. Only Eve Brook and Josh Raven are Yanks. The others are English.' He was inclined to be scathing towards his elders where modern music was concerned. Brindle was too full of good food and drink to do more tonight than glower at him, besides which, he knew he'd never win an argument about modern dance bands, so he contented himself with filling his pipe and puffing out great clouds of smoke.

Angie stuck out her tongue at him; Sid was too preoccupied to concern herself with Keith's cheek.

'Is she asleep?' asked Angie.

'Just. She's had such a happy day.' Her voice shook a little as she blinked back tears, and Angie gave her an anxious look.

The weeks following Christmas passed quietly. 'I reckon that there Hitler's all wind and water,' said Keith contemptuously. 'There's not going to be a real war.'

'Our men are already fighting,' reproved Angie. 'They are being killed or wounded and their families must find war real enough.'

'Yes, I suppose so, but we all know we'll win soon and I'll never get a chance to hold a gun.'

Brindle said, 'Thank your gods that you won't. I was in at the tail-end of the last lot when they took older men, and it was hell on earth.'

'That's all gone and forgotten,' said Keith impatiently. 'It's history. This war's bound to be better, with aeroplanes and tanks and submarines and guns, all of them bigger than you had.'

Brindle shook out his paper and refused to answer. 'Listen to this,' he said. ' "Can any gentleman recommend a really first-class butler for country situation? Fourteen servants kept." Well, that'll all end when the war really gets started. They'll have to do their own work, or beg their old servants to come back; and if the war goes on long enough, they'll call us up too.'

Keith shouted with mirth at the idea of Brindle carrying a gun.

Brindle was annoyed, and Sid said coolly, 'Keith, take this rubbish and don't forget to use the right salvage places, food into the pigbin, paper and cardboard in the sack, bones in the box. Everything's wanted for the war effort.'

Keith looked sulky, but didn't dare disobey Sid when she used that tone of voice.

When Brindle and Patrick joined the small local private army, Keith's derisive laughter didn't ring quite true. 'Silly old josser!' he muttered. 'And Patrick wouldn't know one end of a gun from the other. He'll probably shoot himself. In any case, Jerry will never get to Britain. You don't think he will, do you, Sid? You've got a lot of sense.'

'Thanks,' she said drily. 'I certainly hope he won't, though it would give us all a chance to use a gun.'

Sid decided what her next move must be, and spoke to Mrs Cardell. 'I think I shall apply for a job in munitions. We women must do something to help. I'll have to leave Amy all day and maybe some nights as well, but if I don't volunteer I might be called up and sent away and I wouldn't be near her at all.'

Mrs Cardell nodded. 'Very wise, my dear. The factories need people just as much as the forces. Amy will be cared for while you are away. Even if Angie has to leave us, the Misses Weekley will look after her, and I, of course, will supervise.'

Keith heard Sid's news and asked, 'Why don't you join the Women's Air Force, or the Army girls? That'd be more fun.'

Mrs Cardell and Sid sat together in the back of a taxi bearing them to Aunt Jess's gown shop.

Jess, having been told to expect them, came out to greet them.

'Come in, come in,' she said. 'Mrs Cardell, it's ages since we've met. How well you look.'

'Thank you. Heavens, it is ages ago, and you don't look a day older. I have you to thank for sending Sidonia to me. She and Amy keep me young.'

'Amy? Is she the orphan girl you have adopted? I met one of my sisters and she told me about her.'

'Not adopted. We're just caring for her between us.'

'How very kind you are.'

Several coats had already been selected as possible choices, and Mrs Cardell looked them over. 'This black worsted with a high collar and fur cuffs would be pleasant to wear.'

Aunt Jess watched her as she walked up and down the shop. 'Yes, it's perfect for you, though it needs a little alteration. If you wish, I can have that done and send the coat to you. Now,' she turned to Sid, 'it's your turn.'

Sid laughed. 'No, I've only come to take care of Mrs Cardell.'

'Nonsense,' said Mrs Cardell gently, 'your aunt has my instructions to show you something too.'

'I'm sorry, but I really can't afford – '

'You don't need to, my dear. It's to be a little present. An extra Christmas one if you like.'

'You've already given me enough. I couldn't accept this.'

'I want very much to buy you something special. Remember what I said, wars are cold, and I noticed – forgive me, dear, but I couldn't help noticing – that your coat is getting a little threadbare. You spend almost nothing on yourself. Just try something on. To please me, Sidonia?'

Jess eased Sid's arms into a soft wool tweed coat which suited her perfectly and felt absolutely heavenly.

'You see? It was made for you,' said Jess. 'And here's a matching hat. Very dainty.'

Sid tried on the hat which tipped fashionably over one eye and was embellished by a large quill. 'No, honestly . . .' But she was wavering; suddenly she wanted these lovely garments with all her heart.

Mrs Cardell used her indecision. 'Please, Sidonia. You do so much for me, far more than most girls would. It's a small thank-you.'

Sid looked at her mistress who was seated in a comfortable chair, watching her with eyes bright with pleasure, then at herself again in the full-length mirror. The tweed was a discreet mixture of blues and browns, and had a large collar which could be put up to keep her ears warm in winter winds.

'You can't refuse it,' said Aunt Jess gently.

'No, you can't,' said Mrs Cardell. 'It's impolite to turn down a gift.'

'And it fits you without a single alteration,' said Aunt Jess.

Sid couldn't go on refusing, not when the coat and hat gave her such exquisite pleasure, not when it obviously meant a great deal to her employer for her to accept it. Mrs Cardell added gloves and a scarf, and Sid couldn't summon up a single protest.

'I'll think about the coat for myself,' said Mrs Cardell to Aunt Jess, who smiled, confirming Sid's suspicion that the whole thing had been a charade played to give her a new coat.

Aunt Jess insisted on making them coffee and, as they sat drinking it on small gilded chairs in the alcove where Jess sat between customers, the shop door opened and a girl came in. She had an air of vitality, a presence which drew all eyes to her.

Aunt Jess smiled, 'Mrs Cardell, Sid, may I introduce Miss Susan Morland? She models for us.'

'I'm not surprised,' said Sid, unable to keep a tinge of envy from her voice. Susan Morland was tall, slender without being thin, with perfect skin and clear blue eyes set wide apart and fringed with dark lashes. Her nose was straight and small. She looked, in fact, like the heroine in a romance. She wore a superbly tailored suit and a hat with a small veil, and one of the new net snoods into which her fair hair had been neatly bundled.

Aunt Jess finished the introductions. 'Miss Morland has come to show a small selection of spring outfits to some of my customers. Why not watch for yourselves?' She looked at her watch. 'We shall be closing in a few moments, and our invited clients will arrive. I have wine ready to serve and ratafia cakes. It's always a splendid occasion. Do say you'll stay.'

Sid didn't know whether to be sorry or relieved when Mrs Cardell declined. 'I would rather go home. I feel a little weary.'

Sid forgot her disappointment in anxiety. Her mistress looked unwell and she almost never complained.

'Stay if you would like to, Sidonia,' she said gently.

'I'd rather not leave you.'

Mrs Cardell smiled and turned to say goodbye. To Miss Morland she said, 'You remind me of someone, but I cannot think who.'

'I look a little like my sister. She's Mrs Ware now, one half of the Kissing Cousins. You could have seen her in a theatre, or perhaps her photo in a magazine.'

'The singers?' Sid was fascinated. 'I've heard them on the wireless. They're very good.'

'And I did see them one night a few years ago,' said Mrs Cardell. 'The Bristol Hippodrome was about to be converted into a cinema.'

Susan laughed. 'That's quite right. And now it's back to variety, thank goodness. Eve Brook is her partner, as well as our cousin. They've joined ENSA and now go all over the place entertaining the troops.'

'ENSA?'

'Entertainments National Service Association, popularly known as "Every Night Something Awful".' Susan laughed.

'If the Kissing Cousins are in the show, there is definitely something good,' said Sid, firmly repudiating another surge of envy. She had seen photographs of Tessa Morland and Eve Brook, and knew they were pretty – especially Eve – as well as highly talented.

The taxi returned them to Greystone House. Sid took her treasures to her room and hung them on the wardrobe door, just gazing at them, enchanted by their beauty, trying to work out why a garment cut and sewn by first-class tailors should be so much more marvellous than an ordinary one. She remembered now that Mrs Cardell had sent to the bank for her jewels last November and, later, the jeweller, Mr Harvey, had paid a visit to Greystone House. Along with three pieces of Mrs Cardell's less expensive jewellery, he had taken a valuable brooch. She must have used some of the money on clothes for Sid, and that made them even more precious.

Sid sat in the kitchen reading one of the housekeeper's books. Tomorrow she was to begin work in a small aircraft components' factory near the Centre, and was making notes to leave for Angie. Amy was taking her afternoon nap. She turned the pages slowly, often too absorbed in reading about the splendid past of Greystone House to remember to write in her exercise book, and was startled when Angie came racing into the kitchen.

She was breathless, gasping out, 'He's here. Him and his gran.'
'Who? Calm down, Angie, for goodness' sake and explain.'
Angie sank into a chair, clutching her chest melodramatically. 'Philip Prosser's here with Mrs Prosser. He smiled at me and said I was to tell you he'd like to see you again, just as if nothing had happened. He's got a cheek after what he did to you . . .' Angie stopped, a hand to her mouth.
Sid caught her breath. 'What were you going to say?'
'Nothing. I mean he stole from Madam.'
'That's not what you were talking about. What exactly do you know? You *must* tell me.'
'Amy's his, isn't she?' mumbled Angie.
'Is she?'
'Oh, Sid, she is, isn't she? And – yours.'
Sid said flatly, 'When did you find out?'
'Can't we talk later? What will you do with Amy? Does he know about her? Do you want him to see her?'
Her words jolted Sid into action. 'No, I damned well don't, and she'll wake about now from her nap. I won't have him anywhere near her. He'll only do her harm, the filthy swine.'
Angie's eyes opened wide. 'I've never heard you talk like that.' Then, seeing that Sid's wits had deserted her, continued, 'I'll give her a drink of fruit juice and smuggle her out. We can go to the park.'
She left Sid with her mind in turmoil. Nothing made sense. Perhaps she should have kept Amy here. What if Philip was sorry and wanted to help? When he saw how beautiful she was, he might even wish to get married and give her a name and a family. Surely he was sorry, or why ask to see her? Before she could make a move, he walked into the kitchen in his Air-force-blue uniform. He smiled happily at her. 'Sidonia, it's good to see you again.'
'Is it?' she asked stupidly.
'Of course. Don't say you aren't glad to see me?'

'What do you want?'

'Now, is that a nice way to greet me?' he said, his voice light and teasing.

'Hello.'

'Well, at least you've spoken. Tell me, Sidonia, last time we met you told me you had a little problem. I trust it resolved itself happily.'

She stared at him. 'A little problem?'

'You are better looking than I remember. A lot prettier for one thing. You're one of those women who improve with age. Like wine.'

Sid ignored the remark. 'You've joined the Air Force.'

'Only as a humble ground-crew member. I've no wish to savour the glories of flying, either fighting or bombing.'

'Why? Are you afraid?'

'You bet I am. Wouldn't you be? Anyone who says he isn't is a liar. Sidonia, we're spending the night with Cousin Louisa. You see what I've braved just to be with you? I was worried in case my cousin told Grandmother about the few trinkets I borrowed, but so far she hasn't. She's probably forgotten them.' His eyes shone, he smiled at her confidently. 'So I'm here until tomorrow, and I'm sure you're patriotic enough to give a little home comfort to a fighting man.'

Revulsion coursed through her. Disgust at the idea of his touching her held her tongue fast. Words and phrases chased through her brain, hot, bitter accusations, recriminations, but she couldn't get them out. When she spoke, her words seemed to come from someone else. 'You're not a fighting man. You've just said you're determined to stay on the ground.'

'Airports get bombed.'

'So do cities.'

'Are you angry with me?'

'Angry?'

'I don't think I was kind enough to you in London. I should have offered help. In fact, I wanted to, but as usual Grandmother was keeping me short of the ready.'

'And money would have solved my "little problem"?'

'Of course. It's done so for a couple of the girls in my set. Come on, Sidonia, be friendly. After all, it was just one of those things. You can't be cross with me after all this time.'

'Disgusted would describe it better. You disgust me.'

He glowered. 'You've turned very nasty. I only came to Bristol to see you.'

'You could have saved yourself the trouble. I would prefer never to see you again.'

'Is that so? After I persuaded Grandmother to spend the night here and braved Cousin Louisa, just for you. I think I'll suggest we return.'

'An excellent idea.'

'I suppose you give some other man favours. Why not me? It's damned insulting after we had such a good time in bed. By the way, what did happen to the baby?'

She stared at him with eyes so glowing with hatred he took a step back. 'It died. Our baby died.'

'Your baby, not mine. Did you have it here?'

'No.'

'I suppose not. The old trout would be too disgusted. Still, she took you back again. How much does she know?'

'Nothing.'

He shrugged and walked out of the kitchen, and she sank into a chair, shaking, her teeth chattering. She poured herself a glass of brandy and drank it neat, coughing as the hot liquid stung her throat. How could she have fallen in love, even briefly, with such a vile man? He would never get his hands on Amy. Not that he would care, she thought bleakly.

She served tea to the visitors. Mrs Prosser said, 'We shall be fortunate indeed if we keep our servants, Louisa. So many have enlisted or gone to factories where they earn higher wages than we could ever pay them. It was bad enough after the last war. This one will be the ruination of the old, ordered way of life.'

'Every able-bodied man and woman is needed,' said Mrs Cardell.

'I notice you've still got your cook-housekeeper.'

'Sidonia will soon be working in a munitions factory.'

'So you'll lose her.' Mrs Prosser sounded pleased.

'She will still live under my roof.'

'I see. So you'll have her part-time. I am now reduced to charwomen who never stay long, and a very old couple I pensioned off years ago, who agreed to return for vastly inflated wages. Apart from my maid who's been with me for ever, I'm without help.'

All the time Sid was in the room, Philip's eyes were on her. She handed round the tea as Mrs Cardell poured and offered cakes and sandwiches. It helped her to know that her mistress was aware of the situation and was dealing with it calmly. Perhaps she had even decided to 'forget' the stolen jewels in order to keep everything peaceful.

'Is your chauffeur in the kitchen?' asked Mrs Cardell.

'He left to join the Army. He comes from a good family, you know. He was a spendthrift and his father challenged him to earn his own living for a year. A ridiculous idea, but I must say he took it in good part. Philip drove us down today, but when he's away I have to use taxis. Celia drives me occasionally, but she's a member of the WVS and always off somewhere. This war is horribly inconvenient.'

Sid scarcely slept that night, getting up frequently to check Amy, as if she feared that the presence under the same roof of her father would contaminate her, or spirit her away. Angie was wakeful, aching to comfort Sid, watching her through half-closed eyes in case she needed someone. Both girls were heavy-eyed in the morning, and Sid felt positively ill; she allowed Angie to serve breakfast while she stayed with Amy.

The Prossers left about ten and Amy, who had been rebelling against being kept in the nursery, was allowed downstairs, where Sid cuddled her in frantic relief. Mrs Cardell said little about the visit, asking no questions, for which Sid was grateful.

That night, in the quiet of the nursery suite, Sid asked Angie how she had discovered the truth.

Angie said, 'Remember the night I thought you might be ill and I went looking for you. I'd half suspected Mr Philip was trying to get at you and I was worried. In the end I went to his room and heard you talking to him. Of course, I couldn't hear what was said, I didn't even try, but I did hope that he'd treat you right.'

'Go on.'

'When you began to put on weight I suspected the truth, though I would probably just have accepted it like the others if I hadn't known.'

'And you never said a word.'

'No, I didn't know what to say, but I made up my mind that, if you had to leave, I would go with you and help.'

'Oh, Angie.'

'You've been kinder to me than anyone in the world. I wouldn't let you be alone at a time like that. When you went away with Madam I was relieved. She's such a kind lady. Then when you came back without a baby I was sad for you. I thought you'd had it adopted. Then Mrs Cardell had her brought here and I was really happy for both of you. She's a wonderful child. I love her a lot.'

For the first time, Sid had someone to whom she could open her heart. Mrs Cardell was the dearest lady, but Angie understood better the kind of horror which awaited a girl without money who expected a baby outside marriage. They talked until the early hours.

Mrs Cardell decided to offer hospitality to officers stationed or on leave locally, and the old house became noisy with men's voices and laughter. Some had already been involved in fighting and were recuperating from wounds. Others were eager to engage the enemy, many looking young enough to be at school. In the ordinary way, most of them would be preparing for university.

'That's war for you,' said Mrs Cardell. 'It takes the young men first.'

One day when Sid was playing in the garden with Amy, a tall second lieutenant strode along the path and said, 'Hello.'

Sid looked up surprised, then realised that the man was Barton, the Prosser's former chauffeur.

She straightened up and Amy sat motionless astride her tricycle, indignant that Aunty Sid had stopped playing with her.

'What a beautiful child,' exclaimed Barton. 'Whose is she?'

'She lives here. An orphan,' said Sid, hating as always to give the false explanation.

'Mrs Cardell is a splendid woman, isn't she? And you're still housekeeper?'

'Any reason why I shouldn't be?' she said, suspicious that he was patronising her.

He threw up his hand and smiled. 'None whatsoever. The few hours I spent here were delightful. Good food and comfort were the order of the day. You seemed to be the pivot of the entire establishment. Still are, aren't you?'

He smiled, a genuinely warm and friendly smile, and she decided she had been hasty. He was really very nice. 'Actually, I work in a factory. I'm on the early shift this week.'

'Good gracious. How do you keep up with so much work? And you're a kind of nursemaid as well?'

'I have help. You look very smart.'

He preened himself ridiculously and made her laugh. 'Thanks. I was pleased when I was sent to Bristol.'

'Why are you here?'

'I've been in France. Got a wound. Not serious, I thought, but the medics sent me home to recover.'

'I'm sorry. How do you feel now?'

'All the better for seeing you.'

She frowned. 'Why?'

'Why? I always felt I should like to meet you again.

'Did you? Why?'

He laughed. 'My God, a girl without vanity. I can scarcely believe it. Why shouldn't I? I find you attractive.'

Sid stared at him from beneath drawn brows.

He flinched. 'Don't hit me. I really mean it. I took an instant liking to you when we met. Didn't you feel anything for me?'

She shrugged. 'I thought you were nice-looking and well mannered.'

He gave a shout of laughter which made Amy chuckle. 'What a blow to my pride. I have had better compliments.'

'I hadn't time to get to know you.'

'It only takes a minute to know that someone attracts you.'

'I know,' she said, thinking of Philip.

'Do you, Sidonia – that's your proper name, isn't it? You look sad? Have you lost someone you cared for? People are calling the war phoney, but men are getting killed.'

'I haven't. Not in the way you mean.' He was ready to ask more questions and she said quickly, 'How did you become an officer straight away?'

'I was a fully paid-up member of the Officer Cadet Training Corps at school. I'm only a second lieutenant, the lowest of the low, despised of sergeant-majors. However, I hope to rectify that when I get sent overseas next time.'

'When will that be? No, forget I said that. Walls have ears.'

'Push me,' cried Amy, fed up with the chatter of grown-ups.

'She's been incredibly patient,' said Barton. 'May I push you?'

'I expect so,' said Amy. 'What's your name?'

'What's yours?'

Amy surveyed him solemnly and evidently decided to like him. 'Amy.'

'What a pretty name. Mine is Tom.'

Amy considered. 'Nice name,' she pronounced.

Nice man, thought Sid as she watched him get up a good turn of speed with the tricycle, making Amy shriek with joy. As Sid watched them she felt a terrible yearning. Amy should have a father just like him. She wondered what he'd be like as a husband. Thoughtful. Amusing? Loving? Or treacherous? How could you tell? She'd been such a fool. Never again would she trust a man the way she had Philip.

Chapter Eleven

To Tom Barton it seemed as if he had caught a glimpse of hell. Moments before, the charming little Belgian town of Oudenaarde had been peaceful under the sun; now, after the sudden onslaught of German bombers, it had erupted in black smoke and flames. Red dust from the roof-tiles lingered hazily, adding to the surreal effect. Houses had been chopped in two, furniture lay splintered in the street or hung crazily from gaping holes. Women and children and old men crawled from the cellars weeping and praying, while the dust settled on them like blood.

The British Expeditionary Force was retreating. It was official. That fact alone was enough to weaken a man's spirit, but the sights along the way increased the horror to a kind of numb enduring.

The Army had been ordered to make for the coast from which the men could be rescued, but some must stay behind on guard to enable the battle-weary troops to cross the river. Tom had been sent with a platoon to guard a bridge. The whole thing became a deadly game. A game where the opponents with the quickest wits and the fastest guns survived. The Germans, well dug-in, held up tin hats on sticks, presumably laughing when the British wasted their bullets. In the end, Tom had realised what was happening, and had shot accurately: another soldier lay dead, another family would mourn, a German family. A man wasn't supposed to care about the mourning of enemy women and children. He did. He wasn't cut out to be a soldier.

'When will it be our turn, to leave, sir?' asked a Bren gunner.

'I've no orders yet regarding that.'

'They say there are warships at a place called Dunkirk waiting to take us on board.'

There was a lull, and stretcher-bearers from a Field Ambulance Corps arrived to remove the dead and wounded. Tom watched them pityingly, then beads of perspiration broke out on his face as a man he'd thought was a corpse, with a bullet still sticking from his forehead, sat up and asked for a cigarette. Tom lit one for him, trying to still his shaking hands. The soldier puffed on it once, then died.

The order came to leave the bridge; Tom and the remaining men began the march to the coast. The roads were filled with refugees, pathetic groups mainly of weary grandmothers, frantic wives and children trying desperately to stay together. They were bombed and strafed constantly by machine-guns fired from German planes; the sound of women weeping and screaming and the cries of children became a terrible, endless refrain.

Tom found it almost as unbearable to see domestic animals wandering helplessly, or trapped, in pain, hungry and thirsty, the cows with udders heavy with milk. Some, the hopeless cases, he despatched using his last precious ammunition, unable to let them endure such suffering. Like many another man he released cats and dogs from farmhouses or barns. A dog followed him for a mile or two before sitting down in the road, whining. Some French medics carried compassion further, using revolvers to put women and children out of the agony of their death wounds. In the context of the present horror, Tom could only admire them for their courageous mercy.

He was tired, hungry and thirsty. It seemed reckless beyond belief, but British troops were being ordered to destroy all weapons too big to carry, spoil food, ruin anything which could assist the enemy. Familiar British trucks were left in the fields beside the roads, radiators smashed, engines battered by sledgehammers, tyres slashed. The big guns, their ammunition finished, were rendered equally useless. The retreat could not be orderly, as became fighting men, but was composed of straggling groups made up of soldiers from different regiments, immeasurably weary, unwashed, unfed, the severely wounded being conveyed in overcrowded ambulances, the men with lesser wounds supported as best they could by their mates. Four men clung to the corners of a blanket in which lay a youth as pale as death.

As an officer, Tom felt it his duty to point out that the boy was obviously ill enough to be transported by an ambulance.

A corporal holding one corner of the blanket stared at him, his eyes red-rimmed. 'He didn't seem so bad at first, sir. He's got a lot worse since we began carrying him.'

'I see. Stop the next one you see and ask for help.'

'We'll do that, sir.' He didn't sound hopeful.

The sun blazed, the heat was fierce and unrelenting and Tom's tongue was stuck to the roof of his mouth. He saw a wrecked NAAFI truck and clambered over it, hoping for something to drink. It had been raided by other desperate men, but he found a tin of peaches undamaged. He opened it with his bayonet and shared its contents with a young private who had followed him. He told Tom his name was Stanley, and together they sat in the back of the useless truck.

'Shall we get away all right, sir?'

Tom smiled. The boy was young and understandably terrified. 'I'm sure we will. They won't just abandon us.'

They walked on. Tom's feet were blistered; he was so tired that simply to keep walking was an agony. Now he was ragingly thirsty too. The weather, as if to mock them, remained perfect: that's if you were going to the beach for a picnic. Now it served to give the enemy planes a clear view of their targets. Even the nights never got really dark, and the Germans continued to bombard them with relentless shelling.

The two men stayed together. When they were forced to rest they found a deserted farmhouse and talked a little. Stanley told Tom he was engaged to a girl in his street.

He produced a photograph. 'There she is, sir. As pretty as any film star. And she sews her own clothes and cooks like a dream, too. She wanted us to marry before I left England, but I didn't think it was fair on her. Now I believe she was right. I can't wait to get home and tell her. Have you got a girl, sir? A special one, I mean.'

'Nobody special.' But Tom's memory returned to the charming old house in Bristol and the young woman who ran the place as well as looking after a child and working in a factory. Sid. Curious name for so feminine a creature. Then he had discovered it was short for Sidonia. Now that suited her. It was different and so was she. She wasn't pretty, not with that little bump on her nose and her generous mouth and dark brows. Her hair was fine, and the evening he had talked with her in the garden it had needed attention. In fact, she looked as if she could do with a session in a beauty parlour, the kind his mother and sisters patronised, but she obviously had far too much to do, far too many loads to carry to worry too much about her appearance. In spite of his loathing of the war, Tom was sure it was worse in many ways for women who worked and waited. Like Sidonia. Again his thoughts were filled by her. Her eyes were her best feature, and the look in them when he had pushed the kid on the tricycle in the garden haunted him. He couldn't analyse it. And there was a coolness, a reserve about her which warned him not to get too close. It intrigued him.

He was so deep into his reverie that he jumped when Stanley spoke, which was ridiculous considering the never-ending noise around them. 'I've always been interested in health and I almost volunteered for a medical corps. Thank God I didn't. I've seen wounds that turn a man's stomach. I don't know how the doctors put up with it. And there are nurses too. Brave lassies. One was trying to comfort a boy who'd had his wedding tackle shot away. Poor thing. He was sobbing about being engaged. I wouldn't be able to bear that.'

Tom shuddered.

'It would certainly put a damper on my marriage,' said Stanley, summoning a ghastly smile.

At sunset they found an old farmhouse which still had the kitchen intact. They staggered into its shelter. There were men already stretched out on the floor. They looked up as each newcomer arrived. 'There's food in the pantry and wine in the cellar,' they said. Nothing else. What was there to say?

Tom and Stanley ate stale bread dipped in red wine, then drank deeply and fell asleep. Tom woke to the sound of bombs falling nearby. It was light and the men were dragging themselves up to go on. The room stank with their sweat and the relentless sun had risen on another clear blue day.

They talked a little over their bread and wine.

'What do you want most when you get back to Blighty?' was a favourite question.

'A pint in the local', 'a decent cup of tea, not Army muck', 'a lamb chop with green peas straight from the garden', 'bread thick with butter and honey', 'a night in bed with my lovely old woman'. The answers were varied.

'How about a bath?'

The man who suggested that was jeered. 'Give us the beer and the food and we'll worry about the bath later.'

Stanley and Tom stayed together, finding a measure of comfort in each other's company. They seldom spoke as they tramped on, sometimes giving a helping hand to a civilian refugee, though there was very little they could do. The men in their regulation long-johns got hotter and hotter, until chafing between their legs forced many to walk with a straddle stride which at any other time would have been funny, but very few discarded them, most following strict orders about hanging on to their Army-issue garments at all times.

German Stukas dived low. Some people simply stood and waited in ox-like resignation, their minds beaten beyond thought, their bodies weary beyond belief. Others threw themselves into ditches, at the bottom of which the water was stagnant and added to the general stink. The third time it happened and the plane roared away, Tom got to his feet, but Stanley lay still. He had been grievously and horrendously wounded, his torso a bloody mess. It's better he's dead, thought Tom. Stan's 'wedding tackle' had been neatly sliced off, as if his fear had been father to the deed. He closed his late comrade's eyes. He should get a proper burial, he thought, not left to rot in a ditch like a dead rat. He looked around. Where could he bury him? The adjoining field was pitted with bomb craters, the soil around them rock hard in the sun and impenetrable without a spade. Stanley must lie where he was, along with the dozens of other bodies attracting hordes of flies. He wished he could remember the burial service. The only thing which came to his tired mind was a prayer of his youth, taught him by his Nanny. ' "Now I lay me down to sleep, I pray the Lord my soul to keep. If I should die before I wake, I pray the Lord my soul to take." ' Then he climbed back to the road, where he helped shift a handcart out of the way. A dead middle-aged woman lay beside it, her skirts up, her elastic-legged knickers displayed in a lack of modesty which, living, she would have deplored. In the cart lay an old woman, her hands clasped, as if anticipating the death which had come to her. Her companion was thrown in beside her, landing in a heap.

He walked on. The sight of torn bodies and torsos and detached heads and limbs was now such a common sight he no longer saw them, but he stopped when he noticed some movement from a woman's body. To his ultimate horror a young woman lay dead while her baby still suckled. He lifted the child, looking down into its uncomprehending face. It began to wail, and a woman who was pushing her own baby in a pram held out her arms. Gratefully Tom put the child into them and she opened her blouse and held it to her generous breast.

After that, unwilling to endure any more such ghastly horrors, he left the road and joined other soldiers who were making their way over meadows and fields. Hens still crooned and scratched as if nothing was happening; eggs were quite plentiful. He had never visualised swallowing raw egg, but he did so now, gratefully.

The small seaside town of Dunkirk was detectable for miles, plumes of suffocating sable smoke belching from stricken oil containers. Tom could taste it. Gasometers blew up and flames leapt high into the sky. Planes constantly dropped their screaming bombs. A sergeant asked no one in particular, 'How the devil do they think they're going to evacuate anyone from there?'

'No idea,' said Tom. 'I'm sure they'll do something. They can't just leave us.'

At a road junction, a military policeman with a bandaged head beneath his tin helmet was doing his best to observe some kind of order. 'There are too many men in the harbour already. Go along the coast to La Panne. Wait on the beach. Boats will evacuate everybody.'

The groups of weary soldiers obeyed. Along the shoreline most houses were alight, but some remained almost intact. Tom and the sergeant decided to look for water, climbing through a window where the glass had been blown out. No water ran from the taps, and the milk abandoned in a jug on the table was thick and sour. They were about to give up when the sergeant discovered two bottles of beer which had rolled behind a cupboard. They tasted like nectar. 'There's a basement,' said Tom. 'There may be something to drink down there.'

'That's true, sir. The French are great wine drinkers. There's sure to be a bottle or two.'

If there had been they had been taken by others. The light from the sergeant's torch revealed no further longed-for drink. The beam swept into a corner and they realised that the cellar wasn't empty. A young soldier crouched, terrified, in a corner.

'Come on, son,' said the sergeant. 'You can't stay here, you'll miss the evacuation. The good old navy are coming for us.'

'I won't go any further! I can't!'

'Yes, you can. Now move!' His sudden yell made the boy jump. 'That's an order!'

'I won't obey!' he cried. 'I've had enough.'

'Haven't we all? Come with us, my boy,' said Tom, 'you'll soon be safe home in England.'

'I'm not moving,' the boy shrieked. 'You can't make me.'

'That makes you a deserter!' the sergeant barked.

'Shoot me then. You might as well. I'm going to be killed anyway. So are you. We all are.'

'You probably will be if you stay here. Your only chance is to get on a ship.' The sergeant spoke now as if reasoning with a child.

'None of you will escape. The bombing and strafing and shelling never stop. You're sitting ducks out there. I can't go back. I won't!'

'Don't you want to go home?'

'I'm staying here.'

'We'll help you, won't we, sir? We'll look after you.'

'Of course.' Tom's stomach turned at the sight of the naked terror in the boy's eyes. 'Give me your hand.'

'No!' He went on saying 'no' until his voice rose in a scream and ended in animal-like wails which chilled Tom's blood.

'I'll carry him,' said the sergeant. 'If you could take our guns, sir.'

The young soldier fought like a demon, his shrieks growing more and more hysterical. Then he sank his teeth into the sergeant, who yelled and dropped him. 'I could knock him out,' he growled, sucking his bleeding hand. 'In fact, it would be a pleasure. We could carry him between us.'

'With our guns and what's left of our gear? It's as much as a man can do to get himself over the dunes. He'd regain consciousness, and in his state he could panic the others. Discipline is high at the moment. We'll have to leave him.'

'It goes against the grain, sir.'

'For me, too, but it's a balance of one man against many. And he may see sense and come to the beach.'

'I never will!' shouted the boy.

The sergeant stood looking down at him. 'It goes against the grain,' he said again. 'Poor little devil.'

The military policeman's promise of early rescue proved to be optimistic. As they neared La Panne they stepped over heaped bodies of the dead and wounded. At the head of the beach the two men stood and stared, heedless for the moment of the whining bombs and shells. The dunes were black with a mass of men just waiting, praying to stay alive, enduring constant attack, tortured by thirst and hunger, sharing everything they had. Medical orderlies did their best for the wounded, although they had little first-aid equipment left, and that almost primitive. Tom watched as one sprinkled powder on a gaping shell wound and covered it with Vaseline-soaked bandages. There were too many who would never reach their homeland even for burial, and the stench of human flesh rotting in the hot sun was something Tom would never forget. Here and there somebody's mates had buried him in sand, and placed a rough cross to mark the spot but, as often as not, the next bomb attack blew him out.

'My God,' said the sergeant 'what a filthy mess.' A shell exploded near them, covering them with sand. 'I'm going to try to find my men.'

'Good luck.'

'And you, sir.'

Orders had been given to spread out, and men were struggling as best they could over the dunes.

Tom was cheered by seeing a face he knew, a driver in his regiment. 'Hendy!'

Roy turned round. 'It's you, sir. Glad you made it.'

'What happened to your truck?'

'I kept it going as long as I could. Full of our own men it was. Good old Gloucesters, they fought until their ammo ran out. The buggers strafed us and killed a lot of us. Ambulances turned up to get the wounded, though some were so bad I don't think they'll make it. Not in these conditions. Then I had orders to shove the truck in a field and destroy it. It seemed crazy to me, though I could hardly move it by then: the roads are so full of people. Where do they think they're going? It's as bad here as back in the villages.'

'I don't know.'

'There's only the coast ahead of them. It's terrible. War is supposed to be about men fighting, not all the . . .' Roy stopped and moved his hands, searching for words. 'Women and kids. That's not war. And we've hardly begun and, the way things are, I wonder if Britain can recover from this and go on.'

'We shall,' said Tom. 'We'll fight again.'

'I wish I had your conviction. There are hundreds of dead in the dunes, and we're going to be short of anything to fight with. How will we get enough together to try again? What's to stop Hitler from invading? Did you see how much of our equipment is useless, destroyed? And the men, just lying there beside it, dead, poor sods.'

'We'll get through,' said Tom doggedly. 'We always do.' By now, he was trying to convince himself.

They lay in the hollow of a dune and Roy produced a packet of French cigarettes. 'Like one? They're pretty foul compared to ours, but better than nothing.'

'I definitely would. Where did you get them? No, don't answer that.'

'I took them from a bar. I suppose that's looting, but I shouldn't think I'd get shot for it. The Jerries will take anything we leave.'

Roy smoked his cigarette, staring up at the brilliant sky. One day he'd bring Sid here. The idea surprised him, but it was infinitely soothing and he dreamt on. When the war was over she would marry him and their children would play on the sands with their spades and pails. There was a bandstand at the end of the promenade, still miraculously undamaged. He pictured it peopled by musicians playing merry holiday music for merry dancers. He allowed his mind to drift into pictures, soothing the nerves tormented by incessant gunfire and the groans and cries of the wounded.

There was no respite. At night the bombers rested but the beaches were brilliant with the light from exploding shells. Men pressed themselves as low as they could in the sand, bracing themselves, waiting for death or mutilation. The nightmare went on. Men were tormented by thoughts of escape and home, of remembered kitchens where they would find food and drink, as they watched their mates being killed or slashed to bloody mincemeat, and they shared what meagre supplies they had of water and food. Their spirits were roused when the Germans dropped leaflets urging them to surrender; their answers were crouched in semi-humourous barrack-room language. Small patrols of British planes flew to help, flying in strict V-formation, like ducks, and they lost more planes than they shot down. The men sweating and suffering on the ground muttered imprecations against the Air Force.

'Why don't they send more planes?' said Roy. 'Those stupid sods up there aren't doing much good.'

'They're obeying orders, just like us. It looks as if their training needs to be changed.'

Destroyers had been despatched to lift the men from France, but their size prevented them from coming into shore. Tom was astonished to see small craft of every conceivable kind arriving: ketches and yachts, barges and motor launches, pinnaces, even a Thames fireboat, sailing barges with their distinctive brown sails, a pleasure paddle-steamer, dredgers, rusty, mud-spattered craft, tugs towing ship's lifeboats.

A cheer went up when Devonshire men saw the Portsmouth–Isle-of-Wight car ferry. Then the boats with a suitable draught began to arrive on the beach and the men formed orderly lines.

'Look at that, sir,' said Roy. 'What a sight for sore eyes! Civilian craft. Where have they all come from?'

'Britain,' said Tom. 'Everywhere in Britain. They've come out to rescue us. What courage! God bless them. Now I know we won't be beaten.'

Men were ferried from the shore to the ships. Not everyone made it. Some of the small craft received direct hits, and sailors died and soldiers were killed just as they sighted deliverance.

'Should we go nearer the shoreline?' asked Roy.

'I'll wait,' said Tom. 'It's my duty as an officer.' He thought he sounded pompous. 'I might be needed, though the men are as disciplined as if they were on the parade ground. Marvellous chaps.'

'I'll stay with you, sir,' said Roy. 'I wonder just who is sailing all those little boats?'

The answer came when some men swam ashore after their craft had been overturned in a swell caused by a near miss.

'Lots of our blokes were drowned,' said one, gasping on a cigarette supplied by Roy. 'There was a girl on board, too. Just her and her father. Both gone to the bottom. All the boats are crewed by civilians. That poor girl. Couldn't have been more than fifteen.'

Impatient to escape, desperately eager to get away from the cruel attacks, the queues grew longer, until the leaders were up to their chests in water, heavily weighted by their uniforms, those who still possessed rifles having to hold them above their heads. Caring for their rifles was all that kept them from falling into sleep. Men who succumbed sometimes slid beneath the water and, too heavy for their companions to pull them out, drowned. They were surrounded by debris: wooden planks from sunken boats, tables and chairs, lifebelts, cans, and patches of thick, black oil. There was virtually no panic, and the strong helped the wounded. If someone endangered the rest by rocking the boat, he was quickly hauled into line by threats to throw him overboard. A man unable to drag himself into a boat, encumbered by his waterlogged coat and boots, kept sliding back, until a sailor yelled, 'Come on, you stupid bastard. Some of you others help him.' The rough medicine gave the man the impetus he needed.

Roy and Tom joined a queue. They had nearly reached its head when a plane roared over them, spraying deadly machine-gun bullets. Tom felt as if someone had punched him hard in his shoulder. He looked down and saw his blood pouring into the water.

Roy swore. 'Hold on, sir.' He handed his rifle to the man behind, took out a handkerchief, and bound the bleeding shoulder tightly. A lifeboat appeared, and Tom tried to climb aboard, but his sodden uniform and his hellishly painful shoulder defeated him. A crewman leaned out and, between them, he and Roy got Tom aboard, where one of the lifeboat crew strapped Tom's shoulder as best he could.

The pain really hit Tom now but, in spite of it, he fell into an exhausted sleep, only waking when they docked in Dover. People on shore greeted them with cheers, waving Union Jacks. They were welcomed by the Salvation Army and members of the Women's Voluntary Service; clean, wholesome women, as cheery as if they were serving buns and lemonade on a bank holiday outing as they dished out tea and cigarettes.

'They're treating us like heroes,' said Roy, 'instead of a defeated army.' He said goodbye to Tom. 'I'm off back to the regiment, what's left of it, sir. There're hospital trains for the wounded. Good luck.'

The British leaders had expected to rescue forty-five thousand men. Instead, by use of the improvisation for which Britain was renowned, they had succeeded in evacuating three hundred and thirty-eight thousand British and French soldiers. They left behind six hundred tanks and more than two thousand guns, rendered useless.

Now Britain was wide open to a German invasion. Winston Churchill had become prime minister, ousting Chamberlain who had become unpopular and had been forced out of office by military disasters. Churchill rallied the people with his fighting speeches; he also ordered the distribution of leaflets which told civilians how to deal with German parachutists and what to do in the case of invasion.

Sid and the others read the newspapers and sat by the wireless as often as possible, drinking in the news. Much was censored, but it was clear that the British Army was fighting a rearguard battle around Dunkirk. Only Mrs Cardell had ever heard of the place.

'It's just a little seaside,' she said. 'Quite attractive.'

'It won't be so pretty now,' said Angie.

Later she came to Sid, her face pink with excitement. 'There are trains coming into Bristol packed with men from Dunkirk. They're letting them off in Temple Meads and Stapleton. Do you think we could help? People are giving them tea and things. The WVS have been handing out postcards and they need stamps and someone to post them to let their relations know they're all right.'

'Both of you go,' said Mrs Cardell.

'What about Amy?' asked Sid.

'I'll look after her. Brindle will help.'

Sid hesitated but, although Amy was an independent child, she obeyed and respected Aunt Louisa.

So Sid, Angie, the Misses Weekley and Keith went to Stapleton Road station, each carrying baskets of sandwiches, fruit juice and cigarettes, which they put into the oil-blackened hands of men whose eyes revealed terrible suffering. Sid looked out for the men she knew, but saw no one she recognised.

'I wish I'd been with them,' said Keith as Sid drove the car back.

'You might have been lying dead in France,' pointed out Angie.

'I bet I wouldn't. I'd have got away somehow. Anyway, I shall join up now they're taking younger men.'

On her return, Sid surveyed the contents of the larder. The sandwiches given to the soldiers had used their entire rations of butter for the week. She had used hard-boiled eggs for the filling, and she thanked God for the hens as she beat eggs for omelettes for dinner. There was no meat, and she hadn't had time to queue for offal, but the bacon ration was good, thanks to the 'pig club' which had sprung up. Brindle had suggested that they buy a piglet and fatten it for the pot, but Sid was so horrified at the idea of eating a pet that he let the matter drop, muttering about 'an idiotic woman who'd eat a chicken from the garden, but not a pig.' Dessert would have to be a jar of their own, home-bottled fruit. She had been using it sparingly since the beginning of the war, and there were still some plums in syrup.

Prices had soared, and food was often a problem as Sid struggled to serve meals without bothering her mistress for too much extra money. Men continued to visit, loving the peace of the old house and the way of life, which seemed to them little altered from pre-war, and reminded many of home. She kept a stockpot constantly on the range, adding bones, vegetable water, bacon rinds, making soup which helped. Brindle always saw to it that the wine was correct and the quantity sufficient for any officers who dined at the house. The men, when they could, brought food from the NAAFI, and precious cigarettes.

Sid and Angie found consolation in smoking after their heavy routine duties. Angie now went part-time to a local farmer where she helped on the land. And they all filled sandbags in readiness for the bombing for which everyone waited. So far the action had been confined to daylight raids over positions of military importance, but the young fighter pilots succeeded in causing such heavy losses among the German Luftwaffe, winning what had become known as 'The Battle of Britain', that the Germans turned their attention to night raids.

The expected invasion didn't materialise, and the Army gradually reformed its battalions. They lacked weapons, and had insufficient accommodation for the thousands of men suddenly on their hands. Hotels and private houses were requisitioned, while some houses on the south coast were blown up in the name of defence.

Angie came home from her work on the farm. 'Honestly, you wouldn't know if a German parachutist was here or not. There're people from Holland and France and Denmark and Norway on the land. Anyone could pass themselves off as a refugee. And it's even harder to work nowadays. They've scattered concrete blocks and left old cars in rows about the fields. It's to stop planes landing, I suppose, or maybe tanks driving.'

Sid responded absent-mindedly. She was searching for a recipe she thought she had seen somewhere for mock cream.

'Here it is,' she said.

'Here what is?'

'Mock cream. Cornflour mixed with margarine, milk and sugar. I'll give it a try.'

Four officers were at dinner that night, which began with soup from the stockpot, followed by omelettes with grated cheese and onion and bits of crispy fried bacon. Sid had to open a second jar of plums, and the mock cream proved a success.

'You're so clever,' said Mrs Cardell later. 'Did you give the same cream to Amy? Did she enjoy it?'

'She had a little and thought it was lovely.'

'Children are so good at adapting. I suppose she takes everything for granted.'

'She seems to. Even the aeroplanes are fun to her, theirs or ours.'

Amy was growing fast. She wouldn't be ready for school for a couple of years yet, but already she was beginning to recognise letters in the books read to her. She had a quick memory and knew some of the stories off by heart. Sid had been on early duty; now she sat with her daughter on a blanket on the small patch of grass Brindle and Keith had spared after digging up the rest to grow food. She grew drowsy, and several times her eyes closed. Amy poked her and said, 'Wake up, Aunty Sid. Read to me,' but eventually Sid, overcome by weariness, sank back on the blanket and slept.

Amy looked up at the sound of footsteps and saw a man she remembered. 'I know you.'

'And I know you. You're Amy and I'm Uncle Tom.'

'Aunty Sid's gone to sleep. I want her to read to me.'

'Will I do?' Tom spoke in whispers so as not to disturb Sid.

Sid was astonished to hear a male voice reading the story of the Three Bears. She was still only half awake, but it was a voice she recognised and, embarrassed at being found in so helpless a position, she sat up so quickly she made herself giddy. She put a hand to her head.

'Are you all right?' asked Tom anxiously.

'Quite, thank you. I didn't know you were here.' She tried not to sound irritable.

'I hadn't the heart to disturb you. Mrs Cardell told me how hard you work. I must say, you do look awfully tired.'

'Must you?' Sid's reply was ungracious, even though she had suddenly realised how glad she was to see him again. She wished she had been wearing something better than her factory skirt and blouse. Her hair was all over the place too, and she hadn't got a trace of make-up on.

'I didn't mean to insult you. You're bound to get tired. I wish you had slept on.'

'It doesn't matter,' said Sid, recovering her equilibrium. No matter how nice he seemed, she wasn't about to let another man into her life, so what did it matter how she looked? She took a closer look at him. 'You don't look so good yourself.'

'I was wounded at Dunkirk.'

'I'm sorry. A severe wound?'

'Not too bad. Shrapnel in the shoulder, but infection set in on the way to the hospital, so I was more ill than I should have been.'

'Why wasn't the wound treated properly in the first place?'

Tom was nonplussed. Where could he begin? How to describe the confusion of the retreat to someone who had no idea of battle conditions? Perhaps later on, after the war maybe, some historian would gather up all the facts and make sense of them.

'Things got in a bit of a muddle,' he said. 'We had to leave a lot of the worst wounded behind with their medics, poor chaps. I'm lucky I was a walking wounded.'

'I see. People are talking about the Miracle of Dunkirk. It makes it sound holy.'

'No, I wouldn't have called it holy, but it did seem like a miracle. No one who was there will ever forget it. The Navy was there, of course, but dozens of civilians got us off the beaches. Old people and young boys and girls crewed the small boats. Some of them died.' He paused and repeated softly, 'A miracle, yes, but not holy . . . I've been allowed home for my convalescence.'

'Home?'

'Yes. Didn't you know that my home town was near Bristol? No, of course you wouldn't. It wasn't mentioned when you thought me a mere chauffeur.'

'There's nothing wrong with being a chauffeur.'

'Of course there isn't. As a matter of fact I found it quite a jolly sort of job, driving lovely cars here and there with not much else to do but polish them. My only problem was the people who sat in them.'

'Your employers?'

'Exactly. The Prossers are a sorry bunch. Now if it had been Mrs Cardell, or preferably you . . .'

Sid stared narrowly at him. 'You flatter me.'

'No, I don't. I really would enjoy ferrying you about. You're so refreshingly honest and direct.'

Sid's eyes went to Amy. Refreshingly honest? She thought of the hours she was away from her child. 'I wish I had a car to get to work. Mrs Cardell hasn't owned one for years, and you can't get the petrol anyway. The trams and buses take time and I like to be here as much as possible.'

'You're an absolute brick to do a full-time job and still stay with Mrs Cardell.'

'Angie helps, and we have our cleaning ladies. They're marvellous, both of them. They're fire-watchers for their street and often don't get enough sleep.'

'That seems to be inevitable in war. Never enough sleep.'

'And cold. January was dreadful. The coldest for forty-five years, they said, and everyone was urged to save fuel.'

'It's warm enough today and it's lovely in the garden.'

'It looks more like an allotment after Brindle and Keith's efforts . . . Amy,' she called, 'Come off there. We're growing that stuff to eat.' She smiled. 'It's an experiment. Have you ever heard of prickly spinach?'

'Not a word,' he said solemnly.

She laughed. 'We're told it's full of goodness and withstands the weather. Brindle would dig it up like a shot and plant cabbage, but

Mrs Cardell saw it one day and is interested.'

'Will Keith be joining up?'

'He certainly will. He can't talk of anything else.'

'Who'll see to the garden then? There's quite a bit of land.'

'We'll manage. Perhaps some of the visitors will lend a hand.'

'I certainly would,' said Tom eagerly. 'Especially if you asked me.'

Sid was silent for a moment. 'Everyone is preparing for invasion,' she said. 'Some of the things they do seem quite crazy. Men are dragging derelict cars and lorries and concrete piping – anything they can get hold of – and leaving them in the fields, and some are driving stakes into the ground.'

Tom had been snubbed and he knew it. She was as prickly as the spinach. It made her more interesting. Girls who fell easily into a man's arms didn't attract him. 'Be prepared, that's the British motto. Like the boy scouts.'

'They're even putting concrete blocks by the sides of the roads to stop planes from landing there.'

'It's a pity there weren't a few more obstacles in France.'

'Would it have made a difference?'

'I don't know,' he said, wishing he hadn't brought up the subject again. It haunted him and would do so, he knew, for a long time. His need to talk about it was powerful, but not to a civilian, however sympathetic. He lowered his voice, almost as if he spoke only to himself. 'I suppose no one will ever know. So many men lost, so many lives blighted.'

'War is horrible!'

'Yes.' He paused and said, 'I met your window-cleaner, Roy Hendy, there, by the way. We're in the same battalion.'

'Did he get away?'

'Yes, and with a whole skin. He's gone to a camp somewhere.'

'Thank heaven.'

'Is he a particular friend of yours?' Tom was surprised by a surge of jealousy.

'He's a friend, just as you are. We're making lots of friends these days. The house is full of officers.'

'I see.'

Amy had returned after her reprimand, but realised with disgust that the grown-ups' conversation was still boring, and had gone off again. Now she appeared with her hands full of flowers.

'Oh, Amy,' cried Sid, 'what will Brindle say?' She turned to Tom. 'Brindle is cultivating a few flowers here and there in the garden. Mrs Cardell likes them in the house.'

'Brindle's nice. He won't be cross,' said Amy, but she looked uncertain. There were uncomfortable things happening to the people around her. Her two favourite aunties kept going off to somewhere they called 'work'. Brindle and Patrick went out nearly every night to be soldiers, and Keith was sometimes quite cross. Tears of self-pity filled her eyes.

'Oh, I say, don't cry,' begged Tom. He produced a large khaki handkerchief and dabbed at her eyes. 'Don't cry. What game would you like to play?'

'No game,' said Amy, forcing out more tears.

'Show me round the garden,' said Tom desperately.

Sid looked on, amused. She knew that Amy resented the way the household was disrupted, but other children were suffering far worse problems, and Amy was usually happy. The tales sifting back from the evacuees were not always pleasant, and many children had run away and gone back to their parents.

Amy stopped crying, wiped her eyes, blew her nose in Tom's handkerchief and ordered him to follow her. She showed him the vegetable patches she had memorised as Sid leaned on one elbow to watch them. Tom was very attractive. Here in the quiet garden it seemed incredible that he had been in such danger, twice wounded in a war which here seemed hardly to have begun, and was so far away from the realities of home. He would go back to the fighting and worse might happen to him. The idea upset her. Pessimism was taking her over, and she quietly sprang up and joined the others, who were now inspecting the herb patch. Amy was telling Tom the names of the plants picking a sprig here and there and insisting Tom smelt them.

When Amy had been put to bed that night and dinner had been served, to three officer guests including Tom, Sid sat alone in the quiet kitchen. Angie had gone to a local class in first aid, Brindle and Patrick were drilling with the Home Guard, while Keith was at home spending some time with his parents before he left to join the Army. She had taken a tray of whisky and soda to Mrs Cardell and her guests, and wondered how long their stock of alcohol would survive the onslaught of so many thirsty men. She thought of the way Tom had looked at her, as if he found her attractive. Her whole concept of life had been turned upside-down since she had left her job in the hairdressing salon. First there was Mr Keevil and his sick-making attempts to kiss her. Her parents had made that sound as if it was all her fault. Then Philip. He hadn't meant a word he had said to her. He hadn't been bowled over by her looks or her personality at all; he had simply gone for her because she was a woman and she was there.

Roy was different. He liked her the way she was. Perhaps she should tell him about Amy; if he still wanted her, they could be married. Amy would have the security of a father and Sid could spend more time at home. Women with serving husbands and small children were not encouraged to work, though some factories provided crèches. Amy would grow up in a stable home, but when she tried to picture it, her mind balked. Surely she was entitled to dream of a man she could love wholeheartedly. Was that so selfish? And Amy was happy and safe enough with so many devoted aunts and uncles.

Keith was so bitterly disappointed he could hardly bear to speak. He had gone off to register for enlistment with a bright face and high hopes, only to return after his medical. 'I've been rejected,' he said, struggling with tears.

'What? Impossible!' Angie and Sid spoke together.

'You're as fit as a fiddle,' said Sid.

'You've only got to see you digging the garden to know that,' said Angie.

'I've got a dicky heart. I had rheumatic fever when I was a kid and that's the result. It's only a murmur, the medic said, but enough to keep me at home.'

He was morose for days, then said, 'I'm going to join the Home Guard. They take anybody. Even the vicar, and he's so short-sighted he couldn't tell a Jerry from one of ours unless he got close up. Some of the men are so old they can hardly stand up, but it's the nearest I'll get to being a soldier. I just hope Hitler invades us and I'll show them how I can fight.'

After the Battle of Britain in which so many died, Angie felt restless. 'I'm not doing enough, Sid,' she said one night, her hands busy as always with knitting. Nowadays it was always khaki, Air-force blue, or navy. Balaclavas and socks were made at record speeds.

Sid closed her eyes briefly, shaken by the thought of Angie leaving. 'You already work on the land,' she pointed out.

'I know, but it's not official and it's not enough. I'd like to be somewhere where I can feel really useful, nearer the real war. In the Women's Auxiliary Air Force, if I can. Those girls take on ever so many things to spare the men for fighting. I know it sounds daft, Sid, but I feel the country needs me.'

'We all need you,' Sid blurted out.

Angie looked worried and Sid said quickly. 'Of course you must go. Of course, I shall miss you, we all will, but you must do what's right for you.'

'Thanks. It's Amy I'm really thinking about. She's strong and sturdy and the others will care for her. I'm already out a lot, but I hate to think of upsetting her, and I don't like leaving you when you need me. I've been worrying about it.'

'Amy's lucky to have others who love her. I shall be here, and so will Mrs Cardell. Between us we'll make sure she's all right, though I sometimes wish our factory had a crèche.'

'Why not try for a job in one of the big ones? Filton, perhaps?'

Sid tried to get transferred, but was refused permission. It seemed that everything was regulated nowadays.

The day Angie left was a bleak one for Sid. She'd had to go to work as usual, and the Misses Weekley, Mrs Cardell, Brindle, Patrick and Keith all vowed that Amy would be their first concern. Sid thanked them and smiled, but her stomach was churning when she thought of all the dangers that might come to her child. When she returned from work that evening, Angie's bedroom was neat and clean, most of her civilian clothes folded and lying in the big nursery cupboard. Sid missed her more than she would have believed possible, and Amy kept breaking into wails.

'I've explained it to you, darling,' said Sid, 'and so did Aunty Angie. She has to go away and be a soldier.'

'It's men what are soldiers,' shouted Amy. 'They come here and I see them I *know*.'

'There have to be lady soldiers too.'

Amy refused to be consoled, and Sid sat with her for hours that night until she slept.

Angie's first letter to Sid arrived. 'I'm glad I got into the Air Force. The uniform is much more becoming than the ATS, and after I've done the necessary drilling I shall be posted. I can't help feeling excited by it all. Of course, there are drawbacks – being yelled at by loud-mouthed women sergeants, and inspected by women officers who look at you as if you were dirt – but I've met a lot of girls and made some pals. None of them knows about my past and I'm just taken for granted here. Give Amy my love and a big kiss.'

Sid wrote back and everyone put in a note, telling her how much she was missed and wishing her well.

Mrs Cardell handed hers to Sid one night as she was being helped to bed. She sighed. 'Young women out fighting a war. What will happen to them all? How will they ever settle down when they return?'

'I don't know. I should think most would welcome the end of the war.'

'Maybe. Of course some of the men must be restless too. There are recruits who have hardly had time to go out to work in the world, some young ones are called up straight from school. It was the same last time.' Sid looked at her mistress anxiously. She had grown perceptibly more frail since the war began, following the news avidly, mourning the loss of life.

'We all thought the Great War would end war for ever. We were so wrong.' She climbed into bed and Sid handed her her glass of milk and whisky, without which she couldn't sleep. Sid and Brindle had concealed some bottles for her sole use.

'No telling how long this'll go on,' Brindle had said. 'We'll look after her upstairs as long as we can, won't we, Sid?'

Chapter Twelve

Tom was due to rejoin his regiment. His presence disturbed Sid, and she had decided she'd be glad when he left. Not that she wanted him to go into danger. The idea made her heart beat faster, but she needed more time to give to Amy. Often when she was at work in the noisy factory, the machines by which she was surrounded as they stamped and clattered and whirled so dangerously unnerved her, setting her worrying about her child. She imagined her wandering round the garden in Greystone House, or in the kitchen, perhaps not properly supervised: the horror of possible accidents would blot out everything. She wished that Angie was still with them. There were other women working on the factory floor who had left younger children with friends or parents. War was a spartan time, a time when food and fuel were in short supply, when living standards which had long been taken for granted must give way to the necessities of combat. That was accepted. What was more significant were the compromises which had to be made. Conventions which had ruled strictly for years were thrown out. Women were being encouraged to leave their homes to work in factories, on buses and trams, to join the military services. Many men failed to accept this drastic alteration in their ordered lives, and some of Sid's workmates grumbled, sometimes humorously, sometimes resentfully, about the lack of co-operation from their husbands.

'Tells me to get his tea when I come home more tired than him,' said a young woman. 'Cheek!'

The answers were varied. 'Tell him to get his own.' 'Tell him to get yours as well!' 'Ask him for money for fish and chips.' Some of the suggestions were more than vulgar and made the women laugh, including Sid who had never before heard vulgar jokes.

She had enjoyed Tom's company more than she realised, and now she missed him badly. Then she got news through a brother officer that his wound had broken open and he was quite ill. He had wanted Miss Penrose to know and asked if she would write to him.

Sid complied and received a few shaky words in return. She wrote twice more, just giving him day-to-day news and sounding as cheerful as possible, and after two weeks he turned up looking pale but well.

When he entered the kitchen, Sid was cooking. 'Tom! I'm so glad to see you! Are you really recovered?' Her relief gave her voice such a glad ring that he stared at her, then came nearer. 'Watch out!' she said. 'You don't want your uniform splattered by soup.'

'It would be worth it to be close to you.'

His fervent response startled her. She shrank from intimacy with him, with any man. 'Go and sit down,' she said. 'I'll be with you as soon as I can leave this.'

'Will I get some? It smells good.'

'That depends. If you are staying you will eat it at dinner. Lunches are very simple nowadays. Mostly one course, though I do what I can to satisfy Mrs Cardell's sweet tooth. You could walk round the garden while you wait: you look as if you could do with some fresh air. The flower-beds are full of vegetables now. Brindle and Keith are doing a fine job.'

'I prefer to look at you.'

She didn't answer and, after a moment, he seated himself at the kitchen table.

The soup came to the boil and she left it simmering. 'Would you like some refreshment? Tea? Or coffee? Or even a whisky?'

He laughed. 'Coffee will be fine.'

She made two cups and sat down opposite him. 'How are you? What exactly happened? You still don't look completely well. Is your arm all right now?'

He was pleased by her concern. 'I feel a great deal better. My wound is clear now as far as the medics can tell. I've been granted another two weeks' convalescence, then I go before a medical board to see if I'm fit for duty.'

'Perhaps you'll be given a job at home.'

'I hope not!'

'Why? That's crazy. Surely you don't like fighting. I mean, a soldier has to kill. How can you want to go back?'

'It isn't a matter of killing. Few men enjoy that, but I have to go back. I can't let them down.'

'Who? The men at the top. The ones in charge who stay in safe places and order others to face the enemy?'

'Someone has to work out the overall strategy.' He paused. 'We left men in France. Some were my friends.'

Tom sipped his coffee in silence as his mind ranged over his experiences at Dunkirk. He thought of all the ones left behind, some dying, some to be prisoners of war, so many dead already.

Sid, too, fell silent before the sudden anguish in his face, then put out her hand to him, knowing that he needed comfort. He met it with his and their fingers remained clasped for several seconds.

'It sounds as if someone was neglectful towards you,' said Sid. 'A wound ought to heal if it's been properly treated.'

'It wasn't the medics' fault. It seems the infection wasn't quite contained at first. We had to wait for rescue and proper attention. Remember we spoke of Roy Hendy. He was the one who tied my shoulder with his handkerchief.'

'Well, he didn't do you any favours!' said Sid indignantly.

'He helped save my life.' Again there was something in his expression, something in his tone which precluded further questions. 'They think they've got rid of the infection completely this time. I'm lucky not to have gas gangrene. Some of the chaps did.'

'But how? That happened in the last war, but I've read that the Army Medical Corps is much better equipped this time and know more.'

'They do and it is usually. Those chaps were marvellous. All the chaps were marvellous.' The memory of the terrified boy crouching in the cellar came to plague him as it did so often. He reproached himself. He should have done something, knocked him out perhaps, helped carry him to the beach, not leave him there perhaps to die alone. He wondered if the sergeant was feeling the same way. He was an older man and had seen action before. It had been his decision to leave the boy, but Tom could have countermanded it. He had been the senior man.

'Have you missed me?' he asked.

'I did. I'd got used to our talks. Amy did, too. She is fond of you. Poor little girl, it must seem to her as if all the people she likes best are leaving her. I hope it won't affect her. She has so much love to give and is so generous with it.'

'You really care about her, don't you?'

Sid, lost in her thoughts of Amy, was so startled she almost blurted out the truth. She wanted to tell it. She ached to say, I'm her mother. Of course I care. 'Do you feel like walking in the garden with me?' she asked 'I've a little time to spare.'

'I'd love to. Where's Amy?'

'Having a nap. She'll be delighted to see you again.'

They wandered down the garden path. 'Are you delighted?' he ventured.

'To see you? I'm pleased you are well again,' she said primly.

'Is that all?'

She took a pair of scissors from her apron pocket and cut a few Michaelmas-daisies. 'Brindle allows us a few flowers here and there. Aren't they lovely? Such a delicate shade of mauve, they've always been one of my favourites.'

'Lovely,' he agreed. 'Sid, I'll be leaving Bristol again quite soon.'

She straightened up and said almost angrily, 'You're so eager to get back to the fighting, aren't you?'

The bitterness in her tone had more to do with the degradation she had suffered from Philip Prosser, more to do with her agonising frustration where Amy was concerned, than the war. She didn't want Tom to go and hated herself for her weakness.

'Someone has to go. We can hardly let the women do everything.'

'Sorry. I get rattled at times.'

'We all do. Would you really rather I didn't have to fight again?' She said nothing and he asked. 'Why?'

She bent once more to the flowers. 'I wish none of you had to fight. I can only wait and hope that my friends will come back. Roy Hendy was building a good business when he joined up. I hope it lasts the war out. We get the two old men he engaged to clean our windows now.' She laughed. 'I can't bear to watch. They're quite shaky, even before they climb the ladders, and I've forbidden them to go on the roof. The skylights can get dirty. It'll help with the black-out. And what have I got to grumble about? Many civilians are having a much worse time. Some are getting bombed.'

'It's awful,' agreed Tom, 'but it isn't anything like as bad as we expected. May I take you out tonight?'

She straightened up and stared at him. 'What?'

'I asked if you would give me the pleasure of taking you out. I thought we might go dancing. Or just dinner, if you prefer.'

'Why me? Why not one of your regular girlfriends? You must have plenty in Bristol.'

His gaze lingered on her face. 'My God, but some man has a lot to answer for.'

'What do you mean?' Sid was furious. How dare he speculate about her life?

'Someone has deceived you, hurt you. You don't trust any man, do you?'

She marched off down the garden path, her back stiff with indignation.

He soon caught up with her and held her arm. 'Please, Sid, I'm sorry if I spoke out of turn. I really would like to take you out. I'm sure you must enjoy dancing.'

'Oh, are you?'

'Yes. You've got just the figure for it. Slim and graceful.'

Was he serious? Slim and graceful? She was skinny and awkward. Dad had said so, and Philip Prosser's treatment of her had confirmed her lack of beauty. But Tom looked serious.

'I would like to dance,' she said tentatively.

'So you'll come?'

She thought of an evening away from work and worry. 'Yes, I think I will.'

'Jolly good show! Can you be ready soon after dinner?'

'I'll do my best. Amy has to be settled first, and there'll be the dinner dishes to see to.'

'Hang the dishes for one night. Do them in the morning.'

'In the morning I have a job to go to.'

'Oh, yes, I forgot.'

'I'll make an exception and get up earlier.'

'Just for me?'

She gave him a straight look. 'Just for you. As a friend.'

When Sid told Mrs Cardell about the invitation she said, 'You'll enjoy that. I know his family. Decent people. Father a retired colonel, his mother came from an Army background too. Tom was the last of their children, born late to them. I fear they all spoilt him. He disappointed them, but his enforced stint as a chauffeur seems to have sobered him. Then there's the war. I think he has reformed. I'm sure he can be trusted.'

Sid's lack of belief in herself was never far from the surface, and Mrs Cardell's words seemed to imply doubt of her good sense. Anger rose in her like gall. 'I'll be careful,' she said acerbically.

Mrs Cardell called her back from the door. 'Sidonia, forgive me. I know you are not a fool. I care about you – so much. A member of my own family has been so wicked towards you. I can never forget it. I want you to be safe.'

Sid returned and impulsively kissed her employer. 'I know. It's true I don't really understand him. He must know many girls of his own sort.'

'He's asked you out, Sidonia. Not all men are like Philip, thank God. What will you wear?'

Sid smiled. War or no war, Mrs Cardell – along with millions of other women – still cared for appearance.

'I bought a rayon marocain frock in dark red. It cost twelve-and-six and isn't at all practical, but the sales-lady said the colour suited me, and I wanted something pretty.'

'Dark red? Ideal. And I have just the accessories to go with it. Look in the big drawer at the base of my wardrobe. There's a stole there wrapped in tissue paper.'

Sid lifted the parcel and the paper drifted away in a scent of lavender, revealing a beautiful, fine wool stole embroidered with a great golden dragon. 'It's gorgeous! Are you sure? What if I should damage it?'

'You won't, but even if you did, it wouldn't matter. In fact, you may keep it. Now, what about jewellery?'

'I don't need any. Are you sure about the stole?'

'Absolutely. There is a pearl necklace in my lacquered box. I last wore it in the 1920s and it's long enough to go three times round your neck.'

'I can't borrow pearls!'

'They are not valuable. The fashion in those days was for costume jewellery, and now I remember there's a matching hair ornament. And take a pair of my white kid gloves. Fortunately we both have long fingers. Oh, yes, and you'll need a small handbag. There's a gold one in the next drawer up from the gloves. What a pity I take a different size in shoes. Now go and get ready and let me see you all dressed up.'

It seemed as if Amy would never sleep, as if she sensed the mounting excitement in her mother at the idea of going to a dance in such a resplendent outfit. Sid read story after story to her, but Amy's eyes remained firmly open. In fact, Sid had begun to yawn before Amy gave way, but she finally slept. Sid bent and kissed her face and Amy murmured in her sleep and turned on her side.

Sid raced to the nursery and washed, dried and brushed her hair until it gleamed. She twisted a few curls to the top of her head and pinned them in the new fashion, while the back tresses descended into a shining pageboy. The hair ornament which was a slide in the form of a draped nude woman nestled becomingly among the curls. When she looked into the cheval glass at the overall effect, she was astonished. The dark red dress, the pearls and the stole flung about her shoulders gave her an exotic appearance, and her eyes shone bright with anticipation. Her shoes weren't exactly right. She possessed two pairs only, one of sturdy black leather for work and one black patent for best, but with the black stole they were acceptable.

Mrs Cardell was delighted. 'Oh, my dear, you look lovely, simply lovely.' And for the first time in her life Sid *felt* lovely.

Sid was gratified to see that Tom was impressed though wary. She wondered if Mrs Cardell had given him a warning word or two, knowing that Sid could be edgy. 'You look charming, Sidonia,' he said. 'Absolutely top-hole.'

He had been home and collected a car, a vehicle almost as big as the Prossers' Rolls.

'Goodness, is that yours?'

'My father's. He allowed me to borrow it, bless his cotton socks, and it's filled with his precious petrol, too. He's a good sort, is Father. I'm sure you'd like him.'

'If he's anything like you I'm sure I would,' agreed Sid, convinced that the retired Colonel Barton and the munitions-worker-cum-housekeeper would never meet.

Sid had expected to be taken to The Glen on Blackboy Hill, a place her sisters visited, or somewhere similar. Instead, Tom drove out of town and turned into a driveway as long as the one at Greystone House, pulling up in front of a large building from which came the sound of music. Because of the black-out there wasn't a light to be seen.

'Where are we?'

'A friend's,' said Tom laconically.

A torch was flashed briefly on him. 'Mr Barton, sorry, sir, I should say Lieutenant Barton. Parking is in the stable-yard. There's a carpet laid out there so the ladies won't slip on the cobbles, but if madam would like I'll escort her to the door. Or I can park for you.'

Tom turned inquiringly to Sid, who had no intention of entering this large, strange house without support.

'Come on, Sidonia, let's kick up our heels.'

Sid stayed where she was.

'What's the matter? You do want to dance, don't you?'

'Of course,' she said. She had never had a lesson in her life, but having watched so many stars in films and seen her sisters practising, she was sure she could.

'Then come along. Take my hand.'

Sid decided to permit herself to be cherished for once. It was heavenly to be with a man who treated her so well. Tom took her gloved hand in his and helped her from the car, which was driven away to be parked. She was exceedingly nervous, but held her head up to prove that she wasn't. It required an effort to keep up the pretence when they were admitted to a large hall, then into a ballroom, where dozens of couples were dancing to the strains of a professional band. Their name was stencilled on the big drum.

'Josh Raven and his Melody Men,' she said, forgetting her nervousness. 'Gosh! They play on the wireless. Do you think their singers will be with them? The Kissing Cousins? Do you know of them?'

'I certainly do. Great girls, both of them. Their men are serving abroad. Tessa is married to a chap called Charles Ware, and Eve recently got engaged to a man called David Selby. They are members of ENSA. The band, too, of course. They go anywhere where people need cheering up. Eve and Tessa could even be sent abroad. They've both got tremendous courage and resilience.'

'How do you know so much?'

'Eve Brook is a distant cousin of mine. Not a kissing one, though.'

She laughed, letting go the weight of her melancholy. Tomorrow she would assume it again as she faced the daily strain of work and anxiety over Amy, but tonight she would be happy. Her heart missed a beat when she saw women wearing long gowns, but to her relief there were also girls in short skirts, and even a few in uniform, as were most of the men.

'Come along. darling,' said Tom, 'and I'll introduce you to our host and hostess.'

His endearment alarmed her, yet also gave her a small thrill of pleasure, until she realised that in this company everyone spoke to friends in the most intimate terms. She was introduced to a lady in black velvet, and a man resplendent in a red dress-uniform from another war. She said a murmured word of greeting to them before Tom swept her away into a waltz, a step which was easy to follow.

'Who are they? she asked. 'I didn't catch their names.'

'Sir Greville Mowbray and his wife. They have four sons. Or they had. Now they have only two. The eldest was killed in Belgium, the youngest died of his wounds after Dunkirk. The others are serving abroad and their daughter is in the WAAF.'

'How can they bear to watch us dance? There are so many officers here. They must be reminded of their sons.'

'They've got guts,' said Tom.

'But to lose two of their children! It's too cruel . . . This war . . .'

'I know. It's brutal, but we all have to do the best we can and live for the moment.'

Arguments rose to her tongue, but she bit them back and gradually lost herself in the beauty of the room, the scent of flowers, the atmosphere of gaiety, this brief respite. She sat out with Tom and they drank clear, golden wine.

'Glad you came?' he asked.

'Oh, I am. I've never been to such a place as this. Never thought I would. It's so beautiful. And bigger than Greystone House.'

Tom laughed.

'Do you think I'm naïve?'

'A little. I like it. In fact, I like you any way you want to be.' He sat silently for a while, then said, 'At Dunkirk I doubted that Britain would come through this war, but with people like Sir Greville and his wife, I know we will. In fact, nowadays, there's a marvellous spirit permeating everything and everyone.' He laughed ruefully. 'Lord, I sound like a propaganda film.'

Sid laughed with him. 'Why not? British and proud of it, say I.'

Everyone seemed to know Tom. He knew everyone too, and introduced her to as many as possible. The woman looked her up and down; Sid was sure some of them counted accurately the cost of everything she wore. It didn't matter. It was the men who surprised her. They viewed her with a gleam which made her feel a desirable, attractive woman. It was heady. Tomorrow . . . But she wouldn't think of tomorrow. She and Tom sat with others and she listened to their chatter, dreamily, as if she was on some exalted plane. It was all so unbelievably splendid after the years of self-denial and hard work.

After supper, Josh Raven, a handsome American who had made his home in Britain and preferred to stick with her through the war, announced his singers. 'My lords, ladies and gentlemen, my singers are here. I know you will forgive them for their late arrival, but they have been visiting hospitals and convalescent homes, entertaining the wounded. They reckon they were needed more by them than by you guys and gals.'

'Hurrah!' 'Jolly good show!' 'Wizard!' The cries came from all sides.

The singers walked on stage to frantic applause, and Sid stared at them, mesmerised by their beauty and polished charm, by their long, lovely gowns which clung to their graceful figures, and their shining hair. Eve was the more conventionally beautiful, but there was something special about Tessa. It was generally agreed that she was the better singer. Not that it mattered. People thought of them as a duo and loved them that way.

Eve stepped to the microphone. 'Good evening.'

'Good evening,' came a chorus from the dance floor.

'Tessa and I will sing a medley of favourites. Please feel free to join in if you wish.'

There was further applause, which died away as the two girls began their songs. They had chosen cheerful ones. 'Blue Skies Are Just Around the Corner', 'I've Got a Pocketful of Dreams', 'It's a Hap-Hap-Happy Day', and the dancers sang, too. The band then swung into 'In the Mood' and 'Moonlight Serenade', and Eve and Tessa were beseiged by would-be partners.

Later, after requests, the girls sang, 'We'll Meet Again', the extra-special song which Vera Lynn had made her own. Some people were in tears, some smiling as if they hadn't a single care. The whole evening became for Sid one long, deliriously happy respite, and she couldn't believe it was ending when the last waltz was announced.

'Who's taking you home tonight? After the dance is through?' warbled Tom to her in a nice tenor. 'Who's going to hold you tight?' His arms tightened round her. 'And it had better be me.'

'That last line isn't in the song,' she protested.

'I know. I just put it there.'

'I hate to stop. What time is it?'

'Oh, quite early.'

'Tell me.'

'Two o'clock.'

'What? I'll get no sleep at all. And I've the dishes to wash.'

'Oh, how prosaic! How can you ruin these magic moments?'

'Idiot.' But she melted once more into his arms, until the dance ended and the band and singers wished them goodnight.

'They used to play all night,' said Tom, 'but they work so hard during the day they need more sleep. Not that they'll get much tonight.'

'Some of them seem quite old to be dance-band players,' said Sid, then wished she hadn't. She knew nothing about dance bands.

But Tom said seriously. 'They are getting on a bit, because one by one the young men have been called up. The pianist is a chap called Sammy Jacobs. He used to be a regular, but he retired. Now he helps out when they need him.'

Sid was sorry to see the band leave. This evening was an enchantment out of context, a break in the difficulties of her life. 'I suppose the Mowbrays want everyone to go now?'

'Oh, no. If anyone prefers to go on dancing they'll play gramophone records.'

'Where are they?'

'The records?'

'No, the Mowbrays.'

'Tucked up in bed I should imagine.'

'Fancy the host and hostess leaving their guests.'

'They know at least half of the guests personally. No one expects them to sit up all night.'

'Do all the guests live in Bristol?'

'Some of them. Others are stationed nearby. The Mowbrays are doing their bit for the war, just like you and Mrs Cardell at Greystone House.'

That jolted Sid. What if Amy had awakened and wanted her? Keith was sleeping in the nursery suite for tonight, but she might be ill. Anything could happen, and he was only young and a boy at that. How could she have forgotten her child?

'What's up? You look positively haunted.'

'Sorry. I must go home now.'

'Oh, must you?'

A girl in Air-force blue had put on a record and a voice crooned, 'When they begin the Beguine . . .'

'Listen to that. a South American number.'

'I must go.'

'I suppose you're worrying about the child. I don't see why you should. She's bound to be all right. There are plenty to look after her.'

'I said I wish to go home! Keith does his best, but . . .'

'All right, I'll take you home.'

The atmosphere between them had altered abruptly from one of serene contentment to an uncomfortable prickliness.

In the hall Tom called a maid to fetch her stole, and soon Sid was in the car being driven through the blacked-out streets, slowly, and as safely as the permissible, narrow slits from the mainly blacked-out headlights would allow.

When they arrived at the front door of Greystone House, Tom said, 'Sorry, Sidonia. You are right and I'm wrong. You owe a duty to those you care for.'

She was so relieved she turned to him saying eagerly, 'I'm glad you understand. You're such a nice man.'

He leaned towards her and his lips touched hers. For an instant she let them linger, enjoying the sensation, then she drew back. 'Goodnight. Thank you for a lovely evening.'

She went straight to Amy's room. She was sound asleep, one hand up to her rosy face. Sid bent and kissed her, aching to pick her up and hug her. My child, she thought, leaning over the bed. Mine. I'll never let you down, my darling.

There had been a few minor air-raids and, although the Bristol people were sympathetic towards the handful of people who had died in them, they had begun to look upon the wail of the warning sirens as an interlude from work as they sat in the shelters. Then, on 25 September, the Germans launched a large-scale, unopposed daylight raid on the Bristol Aeroplane Company at Filton, and the shock sent waves of horror through the West Country. The facts and figures soon became known in spite of the authorities' endeavours to cover them up to avoid spreading alarm. However, it proved impossible to hide something that so many had witnessed, and horror stories filtered out to the general public. Fifty-eight bombers escorted by forty fighters had dropped three hundred and fifty bombs, severely damaging the works and nine hundred surrounding houses. Seventy-two civilians had been killed and one hundred and fifty-four injured, some severely. Eleven soldiers marching past the factory had also died. When it was clear that peoples' homes had been destroyed and civilians killed and injured, the war became close and deadly. If the Germans could so easily mount a raid in broad daylight, what might they do next?

'Not a single one of our planes were there,' rasped Brindle, his face almost purple with fury.

'You can't blame the pilots,' pointed out Keith. 'They have to obey orders.'

'I'm not blaming them! It's them at the top I hold responsible. What do they think they're playing at?'

'It's no game,' said Keith bitterly. 'Even a rejected man knows that. I could have shot down Jerry planes if they'd let me.'

'I know you could,' said Brindle indignantly, at one with his junior in this. 'but do *they*?'

They evidently did, because when Filton was again bombed two days later, the Germans were met by Royal Air Force Hurricanes.

But nothing could alter the fact that Bristol was easily reached by determined men in planes, and nerves were stretched as the people waited.

German losses were high in their daytime raids, and they were abandoned, but people watched fearfully as the blitzkrieg began in London, and tons of high explosives were dropped. Then it was

Coventry's turn, followed by Southampton and Birmingham.

As September passed into November and nothing happened, Bristolians began to feel optimistic. Maybe the bombing of Filton had satisfied the enemy.

Brindle said, 'Bristol's a port. The Jerries are bound to come back here.'

'He was always a pessimist,' said Mrs Cardell hopefully.

Susan Morland had agreed to work on Sunday and stay overnight in the flat in Park Street with Mrs Endicott, her employer. Miss Benson, the alteration-hand, had retired, her sight impaired after so many years of close sewing. Susan and Mrs Endicott now coped with alterations as well as selling.

Her parents disapproved of Sunday working, but Mrs Morland had sighed, 'I know things are different now there's a war on. Everyone has to do their bit, and the factories are going seven days a week, twenty-four hours a day. Well, I reckon we had to go to war for people like Sammy and his family, and there's our Tessa and Eve singing practically all the hours God sends, and Joseph and Susan learning how to make people well, and him doing his best to make folk see the light of God, and the Jerries won't care what day it is, they're so wicked.'

Her husband smiled affectionately at this rather garbled speech. He hadn't been able to cope with a full-time job since a car accident in the black-out. This, coupled with repeated chest infections caused by the manual labour he had been forced to undertake during the slump when his carpentry had not been wanted, had affected his health. He hated idleness, so he had joined a Rescue and Demolition Squad as soon as possible.

The Morlands liked Sammy. A Jew, he had lost relatives in Germany, and he and his wife were caring for a refugee cousin and her children as best they could in a small house in Manchester. Joseph Morland, the evangelist son, had failed utterly to convert Sammy to Christianity, and even Mrs Morland was glad when he gave up trying, though she would have died rather than admit it. Joseph was an excellent son, and she and Dad approved wholeheartedly of his militant Christianity, but he was uncomfortable to live with sometimes.

Susan and Mrs Endicott had not had time to unpack a delivery of clothes during the week; now they worked together, smoothing out the dresses and blouses and hanging them on rails, not saying much, comfortable in their relationship.

When the siren sounded at twenty-two minutes past six, they looked at one another.

'I suppose we should go to the shelter,' said Mrs Endicott.

'I suppose so.'

'It seems a pointless waste of time. Not many people bother any more. By the time we get there they'll probably have sounded the all-clear.'

'That's true, and we've nearly finished.' Susan stroked the skirts of a pale blue taffeta evening gown. It had short sleeves, a low V-neckline, and one burgundy velvet motif, an elongated scroll appliqued on to the wide skirt from waist to hem. She had tried it on and loved it, wishing she could afford to buy it. She earned good money now, but took much of it home where it was needed.

She was a member of the Civil Nursing Reserve, and had hoped to be sent abroad, but found herself instead working in Bristol where, as yet, the only calls for her services had been for black-out mishaps and a couple of times to men in over-excited football crowds.

'It's not that I want people to be hurt,' she explained to her family, 'but I would like to do more to help the war effort.'

Mrs Morland smiled encouragingly. 'Of course you would and I'm sure you will,' while she sent up a silent prayer that her daughter would never have to go into danger.

Joseph had asked for non-combatant duties and was serving in a medical corps. He might be posted anywhere, and so, in fact, might Tessa and Eve. War cut through everything; all the hopeful, carefully made plans were wiped out as if they had never existed.

Susan placed the lovely blue gown in the window, where it dominated a tasteful display of a lacy matching snood for the hair, a wide blue chiffon scarf and white kid gloves.

She was checking that the window was sufficiently dressed to attract buyers next day when the sky lit up. She peered upwards through the window, then she and Mrs Endicott went outside. Flares were falling from planes, shedding a brilliance like the blinding silver of fireworks over the city, turning the dark November evening into day. A second wave of planes arrived; this time they dropped incendiaries, and the bells of fire-engines resounded through the night air.

'They've come at last,' gasped Mrs Endicott. 'There are fires everywhere. How will the fire-fighters manage so much?'

Susan ran to check that the buckets of sand and water were ready if needed. The sky grew even brighter as the incendiaries performed their blazing task. More planes came, big heavy engines filled the sky with their throbbing; then came the ultimate horror as they dropped high explosives into the fires, turning them into an inferno.

'It *is* Bristol's turn,' said Mrs Endicott shakily. 'They're after us now. Come on! To the shelter!'

'But I'm supposed to help with first aid!'

Mrs Endicott seized her hand and dragged her along. 'Not now. You can't do anything yet. No one can. Afterwards.'

They grabbed their coats and dashed through to the back to their concrete shelter, which Mrs Endicott had had built into the earth.

The first wave of bombers was followed by others. The town was lit up and wide open to attack.

Susan was sitting in a bottom bunk with her employer opposite. Even had they wished to talk, it would have been impossible to have a normal conversation in the fearful noise of bombs screaming down in a horrific, destructive rain. Crouching below ground level, Susan was sure she felt the impact of every bomb which landed in the city that night. She was frightened and tried to pray for deliverance, but she couldn't remember any of her childhood prayers. How silly, she thought. All my life I've been a member of the chapel and I can't think of a single prayer. She just said, 'Please, God,' over and over in a desperate, silent refrain.

Several times smoke filled the shelter, once thickly, making them cough, bringing streaming tears to their eyes. 'Should we get out?' cried Mrs Endicott shakily.

'Where could we go? They sound as if they're right over us.'

Mrs Endicott stretched out her hand and found Susan's and clung to it.

The barrage of noise seemed endless, as stick after stick of bombs shrieked their way to deliver destruction and death. Then the shelter vibrated and moved, as if the ground beneath had shifted. Dust enveloped them.

'Where did that one land?' Mrs Endicott choked.

'Very near,' gasped Susan.

Sid watched the night sky over Bristol as it turned from black to scarlet. It was Bristol's turn at last. She raced to the nursery and picked Amy up, wrapped her in a blanket and hurried downstairs. Keith and Brindle were in the garden.

'Get to the shelter,' said Sid. 'Here, Brindle, take Amy. Keith go and get Patrick, I'll see to Mrs Cardell.'

Brindle seized the child, who had only just gone to sleep. At first she had been excited by the sudden awakening, the race into the garden and all the pretty lights in the sky, but when Aunty Sid handed her over to Brindle so roughly, she protested and began to struggle.

She wasn't very heavy, but Brindle had difficulty in holding her. 'Keep still. You're like an eel,' he said as he carried her to the air-raid shelter.

'Want Aunty Sid,' she shrieked.

'She'll be along soon.' He was breathless as he negotiated the steps leading down, and was glad to sit with Amy on his knee. At least, that was his intention. She jumped down and made a dash for the entrance.

'Come back!' Brindle grabbed her ankles as she was climbing the steps.

'Let me go!' she screamed. She kicked out and one of her feet hit him in the eye.

Half blinded, his eye paining him, Brindle smacked the backs of her legs.

She screamed even louder. 'Nasty man! Nasty old Brindle! You hit me! You did! You hit me!'

'And I'll do it again if you don't shut up,' he growled in her ear.

Astonishment quietened her, and she sat on the plank bench beside Brindle, swinging her legs defiantly, occasionally glancing up at him.

Keith arrived with Patrick who was arguing. 'We got to get our things and go to Home Guard. That's what we have to do. When the enemy comes we got to be ready. They've come.'

'They're attacking from the sky,' yelled Keith. 'Silly fool,' he added beneath his breath.

Brindle lit a candle, and Sid appeared with Mrs Cardell, who was behaving in as dignified a fashion as if she were about to enter a drawing room.

'Good evening. Are we all here? Good, I trust you are wearing warm clothing. We have been warned to keep some ready.' She was in her fur coat, and Sid wrapped a blanket round her legs. On her feet was a pair of stout boots, and she cuddled her hot-water bottle.

As soon as Amy saw Sid she began wailing. 'Nasty old Brindle smacked me. He did, Aunty Sid, he smacked me right on my legs and it *hurt*.'

Sid took her on her knee and began to thrust Amy's arms into the warm jumper she had brought, following it with leggings and a hat.

'I'm sure he didn't,' she said. 'Now, come along, Amy, put your feet into your shoes.'

'Why? It's bedtime. You said so. I was in *bed*.'

'Stop wriggling, please.'

Amy hated everyone. Even Aunty Sid who was never cross was being nasty. 'I don't like you,' she cried. 'You're all horrid.'

'Do you want to go back to bed?' asked Sid.

'Yes. No. What's all that noise and why are there fireworks?'

'They're to make everything bright,' said Mrs Cardell calmly. 'Now, Amy, do as Aunty Sid tells you.'

The child went quiet at last, and they sat by the light of a candle, the entrance to the shelter protected by a concrete wall and sacking to conceal the candle-flame, though it could scarcely matter tonight. They had practised air-raid drill faithfully, as ordered by the government, but practice was very different from the real thing.

'They seem to be over the middle of the city,' said Mrs Cardell.

'Let's hope they don't shift this way,' muttered Brindle.

'Don't spread gloom and despondency,' reminded Keith.

Brindle glared at him. 'I know what to do better than you, thank you. I remember the last lot.'

'You must have been an old man, even in those days,' jeered Keith who, Sid suspected, was glad that the enemy had brought the war close enough for him to see it.

'Not so much of your cheek!' growled Brindle. 'I wasn't all that young, I grant you, but I was a sergeant and used to respect.'

Sid said quietly, 'Keith, I should start thinking about what's going to happen next. The Home Guard may be called out. Hitler might have plans to invade.'

'I do hope not,' said Mrs Cardell. Her voice was a trifle quavery. 'But we shall have to obey Mr Churchill and fight them wherever they appear.' Sid could at that moment quite easily picture her holding a gun.

Tessa Ware and Eve Morland had been out of town with Josh and the Melody Men giving a show to hundreds of soldiers in a barracks hastily organised after Dunkirk. The band was always in demand. At first Tessa had felt she was useless in a war where everyone seemed to have a vital task; now she believed her husband's prophecy that entertainment would be of immense value. The men, many of them depressed by their defeat, saddened by the death of their friends, worried about the terrible loss of weapons left behind in France and the final possibility that Britain could soon be invaded, lost their strained looks when the music began. They were especially cheered when two extremely attractive women appeared, gowned as if for a pre-war dance, singing as many songs as were demanded: the Kissing Cousins realised then that their wartime contribution was vital to morale.

The train back to their Bristol base had barely arrived when the bombing began. It was not their baptism of fire. That had happened in London on their way through after giving another show, but every raid was fearful, and to the girls at attack on Bristol was an attack on the people they loved best.

'Do you think we'll get home tonight?' asked Eve. Home for her was Cousin Tessa's family and the little cottage near Kingswood. Her father had died horribly by his own hand, her mother was in America, imprisoned in her self-erected barrier of grief. The Morlands gave Eve all the love her starved heart needed.

Except of course the love of a man. That came from David Selby. He was somewhere at sea on escort duty in a warship, trying to protect the men who did their utmost to bring essential supplies to Britain. The merchant seamen were performing one of the most dangerous jobs in the war, and all the splendid efforts of the Navy couldn't give them as much help as they needed. Hitler's deadly U-boats – submarines which moved silently below the surface of the water like hunting sharks, striking without warning – were taking a terrible toll on shipping and lives.

'We must go to the nearest shelter,' said Tessa. 'That's what we've been told.'

'I know. I just wish we were at home. I hate the bombing so much.' Eve's teeth were chattering. She tried to stop them. In fact, it wasn't so much the fear of bombs which undermined her courage, but the actual terror of not becoming David's wife one day, of not having his arms around her while he told her in person how much he loved her. They had said goodbye after a stormy relationship, with tentative verbal pledges of love. Since then he had written to ask her to marry him, his letters growing more passionate with love and longing. Eve too was now free to pour out her emotions on to paper. Sometimes, she thought with a wry grin, calming down as memories of David gave her strength, it was a wonder the paper didn't catch fire.

Chapter Thirteen

When the all-clear sounded shortly after midnight, Sid and the others climbed stiffly out of the shelter to find the sky over the centre of Bristol had become a brilliant crimson. The sounds of bells from ambulances and fire-engines hurrying from the suburbs to assist echoed through the cold November air.

'What have they done?' breathed Sid. 'It looks as if the whole town is on fire.'

They stood watching for a while as the redness flared sometimes into pillars of sparks. They could smell the smoke that drifted in a pall over the horrified citizens.

Mrs Cardell was the first to turn away, with a groan. 'Our beautiful city,' she mourned. 'The poor people. Take the child indoors, Sidonia. We'll follow.'

In spite of her determination to remain awake and enjoy this novel way of spending the night, Amy had fallen asleep. Sid heard her murmur softly as she carried her into the house and back to bed, where she settled her carefully, still wrapped in a blanket. Then Sid hurried back to attend to Mrs Cardell. Keith and Brindle had taken an arm each and helped her to the kitchen, where she had seated herself beside them near the range. Keith had poked the fire into activity; the warm glow eased the cold and cramp in her elderly body.

'How did the range last this long?' she wondered. 'We've been in the shelter for hours.'

Keith said proudly, 'I made it up before I ran for cover.'

'Well done,' said Brindle unexpectedly. He was never quick to bestow praise, and Keith coloured. Since Brindle had been given the rank of sergeant in their unit of the Home Guard, Keith had regarded the old man with new respect. Brindle didn't need to be told what to do. He ordered others about in a voice which Keith had never heard him use before.

Sid made hot drinks for them.

'Come on, Keith,' said Brindle. 'It's time we were off.'

'Off?'

'To join our unit. We'll be needed.'

Keith's face lit up. 'I never thought of that.'

'You're a front-line soldier now. Get your cap and armband.'

So far, that was all the uniform Keith had been allotted. When the authorities had appealed for the elderly, the slightly infirm, the sedentary, those too young to join the forces, or any man who was prepared to defend his land against the enemy, they had expected perhaps one hundred and fifty thousand men. They had got one million seven hundred thousand and, feeling himself a part of such a large, determined army, Keith had regained his manly pride, so deeply dented since his rejection by the regular forces. The colossal numbers meant that there was a race to provide uniforms and arms and, for a while, some men carried gas-pipes fitted with bayonets. Gradually the strangely assorted men had resolved themselves into fighting units, and people who had laughed to see what appeared to be a raggedy collection of males who were supposed to hold back the invading German Army forces, now realised that there was a disciplined force which kept sentry duty on railways and roads, coastal defences and factories.

Susan Morland left the shelter with Mrs Endicott to find that a bomb had dropped just outside the shop. The walls were holed, the windows shattered, and glass pierced the displays. Up and down the street, shops were in ruins, fires raged, often unchecked, because the owners were at home and their sand and water and stirrup-pumps were unused.

'How can I leave you like this?' agonised Susan. 'Yet I can't stay to help.'

'Of course you can't. I'm not hurt. You must get to your post.'

'You'll be all right?'

'Certainly. No German bombs are going to bother me! '

Susan looked once more at what had been the neat little shop. Its interior was lit up clearly by the fires. The blue dress she had so coveted had been slashed to ribbons by shrapnel and glass. It seemed to typify the horror of the night. Park Street was a shambles, with shops destroyed or with fires raging out of control of wardens with stirrup-pumps. On her way to the First Aid Station, she passed what was left of Charles Ware's antique shop, which was burning fiercely. She wondered why the fire-engines were not in attendance. At the first-aid station she greeted the others quietly, changed quickly, and climbed into the driver's seat of her auxiliary ambulance. She and Sheila, her co-worker, drove through the burning streets, looking appalled down others where the flames had been whipped into a fire-storm and where firemen sweated and cursed. No wonder they had no chance to deal with lesser conflagrations. Susan drove on, staring in disbelief at the devastation that had been Bristol's city centre, she and Sheila going wherever they were sent. They picked up a young boy with a gaping chest wound. Little in their training had prepared them for such an injury, but they dressed it, reassured him, and took him to the Central Health Clinic where casualties were being dealt with. He was too ill and shocked to speak; and it would have to be left to others to discover what had happened to his family. The hours became a nightmare of bumping over fire-hoses which snaked their way towards the fires where men and women struggled against these fearful odds with equipment which was proving inadequate.

They picked up the severely injured and comforted the dying. They coped with weeping children who had lost their parents, parents who were frantic for their missing children, the shocked and the terrified. Wherever they went they tried to make a small corner of order amid the chaos. Hearing about the blitzkrieg, reading about it, seeing on the newsreels the bombs dropped in Spain had given no one any idea of the full horror.

Once Susan saw a team of men, grey with dust, digging in the ruins of a house. 'It's my Dad,' she cried, pulling the ambulance to a halt. She leapt out and ran to him, calling him.

He turned and saw her, 'Susan, my love,' he said. 'You doing your duty? That's a good girl. I expect our Joseph's somewhere around. They've called the Army in.' Then he went back to his task of showing the men how to shore up the rubble so that they could get at someone who was buried.

'He's not really all that strong,' said Susan to her companion, holding back tears. 'He had an accident...'

Tessa and Eve hurried home, getting lifts from passing drivers when they could, walking most of the way. Mum met them at the door, characteristically tutting at their filthy state as she served them tea. Neither girl ate anything, which brought more tutting.

'Sorry, Mum,' said Tessa. 'Where are the others?'

'Your Dad's out on his rescue work. He went as soon as the raid began. And I suppose our Susan's out there somewhere too, and Joseph I shouldn't wonder.' Her pride in her family was mingled with terror for their safety. 'All we can see from here is the red sky. There must be some dreadful fires.'

'There are,' said Tessa wearily. She felt helpless and useless again. Surely singing to people could never be as important as saving lives.

She had written these feelings to Charles; his reply had been characteristically clear. 'Darling, you must be saving people's sanity, which is as necessary as saving their lives.'

But she found it hard to accept her role when her mother said, 'It's my turn now. I've been down at the church and I've got to go back. I just wanted to see if any of you were home.' The crypt of a Church of England building was not a place she would normally have set foot in, she being a staunch chapel member, but that was where the Women's Voluntary Services met. 'We've been cutting sandwiches and stocked up our vans to take out refreshments,' said Mum. 'When you see the others you can tell them where I am.'

'Can't we help?' asked Tessa.

Mrs Morland smiled. 'God bless you, no, my love, you and Eve have done your work.'

'It seems too little,' said Eve. 'I don't feel useful.'

'God gave you girls a gift for a purpose, and you use it to His glory, saving His people,' said Mum before marching resolutely down the lane.

Eve looked at Tessa and laughed a little wryly. 'What a difference!

Remember how she thought we were sinful to sing in dance halls and theatres?'

'How could I forget? Come on, Eve, let's get some rest. They'll need us when they come home.'

Neither voiced the fear that one of their loved ones might not come home at all. They had scarcely slept, and now they waited with increasing anxiety. They fed the hens, the dog and the cat, prepared vegetables and made soup, cleaned the cottage, did the washing, and even checked the garden for weeds, though it was an unlikely occupation for November, Tessa admitted. First Susan, then Dad arrived. Both were exhausted, both grey with dust and fatigue. They didn't speak about their experiences, except to say things had been bad, but there was a haunted expression in Susan's eyes which hadn't been there before, and Dad had the same look on his face that he'd worn when Joseph used to question him about his experiences in the trenches in the 1914–1918 war. They swallowed the soup gratefully, but no one could rest while Mum was out. She came back during the afternoon, staggering with fatigue, as filthy as the others had been.

'We made five trips out,' she said. 'I wanted to let you know I was all right, but there didn't seem time. It was awful, but everyone was brave; they even made jokes. The firemen are black with soot and they look like they're ready to drop. What a wicked thing war is. I always knew it was, of course, but I'd never pictured anything like this.' She was voluble with nervous distress, and Eve and Tessa calmed her with hot tea and soup. They had pans of water boiling for washing, and Tessa helped her mother to bed.

Mrs Morland protested. 'They're still out there, the men and women. They still need food and drink.'

'Others can do it now,' said Tessa. 'It's your turn to rest.'

'She's right,' said Dad, climbing into bed beside her. 'Come on, my love, we're both safe, thank God.' He put his arm comfortingly over his wife.

Mrs Morland wasn't comforted. 'Our Joseph must still be out there somewhere.'

'He's a soldier. We've got to get used to that.'

'I never will,' said Mum.

In the morning, Joseph came home. He looked dazed, almost as if he didn't recognize them.

'Are the others safe?'

'All safe and home,' said Eve.

'Come to the fire,' said Tessa gently.

'Fire?' he said angrily. 'I've seen enough of fire. People burnt, buried, suffering. Why? I don't understand. I've prayed so hard. I never expected war to be like this. I never thought to see children in such a state. Nor women. Young girls dead or maimed. I helped nurse men home from Dunkirk, but they were men. Men expect to suffer in war. It's different. I can't think why it's allowed.'

'It's not our fault,' said Tessa. 'We had to fight. Such awful things are happening.'

Sid knew. Everyone in Greystone House knew. Brindle had told them several times as he stormed and ranted.

'You can't blame him,' said Sid when she told the women at work.

'No you bloody well can't,' cried one. 'My house was bombed and our old Gran wouldn't go to the shelter no matter what we said. She was killed in her bed.'

'It was terrible,' said her friend, a large woman, mother of six, four in the forces. 'Poor old soul. And the *Evening Post* printed just seven paragraphs. *Seven!* I ask you? "Casualties comparatively few", it said, and "the firemen brought the fires under control." '

'Like hell they did, poor sods,' said the first woman. 'It took ages. It was like an inferno with flames blowing from building to building.'

They expected more from *Movietone News* at the pictures, but no damage was shown. It depicted Bristol as it was before the raid. To increase their frustration, although the newspapers were censored, the British traitor, William Joyce, christened Lord Haw-Haw because of his fruity public school voice, who made regular broadcasts from Germany, told the world that Britain's factories were in ruins and her people defeated.

'Bloody liar,' was the general reaction, but it was depressing when he so often came very near the truth.

'Spies, that's what it is,' said Brindle. 'Spies sending messages. I hope they get the lot of them and hang them. They won't make us give in.'

Although the Germans had burned the heart out of Bristol, they hadn't torn the heart out of her people.

Sid went to visit her family before one of her late shifts. It was a Wednesday and she knew her aunts would be there. They visited on half-day closing nowadays, because on Saturdays they helped their husbands in the shops.

'You thought you'd come, then,' said Mum. 'For all you knew we could all have been dead and buried by now.'

'I assumed someone would tell me if that were so.'

'Hark at her!' Mrs Penrose turned to her sisters. 'She even talks like them now.'

'Is everyone all right?' asked Sid.

Aunty Maud said harshly, 'I suppose you mean after the raid. We had to sit in the shelters listening to the bombs coming down. Awful, it was.'

'Terrible,' agreed the others.

'I know,' said Sid mildly. 'I was only just down the road.'

'You'd think you could have bothered to visit your parents before now. You must have days off,' said Ella.

They were being deliberately provocative. They knew Sid was working full-time in a factory as well as running Greystone House, but she hung on to her temper. 'Hitler doesn't allow for much time off. I work seven days a week most weeks and there's lots to do at home. You'd be welcome any time you'd like to visit me. Just telephone first to find out if I'm there.'

'You're not the only one with too much work to do,' said Joan. 'All the young assistants have been called up, so we have to help in the shops – and that's not easy, I can tell you. And what with our house-work and cooking and rationing and people not believing you when you tell them there's nothing under the counter, it's getting very difficult.'

Sid's eyes strayed to the plate of ham sandwiches and her mother offered her one. She took it and bit into it. 'Delicious,' she said. 'Plenty of butter, too, and nice thick ham.'

Ella and Douglas, her husband, kept a grocer's shop, and Ella said, 'If you're hinting that your mum uses a lot of butter and ham considering the rations, why don't you come out and say it?'

'All right,' said Sid calmly, surprised to discover that her relatives had lost most of their biting power to hurt. 'She uses a lot of butter and ham.'

'I hope you agree that it's a duty to look after your family first.'

'It's natural,' said Sid, a pacific answer which yet somehow seemed to imply more criticism, and made her mother and aunts frown.

'Aren't you going to ask after Aunty Mattie and Grandma Lacey?' demanded Ella.

Sid knew that both were well, because she had passed the shop twice and seen them, though she hadn't had time to go in and talk to them. She had been to see Aunt Jess in her lunch-break and discovered that happily her gown shop had not been hit. She had met Susan Morland there again. Her employer's place in Park Street had been so badly damaged that it was no longer usable, and Mrs Endicott had gone to stay with a brother near Bath, while Susan had been taken on part-time by Aunt Jess. 'How are they?' she asked.

'As well as can be expected,' said Joan. 'Two lone women on their own in that terrible raid.'

'I'm sure they were very brave. I'm sure you all were.'

The aunts were nonplussed. They wanted to criticise Sid further, but her calm agreement defeated them.

'Where's Dad?' asked Sid, taking advantage of the momentary lull in the conversation.

'In the greenhouse,' said Mum. 'He's potting something.'

'Who's doing the cooking in Greystone House now you're at work all day?' asked Mum.

'The Misses Weekley still come in: the elder one's quite a good cook. I take over when I'm there.'

'You can't do much on one-and-tenpence-worth of meat each,' complained Bea. 'Rations! I bet those that fixed them eat out in hotels half the time.' The others chimed their agreement, discussing dishes which could be stretched by buying the cheaper joints.

'Of course, everyone's after the cheap cuts,' said Ella. 'You have to start queuing early to get what you want. And as for liver and kidneys and the rest of the stuff off-ration, you'd think that animals were born without any nowadays. I suppose the butchers keep it for their families, and what's left over goes to their favourites.'

'Perhaps you could do a swap,' suggested Sid. 'A nice piece of cheese for half a pound of liver.'

Ella gave her a dark look. 'Is that orphan child still at Greystone House?' she asked belligerently.

As always when Amy was mentioned, Sid's insides seemed to cave in. 'She's still there.'

'You'd think her relatives would come and get her. It must be very inconvenient for you to have such a young child to look after when everyone's so busy,' said Mum.

'I do my best and the others all help.'

'Why don't her relatives come for her?' asked Joan.

'Mrs Cardell is a relative. Perhaps Amy doesn't have any others. Perhaps they're all in the services.' Sid stopped speaking. Talk of Amy undermined her confidence; she always worried she might say the wrong thing.

'Well, I think it's very funny,' said Bea. 'How did Mrs Cardell take the air-raid.'

'Courageously. She's not really strong. She has a heart condition.'

'What sort of condition?' demanded Maud.

'I don't know the medical name. I think maybe she's just getting old and tired.'

'How old is she?'

'I don't know.'

This effectively took their attention from Sid as they discussed the possible age of Mrs Cardell, the probable nature of her heart complaint, and the progress and eventual sudden demise of all the heart patients they had known. They hardly noticed when Sid slipped out the back door. Dad was busy with trowel and compost.

'Hello, Dad.'

'Shut the door. Don't let the cold in.'

She obeyed. 'How are you?'

'As well as can be expected. It's not easy at the shop. Some people can't be told anything. They must know I can't get hold of bananas and oranges. Everything seems in short supply, or it's disappeared altogether.'

'We've been used to importing such a lot of goods. The merchant ships do their best.'

'I know, I know.' Dad was ratty. 'I do my best, too.'

'I'm sure you do. I thought you might be at the football.'

'Not much time for it these days. They keep telling us to dig for victory, so I've been planting more stuff in the garden, though it's like carrying coals to Newcastle.'

'If food gets scarcer, you could sell the garden produce.'

'I suppose so.' Dad lapsed into silence.

'How's Raymond?'

'Doing all right.'

'And Audrey and Irene?'

'They're all right. Ask your mother.'

Sid waited a moment longer, but it seemed Dad had exhausted his willingness to talk, and she returned to the house. She peeped into the best room. Mum and the aunts were discussing a neighbour who had just given birth to a baby who, they had decided, looked more like the new young milkman than his soldier father who was stationed away. She made her way back to Greystone House.

Christmas was near and she spent every moment she could spare planning it. War or no war, she, like every other woman, wanted to give the family a happy time. She had spent hours bottling, drying herbs, making jam, marmalade and pickles. Nothing was wasted. The garden soil was good and, although Brindle and Keith spent more time drilling and taking part in Home guard exercises than gardening, it had still yielded fine crops. When she had remonstrated gently with them about the rampant weeds, they had been indignant.

'What if old Hitler comes?' demanded Keith. 'You won't get much to eat if we're invaded.'

'The lad's right,' said Brindle. 'He's said to hate the British, especially since our boys won the Battle of Britain. That Goering thought his Air Force could beat us, but we showed him.'

On Christmas Eve, Sid was working late in the kitchen. She'd saved their meat coupons to buy a large joint of pork, and was pushing sage-and-onion stuffing into the deep cut she'd made in it, when there was a subdued knock at the back door. She looked quickly around. The black-out was in place. Perhaps someone upstairs had inadvertently shown a light. But the Air-raid Wardens would have banged and shouted. She went cautiously to the door and called, 'Who is it?'

'Me. Angie.'

Sid raced to turn off the lights, grab a torch and open the door. Angie stood there in uniform, her kitbag on the ground, a large carrier bag dumped beside it.

'Oh, God, Angie, I *am* glad to see you! Are you home for Christmas? How did you get leave? Why didn't you phone?' Sid pulled her in, hugged her, closed the door and put on the light. 'Let me look at you. You've put on some weight. It suits you. Oh, Angie.' She hugged her friend again until she gasped.

'Heavens, Sid, what muscles you're developing. Can I get a word in edgeways now?'

'Yes, of course. Sit down. I'll make some tea.'

'No, you sit down and I'll make tea. You've got thinner. I suppose you're working your heart out.'

'It's tough going sometimes, but it's the same for everyone.'

'Not quite,' said Angie drily. 'There are plenty of skivers.' She fetched the teapot and put in two teaspoons. When Sid made an involuntary gesture of protest, Angie said, 'I know the ration's only two ounces a week each, but I've got my stuff to add to it. Just for once we'll have a good strong cuppa.'

When they had drunk their tea, Angie stood up and removed her jacket. She fetched an apron from the drawer. 'Now, where do I begin?'

'You must be tired...'

'Look, who's talking. You look like a racoon with those shadows under your eyes.'

'Thanks.'

They laughed; the next hour's work was completed easily to the accompaniment of uninterrupted chatter.

'The work on the station gets as boring as any other work,' said Angie. 'I thought it was all going to be so glamorous. I wasn't very good at clerical stuff, but they discovered I could cook and now I'm in the cookhouse.'

'Don't you like it?'

Angie laughed. 'It's nothing like Greystone House. Everything's cooked in mountains. It's difficult to make the food decent when there's so much of it. Somehow, flavour gets lost, and things get too thick or thin. We do our best.'

'I'm sure you do.'

'Of course, there are compensations. The station is full of lonely men who want a bit of comfort.' At Sid's startled look she laughed. 'Don't worry, I'm not going down my mother's road. A walk, a beer in a local pub, a chat and a few kisses, that's all. No harm in it, and it cheers us up.'

Sid was not at all surprised to learn that she had men friends. Angie was so different from the depressed girl she had first met. She was confident, laughing, optimistic. She was almost pretty, certainly very attractive.

'Your bed's ready for you,' said Sid. 'It's made up with clean stuff, and I've put hot-water bottles in every week to keep it aired.'

Angie threw her arms around her and kissed her. 'Oh, Sid, I've missed you. I'll never make another friend like you!'

Sid made Christmas Day 1940 as good as usual. The tree stood in the hall, bright with lights and decorations, and there were presents piled beneath it, mostly for Amy. Brindle brought up good wines from the cellar.

'Christmas with a child is so much better,' said Mrs Cardell.

Sid glanced anxiously at her. Her words were happy but her voice was weary. She looked strained, unwell, and blue around the lips. It was not surprising, considering the air-raids. The winter was bitterly cold, the central heating no longer worked, the fires were lit in rooms only as they were needed. Officials had tried to fit Patrick into some kind of war-work and failed, so he spent much of his time roaming round gathering wood for fuel. He helped in the house and garden, returning to creep thankfully into his haven below the house.

There had been another terrible blitz on Bristol on 2 December. It had been a freezing night, and it had taken Sid two hours to stop Mrs Cardell shivering from cold. After that, she had decided that they would be as safe in the cellar as anywhere. It wasn't much warmer, but at least they didn't have the stumbling journey across the rock-hard ground. Sid, Keith and Patrick had put up camp-beds.

Everyone was delighted to see Angie. After dinner they all sat in the hall, where Patrick had lit an enormous wood fire, and listened as she recounted her experiences, embellished, Sid suspected, to amuse them. It was good to see Mrs Cardell laugh.

On the doctor's last call, Sid had asked him how ill she was.

'Very ill,' he had said. 'There's nothing to be done. I tried to persuade her to move to somewhere safer, but she refused. She's a stubborn old girl. Thank heaven she's got you. She was very lonely before you came.'

When Sid put Amy to bed she said, 'I like Christmas, Aunty Sid. Can we have it tomorrow?'

Sid thanked heaven for Angie. 'Aunty Angie will be here. I have to work.'

Munitions factories couldn't stop for Christmas and she'd been lucky to get the day off.

'I like Aunty Angie.'

'That's good, darling. Now I'll read to you and you must go to sleep.'

Amy settled down. On the pillow beside her lay a baby doll from Mrs Cardell. It wore a pink frilly dress, a bonnet and jacket, with tiny shoes and socks. Amy loved it, but when her eyes closed she was hugging her familiar battered teddy bear. Sid smiled down at her daughter, loving her with a painful passion.

Angie was home for ten days. On the fourth day she and Sid were in the garden gathering winter greens, their breath steaming in the icy air.

'How's Roy?' asked Angie.

'He's well. We write.'

'Do you hear from Tom?'

'Quite often.' Tom's letters were full of news which he made interesting and amusing. They said how much he missed her. His words warmed her, but when she wrote back, she spoke of work, making light of it, unable to respond to his expressions of affection, finding it impossible to admit how much she missed him. Philip Prosser had left a wound which hadn't healed and it inhibited her pen.

Angie said suddenly, 'I've been wondering whether to tell you, Sid.'

'Oh?' Sid straightened. 'What have you done?'

'Nothing. It's just that – well – Philip Prosser is stationed where I am.'

Sid's stomach contracted. 'He means nothing to me,' she said harshly. She bent again to the crops. 'These leaves are so frosty I wonder if they'll cook into a mush, but we need greenstuff.'

'I just thought you ought to know.'

'Why?'

Angie was thoroughly miserable now. 'I don't know.'

Sid stood upright again. 'I'm being a pig! Sorry. I know you'd never do a thing to hurt me. It's as well to know where he is, I suppose, for Amy's sake. What's he doing?'

'He's training to fly.'

'What? I thought he'd move heaven and earth to stay on the ground.'

'He did. Then he saw how the women flocked round the air crew so he applied and was passed. The opinion is that he won't be a pilot. More likely a navigator. He's quite clever.'

'Have you got a spy system going?'

'Sort of. I go out with one of the clerical chaps.'

'Serious?'

'No. I sometimes wonder if I'll ever meet a man I can love. I'd like to.'

'You will.'

'I don't know. Since I was tiny I saw men as people who appeared and left. Some of them were horrible. I can't forget. I can't seem to trust them.'

Sid sighed. She and Angie had landed in the same, insecure boat. 'Some nice man will recognise a wonderful girl and grab you.'

They walked into the house together, as close as sisters, more so, thought Sid, remembering Irene and Audrey. They worked in the millinery department of a large store. Sid had remonstrated with them, suggesting that they take up war-work.

'Mind your own business,' snapped Audrey. 'Our boss says we lift women's morale. She said women will want pretty hats to wear when they welcome their menfolk home. It'll cheer them up and send them back contented.'

Amy loved Angie's company, and Sid took advantage of this to pay a visit to Aunt Jess. The shop wasn't busy, and she was invited into the back room for tea. Susan Morland was there, stitching a hem. She smiled at Sid. 'Can't stop work. This is an alteration for a lady whose husband is due on leave at any minute. She wants to look as pretty as possible.'

'Please, don't mind me.'

Jess brought tea and a sponge cake served on porcelain china. 'Have you seen the others lately?' she asked.

'The aunts? I've seen them. They're well.'

'Grumbling, I suppose, about lack of staff and having to work in the shops.'

Sid laughed. 'You know them so well. They're doing their best.'

'Of course. Mattie came to see me. I think she'd like to talk to you.'

'Oh, dear. I'm afraid I've neglected her lately. I'll go as soon as I can.'

'Don't worry, she knows how hard pressed you are. You do far too much, my dear. A full-time job, Greystone House. Old Mrs Cardell's a dear, I know, but she must need a lot of attention. And the child. That's an extra you could have done without.' Sid had to quell her quick anger. She lifted her cup with a hand that shook slightly. 'Must you stay there now?' Jess went on. 'I was delighted when you took to the job, and obviously Mrs Cardell is devoted to you, but you have a duty to yourself. You look far too thin and tired.'

'Lots of people do. It's partly lack of sleep from the bombing.'

'Yes, of course.' Jess looked anxiously at her. There was an almost febrile quality about Sid's quick response.

'What would poor Mrs Cardell do without me?'

'I know, I know. Why does God let it happen? He only has to put out His hand and it would all stop. I don't understand.'

'You know He gave us free will,' said Tessa. She had never heard Joseph speak bitterly about God, and she had to draw on her memories of chapel days to try to help him.

'Free will? Free will to allow children to get blown to bits? I'll never forget what I've seen. Never.'

'You must rest.'

'I can't rest.'

'You must try,' said Eve.

'Everyone else is,' said Tessa. 'They may be needed again tonight.'

Joseph stared at her, his red-rimmed eyes revealing his inner torment. 'Tonight? It can't happen again.' He slumped down, his elbows on the kitchen table, his head on his hands, 'Yes, it can. Oh, God, yes it can.'

'Will you take a little brandy?' asked Eve tentatively, knowing his strong teetotal views. 'Just a few sips as medicine. I'm sure it will be forgiven.'

He accepted a glass from her and drank down the golden liquid in a gulp. Eve gave Tessa a significant glance. She hadn't really believed he would accept.

'Have you got leave?' asked Tessa.

'No. I just wanted to come home for a while. I can't stay.'

They helped him to clean himself. He drank two cups of tea and looked a little better. Then he stood up. 'I've got to get back to camp. Give the others my love.' He kissed Tessa, then Eve – a rare gesture – and walked out.

Susan got up at nine. She was bleary-eyed and hadn't been able to get her sooty fingernails clean. 'You should go on resting,' chided Tessa.

'Resting? I've got to get to work.'

'I thought you said the shop had been destroyed.'

'It has, but poor Mrs Endicott lived there. She'll need me to help her salvage what's possible. I suppose you two will be off again.'

'Josh will be back today,' said Eve. 'We've a rehearsal this afternoon for the broadcast tonight. That's if the BBC is still standing.'

'We'll do it from somewhere,' said Tessa.

In that first raid on Bristol, many had been killed, injured and rendered homeless, but the authorities refused to allow the truth to be told.

Brindle, along with other Bristolians, was enraged. 'Why should we be called just "a town in the West"?' he raved. 'Keith and me saw what the buggers did. Everyone with any eyes to look can go and see it if they want to.'

'I suppose it's necessary for secrecy . . .' Sid got no further.

'If it's necessary, why do they keep on about Coventry and the others and their brave citizens? What about ours? Plenty of them are lying dead; others will never be the same again: we've got heroes too. Did you know eight firemen died and more than twenty air-raid wardens and ambulance drivers, as well as two little messenger boys?'

'She could find an older housekeeper who couldn't do factory work.'
'I must stay. They need me.'
'You are so conscientious. I admire you. Are you fond of that child. What's her name by the way?'
'Amy, and yes, I'm fond of her.' Fond! She adored her with an intensity which sometimes threatened her sanity. Amy was safe, respectable, under Mrs Cardell's benevolent roof, loved and pampered. It was best for her. She wondered what Aunt Jess would say if she knew the truth. She might be sympathetic, but she dared not risk telling her. Even liberal-minded women drew the line at illegitimate babies: nothing must spoil Amy's life. The shop door gave out its musical chime and Jess returned with a young soldier. He was medium height, sturdy looking, grave-faced. 'Look who's arrived.'

Susan jumped up, dropping her sewing on to a small table. 'Joseph! How long have you got? Have you been home yet? Sid, this is my brother.'

Joseph shook hands solemnly. 'I came here straight from the station. I hoped you'd be in. I'm going to get the bus home now. Is everything all right there?'

'Fine, thank goodness.'

'Is Mum still going out with the WVS van with refreshments? Is Dad still on the Demolition and Rescue?'

'Of course. You know them.'

'I do. They'll do their duty. And what about you, Susan?'

'Staggering along on the end of a stretcher and generally being helpful to the hurt.'

Joseph nodded solemnly and Sid wondered if he ever smiled. Aunt Jess offered him tea and he sat down and took the cup and saucer with hands which looked too strong for them. 'Where's Tessa?'

'Travelling round with Eve and the band. People love them.'

'It's a way of helping.' said Joseph. 'Men are bored with the everlasting drill and exercises. They want to see action.'

'Joseph is a medical orderly,' explained Susan to Sid.

Aunt Jess said, 'Would you like to go home with your brother, Susan? It's almost closing time.'

'Thank you, but I must finish this. It's promised to a customer, Joseph.'

He nodded. 'That's right. We must all do our duty were it leads us.' His voice was flat, as if he scarcely meant what he said.

'I must be getting back soon,' said Sid.

'You will come again?' said Susan. 'I do so enjoy talking to you.'

Sid felt warmed by her response. Susan's personality was open and honest and appealed to her. 'Could you come to tea in Greystone House on Sunday?' she asked. 'You, too,' she said impulsively to Joseph.

'We'd love to,' cried Susan, before Joseph had time to answer.

After he had left, Susan grimaced at Sid. 'He's a dear man, but not the jolliest in the world.'

'Jollity isn't everything,' smiled Sid as she left.

On Sunday afternoon, a car pulled up in the drive of Greystone House. Sid opened the front door.

'I hope it's all right,' cried Susan, climbing out of the passenger seat. 'My sister and cousin were home and, knowing how you like their singing . . .'

Sid was delighted and rather overawed to recognise the driver as Tessa Ware and a girl in the back seat as Eve Brook. Her mind ran quickly over the food on the kitchen table. Joseph climbed out and stared at the large house rather disapprovingly.

Tessa advanced, her hand out in greeting. 'Sorry about this, but Susan insisted . . .'

'I'm so glad she did. I really admire your singing. I have your records.'

Eve shook hands. Sid, like many others, never got used to her beauty. It was different these days, more haunting: the war had added a fragile vulnerability. 'Susan is so impetuous, but to make amends we've brought you one of Mum's cakes,' she said. In the kitchen Eve looked round. 'What a huge place. It's bigger than Padding House.'

'Where's that?' Angie ventured. She had greeted the unexpected visitors with awe.

'Oh, it's a family place in Frenchay. My cousin, Paul, and his wife live there now.'

'You've made a very cosy corner near the range,' said Tessa. 'Two ranges? Goodness. How do you manage them both?'

'It's lovely and warm,' said Susan. 'Do we eat here?'

'Yes, do sit down,' said Sid. 'There isn't the fuel for both ranges, so we keep the smaller one going. It give us hot water.' She laughed. 'Well, lukewarm water sometimes.'

Keith and Brindle and Patrick were out on Home Guard manoeuvres. Some men might have found the sole company of women embarrassing, but Joseph Morland waited calmly and politely until they had seated themselves then joined them. He was so quiet and still that the others almost forget he was there as they chatted about their various war duties.

'You do such a wonderful job,' said Angie to Tessa and Eve. 'If you could only see the faces of our men when they come back from a difficult strike and some of their friends have bought it. I cook and sometimes serve in the mess and we keep the radio on. When your band starts to play and you sing it helps. You choose good songs about hope and love. Are your men in the forces?'

Tessa swallowed a mouthful of cake carefully. 'My husband is in the Army. Eve's fiancé is serving at sea.'

'You must be proud of them, but anxious?'

Eve said, 'Always. I'm always anxious.'

Angie was disconcerted. 'I'm sorry. I should have known better than to ask. Most women have a loved one doing something dangerous.'

'It's all right,' said Eve. 'Do you girls have anyone special?'

'Not me,' said Angie.

'Not special like you,' said Sid. 'Just friends I write to.'

Angie was wearing civvies, and Joseph had been silently contemplating her for some minutes. 'What do you do?' he asked.

'I'm in the WAAF. I cook.'

'A very necessary occupation,' said Joseph.

'Thanks,' said Angie. She thought: he speaks as if he was in a pulpit.

Joseph pronounced, 'Women are doing a marvellous job in this war. It's wrong to put you in danger, but we need you.'

Angie smiled at him and handed him a plate of shortbread biscuits. 'Did you make these?' he asked.

When she said yes he complimented her.

Angie said, 'Sid told me you volunteered for medical duties because you refuse to fight.'

'That is so.'

'Someone has to do it,' said Eve.

'But not me.'

This was a source of contention between Eve and Joseph and Tessa said quickly, 'We're not all the same.'

'I admire a man who sticks up for his beliefs,' said Angie.

'I'm glad to hear it,' said Joseph. His brief smile lit up his face.

Amy had been put down for her nap and Sid excused herself to fetch her. She was awake, still sleepy, pink and warm.

'Come on, darling,' said Sid, 'there are visitors downstairs.'

Amy brightened. As far as she was concerned, the more people there were, the better she liked it. She thrust her arms into her sweater. Long socks and shoes were pulled on, her hair brushed while she twisted impatiently, a wipe over of face and hands and she was ready.

'What a darling!' exclaimed Eve. She who had never cared for children now ached to hold one of David's in her arms.

Amy regarded her solemnly. 'Have you brought me a present?'

'Amy!' exclaimed Sid.

'Sorry, no,' said Eve, 'but we didn't know we were going to meet a dear little girl.'

'I'm not little. I'm getting big. Aunty Sid says so. And Aunty Angie said she thought my jumper was going to be big enough for me to grow and it just fits, doesn't it, Aunty Angie? And Aunty Louisa said I was getting big too.'

'She's lovely,' said Tessa. 'Whose child is she?'

'She's lost her parents,' said Sid quietly. 'Mrs Cardell has given her a home. They are related.'

'She reminds me of someone,' said Eve. 'I wonder if I knew her family. What were their names?'

'I can't remember.'

'But you know Amy's name?'

'Oh, yes, of course.'

'It's Brown,' said Amy.

'A good plain name,' said Joseph unexpectedly.

Sid couldn't have spoken. She had tried to deny the fact that Amy was growing more like her father every day. She had inherited the best features of both parents, and had her mother's large, beautiful eyes, but there was a slant to them which reminded Sid of Philip.

Amy walked towards Joseph and looked up into his face. 'Can I sit on your lap?'

'Of course.' He lifted her.

'Your clothes are all rough.'

'They're Army things. They have to be rough.'

'Do you have a gun?'

'No.'

'How can you kill people without a gun?'

'I don't kill people. I bandage them when they're hurt.'

'Would you bandage me?'

Joseph looked into the child's clear eyes. 'I hope I'll never need to.'

'But would you?'

'Yes.'

'Thank you.'

Sid asked, 'Eve, Tessa, my employer, Mrs Cardell, is very fond of your singing. May I tell her you're here? Would you mind seeing her, if she's well enough? She's in bed today.'

'Of course,' both girls agreed at once.

Mrs Cardell welcomed them with smiles and congratulations. 'How lovely to meet you. Keep up the good work.' She was too breathless to say much and they soon left. Sid smoothed her sheets, plumped up her pillows, poured fresh water. 'Is there anything you need?'

'No, thank you, my dear fusspot. Go back to your tea party.'

After the visitors had left and Angie and Sid were washing up, Angie said, 'I like Joseph Morley.'

'Do you? I would have thought he was too po-faced for you.'

'I've seen enough of the other sort. You could always trust him.'

'He doesn't smile much.'

'No. He looks terribly sad.'

'There are lots who look like that these days.'

'Yes, that's true, but he's different. I wonder if he's lost someone he cared for.'

Chapter Fourteen

There was a long, savage air-raid on 3 January, during which one of a stray stick of bombs landed near Greystone House, adding to the horrendous noise of planes and anti-aircraft guns, some of which were mobile, so that the residents never knew when to expect a sudden increase in the fearful cacophony. The suburbs were luckier than the more populated districts and suffered fewer bombs, but the strays – dropped sometimes by a plane unloading its cargo because it was in trouble – could just as easily bring death or frightful injuries to the people below. The cold and shortage of fuel had become allies of the enemy. The water froze even as it left the firemen's hoses, so that they were helpless before the raging flames. The cellars in Greystone House were chilly, and although Brindle had produced a couple of oil stoves, they barely lifted the level of cold and damp.

The all-clear finally sounded, but Mrs Cardell was too weak to climb the cellar stairs, and Sid couldn't manage her alone. Angie had returned to camp, the men were out on duty, and Amy was fast asleep in her small bed in the corner. They would have to remain where they were. Sid went to the kitchen to boil water for more hot-water bottles. The electricity had been cut off and she groped around with her shaded torch, wondering why the kitchen was so freezingly cold when they still managed to keep the range going somehow. When her shoes scrunched over glass she realised that the windows had been blown in, and when she tried to fill a kettle for tea, there was no water either. The air coming through the shattered panes was bitter and, in spite of wearing hat, coat, scarf and gloves, she shivered. A large pan of water was always kept full on the range: mercifully it was still hot enough to fill all the bottles, and she tucked them round the old lady, who thanked her gently before she accepted a tablet for the pain in her chest, then closed her eyes. Sid couldn't tell if she slept or not. By this time she was shaking with cold herself, and climbed back into her bunk, wrapped in a blanket, waiting for dawn.

When the others returned, they helped Mrs Cardell to her room. The doctor came to examine her. He shook his head at Sid. 'She should have gone away to a safer place while there was still time.'

Sid was horrified. 'Do you mean . . .?'

'The hospitals are full of the wounded now. If I could get her in she might last a little longer, but there's no guarantee. Besides, bombs are no respecters of hospitals.'

'What shall I do? She can't stay upstairs while there's a risk of raids.'

'She's promised me she'll go to the cellar every night before the raids begin and stay till morning.'

Sid sighed with relief.

The doctor said gently, 'Whatever happens she hasn't very long to live.'

Sid nodded, her throat too constricted to speak. Until that moment she hadn't realised just how much she loved the woman who had given her back her self-esteem and treated her more like a friend than an employee.

Brindle fetched the two paraffin heaters from the glasshouses. 'She'll die of pneumonia if she isn't kept warmer. Poor soul, she's got no resistance to cold. Have you noticed how thin she's got?'

Of course Sid had noticed, but she said nothing, knowing better than to thank him. He adored his mistress. She thanked God for the range and Patrick's devoted application to collecting fuel, which enabled them to cook and to keep a fire going in Mrs Cardell's bedroom. Some of the upper rooms had escaped damage, her room fortunately being one of them, though her sitting room was uninhabitable. Brindle, Keith and Patrick boarded up the windows, which helped, but could not fully keep out the draughts. However, glass or no glass, Sid was still able to simmer nourishing soups, and these, and the bottles and jars of food she had preserved, became their standby when rations were so sparse. Brindle also revealed the existence of a garden well which had been covered over for years. It was found to contain water which lay too deep to freeze. Sid rendered it drinkable by prolonged boiling. No one grumbled, not even Brindle, except – as did everyone else – about the Germans. There had been so many deaths and injuries. There were disturbing accounts too of poor families unable even to afford the rations, let alone extras, so that there was real hunger.

When Tom wrote now he inquired anxiously after Sid's safety. 'We're getting reports of terrible casualties and damage. The men are worried sick about their families. We didn't bargain for our loved ones being in such danger.'

Did he include her in his category of 'loved ones', she wondered? Not that she wanted his anxiety. Life was complicated enough. She wrote back reassuringly about their safety and comfort, only telling him that Mrs Cardell was now very ill.

She could no longer be left without constant attendance, a full-time nurse couldn't be spared and the Misses Weekley, although they did their best, were not able to cope. They took turns in sitting with the invalid, but their own small cottage had suffered and they too were existing as best they could, so with the help of the doctor, Sid had been released from her job to care for her employer under the guidance of an over-stretched district nurse. Electricity was restored, but the tap water remained solid, locked by the unrelenting cold.

Susan Morland dropped in one day and saw the state of the rooms; soon afterwards her father arrived to replace glass in the most needed windows. He couldn't manage to reglaze the kitchen windows, so although the black-out curtains kept out a certain amount of cold, Sid's refuge was no longer so cosy.

Mrs Cardell asked to see Amy every day. Sid was pleased both for her employer's devotion and the fact that, in Aunty Louisa's room, Amy could discard the inevitable coat and hat. Amy liked Aunty Louisa, and enjoyed playing upstairs, watched by her loving eyes, exploring the large, comfortable room, emptying boxes containing costume jewellery, and draping herself with long necklaces, pinning brooches on her jumpers, clipping on earrings. She would stand for ages admiring herself in the long wardrobe mirror while Mrs Cardell looked on, amused.

'I've never seen the like,' said Miss Nellie Weekley. 'You'd think she was the girl's granny, or something. She lets her do almost anything she wants.'

'She's like her father,' Mrs Cardell said one day to Sid.

'Yes.'

'That doesn't please you, my dear?'

'How could it?'

'I meant in appearance, though she has the same sunny disposition he had as a boy. It's a great pity he was spoiled by having too much money at his command too early.'

Amy, as young as she was, had been listening intently. 'I'm like my father?'

'Yes,' said Sid.

'Good,' said Amy.

Spring came and the weather improved and still Mrs Cardell lingered.

'She's a marvel,' said the doctor. He glanced at Amy, who was dressing her doll in a set of new clothes sent by Angie. 'She takes great joy in the child. They're related, aren't they?'

'Yes.'

'You care for her so well. Mrs Cardell never did a better day's work than when she engaged you.'

'Thank you.'

The doctor glanced at Sid, who as usual was tongue-tied and angrily helpless at any mention of Amy's connections which left her out. 'Keep on as you are. We may see the old lady through the summer yet.'

They might have done, had it not been for the raid of 16 March, the deadliest Bristol blitz of all. The doctor attended her the next morning, but could do nothing to save her. Sid was at her side when she opened her eyes, said, 'Thank you,' and quietly died. Sid fell on her knees by the bed, holding the dead woman's hand. She had lost one of her dearest friends and the pain was bitter.

She had kept Mrs Prosser informed of the progress of her employer's illness, and she telephoned the news of her death.

'Why did you not call me sooner?' demanded the irate woman. 'I should have been there.'

Sid resented her reproaches but said only, 'I'm sorry. She's been so close to it for a long time. I had no special reason to expect it today.'

'I shall be down as soon as possible. Prepare a room for me.'

Sid had been busy calling in the appropriate authorities and checking that everything was done properly for her dead employer, but after the phone call she sat down abruptly and faced her future. Probably Mrs Prosser would dismiss her. There was no reason for her to keep on a house of this size. She might try to sell it, but people weren't buying. Why purchase something which might be blown to bits the same night? Greystone House was inconvenient and expensive to run, but she could leave Brindle as caretaker and wait for the war to end. What of Amy? Mrs Prosser would demand proof that she was indeed a relative of her late cousin. If it couldn't be proved – and Sid had no intention of permitting Philip Prosser to know that he was her father – what would Mrs Prosser do with her? She might even try to send her to an orphanage. Sid went cold. She would keep her somehow. She must. She could earn enough at the factory for them both, but where would she leave her during her twelve-hour shifts? She couldn't get evacuated with her, because no one knew she was her mother. She thought of the McGregors. They surely would help if she asked them. But if no way out of the dilemma presented itself, she would have to declare the child her own and she would take the consequences. The idea sent her mind spiralling into the future. Her small daughter who was so open, so fearless and joyous, would probably have to grow up in some dingy lodging house to face a world which usually despised her kind.

'I suppose those two young demons will be coming, too,' said Brindle.

'Who?'

'Mr Philip and Miss Celia.'

Sid managed to hide her alarm. 'Surely Mr Philip will be on duty somewhere.'

'You can get compassionate leave for funerals. If you want to, that is. He don't care a cuss for her, but after the funeral they'll hear the will and he'll want the same chance as the others to poke his nose into her stuff.'

'I hadn't thought of that. I don't suppose she's left much that they'll want.'

'Don't you believe it. Some of the ornaments and pictures are worth quite a bit, and if they can't use the furniture they can store it till after the war.'

'I suppose they could leave stuff here.'

'No. You can be sure they'll try to get rid of this place as soon as ever they can for as much as they can get. Is there any of the good jewellery left?'

'How do you know about that?'

Brindle frowned and said indignantly, 'I was often her only helper before you came. I know she's been selling stuff to Mr Harvey for years, and lately he's called more often.'

'Of course. Sorry. There's a fair bit left. I think the most valuable are her pearl necklace and earrings and a brooch.'

'They were a present from her father on her wedding day,' mused

Brindle. 'She looked handsome in them. Well, they'll lose no time getting their hands on those.'

He stumped out and Sid sat down. The kitchen was quiet and reasonably warm after she had stopped up gaps with torn rags. Would Philip turn up? Somehow she had taken it for granted that only Mrs Prosser and Celia would arrive. What on earth would she do with Amy? She had told Philip that their child had died. Not that he would care one way or the other, but he was malicious and could make trouble.

The problem of the funeral day was solved when the Misses Weekley offered to care for her. 'A funeral's no place for a child,' said Nellie.

'Nor is a house of mourning,' said Selina, 'though many poor children are having to learn some dreadful lessons these wicked days. She can stay with us overnight.'

Amy was pleased to do so. She had visited the little cottage before and was enchanted by the array of china artefacts the two elderly ladies collected. Toby jugs, miniatures, a doll's tea-set which they permitted her to handle under supervision. There were other things she was allowed to play with, including a rocking horse on which she had many adventures. Nellie explained, 'We kept all our own toys for the day when we might have children to use them. That day never came.'

Sid was stuck for an answer to such a sadly significant speech, but Miss Nellie said dispassionately, 'We had our chances, but never came upon the right one. My sister and me have had a happy life together none the less.'

Sid prepared three bedrooms. The tobacco-brown room gave her the shivers. What a gullible fool she had been. She thought: He might not come. I'm worrying needlessly. Of course she could ring and inquire. Or would a housekeeper always be ready and waiting for guests? All her uncertainties had returned with interest on the day Mrs Cardell died.

When the car drew up outside the house, Celia Prosser was driving; the only passenger, Sid realised with relief, was Mrs Prosser. Her relief didn't last long.

'Have our luggage brought in,' ordered Mrs Prosser. 'We shall need three rooms. Mr Philip will be arriving late tonight.'

Sid's tongue would hardly move. 'I'm the only one here at present. If you leave the cases where they are I'll get them brought up later.'

'Has everyone left? Where's that decrepit old fool? What's his name? Brindle?'

'He's a sergeant in the Home Guard, madam. He's on duty and so are the others.'

Mrs Prosser looked as if fate had dealt her a particularly nasty blow. 'Where is my cousin?'

'In her own room, madam.'

'Bring tea here,' said Mrs Prosser, opening the door of the small sitting room. 'It smells damp!'

'Since Mrs Cardell's illness we have used most of the coal for her sick room, madam.'

Perhaps Sid had put undue emphasis on the word 'sick', because

Mrs Prosser frowned and Celia gave her a disdainful look.

Celia yawned. 'God I'm tired. I'll be glad when this damned war is over and we can get a chauffeur again.'

'You don't mind using the car for pleasure,' snapped Mrs Prosser.

'When we can get a little extra petrol,' said Celia languidly.

Mrs Prosser glanced at Sid and threw Celia a warning look.

'Oh, don't worry, Grandmother, Sidonia understands, I'm sure. She must have been buying extra stuff to keep this huge, ghastly place going.'

Sid watched Mrs Prosser move about the room, bending a little to examine the Crown Derby china in a Regency display case, picking up a Dresden ornament from the mantelpiece. She turned impatiently, 'I asked for tea.'

'Yes, madam.'

When Sid returned with the tray of tea she asked, 'Will you be staying long?'

'Why do you want to know?' snapped Celia.

'It's a reasonable question,' said Mrs Prosser unexpectedly.

'If it's a week or more I shall need your ration books.'

'I'm afraid I left them with my housekeeper,' said Mrs Prosser. 'How long we stay will depend on several circumstances.' She smiled thinly, 'I'm sure there are enough stores in the larder to cater for three more.'

'It's as if the war was happening to someone else,' Sid told Brindle when he returned.

'Damn female!' muttered Brindle. Much of his old surliness returned when he contemplated Mrs Cardell's relatives. 'They did nothing for her when she needed it. Not that she wanted them! We looked after her all right. Are *they* with her?'

'Miss Celia is. Mr Philip will be here later.'

'Damn 'em!'

'Could you get Patrick to carry their luggage in, please? I'm preparing dinner, though I dare say they'll grumble. I've made a cottage pie with mince and there's spring greens and peas. I've got apple Charlotte to follow from the stale bread and the last of the cookers.'

'I hope it chokes them,' said Brindle. He mourned Mrs Cardell sincerely.

Sid laid the table in the small sitting room while the two women were upstairs. Twice she was rung for, both women demanding to know why the water for their bathing wasn't very hot, and the extra trips she had to make to their rooms and their lack of grace when she explained did nothing to help her nerves.

Downstairs, Mrs Prosser asked, 'Why are we in here instead of the dining room?'

'I've got used to serving meals here. It's the only room Mrs Cardell used.'

'Well, that won't do for us.'

'No, madam.' Sid thought almost with satisfaction of the large dining room which even in the hottest weather only became mildly warm. But if grandeur was what they wanted, they must make the best of it.

The two women ate well of the expertly cooked food.

After they cleared their plates, Sid took in coffee. 'You gave us a very plain dinner,' said Mrs Prosser.

'Yes, madam.'

'Is that all you have to say?' demanded Celia, taking a cigarette from a gold case, lighting it and blowing smoke over the table.

'Celia!'

'Sorry, Grandmother,' she said laconically.

'Even if you have no other sources for foodstuffs, there are items which may be purchased off the ration,' said Mrs Prosser.

'Yes, madam, but I've not had time to queue.'

'I understood from a letter my cousin wrote to me that you had been granted leave from your factory position to nurse her. You had plenty of time.'

'For several days I haven't dared to leave her. Besides, she's had no appetite, and the rest of us have made do.'

Mrs Prosser frowned. 'How many staff are there now?'

'Four, madam. Myself, of course, Brindle, a young man called Keith and another, the boilerman, Patrick.'

'Both young?'

'Yes, madam.'

'Why are they not in uniform?'

'They are all in the Home Guard.'

'Ridiculous! They should be with the proper fighting men.'

'When they lose their cushy jobs, they'll have to do something constructive,' snapped Celia.

Sid couldn't miss the threat. They were going to get rid of them all and sell up. Mrs Prosser waved her hand towards the coffee tray. Celia took no notice and Sid poured. She finished and straightened her back. 'Neither man was found medically fit to fight, madam.'

'Are we paying wages to unfit specimens?'

The word 'we' was like a stab in the heart. Evidently, in her mind, Mrs Prosser had already taken over the house.

Celia lit another cigarette.

'Celia, that is the third since we began dinner.'

'Will you be needing anything else, madam?' asked Sid.

'No, but I trust you have kept a meal for Mr Philip.'

'Yes, madam. The cottage pie only just went round, but I'll no doubt find something.' She left quickly.

Celia's voice floated after her. 'She's an insolent piece. She acts as if we were not welcome here. In our own house!'

When Sid went to clear the table, the two women were still in the small sitting room, seated near the fire which they had piled with wood. Celia was sprawled in Mrs Cardell's favourite armchair, still smoking, turning the pages of a magazine. 'These magazines are ages old. Didn't Mrs Cardell ever buy up-to-date ones?'

'I don't suppose she cared for them any more than I do,' said her grandmother. She glanced up at the clock. 'Philip is taking longer than I expected.'

'He's probably met some floosie on the train.'
'I wish you would not use such terms to me.'
'Sorry, Grandmother.'

Sid was almost at the door with the heavy butler's tray when Mrs Prosser asked, 'What happened to the child my cousin took in?'

Sid turned round so quickly the spoons clattered in the saucers.

'Mrs Cardell mentioned her name once in a letter. I have forgotten what it was.' She waited but Sid said nothing. Mrs Prosser frowned and continued. 'I wrote back and inquired about the child, but she did not answer. I suppose you must have got rid of her by now. A child is just an extra burden. I can't think why she did it.'

Celia said, 'Neither can I. Has she been sent away?'

Sid glanced at Celia, who was staring at her. She received a further shock as she realised for the first time that Any resembled Celia much more than she did her father.

'She isn't here at present,' she gasped as she backed out with the tray. Her knees felt as if they might give way. Thankfully, the kitchen was empty, and she sank down by the table, feeling as if a huge weight was rolling inexorably towards her.

Philip Prosser arrived at eleven o'clock, after his grandmother and sister had retired. Mrs Prosser had said she was tired, and declared that Celia should not go pleasure-seeking from a house of mourning. Celia complained monotonously that she was bored and wished she hadn't bothered to come.

Brindle had insisted on waiting up with Sid, and he answered the door, greeting Philip with a scowl.

Philip dropped his case in the hall for the old man to deal with and made his way straight to the kitchen.

'Hello, Sidonia,' he said. 'How are you?'

'The table is laid for you in the small sitting room,' said Sid. 'We have kept the fire going.'

'It's not all that warm in here.'

Sid's nervousness kept her talking. 'We have to let the fire die down at night because of the fuel shortage. Our windows were blown out in a blitz. We can't get them all repaired.'

'Really? I knew Bristol had had some raids, but I didn't realise it had affected you. London is getting it very badly. My grandmother is thinking of moving out.'

'I have soup for you. Brindle will serve you upstairs.'

'I don't think he likes me.'

Sid didn't answer.

'I don't think you like me, either. That makes me sad.'

She looked at him then, her eyes filled with contempt. How could he speak to her like that? Did he really believe he could walk back into her life after all that had happened, and act as if she were annoying him in some way by withholding her friendship? 'I don't,' she said.

'Don't hold that episode in the past against me, Sidonia. Remember what good times we had?'

Brindle marched through the kitchen. They heard him crashing around in his pantry, slamming down what was left of the silverware in a way which would have made Mrs Cardell wince. Sid couldn't find words to express her anger and disgust with Philip. Besides, if her self-control went, she might let something out. Mrs Cardell had already made one slip by mentioning Amy to her cousin. How had she ever believed she loved this man? He was without principles, without a trace of empathy, without even the grace to be sorry for what he had done to her.

'Do you want your food or don't you? I have a busy day tomorrow.'

'Ah, yes, the funeral. Will there be many guests?'

'I believe not. Many of Mrs Cardell's contemporaries have died or moved into the country since the raids began. I've prepared a light buffet for a dozen or so.'

Philip waited for more, then walked angrily out of the room. She followed with soup and a platter of bread and cheese.

'No butter?' he asked sulkily.

It gave her a somewhat petty pleasure to say no.

The funeral was a small affair. The only ones outside family and staff to attend were Mr Mapleton her solicitor, her doctor, and Mr Harvey, the jeweller. The local vicar read the service. There were no hymns. For once Sid had agreed with Mrs Prosser. For so few to attempt to sing would sound frightful. Brindle wiped away a few tears, the Misses Weekley dabbed at their eyes, Patrick wept copiously, sobbing so loudly that he earned furious frowns from Mrs Prosser. Sid was so locked in by sadness and worry she felt her throat would burst with the lump in it.

Back at the house, after the servants had dispensed drinks and sandwiches, the guests left and the family adjourned to the library to hear Mr Mapleton read the will.

Sid went to the kitchen and sat down. She felt utterly weary and lethargic. Mrs Prosser would not waste time in ridding herself of the servants. She should have made plans, but somehow there hadn't been time.

Brindle hurried into the kitchen. 'They want you in the library, Sid,' he said breathlessly.

'What for?'

'How should I know? They sound edgy.'

'How do you know that?' asked Sid.

'He was listening at the door as hard as he could,' said Keith.

Brindle glowered at him. 'Just because you've been made a lance-corporal doesn't mean you can cheek me.'

'No, sergeant.'

When Sid walked through the library door she was regarded by the Prossers with cold animosity.

'For some reason your presence here is required,' said Mrs Prosser icily. 'I suppose you have been left some small legacy, though the information could have been conveyed to you later.'

Mr Mapleton began his solemn reading of the will. It was short.

After the payment of a few outstanding debts, Mrs Cardell had left the house and its entire contents to 'my dear and devoted housekeeper and companion, Sidonia Penrose, in the earnest hope that it will not prove to be a white elephant, and on the understanding that she keeps the services of Isaac Brindle until his decease or his wish to retire.' Brindle was also granted a small annuity.

During the sonorous drone of Mr Mapleton, gasps of disbelief could be heard from the Prossers.

As soon as he stopped, Celia cried, 'Outrageous! Grandmother, you will of course contest the will!'

Philip said, 'What a clever, conniving woman you turned out to be, Miss Penrose.'

'They are right,' said Mrs Prosser to Mr Mapleton, 'I shall of course contest this infamous will. It is obvious that my cousin was not in possession of her senses when she had it drawn up.'

'On the contrary, she was as sharp-witted as ever, as her doctor will testify if needs be. A weak heart need not affect the brain.'

'It may affect the emotions,' said Mrs Prosser, 'and Miss Penrose had every opportunity to influence her. Now I see why she didn't call upon the services of a trained nurse. What an opportunity for a fortune-hunter!'

'Your cousin could scarcely have afforded to pay for all the medical help she required,' said Mr Mapleton, 'even if they didn't have their hands full these days. And in any case, she particularly wanted Miss Penrose, who made her last months as comfortable and happy as possible in spite of the war shortages.'

'When did she make the will?' asked Philip.

'Over a year ago.'

'That means nothing,' said Mrs Prosser. 'This woman has had years to exert domination over her. I shall insist on contesting the will.'

'You may do so,' the solicitor said dispassionately, 'but it is watertight and your claim is merely that of a distant relative. You will fail.'

'We may fail,' said Philip, 'but her defence will cost Miss Penrose every penny she can raise, and leave her with nothing. That will teach her a lesson.'

Mr Mapleton gave him a contemptuous look. 'It will also cost Mrs Prosser a large sum, and will bring neither credit nor success.'

Sid had been only half listening to the vilification, overcome by her late employer's generosity. She had done it to help Amy as well as herself. She had given them as good a measure of security as she could.

'What have you to say, Miss Penrose?' asked Mr Mapleton.

'What could she have to say?' said Celia. 'A female like that to inherit this house! To be the owner of valuable pictures and furniture. And I've seen some nice bits of porcelain. And what of the jewels? They are worth a great deal of money.'

'Many of the best have already been sold.'

'By this woman?' snapped Mrs Prosser, staring at Sid.

'You are making a most serious accusation. Fortunately it can easily be disproved. I knew of the transactions between Mrs Cardell and her jeweller.'

Mrs Prosser went an unattractive shade of red. 'Are you saying that my cousin sold the stuff just to keep up this run-down mausoleum?'

'If you think it's such a run-down mausoleum, I wonder why you resent my having it,' said Sid, goaded to a retort.

'That is hardly the point! Money can still be made from it, money which should remain in Mrs Cardell's family,' said Celia.

'She did not think so,' said Mr Mapleton calmly, closing his briefcase. 'Now, if you will excuse me, I have another appointment.' He turned to Sid and said gently, 'Miss Penrose, Mrs Cardell left a letter with me to give you on the occasion of her demise. It is for your eyes only.' He handed her a long white envelope sealed with wax, on which was imprinted an official-looking stamp. 'Come to my office and we'll go over the details of the will. I can then answer any queries you have. Meanwhile, if there is anything you need to know urgently, or any help you require, please don't hesitate to call me. And please ask Mr Brindle to come to my office at his convenience.'

Sid nodded. She wanted to leave, to go downstairs and start to come to terms with this enormous lift in her fortunes, but she felt numb. The solicitor packed the papers into his briefcase, smiled at her and departed, leaving behind him an appalled silence.

It didn't last for long. The three Prossers all began to speak at once, discussing the will, the possible state of Mrs Cardell's mind, the value of the property, the evil machinations of her damned housekeeper.

'What's in the letter?' suddenly demanded Mrs Prosser.

Sid gazed at her abstractedly. 'If Mrs Cardell had wanted others to know, she wouldn't have sealed it.'

'I bet it's full of money,' snarled Celia. 'Conniving little cat! Or it's about money hidden away.'

The uproar broke out again, and they hardly noticed when Sid got up and walked out. Back in the kitchen, Keith and Brindle were waiting.

'Well?' they demanded. 'Did you get anything?'

'Did she leave me something?' asked Brindle anxiously. 'I've been with her so long . . . I haven't got much saved.'

'Of course she remembered you. How could she not leave something to her most faithful servant? You have an annuity for life; Mr Mapleton wants you to go to his office when you can. He said "a small annuity" but what someone like him thinks is small is probably a lot to us. I dare say it's enough to keep you.'

Brindle smiled. 'What a good old soul she was.'

'Did you get anything?' asked Keith. 'You've been a brick to her.'

'Why, thank you. As a matter of fact I did. I got Greystone House and everything in it.'

The others stared at her, then laughed. 'Come off it,' said Keith. 'What did you really get?'

'I just told you. I mean it.'

'She does mean it,' said Brindle slowly.

Keith gave a shout of laughter which brought Patrick up from the cellar. 'What's funny? I like laughing.'

227

'Sid's our new boss.'

'Sid is the boss now,' he said, puzzled.

'Mrs Cardell left her the house.'

'Did she? That's nice.' He vanished again.

'He doesn't understand,' said Keith. 'I suppose you'll sell up if you can. It should give you a nice nest-egg.'

'No,' said Sid, coming to an immediate decision. 'I shall keep it on. I don't know how yet, or how I'll cope with Amy and the house and my job, but somehow I will.'

She read the letter in the privacy of her room.

My dear Sidonia [it said],

I find it difficult to put into words what you have meant to me over these past years. You changed a life which was becoming too grim to bear into one of lightness and joy. I am deeply grieved that you should have suffered at the hands of one of my relatives, but cannot regret Amy's birth. She has been the source of so much happiness to me and I know how much you care for her. The legacy, of which by now you will have learned, may help you to keep her without too much worry. There will be a small income from my late husband's estate, and I do advise you to take advantage of the sale of any of the artefacts which you can sell. They will help you whatever you decide to do. My race is almost run, but yours and Amy's are scarcely begun. I love you both. My heartfelt prayers for your future and God's blessing on you.

Your loving friend, Louisa Cardell.'

The tears Sid had been unable to shed came now, though this was no occasion for weeping. Mrs Cardell had not been sorry to die, to relinquish her pain and infirmity. She must think and plan for the future. Hers, Brindle's, Keith's, Patrick's and Amy's, and maybe Angie's too.

Mrs Prosser announced that they would not be leaving until the following day. She rang the bell to tell Sid the news. Cheek, thought Sid, in her new-found position as owner of Greystone House, but she answered the summons. 'I would much prefer not to stay one more night beneath this roof,' said Mrs Prosser, 'but I am fatigued and do not see why I need go to the expense of a hotel. I trust you have no objection.'

'You're welcome,' said Sid.

Mrs Prosser gave her a look which would have frozen an Eskimo, but left Sid unmoved. As willing as she had been to give Mrs Cardell everything that was her due and more, she had still been a servant with an uncertain future. Now she had been liberated from servitude and owed nothing to the ill-tempered Mrs Prosser.

But she carried on with her work and served a good dinner, sacrificing precious rations, though she received no thanks for it. She hurried to the Misses Weekleys' cottage. Amy was thoroughly enjoying playing with their old toys and being spoiled, and they happily agreed to keep her another night.

That night, the men were out on duty as usual, and Sid sat down to write to Angie. In the background the wireless was playing from a hotel where Josh Raven's band and the Kissing Cousins were performing.

She was astonished when the door opened and Philip walked in. 'Writing to your latest lover?'

She looked at him, her contempt clearly displayed.

'By God, you're an insolent bitch. And far more clever than I gave you credit for.'

'Is that all you came to say?' Her words were crisp but her heart was thudding slowly and heavily. She wondered how it was possible for her to loath someone so much and not burst. 'I didn't invite you to the kitchen.'

'No, you didn't, and of course it's all yours now, isn't it?' He sat down opposite her. 'I want a cup of coffee. There wasn't much at dinner-time.'

'How sad for you. The war affects civilians too, though I don't suppose you've given much thought to that. Coffee isn't always easy to get, and I've had little time for shopping.'

'You must have some somewhere. Make me a cup.' She leaned back in her chair and gave him a steady stare. 'What are you staring at? It isn't the least bit of use putting on airs and graces. You'll always have a servant's mentality.'

'Well, if I do, I shan't have a servant's responsibilities. I shall serve breakfast before you leave tomorrow because your grandmother is elderly and needs to be cared for, but if you want coffee now you can make it yourself.'

He stayed where he was and she picked up her pen. On the radio, Eve and Tessa were singing softly in harmony, 'Love is all', investing the words with intense meaning, Eve's sweet soprano and Tessa's mezzo-soprano blending brilliantly.

'Love is all!' said Philip sceptically. 'That's just what Eve Brook thinks. She's anybody's you know: if there's a man she fancies she just goes right to bed with him.'

'What a vile thing to say! She loves her fiancé!'

'If I were him I wouldn't trust her an inch.'

Sid wanted to flay him with words. She attacked his vanity. 'What's the matter? Did she turn you down?' It was a random shot, but it struck home.

'Uppity little cow,' he snapped. 'Her head is so swelled I wonder she can get her hat on.'

Sid laughed. 'She did turn you down.'

'Which is more than you did! Any more than you do your other lovers.'

'You can leave any time you like,' said Sid, picking up her pen again. Her tone was calmness itself, though inside she was seething. Thank God she hadn't told him his child was alive. He was despicable. He could have hurt Amy with as little thought as he had so cruelly hurt her mother.

Tom wrote to say he was coming home on leave and would visit her. When she read his decisive words her eyebrows lifted. He hadn't asked if he could come, he had stated that he would. He arrived the week after Sid had thankfully seen the Prossers depart. He was so strong, so good-looking, with his customary gentleness of manner towards her. She was glad he had come.

He seated himself in the kitchen. 'You've had bombs here, too. Thank God you're all right. I heard about Mrs Cardell. I'm so sorry. You were very fond of her, I know.'

'Yes, I was.'

'I suppose the ghastly Prossers have ordered you to leave. What will you all do? And how about the child? She's going to miss Greystone House and Aunt Louisa and all of you. You'll have to be sensible now and find some relatives. She must have others. You can't look after her in a bed-sit somewhere.'

'Nice of you to be concerned.'

'That was your sarcastic voice. What did I say?'

'Everyone has plans for Amy, as if she were a lost kitten or a stray dog.'

He flushed. 'Sorry, I didn't mean it that way. I was thinking first of you.'

'And I am trying to think for everyone.'

'So like you. You're the kindest girl I've ever met. But I wonder the Prossers didn't arrange for Amy's future. Or perhaps they are going to.'

'No.'

'I suppose it was too much to expect of them.'

'I'm sure it would have been, but there was no necessity for it. Mrs Cardell left everything to me.'

Tom was amazed. 'You can't be joking. Not about a thing like that. Well, who'd have thought the old girl had it in her.' He gave a yell of laughter which echoed to the high kitchen ceiling. 'How priceless! I wish I'd been here when they found out. What did they say?'

'They were quite rude.'

Tom's laugh burst out again. 'Quite rude? That must be the understatement of the century. I wonder they haven't threatened to contest the will.'

'They want to, but the lawyer said they had no chance. In the end, they gave up and left. You just missed them.'

'Thank God for that.' Tom looked round him, at the yards and yards of wall; the dozens of hanging utensils – mostly unused nowadays, many tarnished and still rather grimy from the dust which seemed to seep through the rags; at the blocked-up windows; at the enormous ranges. 'I've never seen such a huge kitchen.'

'How many have you seen?'

'You have me there. Hardly any. Well, one actually. Our own. I used to go there as a boy and Cook gave me gingerbread and home-made fudge. Everything here is so big. It needs an army of servants. I don't know how you've managed. Will you sell up?'

'I doubt if it would sell at present.'

'Perhaps not. After the war it could fetch a fair price, but you'll need to keep it in order.'

'I know.'

'What about all the stuff? Prices for anything large have sunk to rock bottom, but people are still buying good pictures and small furniture.'

'I shan't sell anything unless I have to.'

'Is this because you feel you owe something to Mrs Cardell?'

'She left me a letter. I can do what I like.'

'She was a grand old girl.'

'She was.' Sid got up to make coffee, blinking the moisture from her eyes.

The Misses Weekley arrived to clean, bringing Amy with them. She was full of chatter about Aunty Selina and Aunty Nellie and their collection of dolls, fluffy rabbits and dogs and other toys. In her excitement she ignored Tom until, turning to him, she asked suddenly, 'Have you got lots of aunties like me?'

'Too many,' he grinned.

'Why?'

'You don't have to explain,' said Sid, smiling. ' "Why" is her favourite word just now.'

'Why?' asked Amy again. She was always single-minded in her purpose.

'Because they keep knitting things for me. Socks and pullovers and balaclavas.'

'What's one of them?'

'A balaclava?'

'Yes.'

'It's a hat which goes over your face.'

'How can you see then?'

'They leave a space for your eyes.'

'Why?'

'Why what?'

'Why don't you like all the things?'

'I've got one aunty who knits one sock longer than the other, and another who makes pullovers big enough for an elephant.'

Sid groaned. 'Now you've done it. She takes everything literally.'

By the time Tom had stumbled his way through an explanation concerning elephants and pullovers, it was well into the morning.

'I must set to work,' she said. 'I'm returning to the factory in three days' time, and I want to check Mrs Cardell's things. There will be garments I can give to the WVS or the Salvation Army for the poor souls who've been bombed out and lost everything.'

'Am I being ejected?'

'You can stay if you like, but I don't know what you'll do.'

'There must be something.'

'I've boiled the hens' food, but it needs mashing and the garden needs tidying up. Brindle's getting too old for much stooping, Keith is so besotted with the Home Guard he can't settle to anything for long, and Patrick tends to pull up the vegetables, thinking they're weeds. Of course, you can't do much, the ground is still frozen.'

Tom borrowed an old leather apron and mashed away at the boiled vegetable peelings, whistling along with the music on the wireless, then went outside. Sid saw him occasionally through a window as he methodically worked with a fork, dragging dead leaves and twigs to the compost heap. He really was a very nice man.

The three men servants had been out helping to clear up after stray sticks of incendiaries and bombs.

Brindle walked into the kitchen, 'What's *he* doing in my garden?'

'Helping you,' said Sid. 'He knows you have heavy duties with the Home Guard.'

This rendered Brindle temporarily speechless, which annoyed him further. 'I hope he knows what he's doing. That idiot – jerking his thumb at Patrick – 'pulled all the tops off the cabbages the other day. Heaven only knows if they'll thrive.'

'I'm sure they will,' Sid assured him. 'We all know you've got green fingers.'

'Is there any cocoa?'

'You know you don't like it made with water.'

'I'll just have to get used to it. Isn't there any milk at all?'

'Just enough for tea. And Amy's special allowance, but she needs every drop.'

'Kids get everything now. Milk, orange juice . . .' He went grumbling towards his pantry, then stuck his head round the door to say, 'I'll have it made with water then.'

Sid took pity on him and allowed him some milk. After Mrs Cardell's death, he had seemed to shrink. For years he had cared for her single-handedly; losing her had been to lose his dearest friend. But he had put his shoulders back and resumed his duties. She wondered how old he was. Far older than he admitted: she was certain he had lied about his age when he joined the Home Guard. She handed him his cocoa with milk, which pleased him, and when he tasted the generous amount of sugar she'd added, he smiled. Only a little, but his face definitely broke into happy creases for a moment. He supped it loudly, smacking his lips. Keith called Tom who joined them, accepting milkless tea without comment and helping himself frugally to one biscuit only.

'How are you getting on with sorting things out?' he asked.

'It's slow work. I've begun with the downstairs stuff. There are piles of papers and notebooks. I've put them into drawers in the library. I'll have a go at them later, though they all seem to deal with personal matters, so I'll probably destroy them unread.'

Tom left quite late that night. When he had finished gardening he washed in cool water, then came to the kitchen where Sid was baking.

'You work so hard,' he said.

'Good job I'm strong then.'

'If you ever needed me, you would ask, wouldn't you?'

She kept looking down into her pastry mix. 'I shan't need to ask.'

'But you would, Sidonia? You know I care about you.'

He came up behind her and held her waist in his large hands. 'Such a slender waist. You do eat properly, don't you? You don't give all the food to the others?'

'That would be an exceedingly stupid thing to do. I need my energy to keep going. Thank you for the gardening and the hens.'

She turned round. She hadn't given a thought to how close to her he was standing, and her face was very near his. Without hesitation he kissed her, his lips warm and gentle. She longed to relax into his caress. It would be sweet to lean on him just for a moment, to take what he had to offer. What had he to offer? Another shameful episode? Philip had been charm personified until she had told him about their child. She remained passive and, after a moment, he released her.

Sid went to see some of the results of the savage Easter raid, wondering if she could do anything to help. It had caused terrible damage to hundreds of homes and left many people dead and injured. She saw families struggling as best they could in their half-ruined houses, reluctantly moving out as they were declared unsafe, camping in chapels, dance halls, anywhere they could sleep under cover. Ironically, there were many who had been evacuated to Bristol when it was considered a safer place. The older children were kept busy at school, though the classrooms were now so overcrowded the teachers were getting desperate. The weary mothers, hanging around empty halls with toddlers and babies who had nowhere to play properly, looked grey with anxiety as their younger ones worked off their energy. Quarrels broke out among both the women and children as they struggled for space. The WVS were much in evidence, handing out donated clothes and shoes, sorting blankets and allocating them, making sure everyone was fed. Sid returned to Greystone House feeling very thoughtful. She stopped outside the front door and looked up at the old stones. 'There's plenty of room here,' she said aloud. 'I could easily offer help.'

She telephoned the WVS, who sent two women round at once. One of them, plummy-voiced, was dressed in lovely tweeds. The other was short and plump with a kind face. Sid showed them into the small sitting room. The weather was still bitterly cold and the room was icy, but people were getting accustomed to the cold both inside and out.

They introduced themselves as Mrs Arlington and Mrs Morland.

'I don't suppose you're any relation to Tessa Morland – Ware now, of course – one of the Kissing Cousins?' asked Sid. 'I know she's a Bristol girl.'

The plump lady preened herself. 'I'm her mother.'

'How wonderful! I just love her records. She writes some of her songs herself, doesn't she? I met her. She's a marvellous person.'

'She is that,' agreed Tessa's mother happily. 'A lovely girl and thinks a lot of her family. Her cousin Eve's lovely, too. She's like one of our own. They told me about you. That's why I came – one of the reasons. I feel I know you already.'

Sid wondered what it must be like to have such a sweet, good-natured little roly-poly mother with kind eyes.

Her thoughts were interrupted by Mrs Arlington. 'I understand you are willing to give accommodation to some of our distressed families?'

'To the bombed-out people? Yes.'

'I also understand that you have been left this house and contents unconditionally.'

'It doesn't take long for news to get about.'

Mrs Arlington's eyebrows rose. 'Mrs Cardell's will is no secret.'

'No, of course not.'

'What war-work do you do?'

Sid could see no relevance in the question, but said mildly, 'I work in an aircraft components factory.'

'I'm happy to hear it,' said Mrs Arlington. 'There are too many young women who seem content to remain in quite unnecessary occupations.'

Mrs Morley bridled. 'My Tessa and Eve are doing vital war-work. Everyone says people's morale needs lifting.'

Mrs Arlington had enough grace to blush. 'Of course they are doing their duty. I know they go all over the place, including London, where the raids are simply dreadful. I was not referring to them.'

'That's all right then.'

Sid, thinking of her sisters still in their comfortable jobs in millinery, said nothing.

'I suppose you work long hours. Shift work, too.'

'We all do,' replied Sid.

'Mrs Arlington is wondering how you'll manage when you're out such a lot.'

'Thank you, Mrs Morland, I am capable of expressing myself.'

Mrs Morland flushed. 'Of course you are, dear. I'm just trying to help.'

'The women are generally disorganised,' said Mrs Arlington.

'They're mostly a good-hearted lot,' said Mrs Morland, 'but a bit feckless.'

'Decidedly feckless,' said Mrs Arlington. 'When I see them lounging about, smoking as many cigarettes as they can buy, their children none too clean . . .'

'They can't do much stuck in church halls and the like,' said Mrs Morland, 'and the washing facilities are very poor. They go down to the public baths and wash-houses, though they've little left to wash, poor souls.'

'Are you sure you'll be able to manage?' asked Mrs Arlington, trying to ignore Mrs Morland. 'Their children are not on the whole well disciplined.'

'I have to admit,' said Mrs Morland, 'that some of the children do run a bit wild.'

Mrs Arlington persevered. 'You have some valuable things in this room; I suppose there's more elsewhere in the house.'

'The valuables can be stored. There's a dry stable outside, and I can take quite a few into my rooms.'

'That would be advisable. You'll need to make rules about bathroom and kitchen access, cooking facilities, that kind of thing. May we see over the house?'

'Of course.'

They went from room to room, Mrs Arlington taking notes. When they reached the nursery suite she looked pleased. 'This is so suitable for the mothers with young babies. We can set up more beds. I see there is a wash-basin too. Who uses it at present?'

'I sleep here with a child, and a maid returns here for her leaves. She's in the WAAF.'

'Ah, yes, I had heard of a child. One of Mrs Cardell's relatives? I imagine arrangements have been made to remove her.'

'No. She has nowhere to go.'

'Nowhere? Has she no family?'

'No.'

'Or none that will recognise her? A war baby? A victim of promiscuity perhaps? There will be many such godless children born before the war is finally over.' Mrs Arlington's thin nose twitched.

Sid resented her prurience and intolerant attitude, but before she could speak, Mrs Morland said loudly, 'All children are equal in the sight of God.'

Sid felt an overwhelming desire to kiss her. 'We can move out of here,' she said. 'I could take Mrs Cardell's room for both of us, and a lot of her better stuff could be stored there. It's a big room.'

Both women exclaimed at the size of the kitchen. Mrs Arlington looked even more pleased. 'Excellent. There's space here for everyone to eat at once. I'll requisition some trestle tables and have them sent down with some chairs. We also have playpens and high-chairs and rubber sheeting. I'm afraid you'll find plenty of bed-wetters among the children. It is one of the most frequent complaints we have had to deal with from people who have taken evacuees. I see you have good fireguards, and the children will be able to use the garden.'

'As long as they don't upset the gardener. We've been digging for victory, and lots of our food comes from there. But there are no vegetables planted in front of the house, and they can play among the trees as well.'

'Excellent,' said Mrs Arlington again, scribbling away. 'Of course, there are not really enough bathrooms and lavatories, and in ordinary circumstances I would consider the place unsuitable for a number of children. However, they are infinitely better than we can at present offer, and most of them are unused to bathrooms anyway. We can supply tin baths and chamber-pots. I can't promise fuel for central heating, but you'll get extra coal for the fires. Do you need more fireguards? I'll have them sent. Let me know if there is anything else required. When I return to headquarters we shall decide how many families you can take. Meanwhile, I suggest you begin to prepare the place. There is talk now of evacuating Bristol, so it may not be for long.'

Sid wrote immediately to Angie to tell her what had happened. 'Please, don't mind,' she begged. 'I remember how glad you were to have your own room when you came on leave, after sharing with so many others, but this will always be your home and now you'll only have to share with Amy and me.'

The reply came by return. 'You're doing the right thing. I'll gladly share with you and Amy. I just hope it won't all be too much for you to manage.'

Chapter Fifteen

Men arrived with two long trestle tables which they put up in the kitchen. 'What a whopper of a place,' one of them remarked. 'You'll need it, too. Some of the kids are right little devils. They need a lot of space.'

Sid signed for the tables, extra chairs, all the things Mrs Arlington had promised, as well as a number of camp-beds and blankets. As the men were leaving, one said, 'Oh, I nearly forgot, there's a note from Mrs A.'

Sid read the hastily penned words: 'Dear Miss Penrose, the women will be bringing their ration books along. It is up to you to decide whether or not they should purchase and cook their own food. My advice is for you to avoid any complications which might ensue by taking all the books and catering for the household. Yours, Penelope Arlington.'

Later that day, Sid answered the door to find Mrs Keevil standing there. Sid was so surprised that she asked her straight in, taking her to the small sitting room. 'What can I do for you?' she asked politely.

Mrs Keevil, whose eyes had missed nothing on the way there, looked round the room. 'Well, you landed nicely on your feet, didn't you?' she said.

Sid decided to be polite. 'What can I do for you?' she repeated.

'It's what I've come to do for you. I'm a member of the Women's Voluntary Service. I work closely with Mrs Arlington.'

Sid doubted their closeness. Mrs Arlington was autocratic and domineering, but she could have little else in common with Mrs Keevil. Mrs Keevil was wearing a costume whose undoubted smartness was spoilt by too much glittering jewellery, her nails were long and red and her face was still over-painted.

Mrs Keevil said, 'Oh, you're thinking I don't look the part. I fail to see why helping out in wartime should mean one has to wear a dowdy uniform. I only do when I'm meeting someone important, like the mayor. When Mr Winston Churchill visited Bristol, I was able to greet him and welcome him to Bedminster.'

'Were you? Why were you in Bedminster?'

'Because that's where he was going to be. Of course, not everyone knew that. It had to be a secret because there are those who wish him harm, even people in this country of ours. That wonderful man!'

'I think people who have lost everything, including some of their loved ones, don't really want dignitaries to visit them.'

'I should have known you'd be on the wrong side!'

'I didn't know we were taking sides, except against Hitler.'

Mrs Keevil frowned and looked Sid up and down. She was without make-up, dressed in a brown overall borrowed from the servants' cupboard. Her hands were rough with broken fingernails. She realised she didn't care what Mrs Keevil thought about her, and when she asked to see the kitchen she had heard so much about, Sid escorted her downstairs.

Mrs Keevil looked round at the kitchen. 'Is this where you work nowadays? Though I don't suppose you do much work any more. I read about the legacy in the newspapers. They said you were rich; they called you a modern Cinderella.'

'You shouldn't believe all you read in the newspapers,' said Sid coolly.

Mrs Keevil bridled. 'Oh, I don't, of course, but you do own this house now, don't you? No smoke without fire. I heard it said that you got the old lady nicely under your thumb. Clever of you.'

Sid kept a hold on her flare of anger. 'How's Mr Keevil?' she asked. She was immediately ashamed of the innuendo in her voice. 'Is he the bank manager yet?'

Mrs Keevil flushed. 'The promotion will come in due course. I came here to talk business.'

'Good, so shall we get down to it? As you can imagine, I am very busy.'

'And I suppose you think I'm not!'

Sid didn't bother to answer.

Sid's silence and the slight, sardonic, irrepressible lift of her eyebrows clearly irritated Mrs Keevil. She spoke quickly. 'We are sending you five mothers and fifteen children, six of whom belong to a woman called Daisy Brown. She's been bombed out twice. The first time she lost her own house in London, and in the last Bristol raid her sister's house went. They are needy women who will probably be overwhelmed by Greystone House. It's up to you to make them welcome.'

Sid forgot her dislike of Mrs Keevil. 'Poor souls. Is Mrs Brown's sister coming with her?'

'No, she's gone to Devon to stay with an aunt. There wasn't room there for Mrs Brown's family. She is a widow. Her older sons and daughters are in the services. Presumably you can put them up when they are on leave.'

'Goodness! How many children has she got altogether?'

'I really couldn't say. Have you prepared the rooms?'

'Yes. We've made up all the camp-beds too, though they won't be very comfortable, and it was difficult to fit the rubber sheets securely.'

Mrs Keevil was not interested in such mundane problems. 'Nothing is easy in wartime,' she said without interest, scanning a sheaf of papers she carried. 'They will be arriving at tea-time.'

'Does that mean four o'clock or five?'

'Just before six. Tea to them is dinner and supper combined; they usually have something cooked, or cold meat. Have you enough food for this evening?'

'We'll manage, though it'll be plain.'

'They won't mind that. Some of the children are far too thin. They are said to be undernourished. Their mothers insist they can't afford to buy all the rations, but in my opinion their money goes on drink and cigarettes.'

Mrs Keevil left. Sid and the residents of Greystone House awaited the arrival of the unusual guests somewhat apprehensively. Brindle produced vegetables he'd had stored in sand, grumbling beneath his breath about them not lasting out the cold weather. Sid, who was busy turning them into an enormous pan of soup, hoping that three precious onions and the two ham-bones she'd acquired would give it sufficient flavour, caught the words, 'filthy brats', 'turn in her grave'.

'I hope you'll be kind to the new arrivals,' she said sternly. 'They've had a rotten time.'

'That's not my fault!'

'Nor mine, nor theirs.'

Brindle still grumbled, but more from habit now than conviction.

While Sid prepared food, Patrick and Keith filled all the hot-water bottles they could muster and put them into the beds, then built up the range fire. Sid had decided to open up the schoolroom where, long ago, generations of children had played, and where the furniture was large, heavy and already scuffed and kicked so that there was nothing which even the most rumbustious child could damage. Patrick lit a fire there too.

Amy danced up and down with excitement. The fact that one of the families was called Brown had interested her tremendously. 'Will I have brothers and sisters?' she asked. 'Can they play with me? Do they know any good games? They won't break my toys, will they?'

A fleet of cars came slowly up the drive and one by one ejected their passengers. A drab, dejected group of women and children stood looking fearfully at Greystone House. Any reservations Sid might have had couldn't have been sustained at the sight of these needy ones, and even Brindle unbent and muttered a few kind words.

'Are you all here?' asked Sid. 'I thought there were to be five mothers and fifteen children.'

'That's right,' said a thin woman. 'Mrs Brown wouldn't move unless all her kids were in the same car, and she got the driver to stop and buy food for tonight.'

Sid warmed to Mrs Brown.

The last car swept up the drive and pulled to a halt. A rather desperate-looking young woman climbed out of the driver's seat. The other doors burst open and a noisy brood of children, aged from about ten to two years old, erupted on to the driveway, followed by a woman who was almost six feet tall and brawny with it.

'Hello,' she said raucously in a broad cockney accent, 'I'm Daisy Brown and these are my kids. I've brought some fish an' chips.'

Sid welcomed her. She must have looked apprehensive at meeting this overwhelming woman, because Daisy let out a loud guffaw. 'Don't be scared, my love. My kids'll behave. If they don't, they know what they can expect.'

'A bloody good clout,' said her eldest boy.

Sid expected his mother to reprimand him but she didn't.

The soup was quickly demolished with loud slurpings and plenty of bread, followed by sandwiches eaten with Mrs Brown's fish and chips, which she insisted on sharing. The children gobbled their food like starving animals, with casual table manners which caused Brindle to tut loudly.

'What's for puddin'?' demanded one of the Brown boys.

'Less of your "what's for puddin' " ', cried Mrs Brown. 'Your Aunty Sid's got enough to do without worryin' about puddin'.' Mrs Brown explained, 'They told us the kids could call you Aunty. If you don't like it – '

'It's perfectly all right. I want us to be friends.'

Another Brown boy said belligerently, 'Sid's a boy's name.'

'Well, it's hers as well,' said his mother, 'an' you treat her with respect, or you'll get what-for! What's your real name, ducks?'

'Sidonia.'

'Cor, what a mouthful,' yelled the boy.

Mrs Brown almost absent-mindedly swiped his head while he, with practised ease, ducked so that her hand merely brushed his hair. 'You can call me Daisy,' she said magnanimously. Immediately the boy shouted, 'Hey, Daisy . . .' Before he got any further she reached out and, with a hand like a ham, slapped him hard. This time she connected. He yelped, but said no more.

During the next hectic hours, during which Sid gave up trying to remember all the children's names, she discovered that the families had been living in Lawrence Hill and that all, even Daisy, for all her brash ways, were still in a state of shock and feeling miserable.

'Lost everythin' we did,' muttered Mrs Wallace. 'Everythin'. An' expected to be grateful to the WVS for givin' us bloody cast-offs.'

'We're lucky to get them,' said Mrs Brown. 'We're all in the same boat an' we're still alive an' that's more than you can say about some of our neighbours.'

'That's true,' sighed Mrs Curtis. The three women were inspecting the rooms, leaving the children in the kitchen in the charge of the other two, who had argued mutinously about this arrangement, saying, 'They'll go an' take all the best places.'

'No, we won't,' said Daisy. 'We'll decide what's fair.'

Daisy, by the sheer weight of her overwhelming personality and her size, seemed to exert some kind of influence over the others, who gave way before her decisions, though still grumbling.

The rooms were allocated. Two of the mothers, Mrs Dawson and Mrs Partridge, with four children under five and a suckling baby, were given the nursery suite. 'We'll make sure there's a fire kept in here,' said Sid. 'Clean rubber sheets, linen and blankets are in the big cupboard.' They left the women there with their pathetic bundles.

Daisy said confidentially, 'Don't take any notice of them bein' miserable, ducks. They've had a terrible time, poor things.'

'Hasn't it been terrible for you?'

'Oh, yes, an' I still feel the effects, but my husband died at Dunkirk an' I've had to get used to doin' for myself. He needn't have gone at his age, but you know what men are, he wanted to do his bit. Not that he was much good when he was alive, couldn't keep a job to save his life, but I was ever so fond of him, though he was a right elbow-shaker an' never brought much money in. I worked in a laundry. Elbow-shaker? That's a gambler. Always believed he'd win, but he lost, just as he lost at Dunkirk, poor bugger. You engaged, ducks?'

'No,' Sid blurted, startled.

'No one in mind? A lover in the forces, perhaps?'

'No one.'

Daisy glanced at her curiously, and Sid could imagine what she saw. A thin woman with dark shadows beneath her eyes, a sallow complexion, a bump on her nose, lank hair. She'd had no time for beautifying herself lately.

She was surprised when Daisy said frankly, 'You're not a beauty, not like a film star, but you've got somethin' in you. Some man will see you for what you are.'

Sid was indignant at first, but she realised Daisy had meant no offence and she smiled ruefully, 'Can you tell so much about me with just one meeting?'

'I'm quite a good judge of character. I knew my man was weak-willed when I wed him, but he suited me. I'm not one that likes to be ruled. An' you're openin' your house to us proves I'm right about you.'

During the next weeks, Sid thanked God over and over for Daisy Brown. She made sure the older children went to school, insisted on the house being kept clean, giving the others duties but deferring to the Misses Weekley so that their feelings were never ruffled. She shopped for food and bought sensibly. True, there was too much starch on her menu for Sid's taste, but she said the kids had to have their bellies filled somehow, and starchy food helped. Sid ate what she was given. Besides, it was comforting to go to work knowing that Amy would be well cared for, return home to a kitchen occupied by the big woman, and sit down to a plate of chips and a poached egg, followed by rather heavy-handed pastry filled with a mixture of jam and fruit, with thick, sweet custard. She even began to gain a little weight.

Brindle ate anything he was given. He seemed to have accepted Daisy – as they all had – as a kind of mother-figure, or perhaps a mother hen who kept all her chicks beneath her wing. She couldn't do anything about the bed-wetters – among the fifteen children there were eight who were never dry – but she insisted on a daily wash and coped with damp beds and blankets.

The final blessing was to discover, when the frost finally broke, that Daisy enjoyed gardening. Brindle's protests at her messing about in 'his' garden died when she said, 'I don't know much, but I've always loved gardens, though I never had one. I'd take it as a favour if you'd teach me.' She was as strong as a man and dug and planted and weeded and bullied the others to work under his supervision until the vegetable beds recovered from the winter and began to flourish.

Bristol had proved more dangerous than expected, and women with young children were being evacuated. Sid hated to think of losing Daisy, and awaited news of her leaving with a sense of impending loss.

Amy, taken aback by the invasion, had at first regarded the intruders with a certain reservation, but when she realised that she now shared the house with six children all named Brown, she was delighted, especially when they included her in their own 'gang'.

'Am I your girl?' she asked Daisy.

'No, ducks.' Daisy could be gentle when she wished. She had been told that Amy was a war orphan, and when the child's face fell she said, 'But you can pretend to be my girl if you like.'

'Ooh, yes!' cried Amy. 'Pretending is as good as real. Better.'

Afterwards, in the kitchen, when Daisy and Sid were inspecting the store cupboards, Daisy said, 'I hope she won't be too upset when I have to leave.'

'We'll cross that one when we come to it,' said Sid.

There were a number of bridges which needed to be crossed. The language of both mothers and children was colourful, to say the least. When Sid spoke hesitantly to Daisy about it, she was puzzled. 'We don't use really bad language,' she said. 'You should hear some of 'em.'

The mothers took to regular evening bathing of their offspring, amid screams from those who had been used to the weekly bath by the fire and a wipe-over with a flannel the rest of the week. No doors were ever locked, and boys and girls were scrubbed together, including Amy, a fact Sid discovered after coming off the daytime shift at the factory.

'Boys have got a dangly thing,' Amy informed Sid at supper. She saw no reason to keep her voice down. The children and their mothers hooted with mirth, Brindle frowned, and Keith smothered a grin.

'I know, darling,' said Sid. 'Eat up your fruit.'

'Why have they?' persisted Amy.

'Because boys and girls are different.'

'I know that. Why?'

'Because they are,' said Sid, exasperated and embarrassed.

Amy attacked her fruit. Later Sid explained the sexual difference as well as she could to such a small child.

The women seemed to require endless tea. To make sure they got it they had no hesitation in making it in a large kettle in the morning and leaving it to simmer all day. Sid found the resultant brew indescribably nasty, but she shrugged her shoulders and drank it. If she had complained, the answer would have been, 'Don't you know there's a war on?' It had become the phrase on everyone's lips. Ask for something off ration, beg for a few extra cigarettes, a bag of sweets for the children, and the inevitable answer came.

Daisy and her troop of workers, often unwilling but bullied into submission, supplemented the rations with the garden produce. Daisy also cooked food which Sid had never considered using. Tripe, for instance. White and rubbery, Daisy cooked it with onions. Chitterlings – actually pork intestines – served cold, white and greasy, with vinegar, were adored by everyone except Sid and Brindle. Amy ate them without grumbling because all her new-found friends did. Faggots, a dish which had once been meat-filled but, like sausages, were now mostly bread, also appeared on the menu. One night Daisy came up with a large, succulent dish of chicken. When Sid praised it and asked where she had managed to buy it, Daisy said serenely, 'It isn't chicken. It's rabbit.'

Amy cried, 'A dear little furry rabbit?'

'That's right, ducks,' said Daisy.

Amy considered the answer, while everyone held their breath. She was subject occasionally to tantrums, which set off the other children. Then she said, 'Rabbit. Can we play before bed, Aunty Daisy?'

Sometimes Sid had to suppress a twinge of jealousy of this woman who had taken over her child's affection and obedience, but she was deeply grateful to be able to go to work in the knowledge that Amy would be well cared for. The mothers let her scramble up the easy trees behind the boys, make dens in the woods, stalk with pretend guns, and race shrieking round the old house when it rained, but she was happy, and any scratches or bruises were tended meticulously by Daisy.

The Misses Weekley came to Sid one day. 'We're handing in our notice,' said Nellie, the elder. 'We can't be doing with all the goings-on here.'

'It's not that we think you shouldn't have invited them,' said Selina.

'But that Mrs Brown makes everyone clean, so you don't need us,' said Nellie. 'They've not been bothersome, I have to say that, but my sister and me liked the quietness of the house, and now it's nothing but noise.'

'I'm so sorry,' said Sid. 'They may be evacuated soon, of course. Would you consider coming back if that happens?'

'We might,' said Nellie, 'but we're not getting any younger and we've been thrifty. We might just get a little job somewhere else to boost our income.'

'I shall miss you terribly. You've been so kind.'

Both ladies shed a few tears, but left anyway.

'Good riddance,' said Mrs Partridge. She sat in the kitchen suckling her infant, unaffected by the presence of Keith, or Brindle, who kept his eyes averted. 'Pokin' an' pryin' into what we was doin'.'

Mrs Arlington and Mrs Morland came to inspect the arrangements sometimes, and even Mrs Arlington was impressed. She tutted at the drawings, sketched by a budding artist on the fine old wallpaper, frowned at the sight of scuff-marks on the doors and skirtings, and at the grubby patches left on expensive carpets by dirty shoes; but the women looked far less strained and the children were blooming.

'I congratulate you, Miss Penrose. You are doing excellent work.'

Mrs Morland lingered behind for a moment. 'You're doing too much, my dear. You look tired.'

'Most people look tired these days.'

'That's true. Tessa and Eve have been on a tour of the camps but they're coming home in about a week. They'll need a rest. They don't spare themselves. Can they come and visit? They enjoyed themselves last time.'

'Of course. I should be delighted.'

Mrs Morland began to walk away then turned back, 'Is Angie going to be here?'

'Not that I know of.' Mrs Morland and Angie hadn't met as far as Sid knew.

Mrs Morland enlightened her. 'Our Joseph is stationed quite near. He told me he'd like to see her again.'

'I see.' Sid felt pleased. Joseph was solemn, almost lugubrious, but he was undoubtedly respectable and she remembered Angie saying she liked him.

'Perhaps she wouldn't mind writing to him. Our Joseph...' Mrs Morland got no further as a tooting on the horn indicated that Mrs Arlington was becoming impatient. 'Oh, dear, I shall have to go. We've got other houses to visit.'

Sid accompanied Mrs Morland outside to find the car surrounded by children who were eating home-made toffee produced by Daisy. To Mrs Arlington's annoyance, there were sticky fingermarks all over the immaculate paintwork. Sid had to suppress a smile as she waved the two ladies goodbye.

Tessa Ware and Eve Brook paid their visit. Eve looked with astonishment at the assortment of children playing under the trees while the hens pecked and squawked around them. The snow and ice had gone at last, and everything was burgeoning with life. 'How on earth do you put up with the mess and racket?' she asked.

Tessa laughed, 'The same way we put up with long waits for over-crowded, freezing trains, plain meals, performing in our coats because it's been so bitterly cold...'

'All right, all right, I capitulate,' said Eve smiling, and again Sid was struck by her extraordinary beauty.

'You an' your friends can have tea in the library,' said Daisy. 'I'll bring it there for you.' She seldom read anything, but was overwhelmed by the number of books in the library, which she always referred to in awed tones. Eating in the library was considered the ultimate in gentility.

'Do you usually eat with the others?' asked Eve.

'Yes, they're a good-hearted lot.'

'Jolly, too,' said Eve. 'Any husbands here?'

'No, they've either lost them or they're serving somewhere. One poor soul hasn't heard from hers for ages.'

Eve put down her cup and saucer with a small clatter. 'If you'll excuse me...' She hurried from the room.

'Oh dear, did I offend her?' asked Sid.

'Not intentionally, and it isn't offence. It's grief. You couldn't know that her fiancé is missing at sea, believed drowned.'

'How terrible! I'm really sorry.'

'Don't blame yourself,' said Tessa kindly. 'He was in the Navy, escorting merchant ships. The men who bring our supplies home have a fearful time. So many of the ships are sunk, so many men die. David was unlucky enough to be on a battle-cruiser that was torpedoed.'

'I've heard of the carnage at sea. It's so awful. We manage on the rations in this house and buy as few clothes as possible. In fact, we've been making stuff from Mrs Cardell's clothes. I found masses of them stored in trunks in all kinds of materials. I can't sew, but Daisy and two of the others can, and they've done wonders. I don't know how anyone can bring themselves to buy on the black market when it might mean more lives lost.'

Eve wandered down the garden. The children were shrieking noisily among the trees, their voices echoing. She stopped at the tall perimeter wall and leaned on it. It was in the shade now, but still held a little warmth from the afternoon sun. David was missing, believed drowned. She had to accept that he was dead. Anyone who was thrown into the icy waters in the depths of winter couldn't survive for long. She must keep reminding herself that she'd never see him again, but still she couldn't believe it when her heart told her that he would return. All her life she had been looking for love; now she had found it, surely fate couldn't be so cruel as to take it away before she had even had time to savour it? His last leave had been so short. He had held her in his arms as if he'd never let her go.

'I love you, Eve,' he had said, over and over, kissing her face, her lips. 'I think of you all the time.'

'I go crazy with missing you.'

'On my next leave we'll get married.'

She had wanted him with all her mind and soul. Her body ached for him to make love to her. She had once had a scandalous reputation and, before they had realised what they would one day mean to each other, she had slept with him more than once, treating him as a casual lover. When she had fallen in love with him she believed it a hopeless love, but miraculously he came to care for her. The subject hadn't been discussed, but their minds were in unison: both wanted to marry before making love again. It was as if they were testing their power to refrain from sexual attachment, as if by yielding they would resurrect the past Eve had striven to forget. What had they been trying to prove? she wondered, fighting back tears. David. David. The name went round her head in a refrain. If she thought about him often enough, if she begged for a miracle, perhaps he'd come back. But men too often didn't. They sank down, deeper and deeper, food for fish; or their bloated bodies were washed up on some shore. She must face it. She must face all possibilities. David, she breathed, turning to lean her head on the rough stones. Then she took a deep breath. How impolite of her to walk out like that and stay out so long. What must Sid have thought?

When she entered the library she said, 'Sorry, I felt like a breath of air.'

If Sidonia had said one word of sympathy at that point, Eve felt she would have exploded in impotent rage and frustration, but she said only, 'Would you like some more tea?' Eve appreciated her thoughtfulness, but it didn't surprise her. Sidonia had a quality about her of warmth and loving kindness. It shone from her eyes, by far her best feature.

Sid saw the suffering in Eve's eyes, and added another black mark to her memories of Philip Prosser, recalling how vicious he had been about her. Angie's letters referred to the conquests he made among the local girls. She hoped they had more sense than she'd had. Angie had also said he had returned from Mrs Cardell's funeral in such a filthy temper that no one had spoken to him for days unless they had to.

Later that week, Susan Morland called. There had been a lot of rain, and it was impossible to dry all the drawsheets needed for the bed-wetters, so Sid had rooted around until she found some ancient flannelette sheets which she had piled on the kitchen table and which she was cutting into suitable sizes. Daisy was at the stove stirring an enormous pot of soup.

'What are you doing that for?' asked Susan, when Daisy had settled her with a cup of dark brown tea.

Sid explained.

'Are all the children babies, then?'

'No. Some of the older ones have suffered a lot in the raids and it's upset their control.'

Daisy said, grimacing, 'Most of the little devils were bed-wetters before the air-raids. Their mothers believe they do it to annoy them.'

Susan smiled at her, then said to Sid, 'Can I help?'

'Would you? I ought to be doing the weekly ration-book check.'

Sue snipped happily away, while Sid and Daisy worked out the food for the next week. Sid smiled to herself when she noticed that Susan was trying to be polite and drink the tea. She gave it up in the end.

'Will Angie be coming home on leave soon?' she asked a shade too casually.

'Yes, in a couple of weeks.'

'Would she mind – would you mind – if my brother Joseph called on her?'

Sid felt excited at the idea of a romance for Angie, who had been so certain that no man would love her. Joseph Morland was not a man Sid would choose for herself, he was far too lugubrious and quiet; but perhaps he was just the anchor Angie needed.

When Angie arrived she looked fit and attractive. She dropped her bags and threw her arms round Sid. 'Oh, it's so wonderful to be home. What a brick Mrs Cardell turned out to be. Fancy leaving you the house and everything.'

Sid hugged her. 'Sit down. The women are all out. The young ones are at school, and Daisy insisted they take a picnic to the park with the babies. I'll make you a cup of tea. The women here must have dark brown stomachs with all the strong brew they swallow.'

'I'm longing to meet Daisy. Your letters made me laugh. Don't worry about the tea. I've had to eat and drink all sorts since I joined the WAAF.'

They chattered for nearly an hour, exchanging news, scarcely having time to listen to the other's reply. Then Daisy returned. Angie's eyes opened wide at the sight of this enormous woman.

'I've left the others in the park, but they'll come back soon.' She smiled at Angie.

'This is Daisy,' said Sid.

Daisy shook hands heartily. 'Pleased to meet you, ducks.'

'Same here,' said Angie, looking at her hand as if to check that nothing was broken.

'Did I hurt you?' Daisy's loud laugh rang out. 'I've been diggin' the garden, an' it's made my muscles bigger than ever. I don't know me own strength. Sid, love, it's time to get the vegetables ready for tea.'

'Heavens,' Sid sprang to her feet. 'And I must eat and go to work. I'm on late shift, Angie. You'll be all right, won't you? I wish I didn't have to leave you . . .'

'I'll be fine. I'm sure there's something I can do to help Daisy.' As Sid got up to leave, Angie said casually, 'Do you ever meet any of the Morlands these days?'

'They visit occasionally.'

'I see. That's good.'

Sid decided to end her suspense. 'Joseph is still stationed in Bristol.'

'Is he? I suppose he's as fed up as everyone else. When will we begin to fight back properly?' She spoke rapidly, embarrassed because they were discussing Joseph.

'He wants to see you. His family will let him know you've arrived if you telephone them.'

Angie's face lit up. 'I'll do that now.'

Joseph Morland walked from his parents' home to Greystone House. It wasn't a particularly long walk, but it gave him a little time to think. In the barracks there was never an opportunity just to think. All the men were kept busy at tasks which were frequently repetitive, boring and useless, simply because their superiors wanted to fill the time of waiting. There was endless drilling and cleaning of weapons, endless sweeping and cleaning, anything which the officers decided would keep discontented men from rebelling. His training as a medical orderly had reached new heights, and some of the wounds he had been told he might encounter had made him feel sick and angry. War! Bloody war! He wasn't cursing. He never had yet. He meant it. War was bloody – always had been and always would. He lived his life surrounded by people who wanted to get back at the enemy and said so in strong terms, adding what they'd like to do to Hitler if they personally got hold of him. Men who were newly recruited boasted loudest, but those who had been in the fighting and escaped from Dunkirk spoke with a deeper bitterness. They wanted revenge on the enemy who had killed and maimed their mates; they couldn't wait. Joseph was unable to understand them. He sympathised with their grief for the loss of their friends, but the thought of killing anyone was unbearable to him. He was ragged unmercifully at times about his attitude, at others he had been badly treated, even roughed up, but that only made him the more determined to resist violence.

He accepted the response his position provoked, but what he had failed utterly to come to terms with was the shaking of his faith in God. It hadn't completely gone. He still prayed, but always in his mind lingered the horrors of the blitz, of digging out the dead: old men and women who should have been enjoying their twilight years in peace and happiness; young women, some still clutching their lifeless babies in stiffening arms; children unable to comprehend why suddenly their world had gone, their parents, brothers, sisters, homes, all wiped out, leaving them trying to grasp reality, trapped in broken bodies in an insane landscape.

He arrived at Greystone House and hesitated. He felt drawn to Angie, but wondered if he had any right to pursue her acquaintance when all he had to offer were doubts and fears. Mum had said she sounded eager on the telephone. He had taken a liking to her the moment they met, but could he cope with an eager woman who made it so clear she wanted to get to know him better, while he was trying to hide his agitated, turbulent thoughts? Well, he was here now, and he wasn't one for turning back. He made his way to the kitchen. His mother had warned him that the place was filled with refugees, so he had chosen a time when the older ones would be at school and hopefully the young ones put down for their after-dinner naps. The kitchen seemed at first to be absolutely full of women.

A very large one called, 'Hello, soldier. Do you want our Sid?'

'I hoped to see Angie . . .'

She was there. She stood up and walked towards him, welcome shining from her eyes. 'Hello, Joseph.'

'Hello, Angie.'

They paused, not moving. 'Will you two stand there all day?' cried Daisy. 'Go on, Angie, take him upstairs to the small sitting room. Small, they call it,' rolling her eyes at the others. 'You could have got two or three of my livin' rooms in it.'

Amid raucous mirth, Joseph escorted Angie upstairs. They sat opposite one another in two easy chairs.

'How are you getting on?' asked Angie formally.

'All right. How about you?'

'All right.'

'I still don't believe in war,' said Joseph, anxious to establish this quickly.

'Who does, but we've got to fight to save all the poor oppressed people.'

'So they say.'

'Would you leave them to Hitler's mercy?'

'I'd leave them to God's.'

Angie, who in her childhood had been packed off to Sunday school to get her out of the way, said, 'Aren't we the instruments of God? He needs help sometimes.'

Joseph said, 'Blessed are the peacemakers.' The words came naturally out of his mouth, but were at odds with his wavering faith; nowadays they sounded priggish to him.

'I agree wars are awful. You've been helping out in the raids, haven't you?'

He nodded. The grim nightmares intruded all too easily into the daylight hours.

Angie took the initiative. 'Shall we walk round the garden? Daisy and the others have been very busy.'

'I thought there was a sort of gardener-cum-handyman.'

'Brindle? He's a sergeant in the Home Guard and takes his duties very seriously. Honestly, I'm sure he would willingly die fighting if the Jerries invaded, but since Mrs Cardell went, he's lost a lot of energy. It's easier for him to forget her when he's on duty.'

'He must have cared a lot for her.'

'He did. He seems to have shrunk since she died. I don't know how old he is, but I'm sure he's over seventy.'

They wandered along the narrow paths between the vegetable patches.

Joseph said, 'They grow a lot of stuff, don't they? My father keeps us in vegetables and Mum has always had a few hens.'

'Sid speaks of your mother so nicely. She thinks she's a lovely lady.'

'So she is. She and Dad gave us a good Christian upbringing.'

'So you've always been a good boy?' Angie smiled at him, daring to tease him a little.

'Not at all.' She was pleased to see him manage a smile. 'I was a mischievous little devil, but then I found the Lord and began my evangelical preaching.'

Angie said nothing for a moment. 'Do you preach nowadays?'

'No. Mum thought I'd be glad to when I was on leave, but . . .'

Angie felt his distress. 'I dare say you'll get back to it after the war.'

'I dare say I will.' They wandered on. 'Dad's always out during raids doing rescue and demolition work, and Mum goes on a WVS van with sandwiches and hot drinks. They both run terrible risks.'

'Susan, too,' said Angie. 'She does great work in the raids.'

'Yes, I have a wonderful family.' He stooped and picked a piece of parsley, rubbing it between his fingers and sniffing it. 'My father fought in the Great War. When I was small I used to ask him about his experiences. He would never tell me, but a certain look came into his eyes. I understand why now.'

'Is he tolerant of your refusal to fight?'

'He accepts it. He's a tolerant man, a good man. Far better than I'll ever be.'

'Yet he fought.'

'Yes. But it didn't damage his faith.'

Angie's heart twisted in pity. He was suffering so bitterly and she didn't know how to help him. 'Do you have any other brothers or sisters?' she asked. 'Apart from Tessa and Susan?'

'No, although we look upon our cousin Eve as a sister.'

'She and Tessa often go to dangerous places, don't they? Civilians are in the battle nowadays: anyone can get bombed. You never know where a pilot will let his cargo drop. People need someone to pray for them.' The last sentence left her lips awkwardly. She never prayed. Never really had.

'Are you church or chapel?' asked Joseph.

She thought of lying. What answer did he want? He wants the truth, common sense told her. 'I don't go to either. At least, I have to attend worship on the base, but that's all.'

'You spoke as if you understood the Christian faith.'

'I know. I was made to go to Sunday school.' Angie's heart felt like lead. When he found out what kind of background she had sprung from he would despise her. She realised she wanted his good opinion very much indeed.

'I'm chapel,' said Joseph. 'Did your parents never take you to worship?'

'I don't know if my mother's ever been to church in her life.' Angie paused. 'I don't know who my father was.' She paused again, decided that he had best know all there was. 'He could have been one of a number of men,' she blurted out. 'My mother doesn't know either.'

Joseph stopped and turned her to look at him. She met his eyes and held up her head. 'What a courageous girl you are. I admire you for telling the truth.'

And that was all. They continued their walk round the garden and he left soon after. He didn't ask to see her again, or if she'd write to him. Angie wanted to weep. A courageous fool, that's what she had been. She should have told a few lies, made certain of holding his interest. She sensed that he was deeply troubled about something; she was sure she had made things worse for him. He was such a decent man. She smiled ironically. What decent man would want a prostitute for a mother-in-law?

The raids continued, though it was some consolation to know that the Royal Air Force was bombing Germany. The authorities had at last declared Bristol an unsafe area and began evacuating children and women with babies. Mrs Arlington had called at Greystone House to tell the mothers to prepare to go, and had been met by a wall of repudiation.

Daisy spoke for them all. 'We're every so happy here, Mrs Arlington, an' we've decided we'll stay.'

'But you can't! You are all in danger. Think of the children.'

'An' you think of the out-of-the-way places that have had bombs dropped on them. We could be hit anywhere.'

'But at least in Devon or Cornwall or Wales you'd be safer than here.'

It was no use. The women had suffered a great deal. In Greystone House they had found a congenial home and there they would remain.

Before Angie went back off leave, Joseph Morland called to ask her out. Angie's face gave her away. She was in love and couldn't hide it, and Sid was frightened for her. Joseph had succeeded in schooling his face to betray no emotion, so that sometimes he presented a mask-like appearance. But Angie was happy.

'He's asked me if I'll write to him,' she told Sid and Daisy.

'That's always a good sign,' said Daisy. 'You'll get him if you play your cards right.'

Angie flushed. 'That sounds so calculating.'

'What's the matter with that?' asked Daisy with a laugh that made the pans rattle. 'If we women want a man we've damn well got to be calculating. The little dears never know what they want, an' if we waited till they found out, most of us would be old. At least, that's not quite true. They all want a roll in the blankets, an' it's up to us to keep them danglin' until they do the right thing, otherwise they'd leave us with somethin' we definitely don't want. I've seen it happen too many times. A girl believes a man's lies, gives in, an' the next thing you know she's expectin' an' he's off like a shot to some other girl.'

Angie was embarrassed for Sid's sake as well as her own. Thank God only she and Sid knew the truth of Amy's birth.

Tom Barton telephoned. He was due some leave and asked Sid if he could take her out. His letters had begun getting warmer; she had deliberately made her replies friendly but cool. She had no doubt at all that he had grown fond of her but, like Philip Prosser, he was from a different stratum of society, and she had no intention of ever being used to amuse a man again. However, he was fighting for his country, so she agreed to see him, wondering if she had come to a wise decision.

He telephoned again as soon as he reached home. 'Are you working tonight? No? I'll be round after dinner. Can't leave the folks until then.'

Sid changed into her prettiest cotton frock. She had found some Liberty material which Mrs Cardell had stored in lavender years before and apparently forgotten. Susan saw the two swathes of material and exclaimed with delight. 'Are they for you, Sidonia? Where did they come from? Mrs Cardell? Oh, let me help, please. I adore dressmaking. Clothes can be such a bore nowadays, with everyone told they mustn't use too much material. I understand of course about our merchant seamen, but we don't need to be drab – and anyway, this was bought ages ago.'

When she paused for breath, Sid said mildly, 'I wish you would help. I'm hopeless with a needle.'

'Wonderful!' Susan opened up the materials. 'These could have been bought with you in mind. Your eyes are your best feature, and this golden brown with the scattering of tiny rose-pink flowers and green leaves will suit them perfectly. And the multi-coloured one has a coral background. Lovely! Gorgeous!'

So Susan cut and she and Daisy sewed, and when Sid met Tom she was wearing the golden-brown frock which was nipped in at the waist to emphasise her slenderness, curved softly over the bodice, and flared slightly over her hips. Susan had added a small frill round the neck: the effect, declared Daisy, was 'really ducky'.

Tom's eyes lit up when he saw her. 'How nice you look. One gets tired of seeing girls in uniform.'

'You might get a lot more tired if they weren't around to help.'

'I appreciate them, of course I do, but all the same . . . I couldn't get a car, I'm afraid. Petrol's so damnably short.'

'It doesn't matter. We can walk. It's nice just to get away.'

'Is it all too much for you?' He was genuinely concerned. 'I'm surprised to find the women and children still in residence. I thought they would have been evacuated.'

Sid laughed. 'They wouldn't go, and to tell you the truth I was pleased. They are good company, and although their contributions aren't very big, the extra money helps me to keep the house in order. At least we don't have any leaks any more, and the glass is back in the windows. Housing the children gave us priority. Where are we going?'

'There's a small hotel quite near which still serves a reasonable dinner. Would you like that?'

'Wonderful. Our food in Greystone House tends to be on the stodgy side.'

He laughed. 'I've never seen you look better. You get prettier each time. Oh! now you've become remote. May I not congratulate you on anything?'

'Of course you may, and I'm not at all remote. I just don't like flattery.'

He didn't argue. He slid his arm around her trim waist and she let it remain there, enjoying the feel of his strong hand, as she enjoyed the maleness of him, the faint scents of his soap and shaving cream. She enjoyed them too much. She had buried the memory of the passion she had shared with Philip deep inside her, guarding herself so that it couldn't engulf her with longing. Not for Philip, but for the sexual joy he had given her. Her mind was frequently a jumble of loathing for his behaviour and longing for love.

They were crossing a bridge, and she twisted from Tom's arm and ran to look over the parapet.

He joined her. 'Did you ever play Pooh sticks?'

'No, but I know what they are.'

'Good.' Tom found some twigs and they dropped them in the stream, then ran to the other side of the bridge to watch them float into view. They kept on until they laughed helplessly.

Tom dabbed at his eyes. 'God, it's good to laugh. There's little enough laughter around these days.'

'I thought everyone was determined to be happy,' said Sid, still leaning over the bridge, watching the flow of water and seeing the occasional dart of a small fish. 'It's known as morale.'

' "Determined" is the right word. The war, the bombing, living in close proximity to strangers has given us all a kind of mateyness we never had before, but real deep-down belly-laughs are not very thick on the ground.'

'I suppose not, though Daisy makes us laugh. I don't know how I would have coped without her. I can't tell you how glad I was when she refused to leave.'

Tom stood behind her and clasped her in his arms, his body bending over hers. His muscles were taut, his breath fanned the back of her neck. 'I love you, Sidonia.'

She froze and he released her. 'Sorry. But I mean it. I love you.'

'No, you don't. I know you're sincere, but in times like these it's easy to make mistakes. We get on well together now, but we see one another so very rarely. One day the war will end.'

'And you think I'm the kind of man who would take advantage of you, then leave you?'

'No,' she said seriously, 'I don't think that at all. But love needs to have a future.'

'We may be killed, do you mean?'

'Oh, no!' She shuddered.

'What did you mean?'

'Must you keep asking questions?'

'Yes, I must. I want some answers. I offer you love and you fob me off with trite statements.'

'They aren't meant to be trite. So many couples are jumping into marriage because they are panicked into thinking they don't have a future.'

'For many that's proved to be true.'

'I know, and that's what's so awful.'

'Oh, Sidonia, surely it's better for them to have shared love even for a short time.'

'Perhaps. I'm thinking of the women left with families to bring up. Life is going to be terribly hard for them.'

'I didn't think you were a woman to fear hardship.'

'I don't, not physical, anyway.'

'You're afraid of commitment?'

She was silent for a moment as memories of Philip Prosser flooded into her. She wanted to tell Tom the truth, but couldn't bear to test his reaction, not now. Maybe later. Maybe when Amy was a little older. Maybe. 'Yes,' she said slowly, 'I believe I am.'

'Do you care for me at all?' He held out his arms, and the temptation to go into them almost overwhelmed her.

'Of course I do. I look upon you as one of my best friends.'

'I see. But you don't see me as a lover?'

'I'm sorry.'

He pulled her close and touched her mouth with his. 'Then I'll try to be content with friendship. For now.'

During his leave they met several more times. Tom kept his promise until the final evening, when he was restless through the meal they shared in a small hotel, choosing his food almost at random and not finishing it. His nervousness upset Sid, and she didn't do justice to her dinner either. Both drank more wine than usual. They strolled through the lanes on their way back to Greystone House. The leaves were beginning to turn brown, a sudden breeze lifted her skirt a little, ruffled her hair, shook the overhanging trees, so that for a moment they were in a rain of dead leaves. Death might be waiting for one of them, or both.

She shuddered and stopped and turned to him. 'Tom, I shall pray for your safety.'

'I'm sure that will help,' he said gravely. 'Do you pray a lot?'

'No,' she said, walking on. 'Sometimes I do. Angie's friend, Joseph Morland, is very religious. He taught her to say prayers.' She frowned.

'Is that so bad?'

'Not if it helps. I was just thinking of Joseph. He looks desperately sad at times.'

'I want you to think only of me tonight. You'll pray for me?'

'Yes. Promise.'

He stopped and tugged her gently round to face him. 'Sidonia, this is my embarkation leave.'

'No!'

'Tomorrow I return to camp and then we're off.'

'I didn't know. I wish . . . this damned war . . .'

'Sidonia, my love, I want more than your prayers. I want you. I lie awake thinking of you, and when I sleep I dream of you. Give me this one last night.'

All her suspicions were reactivated. 'You want me to go to bed with you?'

'It's a natural thing for lovers to do.'

'You're not my lover! You're not! You've been softening me for the big surrender.' Sid hurried away from him, her aching disappointment bringing tears of rage and sorrow to her eyes.

He caught her up and grabbed her arm, twisting her to face him again. 'I have not been softening you for surrender as you so melodramatically put it. I told you. I love you. I want you.'

'I'm sorry. I don't want you. You're being unfair.'

'Is that all you have to say to me?'

'Yes.' Even as she spoke, she wanted to mould her body against his, to feel his kisses hot on her mouth, to enjoy the touch of his hands. Dangerous thoughts.

He saw her to the gates of the house and saluted her. The hurt in his eyes hurt her too. Then he marched away. She watched his retreating back before racing straight to her room to weep.

Chapter Sixteen

Sid visited her family as often as possible, though it was never often enough to please them. They capriciously refused to recognise that she worked constantly.

On one visit, Mum had been chatting to Ella who had turned up alone. They stopped talking when Sid entered, but then Ella said, 'She's old enough to know about things. I forget sometimes she's as old as she is.'

Mum decided to take this as a personal slight, and the atmosphere became frosty, but the sisters were far too fond of a bit of gossip to remain on cool terms.

Mum said, 'Sit down, Sid. Your Aunty Ella's just telling me about Aunty Mattie.'

Alarmed by their air of suppressed excitement, Sid demanded, 'What's happened to her? Nothing bad, I hope?'

'That depends on the way you look at it,' said Ella. 'She's courting a man.'

Sid had a job to keep from smiling. 'Really?'

'It's one she knew years ago,' supplied Mum. 'She's met him again down at the ARP Post.'

'I knew no good would come of her joining that,' snapped Ella.

'If he's nice it sounds good to me,' said Sid. The two women glared at her. 'Unless he's married,' she finished.

'The very idea!' Ella was genuinely shocked. 'He's a widower.'

When Sid saw Mattie she looked happy and years younger. 'Remember the man I gave up to look after Mum? We've been out quite a few times, and there are hours down at the ARP when we can just talk between our duties. Fancy him remembering me so clearly after nearly twenty years!' Her eyes shone with pleasure. 'His wife was a nice woman, but she died. They've got two grown-up sons and a little girl who was born later. That's what killed his wife, poor soul. The child's only five. Wilfred has known our family for years, but after I gave him up we didn't have any contact. He's a bit older than me. When we were children I used to watch him playing cricket and football in the street, and sometimes he'd give me a sweet or a lump of chocolate. We've always liked one another.'

'Do you love him?'

'I do. In fact, I don't think I ever stopped, though that's only for your ears, Sid. I wouldn't want anyone to imagine I've been pining for years. I haven't. My life has been the way I chose to make it, and most of the time I've been content.'

'But not any more?'

'No, not any more.'

Sid went to visit her family. There were the aunts, looking a little weary, as most people did these days from lack of sleep and anxiety; but their tongues never seemed to flag.

As Sid walked to the best room door she heard her name followed by lowered voices.

When she opened the door they all stopped speaking, then Mrs Penrose said, 'Oh, it's you.'

'Yes, it's me.'

'What's this we hear about you filling Greystone House with slum women and children?' asked Aunty Maud.

'Evacuees from the raids,' said Sid. 'Is there a cup of tea in the pot, Mum?'

'If old Mrs Cardell had known what you'd do she'd never have left her house to you,' said Maud aggressively. She could never get over Sid's amazing new position, not just a house owner, but a stately-house owner.

Sid drank her tea. 'That's a nice cuppa, Mum. My evacuee ladies make tea far too strong.'

'No proper upbringing,' sniffed Ella.

The sisters had been so overcome and annoyed by Sid's luck that they had almost ignored the subject of the inheritance. Now the advent of the women and children was raised, they had a fine chance to criticise.

'Of course,' said Ella, 'you had a lot of time to get friendly with the old lady.'

Mum looked affronted. 'I hope you're not suggesting there was anything underhand in Sid's inheritance. No one in *my* family would do anything underhand.'

'Did we say that?' Ella demanded, glaring around. 'Did I say a word . . .?'

Sid helped herself to a small iced cake. 'Icing sugar!' she exclaimed. 'I haven't seen any for ages, though it must be easier to get hold of if you sell it.'

This was received with dark looks. Sid found she wanted to laugh. Owning property, however much of a white elephant, gave her courage.

'How do you keep a place that size going?' asked Joan. 'It's all we can do these days to keep up appearances. Food keeps rising in price, and customers can't buy as much as they used to.'

'I thought they were better off. The women in the factories get paid well, though still not as much as the men.'

'So I should hope,' said Mum. 'Men have got families to keep.'

'After the war there'll be a lot of women with families to keep,' pointed out Sid. 'So many men have died already, and I suppose there will be more.' She choked on her cake as she remembered Tom and the way they had parted.

'I suppose the old lady left money, too,' said Bea, 'though she was never one for throwing it around.'

'No, tight-fisted, we thought,' said Maud.

'Speak for yourself,' said Mum. 'I never thought that about her.'

'Yes, you did,' Ella argued. 'I remember we were at our Mum's and we all said we thought the old lady was – '

'Do you mind?' Sid spoke loudly enough to stop them. She wanted to laugh at their indignant looks. 'My late employer had a name. Mrs Cardell, remember? And she was never tight-fisted. She hadn't much money, but what there was she's left me, along with the house contents.'

There was a short silence. 'Is it true that those children have kicked the furniture to pieces and all wet their beds?' asked Ella.

Sid said coldly, 'No, and I'd be happier if you would stop running my paying guests down. I have taken in five families made homeless in the bombing, and they all chip in to the housekeeping.'

'The garden's overrun with them, the milkman told me,' said Ella. 'We're supposed to grow vegetables. 'Dig for Victory' the posters say.'

'The children have to play somewhere. They stay away from the vegetable beds.'

'Weren't there any respectable women you could have given house-room to?' asked Bea.

'The women are all perfectly respectable. They just had nowhere to go. Others have been able to make arrangements to live with relatives.'

'That's what the government advised,' said Joan. 'They said we should all make sure we've somewhere to go in case we're bombed out.'

'I suppose you couldn't expect women of that class to do something so sensible, even if their relations would take them in,' said Maud.

Sid clung to her patience. 'Many people have already been bombed out in London and came to relatives in Bristol for some peace. One of my ladies is in that position. She's been bombed out twice. Whole streets are down in parts of Bristol.'

'As if we don't know that,' sniffed Ella.

'If those children were never properly trained,' said Mum, 'they'll tear the place to pieces.'

'We have things well organised.'

The family surveyed Sid as she helped herself to another cake. She wished she hadn't. She was so indignant that she had to force it down her throat.

'When you came in we were talking about your Aunty Mattie,' said Maud.

Sid chewed on her cake and waited. 'Don't you want to know about her?' demanded Maud.

'What's she done now?' asked Sid obligingly.

'*Only* got serious about a man!' said Joan. 'At her age!'

'I already know that,' said Sid. 'And she's not old. She's the youngest of you.'

Bea frowned. 'She's getting on for forty. It's just not right.'

'She's still got three or four years to go to forty,' said Sid.

'Well, it's too old to be thinking of men,' snapped Maud.

'And he isn't suitable for a woman from a family like ours,' said

Ella. 'He never was. I remember Mum saying so when she first knew him and –'

'So he's an old friend, is he?' asked Sid innocently.

'That doesn't make him suitable,' snapped Maud. 'A widower with grown-up sons and a young daughter. Fancy inflicting a baby on a wife in her forties. No wonder the poor thing passed away.'

'Lots of women have babies when they're forty or more,' said Sid. 'One of the women in Greystone House is forty-two and she's expecting.'

'Well, I don't think that's nice,' said Mum.

'It seems,' said Bea, 'that she's been going out with him on the sly.'

'On the sly! Surely at her age she's entitled to go out with anyone she pleases.' Sid laughed, annoying her family still further.

'She tells her mother that she's on fire-watch duty, then has a date with a man?' Ella lowered her voice. 'They were seen.'

'*Seen*? What were they doing?'

'Watching a film. They were at the pictures.'

'That seems harmless enough.'

'Stop arguing with your aunties,' said Mrs Penrose. Sid obeyed. She'd only been half teasing them anyway. For her it was a new and interesting occupation.

'How are Irene and Audrey getting on?' she asked.

Mum frowned ferociously. 'You've heard that they both got conscripted, I suppose. They're working in a *factory*. Their poor hands are getting ruined.'

'Do they rub them with Vaseline and wear cotton gloves at night?' asked Joan.

'They've tried everything, but nothing works.'

'I work in a factory,' said Sid.

Mum and the aunts gazed at her. She knew they were bursting to pull her down in some way, but they couldn't come to terms with this new Sid who refused to go red with embarrassment and behaved as if she owned the place. 'They're only doing what thousands of other women do,' said Sid. 'My hands aren't much to look at.'

Sid held out her hands and noted ruefully their general roughness. She had tried the Vaseline-and-glove treatment herself on occasion, but often she was too tired to bother.

'Well, you never did take the same care of yourself as the girls, so I suppose you won't mind,' said Mum.

Husbands were summoned from the garden where they'd been chatting and smoking and grumbling about petrol rationing, then Sid walked with her family to visit Grandma Lacey, who was wearing a black silk dress and jet beads and looking tragic.

'She's out with him again,' she announced as they all trooped in: wives, followed by children, followed by dutiful husbands.

'I hoped I'd see her,' said Sid.

'Oh, you're there, are you? Well, it's nice that you can find the time to visit your grandmother sometimes, though I suppose you've got to get back soon to that houseful of common women and their children.

I'll never know what Mrs Cardell was thinking of to go and leave you a place that size. It belongs in her family. They'd never have taken in a parcel of slum people. I've heard things about those women.'

Sid was exasperated. 'Just what have you heard?'

'They go to pubs and all smoke like chimneys.'

'They've been bombed out. Their husbands are away, all except one, and he was killed at Dunkirk. They do the best they can to keep their families together. They deserve a little recreation.'

'We have plenty of recreation, and we don't need to go to pubs to get it.'

'They like pubs. They've always been used to them and I can't see the harm.'

'Hoity toity!' said Grandma Lacey.

Sid went to fetch in the sandwiches and cakes which Mattie had thoughtfully prepared before she had left. She wondered how soon she could get away. To her surprise and delight, Mattie came home earlier than expected and walked straight into the living room. There was an air of joy about her.

'What's happened?' asked Grandma Lacey. 'Has he got fed up with you today?'

Mattie faced them all and said bravely, though with a quiver in her voice. 'He's asked me to marry him and I've said I would.'

There was stunned silence. Sid broke it by jumping to her feet and embracing her. 'Congratulations, Aunty Mattie. Well done. I hope you'll be very happy.'

'Fat chance,' muttered Ella.

Grandma Lacey looked appalled. 'You'll marry him? A man getting on for fifty with children to look after?'

'Only one,' said Mattie. 'The boys are in the forces. And he's nearer forty than fifty.'

'Well, those boys will come back some day.'

'I certainly hope so,' said Mattie quietly.

There was little about that which anyone could argue with, so Joan asked the question which was in all their minds. 'Who's going to look after Mum?'

'We can't come every day, much as we'd like to,' said Bea quickly. 'The shops are always full of customers, and more queuing outside.'

'I thought you said people didn't have the money to spend,' said Sid.

'You're arguing again,' said Mum crossly.

Mattie said, 'I shall still be here every day – every working day, that is. You will all see Mum on Sundays, and if she needs me I'll be near by. Wilfred doesn't expect me to relinquish all my duties.'

'Kind of him, I'm sure,' said Bea.

'Well, actually, it is kind of him,' said Mattie, looking calmer now the first surprise was over. 'But then, he's a very kind man.'

'That doesn't put food on the table,' snapped Mrs Penrose.

'He isn't poor.'

'He used to be,' said Grandma Lacey. 'He came from a poor family.'

'He works in an office in the city. At least, it was there until it was bombed. They've moved to a place in Clifton. Anyway, he holds a good position. I shan't want for food on the table.'

The others stared at her in helpless frustration.

'Why didn't he come with you to break the news? What's he afraid of?' asked Grandma Lacey.

'He isn't afraid. He wanted to come, but I preferred to tell you on my own.'

'Why?' demanded Ella.

'Because I knew you'd all say the things you've just said.'

There was another silence and Sid smothered a laugh.

'When's the great event going to happen?' asked Joan.

'In three weeks' time.'

'What? So soon? Can't you wait till after the war? Mum can't be left alone at night.'

'We've waited long enough,' said Mattie. 'Twenty years. I gave him up once to look after Mum, if you remember. I've had to watch all of you with your husbands and children. It never seemed to occur to you that I might want them too.'

'Well, we weren't to know,' muttered Bea. 'We thought you were happy.'

'And so I have been.'

'Was he happy with his first wife?' asked Joan.

'She was a good woman, Wilfred says, but deep down he never stopped loving me. As for Mum being alone, he's already thought of that. Actually, he said if it's acceptable he's willing to move in here with his daughter and share my room with me. There's space enough for little Elsie's bed in the box room.'

'Move in with Mum!' cried Bea, 'that's ridiculous. A child of five living here!' Sentiments which were echoed by the others.

But Grandma Lacey looked thoughtful. She had always liked having a man to order around. Mattie had no illusions about her mother, and would have told Wilfred what to expect. It might work out.

Amy had started school and, with her usual aplomb, settled quite happily. The fact that so many of the children from Greystone House attended the same school was a help. She proved as quick to learn as she had been to talk, and she seemed to grow more beautiful by the day. Sid had hoped – believed perhaps – that as the years passed she would become more immune to the hurt of having to lie about her child's origins, but instead it became more difficult. Every time Amy arrived home with an exercise book containing her latest work, or a drawing executed with unusual skill in one so young, or looked particularly pretty, she longed to tell someone that the child was hers.

Amy had stopped asking what had happened to her parents, and simply accepted that they were dead. She understood from when one of the cats had been killed on the road that being dead meant no return. She had mourned him with the others, watched his burial in the garden, wept, then welcomed two new kittens. She was excited because Aunty Mattie was going to marry her friend, Wilfred – another uncle for Amy – and she and his small daughter, Elsie, were to be flower girls. Mattie had been saving her clothing coupons, and Sid and Daisy sacrificed some of theirs to help buy a new costume and coat. Some parachute silk sent by Angie was dyed and made into pretty underwear and nightgowns.

'Such frippery!' said Grandma Lacey. 'In wartime and at *her* age.'

'She's never been married before,' Sid pointed out, 'so why shouldn't she have a pretty wedding and a nice honeymoon? We have to do the best we can for each other these days.'

'I hope you're not presuming to tell me how to behave,' said Grandma Lacey.

'Of course not.'

'She should wait till the war's over,' said Ella. 'There's no telling what might happen . . . And with the raids and everything . . . I mean to say . . .' She stopped, flushing.

'What *exactly* do you mean to say?' asked Maud. 'You surely don't think . . . Not at her age . . .!'

'What *are* you talking about?' cried Grandma Lacey. 'I hope it's not what I think it is.'

'She could have a child,' said Maud, putting into words the thoughts of them all. 'She's not yet forty, and she still sees her monthly visitor.'

Grandma was aghast. 'She wouldn't be such a fool.' She turned a glare in Sid's direction. 'I suppose you'd approve of that too.'

'It's hardly for me to approve – or for anyone else, for that matter, except Aunty Mattie and Wilfred.'

'Cheeky to her grandma!' said Ella, as if Sid weren't there.

On the wedding day in November, Amy was wild with delight. Mrs Cardell's wardrobe was still producing useful and often glamorous materials from long-since-discarded gowns, capes and furs. From these Daisy made Amy a rose velvet dress with a small, fur-edged jacket. Wilfred's small daughter was the other flower girl, and Amy chattered away so unselfconsciously that she forgot to be shy, especially when enough pale blue velvet was found to make her a similar outfit to Amy's. Two tiny coronets of pink and blue flowers in their hair made them hold up their heads like princesses; they were a picture to delight the eye.

Grandma Lacey, and all the aunties, uncles and cousins from both sides who could manage it attended the wedding, many curious to see the man who had returned and carried off Mattie at last.

Audrey and Irene contrived to get a day off, and arrived wearing the latest in smart costumes, even if they were cut to the prescribed utility pattern. Their hair was beautifully coiffured and both wore gloves even when eating, unwilling to display their imperfect hands.

Wilfred's younger son was abroad somewhere in Africa, but the other was on leave and acted as best man. He was quite heavy, of a similar build to Wilfred, and was already showing signs of the baldness which afflicted his father and at which Grandma Lacey sniffed derisively.

'As if being a bit bald was a sin,' said Mattie, giggling, to Sid. Her attack of girlishness was entirely due to Brindle having produced some champagne from Mrs Cardell's cellar. Even Grandma and the aunties had been impressed by this token of affluence. There was no opportunity for a long honeymoon. The happy pair went to Clevedon for a weekend, then were back performing their duties.

It had been decided, much to Mattie's secret relief, that there was no need for Wilfred and his daughter to live with Grandma Lacey; the older cousins would take turns to stay overnight with her. Sid's brother Raymond, who had, to his mother's horror, recently been conscripted into the Army and was about to leave, stayed with Grandma on the wedding night. Her aggressive attitude was somewhat diluted by discovering that Wilfred was far more affluent than she had realised.

Sid had never seen her mother look so miserable. She managed to smile wanly until Mattie had left, but then reverted to her previous tearful state.

'Don't worry, Mum,' Raymond kept saying. 'I'll be all right. I'll be back.' But Mum wouldn't be consoled, and even Dad showed rare emotion when the subject was discussed.

Amy couldn't be calmed after the thrill of the wedding, and seemed never to be still. At school her teachers said she was restless, but that she picked up information as easily as a bee took pollen, even while inciting the other children to naughtiness.

Sid took her into the small sitting room one day to give her a lecture, though it was difficult to be cross with her when she looked deep into her eyes and said, 'Sorry, Aunty Sid. I expect it's because I don't have a mummy and daddy like other little girls.' She was manipulative and Sid knew it, but still couldn't resist her. 'If you'd let me wear my velvet dress to school, I'd be ever so good.'

'You can't wear rose velvet to school,' said Sid, 'but I'll let you wear it on Sundays.'

'And Saturdays.'

'Only if you promise to sit in the house all day and read a book, or draw.'

'I can't do that. I've got to play games with the others!'

'Well, you can't climb trees in a flower-girl's frock.'

Amy thought for a moment. 'All right. I'll wear ordinary clothes all day and change into my rose frock for tea.' And with that they were both satisfied.

Daisy arrived to sweeten the proceedings with a tray of tea and little cakes. Sid thanked her with a smile. 'You shouldn't. You have enough to do.'

'You can say that again.' Daisy rolled her eyes. 'The Dawson brat, sorry, I mean cherub, has just been sick again on the clean tablecloth. I told her not to bring the child to the table, but she won't listen. That kid is sicker than a sick donkey.'

'How sick's a sick donkey?' asked Amy.

'Very, very sick,' said Daisy, and left before she could be questioned further. As Amy opened her mouth to ask another question, Sid thrust the plate of cakes towards her. 'Here, have one.'

'They've got no icing. We had iced cake at Auntie Mattie's wedding.'

'That was special.'

'I haven't eaten any bread and butter yet.'

'Never mind. Just for once you can have cake first.'

When the door opened, Sid said, 'These cakes are delicious, Daisy.' Then she looked up and jumped so violently she almost tipped over her teacup.

Mrs Prosser was standing in the doorway. She advanced, followed by Celia. Neither said a word. Both had their eyes riveted on Amy who looked up at them, not in the least disconcerted, and smiled. Mrs Prosser's breath caught in her throat. 'That child . . .' she said. 'Who is she? What is your name, child?'

Sid's heart was thundering against her ribs.

'Amy. I'm a war orphan.' This piece of information usually elicited a lot of kindly sympathy, often a sweet, and once a whole sixpence.

Mrs Prosser sat down. She was staring now at Celia, her eyes narrowed, her elderly mouth turned down, her face set in grim lines which displayed all her wrinkles. 'She looks like you.'

Celia snapped, 'Nonsense!', but in spite of herself she was agitated.

'Run along downstairs, Amy,' said Sid. 'Go along now. At once!'

Awed by the unaccustomed severity in Sid's voice, Amy obeyed.

'You weren't announced,' Sid said to Mrs Prosser. 'I can't think why. Did you ring the front-door bell?'

'We did and no one answered, so we walked in. I am not at all surprised we weren't heard. The noise coming from the kitchen is enough to drown out an air-raid siren. So we decided to come up here. Celia was then going to call you.'

'This is my house!' Sid hadn't meant to speak so belligerently, but anger and shock had combined to throw her off balance.

'I wish to have another look at that child,' demanded Mrs Prosser.

'Surely you haven't travelled all the way here just to say that.'

'Of course not. We were visiting in the vicinity and heard about the shambles you have been making of my cousin's beautiful house. I wanted to see if it could possibly be true.'

'And is it?' Sid gathered her composure as best she could.

'You know damn well it is,' said Celia. 'We looked into a couple of rooms on our way here. Everything is in disorder. The paintwork is kicked about, the carpets are frayed, and at least two cracked windows have been patched with glue and brown paper.'

'The paintwork can be renewed, the carpets were frayed when I came here, and the broken windows are nothing compared with air-raid damage.' Sid said. 'And I think it inquisitive of you to go poking about without asking my permission.'

Mrs Prosser drew back her chin. 'Your permission! You have no need to remind me of the way you acquired this house. I have never been convinced that you didn't influence my cousin in the making of her will.'

'If I did it was purely unintentional.'

'I wish to see the child,' said Mrs Prosser again.

'Oh, Grandmother, do forget her,' begged Celia. 'I never want to set eyes on the brat ever again.'

'I do.'

'Well, I shall return to the car and wait for you.' Celia swept out.

'I am waiting,' said Mrs Prosser.

Sid looked at her. She was thinner, but that was the only change. She looked as hard as she had at the reading of the will. It was obvious that she had seen Amy's almost uncanny resemblance to Celia, and God knew what she would do. She couldn't want to claim a relationship with the child; she was perhaps merely inquisitive; but for whatever reason she was being stubborn, and Sid was sure it spelled trouble.

'Amy will be having tea in the kitchen and then playing with her friends. I don't want to disturb her.'

Mrs Prosser stood up, white with fury. 'In other words, you refuse to allow me to see the child.'

'There's no reason why you should.'

'There is every reason. In the garden, you say?'

'I hope you're not thinking of going among the children to sneak another look.' The words burst irresistibly from Sid.

'Sneak! How dare you? If anyone has behaved in an underhand way, it is certainly you. Who is the mother of that child? Who was her father?'

'Amy told you, she's a war orphan.'

'Liar! And you've made a liar out of her. She is no such thing. I know you are keeping something from me. There is a memory in the back of my mind of something which surprised me at the time. Something to do with a holiday my cousin once took. I shall recall all the circumstances soon. You are a deceitful, unpleasant woman, Miss Penrose.'

Mrs Prosser waited a moment longer, then stalked out and went downstairs, followed closely by Sid, who opened the front door for her.

Sid didn't expect to hear from Tom again. She had lost him and the loss was a void in her life. The memory of their last evening stayed with her. She should have let him make love to her, or at least given him hope. What cowardice she'd shown! Then she would catch sight of Amy and return to her senses. She wanted marriage or nothing. And if she had been a coward, it was more from fear for Amy than herself. How many men would accept another man's child? How could she explain to him what had happened?

Roy Hendy had also been home on embarkation leave and taken her to a cinema a couple of times. The raids were sporadic now and less concentrated, though London was still suffering horribly. He had made few demands on her. His kisses were still warm and, being fond of him, she permitted them, but she knew that really she wanted no man's lips on hers but Tom's.

Susan Morland paid regular visits, and was able to tell Sid that David Selby, Eve Brook's fiancé, had not drowned. With other survivors he had been in a lifeboat on the open sea for six weeks with a sparse supply of food and water, before being spotted by a ship and taken on board, more dead than alive. But he had recovered, and he and Eve had got married in a quiet ceremony.

'She was so happy,' sighed Susan. 'I wonder if I'll ever meet someone special.'

'You must have had a boyfriend,' said Daisy. 'With your looks an' figure you must have to fight 'em off.'

'Oh, yes, *boyfriends*, plenty of *them*! I want someone I can fall in love with and who'll love me like David loves Eve. I want to be like Tessa and her Charles. You've never seen such a pair of lovebirds as them. Unless you're looking at Eve and David,' she added gloomily.

'It'll happen to you,' Sid assured her.

Mind you,' said Daisy reflectively, 'it doesn't always pay to be choosy. Now, I wasn't a bad looker, but I was so big an' strong I frightened men off. Not many of 'em wanted to wed a woman who could pick 'em up and throw 'em over her shoulder.' She laughed her great laugh. 'So when I saw the man I wanted, I went after him for all I was worth.'

'Did he try to run away?' asked Susan, fascinated.

'He might have tried, but I was too quick for him! We went out a few times, then I got him home in our front room an' asked him if he loved me. He said he did. I think he was so took by surprise that he couldn't think of anythin' else, especially with me loomin' over him like a dragon.'

'What happened next?' asked Susan, her face filled with laughter.

'I said, "Good, that's us settled then. We'll get married in six weeks." He didn't have the heart to argue, an' I don't think he ever regretted his bargain. He loved me an' he loved all his kids. I miss him,' she ended bleakly. 'At least he died quick. That's what his mates said. He was in a sand-dune with a few others an' there was a direct hit an' they never found anything but bits of the poor devils.'

Susan's face expressed all the compassion she felt. 'I'm so sorry. But you're right, it's better to die quickly than suffer. I've seen too much of that in the raids.'

To Sid's overwhelming relief, Tom began to write regularly. Sid always answered quickly. He was out east and his experiences in Singapore sounded amusing. 'The place is invincible,' he wrote, 'and men stationed here have a good time. I feel quite guilty thinking of you civilians having to suffer the bombing, cold, rationing and all the other ills, while I'm living quite a soft life.' Singapore society seemed to be much the same as pre-war, with food and drink and parties: oases in a desert of irritation and tedium. She might have found his letters frustrating, had they not been so witty and humorous as he described the various types he met. She was sure it couldn't all be fun and games, though, not any more. Japanese troops were advancing steadily, taking island after island, showing no mercy to officials and planters and missionaries.

In Britain there were plenty of annoyances, minor in themselves, but adding up to deprivation and irritation. Soap was rationed to one bar each a month; even with the numbers of people in Greystone House, there was never enough.

'This is hard water,' grumbled Daisy. 'We ought to get a bigger ration for hard water. You can't get a good lather.'

On 7 December 1941, without any warning or declaration of war, the Japanese had bombed Pearl Harbor, where the United States Navy was anchored, destroying ships and men and causing an outraged America to enter the war.

'I'll say one thing for the Yanks,' said Daisy, 'they send us some nice food, though dried egg's not all it's cracked up to be. Did you hear that, Sid? I made a joke and didn't know it.'

The orders now were to save. Everything. Money to lend the government for the continuation of the war, metal, paper, food for pigs, rags, anything which could be recycled and used in an effort to cut down importations. Iron railings and gates were carted away by the ton to be melted down for weapons, though the gates of Greystone House were left intact when it was pointed out that there were a number of children who might stray out on to the road. But the salvage men took all the pots and pans that could be dispensed with.

As if a malignant fate was trying to test their endurance to its limit, the winter proved to be another bitterly cold one with snow and severe frost. The men returned from their Home Guard duties, shivering, glad to sit in the kitchen and drink something hot. The kitchen had become the hub of the house. Fuel couldn't always be found for the schoolroom, and the kitchen was where the mothers and children spent much of their time. Brindle had almost given over grumbling. In fact, he looked so old and tired that Sid feared for him. Keith had grown strong and fearless. He had also learned to be kinder, and frequently helped Brindle so tactfully that the old man was unaware of it. Patrick had neither developed nor regressed. He would always be a big child.

Daisy and the others had taken prams full of babies to watch the Home Guard drilling, and had come back pink-cheeked with cold and laughter.

'You should see them, Sid,' cried Daisy. 'It'd do you good to have a laugh.'

Mrs Dawson said, 'When Brindle says "Left turn", Patrick turns right.'

'And when he says "Right turn", Patrick goes left,' said Mrs Partridge. Her husband had been home on leave and she was pregnant again.

'They get into an awful muddle,' said Mrs Dawson. 'Talk about laugh.'

'They go on tactical exercises,' said Daisy, 'creepin' about through the woods, pretendin' that one lot's Jerries an' the others are British soldiers. Our Billy followed them one day an' said Patrick crashes about like a bull in a thicket. I hope nobody ever gives him a loaded gun. God knows who he'd shoot. If someone tells him the other side is the enemy he believes it, even when he knows it's Keith.'

'Patrick's all right,' said Keith, who heard the tail-end of this conversation.

Patrick, the women agreed, was definitely all right. He came out of his cellar a lot since the arrival of the children. He watched over them, rode them round on his shoulders, was never too busy to play their games, taking as much delight in them as they did. He was gentle and laughed easily. And he still went out scouring the countryside for fuel and kept the fires going as much as possible all through the long, terrible winter.

Sid's chief problem was boredom. Her job at the factory was repetitive and the journeys to and from work were tedious, only enlivened – if you could call it that – by air-raids, when everyone dashed for the nearest shelter and waited for the all-clear. Once home she discussed with Daisy all the problems which had to be faced daily. From time to time the children fell ill. At one time they all succumbed to chicken-pox. Rations dwindled. On one occasion the smallest children got into the larder and ate two pounds of biscuits, for which precious points had been relinquished. The fact that they vomited later seemed a just retribution but a terrible waste.

The cats had to be fed. They spent their days hiding from the boys who, however often they were chided, still teased them, but came out at night to keep the house clear of vermin. Of the mouse kind, that was. Three of the girls came home from school with head-lice and gave them to everyone in the house, a shuddery experience which Daisy dealt with calmly.

Sometimes Sid wished she was a member of one of the women's services, instead of having to stay behind and cope with all the mundane tasks of a worker-housewife. Those women did all kinds of exciting things, toiling beside the men who fired guns at encroaching aircraft, controlling the huge barrage balloons raised for protection against low-flying planes; they were in communications, driving, having so many different experiences. She never blamed Amy, of course, but she couldn't think of Philip Prosser without a surge of loathing filling her mouth with gall.

Then, like a hammer blow, the unthinkable occurred. In February 1942, Japan took Singapore. The people had been bombed and shelled incessantly, fires were raging, and the enemy took the supply depots, but the final blow came when they overran the water supplies. There was panic as soldiers and civilians, aware of the atrocities which were daily being committed by the enemy, scrambled to find places on ships leaving the harbour. Many were left behind and taken prisoner, Tom among them. A naval officer brought her a letter which he had written to her hurriedly in wavering handwriting.

Sid saw the officer in the small sitting room. 'Sorry, it's so cold,' she said, 'but most of the fuel goes to the kitchen and nursery.'

'I understand.' Lieutenant Grigson accepted a cup of milkless coffee and a Spam sandwich.

She fell silent, desperate to hear about Tom. Wordlessly, he handed her the note. It stated simply that he was ill and unable to escape. The final words, 'I love you', hurt.

'Do you know what's happening to Tom now?'

'He's a prisoner. Bound to be.'

'I've read awful things about the Japanese. They seem to kill for no good reason. That's if there's ever a good reason for killing.'

'They see things differently from us.'

'Does that mean they'll kill their prisoners?'

'Of course not,' said Lieutenant Grigson, a shade too heartily. 'They tend to use military prisoners as a workforce.'

'How can he work? How ill is he? He must have been laid very low not to try to get away.'

'Some tropical bug he picked up, I don't know what, I'm not a doctor, we all got them from time to time. I'm afraid he was very weak. I'm sorry to be so blunt, but . . . you should know.'

Sid stared at him, unable to say the words which would express her fear. If healthy men died beneath Japanese treatment, how could a sick man have any hope?

'Couldn't he have been carried to a hospital ship?'

The officer stared at her and gave a hopeless shrug. 'I'm so sorry. It just wasn't possible. You've no idea . . .'

'How could Singapore have fallen? It was supposed to be impregnable.'

'The big guns were facing the wrong way. The powers-that-be got it wrong. We outnumbered the Japs three to one and it should never have happened. Our strategy was hopeless.'

'I thought the British were the best fighters in the world.'

'All the men were anxious and willing to fight – British, Australians and Indians – but many of our men had only just arrived and had no experience in jungle warfare. The Japs are like fighting machines; they carry their guns as if they'd been born holding them. They are used to fighting in the jungle and they seem to be able to survive on an incredibly sparse diet.'

'It all sounds like terrible negligence to me,' said Sid angrily.

'In war it's not always easy to know what to do. Try not to worry. You're sure to get word through the Red Cross.'

Weeks passed before Sid heard that Tom was indeed a prisoner of the Japanese. Later, short, stereotyped cards told her that he was 'well' and 'working for pay'. The last printed words were, 'My love to you.' She was glad simply to know he was alive; just how glad, she only realised when the cards stopped coming.

Then she knew just how much he meant to her. As if his disappearance were a catalyst, he now filled her thoughts. She began to dream of him. Tom holding her. Tom kissing her. Tom making love to her. She was happy with him, warm and safe in the surety of his love, until she awoke to cold reality and the admission that she had been a cowardly fool, afraid to show her true feelings because once she had been badly treated by another man.

Roy Hendy wrote still from Africa, where battles were being fought in the desert. Desert Rats, the men were popularly named, and members of ENSA went out to entertain them, among them Tessa and Eve.

'Joseph's there, too,' said Angie when she came home on leave. 'His letters are awful peculiar these days. He talks a lot about God and death and cruelty. It all seems mixed up in his mind.'

Joseph Morland had seen his sister Tessa and their cousin Eve in the desert and enjoyed their singing. He recalled the days when he had thought them sinful because they hadn't devoted their voices to the glory of God. That seemed an eternity ago. These days it wasn't easy to find God. As he toiled in the scorching heat by day and cold by night, in sandstorms, constantly trying to beat back the swarms of flies, he tried not to think at all. If he did he feared he might go mad. He saw men wounded in such ghastly ways his whole being revolted. His first aid during the air-raids had only partly prepared him for the present horrors. During his training he had assimilated knowledge along with the appropriate words. 'Abdominal cases', 'open wounds of the thorax', 'amputation' 'open fractures', but worst of all, he decided now, 'maxillo-facial' wounds. Even if these men without faces could be patched up, they could never go back to normal living. He hoped they had people who could still love them.

The medical corps also tended enemy prisoners. Joseph couldn't see them as enemies. They were men, just like the Allies were men, their flesh and blood, their skin and bone, destroyed with equal facility; their legs and arms lost, or amputated with equal efficiency.

The only comfort to which he was able to cling was his early insistence on non-combatant duties. He could never have shot a man, never have plunged a bayonet into the warm, living body of another human being, never have inflicted the kinds of wounds with which the field-dressing tents dealt every day. He earned high praise from the officers because of his dedication to duty, but the truth was, utter dedication was the only way to fight the demons in his head. He pitied the suffering men, but there were times when he would willingly have exchanged the agony of their bodies for the agony of his mind. He had eaten, drunk, lived and preached the love of God, his belief as unshakeable as the Rock of Gibraltar, and increasingly he couldn't find Him at all. He watched the priests from various religions as they prayed over the injured and dying, watched the Catholics giving absolution to men who died easier for the blessing, and all the time he wondered if the prayers went further than the confines of the tents.

Angie was the only bright spot in his life. He wrote to her, trying to explain the way he felt. She wasn't capable of comprehending the depths of his despair, but her replies to his letters were kind, loving and caring. She was the first woman who had attracted him, and he longed for the day when he could return to her. He tried not to think of her on an air-field surrounded by men who were free to take her out and whose minds were whole. He would ask her to marry him one day, but often he couldn't sleep during his few hours off duty, wondering if she had only friendship for him. He tried to put into words what he felt for her but he, who had been a master of oratory, couldn't relay his thoughts.

One day, the battle ranged so close, the commandant decided that the Field Dressing Station must be moved back to the Advance Surgical Centre before the enemy broke through. Fighting was intense, and Joseph had worked in furious, angry despair on the bodies of men who went out whole to fight and were carried back in a welter of blood and pain. The evacuation of the wounded was completed, except for one patient, a boy of eighteen who was too shocked to be moved without endangering his life still further. Joseph had volunteered to stay with him. The boy had been given a small dose of morphia and kept begging for further relief. Joseph had explained that to give a larger dose could raise his intracranial pressure and increase his liability to haemorrhage. 'I don't care,' the soldier moaned. 'I don't care if I die. I can't stand it. Please. Please.' He slipped in and out of consciousness, and Joseph wondered if he would die. He went to pray for him, but his tongue wouldn't move in the familiar words. He stood at the foot of the boy's bed, his whole being aching with the misery he felt at his inability to help. He wanted to fetch water to moisten his lips. When he returned, a German soldier was standing by the boy, staring down at him.

The young soldier was muttering almost incoherently, 'I want to die. Let me go.'

The German grunted and lifted his bayonet and, as he did so, the boy returned to full consciousness, saw the raised bayonet, and screamed.

Joseph could never recall the details of the next few moments. All he could remember was that he was standing over the German, who had collapsed face down on the bed. A scalpel stuck at right-angles from the German's back. He was dead. Joseph's hand had struck him down. With him died the remnants of his faith. Feeling sick, he removed the scalpel, and automatically laid the body out decently.

When the short skirmish ended and a surgeon returned, the boy stuttered out his story. 'He saved my life,' he gasped.

Joseph was praised and hated it. He hated the war. He hated himself. And he could no longer even attempt to pray because now he was sure there was no one to listen.

Chapter Seventeen

The Allies bombed the German cities without mercy. Hitler retaliated, and in the summer of 1942, Bath was attacked. The people were accustomed to seeing the sky glowing red with fire from Bristol, but had decided, mistakenly, that they were safe. Bristol immediately sent teams of experienced Civil Defence Workers to their aid. Then it was the turn of Weston-Super-Mare, where, among others, people from the Midlands were holidaying during their Wakes Week, so that no one knew just how many had died beneath the hail of bombs. Again the Bristolians came to their rescue.

Susan visited Sid, her eyes red, her face pallid. 'My Dad's dead,' she said. She spoke almost without inflexion, as if what she said was simply an exercise in words and couldn't possibly be true. 'He crawled under a pile of rubble to help a young girl. He knew the building was likely to come down any minute, and he knew how to make it safer, but she was screaming in agony and terrified. They told us he said something about "daughters of my own", and insisted on trying to get to her. He reached her all right and helped get her out, but before he was clear he was buried under tons of concrete. I can't believe he's gone. Not my Dad.' She lost control and began to sob: deep, tearing sobs of anguish. Sid was appalled and offered what little consolation she could.

'And Tessa and Eve and Joseph are all in Africa,' sobbed Susan, 'and they'll want to be at the funeral, but I don't suppose they can manage it. Mum's in a shocking state. They were always very happy together were my mum and dad.'

Sid attended the funeral. The chapel was packed with members of the congregation, to whom Mr Morland had preached so often, as well as friends and neighbours, and some of those he had tended during the raids, including the family of the girl he had saved. She was still in hospital recovering, having had a leg amputated. The chapel was plain, the service a simple one, and Walter Morland was laid to rest in the tiny graveyard.

'Will you come back to the house?' asked Susan.

Sid nodded. Daisy had told her to stay out as long as she needed. 'Poor things, I know what they're goin' through.'

The Morland cottage was small, spotlessly clean, the garden rich with vegetables of all kinds and a few flowers.

'Dad always tended the garden,' said Mrs Morland, whose eyes looked blank, as if she had shut out all emotion.

'I'll help,' said Susan.

'I know, love.'

Mrs Morland went through to the best room, followed by Sid, a few relatives and invited close friends. Sherry and biscuits were served; some, with rationing in mind, had brought cakes or sandwiches. When the guests had eaten, drunk and talked, they went home, and Sid was left with the grieving wife and Susan who clung to her.

'I must get back,' Sid said reluctantly. 'I'm on duty tonight.'

'You should have been getting your sleep,' said Mrs Morland. 'It was good of you to come.'

'Not at all,' said Sid awkwardly.

Susan walked with her to the bottom of the lane. 'I wish you didn't have to go. You remind me a lot of Tessa. She's the strong one in our family. Can I visit you again soon, please?'

'Of course. Any time you like. If I'm not there the others will be. Daisy lost her husband, you know. She looks rough and tough, but she's really very gentle underneath.'

Sid went home and told the women about the Morlands' garden. A light of battle came into Daisy's eyes. 'They'll not need to worry. We've got time to spare. We'll help.'

'War brings out the best in people,' said Mrs Partridge.

'We must all pull together,' said Mrs Wallace.

They were trite words heard on hundreds of pairs of lips, but when they were genuinely meant they were comforting.

Stories of fresh and even more terrifying atrocities against the Jewish people had been seeping out of Poland. They had been incarcerated in a ghetto in Warsaw, where they had starved and died. Those who were left had put up a resistance as best they could, and the Germans, held at bay by people they despised, eventually slaughtered them. If Germany, a so-called Christian country, could behave in so evil a way, might not the Japanese be worse, or at least as bad? At night Sid lay thinking of Tom. Since the raids, Amy had become a restless sleeper, and Sid dared not put on a light to read. She pictured him ill-treated and sick. At other times she ached to hold him with a longing which wouldn't be stilled. Would he ever come back? And if he did, might he not have changed? War did terrible things to men. Why had she treated him badly? Why hadn't she recognised her strong feelings for him? Why hadn't she done what hundreds of others did and given him a night of happiness to remember? She tossed and turned, but even when she slept his image permeated her dreams and she awoke aching with need.

Early in 1943 she saw one effect the fighting had at first hand. On a day of lashing rain, Daisy came to her room, where she was resting after a late shift the night before. 'Sorry to disturb you, Sid, but there's an officer downstairs asking to see you.'

Sid sat up so quickly she went dizzy. With a hand to her head she asked, 'Tom?'

'No, love. Sorry, I should have said at once. His name's Robert Felgate.'

Sid sank back on her pillows, disappointment washing over her. 'I've never heard of him. What does he want?'

'To stay here.'

'What?' Sid sat up again, slowly this time.

'He says he heard that Mrs Cardell welcomed officers.'

'Did you tell him that was some time ago? That she's dead?'

'I told him, but he didn't seem to hear. He's in a kind of daze. He's absolutely soaking wet. He isn't even wearing an overcoat and his eyes frightened me, they hardly seem to see me. He wasn't really listening to what I said.'

'You? Frightened?' Sid had not known Daisy afraid of anything. She got out of bed and pulled on the slacks she had taken to wearing.

'Women in trousers!' Mum had said disgustedly. 'It's not decent.'

'I'll tell him you'll be down then,' said Daisy.

Sid slid her arms into the warm pullover Angie had knitted her. Good old Angie. Apparently she went to jumble sales and bought all the old woollens she could, washed them, unravelled them, and knitted them up for her friends. Consequently the sweater was bright with vari-coloured stripes, the end product of several discarded garments.

In the small sitting room a man in officer's khaki uniform rose to greet her. 'Mrs Cardell?'

Sid saw what Daisy meant about his eyes. 'I'm Miss Penrose. I'm so sorry, but Mrs Cardell passed away.'

'Did she? Sorry, but I never knew her.' Sid waited and he spoke again. 'I met a chap who told me that she was kind to men in need of a bit of peace and quiet.'

There was a burst of noise from downstairs in the kitchen, and Sid guessed that the mothers were having one of their arguments as to whose turn it was to do something or other. On the whole they worked well together, but it never seemed to stop raining, and the mothers of the bed-wetters argued incessantly. There was friction over the amount of soap used for the washing, and over the use of the airing horses and their proximity to the fire. And Mrs Dawson was pregnant, feeling unwell and perpetually cross.

'As you can hear, it isn't very peaceful here,' she said. 'The place is full of women and children.'

'I wouldn't mind that. I need somewhere to stay. I wouldn't get in their way.'

'Surely you have a family you can go to?'

'Yes, I've a home and a brother and a sister with their own establishments, but I don't want to be with them. They fuss and fuss and my father thinks . . .' He stopped, his lips trembling so much that Sid was horribly afraid he was going to weep. 'My father thinks I'm a coward. You see, I've been in Africa and the desert fighting got on my nerves. Lots of chaps hate it, but in the end I couldn't seem to manage it at all. I'm on sick leave. Indefinite sick leave.'

They used to call it shell-shock, thought Sid, or lack of moral fibre, for which they shot soldiers. Thank God people were more tolerant in this war. She said gently, 'Every room is full. I'm so sorry.'

'You must have a corner somewhere. I don't care where. I just want to stay here. Don't send me away.'

He was being completely irrational, but that was part of his illness. She wondered if Tom was suffering this way. Or the Morland's son, Joseph. Or Roy. She couldn't refuse him.

'There's an attic room. I've stored some of Mrs Cardell's things there, but there's a narrow bed and a small wardrobe. It was once a servants' bedroom and it's cold.'

'I don't care what it is or was. May I have it?'

The strain torturing his nerves was beginning to tell. Small beads of perspiration moistened his upper lip and forehead.

'You can have it,' she said. 'But first you must get warm and that, I'm afraid, means sitting in the kitchen.'

'No, I'm not cold.'

'You're shivering.'

'Am I? Yes, I suppose I am.'

Sid thought of the kitchen filled with children, babies and mothers. 'You can stay here for now. I'll send someone to light the fire. The mattress needs airing and I have to make up the bed. Have you eaten lately?'

'I can't remember. I'm not hungry.'

Patrick lit the fire and stoked it well, then helped Sid carry the mattress downstairs to the kitchen, where they put it to air, using all the space in front of the fire, thereby ending for the time-being the arguments. When the women heard of the plight of the man upstairs, reaction was mixed. Daisy, Mrs Wallace and Mrs Curtis were sympathetic, but Mrs Dawson said, 'What's wrong with him? Frightened, is he? I'll give him frightened when my man has to go abroad.'

Sid straightened up. 'Mrs Dawson, if you say one word to hurt Captain Felgate I shall be extremely put out.'

'And so shall I,' said Daisy, glowering. 'The war does funny things to people. He's just as much a casualty as if he was wounded in his body. His poor mind! It makes you shudder to think of it.'

'Quite,' agreed Sid, 'and at his age he could probably have wangled a desk job, but he chose to fight.'

'All right, all right,' said a chastened Mrs Dawson.

In the weeks following, there were times when Sid wished that she had been harder-hearted over Robert Felgate. In spite of the cold, he spent his time in the attic, from which Patrick and Keith had moved some of the furniture into Sid's already overcrowded room. He wouldn't come down even for meals, so these had to be carried up to him. When Keith rebelled, Brindle said angrily, 'Don't you dare to grouse about that man. I know what it's like to be fighting. Poor bloke can't help it.'

Keith, astonished by Brindle's unexpected tolerance, said no more. An Army chaplain had called several times, and the help of a psychiatrist was enlisted, much against the captain's wish; but their efforts met with some success, and gradually his attitude improved. He began to come downstairs, at first when he knew the children would be in bed.

Sid welcomed him, and kept a fire laid in the small sitting room. He sat there for hours, not reading, not listening to the radio, simply sitting and staring into space.

'It's scary,' said Daisy. 'He looks half mad sometimes.'

'He's getting better,' protested Sid.

'Well, I wouldn't like to be with him on my own,' said Mrs Dawson.

'Nobody's askin' you to,' was Daisy's swift reply.

Captain Felgate liked Sid. She carried a tray of tea to him one afternoon and placed it on the table beside him. 'Stay with me, please,' he said.

She was due on late shift and had no time to spare, then she looked into his eyes and realised that for the first time he appeared normal. She couldn't just abandon him.

She said, 'I'll bring another cup and saucer.'

They drank tea together and ate a couple of scones, in a silence which actually felt companionable. Sid had wondered often if he had been unstable to begin with, but she decided now that he was just an ordinary man who had been caught up in events which had damaged his spirit. She decided she liked him, and it became habitual for her to take coffee or tea with him. Gradually he became more expansive, telling her about his home in north Gloucestershire, his parents, his two younger brothers who were serving in the Air Force.

'Pilots, both of them,' he said proudly. 'Only twenty and twenty-one, and both fought in the Battle of Britain and survived. A miracle, my step-mother always calls it.'

'They're quite a bit younger than you,' remarked Sid.

'They are indeed. My mother died and Father married again.'

'Did you ever hear the Kissing Cousins when you were in Africa?' she asked one day.

'I did. Great girls, aren't they? And the band is excellent. I wonder if they'll ever know how they helped the fighting men. I know some of Eve's family. She's extra brave to be out there in her condition.'

'Her condition?'

'She's going to have a child. She'll have to come home, but she insists on finishing the tour.'

Robert went for a medical check-up and was invalided out of the Army. He came straight to Sid. 'I feel such a damned failure,' he said angrily. 'I said I was perfectly fit to return to duty, but the medics say otherwise.'

'What will you do?'

'Get a job, I suppose. I must do something to help.'

He spoke both German and French fluently, and obtained a position with the BBC in Bristol, broadcasting to occupied France to people who risked their lives to listen to messages from Britain, sending propaganda messages to Germany.

'At least, I'm doing something, Sidonia, and I would like to stay in

Bristol. I value your friendship. An old school friend has a flat I can use. He's being posted.'

Sid liked Robert, in spite of his damaged personality. A visit home had sent him back looking haunted. She discovered that his father had been unbelievably scathing about the grounds for his discharge, and Robert had failed to stand up to him.

Amy was delighted with him. He was yet another uncle to pamper and spoil her. She was incredibly adaptable. With the older children she held her own in their rough games, and she joined in with the pretend mothers' and babies' games with the gentler girls. With grown-ups she appeared to have an inbuilt perception of how to approach them. Sid wondered about her. She was so self-possessed, so sure, so charming. Philip was the same. She hoped that Amy hadn't inherited his lack of conscience.

Robert Felgate often visited Greystone House. He had regained his physical health to a large extent, though he knew his nerves would always give him bouts of panic. The old house was still full of raucous, uneducated women and fearfully noisy children. Rationing was severe and the length of the war was taking its toll on everyone; yet somehow Sid managed to hold everything together, to create a haven for them all while still toiling in a factory. She had been his staunch support when he needed it most, and he was inclined to cling to her strength.

He was quite jealous when a young soldier who was strong and apparently coping with ease came home on leave and visited. Roy Hendy seemed to have a lot in common with Sidonia and, having been wounded, was at present a recipient of her boundless charity and compassion. He always called her Sid, a diminutive which Robert disliked intensely, being a masculine name and, in his opinion, not a very nice one either. With Roy she laughed a lot.

Robert felt uncomfortable when Roy and Sidonia shared a joke. He had never laughed easily, and speech came haltingly to him. He put it down to his years at a public school, which he had hated and where he had been bullied unmercifully. He put most things down to that school, even the fact of his shell-shock. He was sure that had his nerves been stronger to begin with, he would not have ended up such a wreck.

Roy Hendy was lucky. He'd been reared in his own home to which he had returned from school each night to be greeted by loving parents. Robert had asked him about his schooldays and to him they sounded idyllic, though Roy made no bones about the fact that he hadn't been clever and didn't read much of anything. He had left a small business to go to war, and it was still being run fairly efficiently by a couple of old men. Robert wondered if Sidonia saw herself married to Roy, supervising his book-keeping perhaps, cooking his meals, washing his clothes, bearing his children. He was aware that she came from a background very dissimilar from his own, but he was sure she was the kind who could fit in anywhere. Sid spoke well, she could look smart and although not especially pretty she looked quite distinguished. She would pass as a lady to most people. He decided to test his theory some time, a kind of experiment. If George Bernard Shaw could elevate Pygmalion in his play he could try with Sid. He was sure it would do her good to meet his people.

On his next visit to Greystone House he took Sid to see the film *In Which We Serve*, which left her wiping her eyes.

'I've never seen you cry before,' he said. The film had been her choice and, afraid to reveal his reluctance to watch men suffer, he had quietly acquiesced.

'I enjoy a good cry at the cinema,' she said. 'It was a lovely film, wasn't it? I saw *Casablanca* again last week. That's even more wonderful.'

Before they parted he asked, 'Do you have a holiday due?'

'Yes, a long weekend.'

'It isn't much after all the hours you put in.'

'It'll have to do. We're pushing the enemy back at last and we can't afford to let up on munitions.'

Robert's memory of Roy's active participation in the war made him cringe inwardly. He had fought hard against his sickness. He had been assured by doctors that he had given enough in his service to his country, and that his injuries, although unseen, were as devastating and crippling as an amputation, but he couldn't accept it. He did not even look ill.

'I was wondering if you would care to come with me on a visit to my home?' he said carefully.

Sidonia was astonished. 'But, why? I'm sorry, that sounds awful, but I can't think of any reason your family would want to meet me and anyway when I have time off I like to spent it with – ' She had almost said Amy, but inbuilt caution changed it to 'my friends here and the children.'

'Don't you see enough of them?'

Never, Sid's tormented soul replied silently. Never have I seen enough of my own child and she's growing up not knowing how dear she is to me, not knowing that she has a mother who adores her. 'I'm always so busy. It would be pleasant just to relax at home. Daisy and the others are very good to me. Whenever I have a day off they conspire to make me rest, for at least part of it.'

'So they should! You've done a lot for them. Not everyone would have opened her home to a collection of such women.' He hadn't meant his tone to sound scornful, but his upbringing had never prepared him for social contact with people he considered beneath him. He had made Sidonia angry though, and he said quickly, 'I'm so sorry. I know they're your friends and all good, decent people. I'm a clumsy oaf.'

'It's all right,' said Sid with a sigh. 'We can't help the way we are. I don't think anyone ever really changes.'

'I've changed since meeting you.'

'Have you?'

'You've been so good for me. I'm sure you know I'm very fond of you.'

'I know, Robert, and I am of you. But to visit your home!'

'My parents would enjoy meeting the woman who helped me to get well.'

'Maybe.'

'They would, I know they would.' Robert was getting flushed and his voice was rising.

She said gently, 'Robert, I'm happy to have helped you though I think you make too much of my part—'

'Never!'

'All right, Robert, if you insist on giving me credit—'

'You are mocking me!' he cried.

'I am not! I admire the way you've coped.'

'Say you'll visit my home, please.'

She saw that such a visit meant a great deal to him. 'I may. Give me time to think.'

He left then, turning at the door to give her a smile which hurt her. She sat alone, thinking about Robert, before her thoughts turned inevitably to Tom. She wondered if she would ever get him out of her mind. She was aware that communication between the Red Cross and the Japanese was almost non-existent, but surely he would have got a message to her somehow. Perhaps he had fallen in love with someone while in Singapore. Perhaps another woman was receiving all his loving messages. Perhaps he was dead. The thought slipped past her guard.

Robert renewed his pleas. He was honest and straightforward, his weaknesses were those of a humane man who couldn't cope with endless scenes of death and destruction. Surely it couldn't hurt to give way to him in this.

She forgot Robert when she received a letter from Mrs Prosser to say she would be in Bristol again quite soon and trusted she might meet the child. Surely she didn't intend to acknowledge an illegitimate child, even her grandson's. No, the woman was merely curious. Or perhaps she was so angry over not getting Greystone House she would stoop to take revenge of some kind.

She wondered how Robert would take the truth of Amy's birth if ever she told him? She had kept silent for so long she couldn't think how she would speak of it. Would Tom have reacted favourably? Or Roy? No man, her mother had always said, wanted another man's cast-offs. Roy had told her he cared for her. He had made friends with another woman, but it had all fallen through. He put it down to the fact that Sid was always in his mind. His background was similar to hers, one into which she and Amy could slide.

She had scarcely slept when Robert arrived and was grey with weariness after a twelve-hour stint at work beginning at six in the morning.

He looked anxiously at her. 'You really should accept my invitation, you know. A short break in the country would do you good.'

Roy returned to his regiment and Robert was glad to see him go.

Robert and Sidonia talked a lot about the war. His part had become minimal, but like everyone, he followed it closely. 'There's something brewing,' he said, one day in June. 'There have been great movements of troops.'

'There seem to have been great movements of troops ever since the war began,' sighed Sid. She was idle for once, trying to relax in the sitting room, thinking again of Tom. He came into her mind so often. She dreamt of him, too; dreams in which they strolled together, held one another close.

'This is something very big. In fact,' said Robert carefully, 'I believe we're going to return to France at last.'

Sidonia stared. 'Is that possible? I knew the war was swinging our way, with Russia beating the Germans back and the Allies winning in Burma – ' She stopped, her mind swinging to Tom again. Could he be in Burma? Would the prison camps soon be liberated? 'Freeing Europe. That would bring the end of this terrible war closer, wouldn't it?'

The Allies were at last progressing through the occupied countries. It was wonderful to know that they were greeted by men, women and children, with kisses and flowers and sobs of relief. Always the cheers were mingled with tears over the death of so many, especially the young, whose promise of a full life was snatched away.

One of the dead was Roy Hendy. He had been killed after fighting his way from the landing beaches. Sid remembered his first cheeky winks, his determination to succeed, his gentle kindness, the fun they had had together, and mourned. She visited his home where she had been a few times before, and offered what comfort she could to his grieving family, she attended his memorial service, but the words made little sense to her. He was her first close friend to die, at least of whose death she was certain. Her initial shock passed, leaving behind strong remnants of grief which would never quite be assuaged.

Celia Prosser turned up out of the blue. Daisy was waiting at the front gate when Sid arrived home from work and told her.

'She's been askin' if she could watch the children play in the garden,' said Daisy. 'She was as nice as pie about it, but I don't trust her. There's somethin' about the way she asked, kind of sly.'

'What did you say?' asked Sid, hurrying into the house.

'I handed her a ball and told her she could go an' have fun and games if she liked, though it was a bit muddy after the shower. She went, too, though I'd not expected her to.'

Sid stopped moving. 'What happened?'

'Nothin'. I whisked Amy round to visit the Misses Weekley. I knew they'd be pleased and so was Amy, an' I knew you wouldn't want that madam to see Amy because . . .'

Daisy stopped speaking, her hand to her mouth, and Sid turned to stare at her. 'You know who Amy is, don't you?'

'Yes. I'm sorry, ducks, but I guessed. I didn't mean to come out with it like that. Damn it, I meant to say that Amy had been invited out or somethin'. I'm really sorry.'

'How do you know?'

'I can't help seein' how much you love that kid. An' she's the image of Celia.'

'Then the others know, too?'

'No, don't worry. They don't see further than their own noses. Too wrapped up in their bickering an' their rights as residents. Don't mind me. I've never said a word to anyone an' I never will, but I couldn't let that bitch upstairs spoil things for you.'

Sid kept Celia waiting while she drank tea in the kitchen, the voices of the women flowing around her like the sound of waves, a perpetual swirling without definition. Then she went to the small sitting room.

Celia was standing at a window. She turned. 'Decided you'd bother to come, have you?'

Sid realised that she must have seen her arrival. 'I needed a cup of tea. Would you like one?'

'No. Thanks,' Celia added belatedly. 'One of your ghastly women, that large one – the most ghastly of them all in my opinion – tells me that Amy is away visiting friends.'

Sid said nothing.

'Is she or isn't she?'

'Daisy told you the truth. I can't imagine why you should doubt her.'

'Can't you, really?'

'You are in Bristol with your grandmother?'

'Yes. We've moved here for a while.'

'You're lucky to be able to come and go so freely. Don't you work?'

'Of course.' Celia looked bored. 'I'm an interpreter. I've always been quick at languages so my travels abroad have come in useful after all. Grandmother always said I was wasting money. I've been transferred to the BBC.'

'I see.' Sid waited.

Celia said, 'My grandmother has been thinking a lot about that kid. In fact, she's quite tedious on the subject. I can't imagine why she cares who the brat is. I thought I'd come and see if I could get the mystery cleared up. Then maybe she'll shut up about her.'

'You've nothing better to do than pester me?'

'I take exception to the word pester! Besides, I wouldn't admit it to Grandmother, but Amy does look like me and my brother was a visitor about the time she would have been conceived, wasn't he?'

'What nonsense! There are so many war orphans, poor little souls. There's nothing strange about Mrs Cardell giving refuge to one.'

'War orphan be damned!' Celia declared loudly. 'That child is my brother's.'

'That's a ridiculous assumption!'

'No, it isn't. I have no illusions about him.'

'How comforting that must be for him.'

'Well, actually he used to confide in me, but he didn't mention this little episode.'

280

No, of course, he wouldn't, thought Sid. Seducing his cousin's companion under her own roof would, for his relatives, constitute fouling your own nest. He wouldn't have wanted to incur the wrath of either his grandmother or Mrs Cardell, especially when he had expected his family to inherit her possessions.

'I suppose you've written a nice confiding letter to your brother,' she said sarcastically.

'Good God, no, and I don't propose to tell him. Heavens, we can't be responsible for his bastard brats, and neither can he. We don't know if there are more and we care even less. If a woman is fool enough to give in to a man, she has only herself to blame if she gets caught.'

Sid seethed with anger. 'I want you to leave Greystone House. You were admitted because my friends are courteous, far more so than you.'

Celia coloured. 'Don't compare me to those fearful creatures. Look, why not just admit that Amy is my brother's child? I find it so curious that Cousin Louisa decided to protect her.'

'Then it's a pity that Mrs Cardell isn't here to answer your impertinent suggestions herself. But you would never have dared question her like this, would you?'

'Probably not.' Celia opened her cigarette case and fitted a cigarette into a long holder. 'Smokes are damned difficult to get nowadays.'

'I believe they send them to our fighting men.'

Celia, ignoring Sid's sarcasm, took a drag and blew out smoke in a long stream. 'Just tell me what I want to know and I'll leave. And it's no good your keeping up with your lies. Cousin Louisa thought the sun shone from your derrière. She'd have told you who Amy really was, except of course that you know all about her parentage, don't you, Miss Penrose?'

'Why don't you mind your own business?'

Celia laughed nastily. 'As a matter of fact, I've remembered about that long, so-called holiday Cousin Louisa took. It was to Scotland and you went with her. For her health, wasn't it? But I believe it had more to do with your health. Or rather, the birth of your baby. That's what happened, isn't it? My brother got you pregnant and Amy is the result.'

'I have already asked you to leave. I ask you again.'

'Not until you tell me the truth.'

'Why should Amy interest you? How dare you invade my house with your unwelcome presence and your disgusting curiosity. You appal me.'

'My goodness, you have learned some high-faultin' ways since you left the kitchen. As for Amy interesting me she doesn't, except that I'm positive that she's your child. You've gone to such extreme lengths to keep her identity a secret I imagine you would sacrifice quite a lot to continue the charade. After all, it wouldn't do Amy's future any good for people to learn she's illegitimate.' Celia tapped ash into the fireplace. 'I've always loved Cousin Louisa's pearls,' she said reflectively, 'and those Regency bedside cabinets are a dream. And a couple of the pictures – '

Sid cut through Celia's soft, menacing tones. 'Blackmail! How disgusting!'

'Blackmail,' repeated Celia angrily. 'How dare you!'

'I don't think you'll tell. After all, it wouldn't put your brother in a very good light, would it? And I wonder what people would think of you if they learned about this.' Sid turned and walked out and up the stairs. She sat on the edge of her bed in the room which was crowded with Mrs Cardell's possessions. Had all their contrivances been in vain? Celia Prosser had guessed accurately. It couldn't have been difficult given the facts. Would she descend to spreading gossip? Perhaps Sid should have placated her, soothed her, tried to get her on Amy's side. She half rose, then sank back. If the Prossers had shown a hint of sympathy or compassion, she might have told them the truth. It seemed as if her early misplaced love, her reckless yielding to passion would never cease to bring her grief.

Celia might voice her suspicions. In her intimate circle it was unlikely that anyone would care that Philip had fathered a child on a servant. They would laugh and sneer, but one day Amy could be wounded. Sid held her head in her hands. She was almost beyond coherent thought.

Daisy came to tell her that Celia had left. 'She was in a right temper, too.'

'She tried to blackmail me. She wanted some of Mrs Cardell's things to keep her mouth shut.'

'The bitch! How does she know? Did you give yourself away?'

'No. She's guessed about Amy. It isn't difficult. You saw the resemblance.'

'Do you think she'll tell?'

'I don't know.'

'Well, her family won't want a scandal. I shouldn't worry, Sid.'

Sid received a letter from Susan Morland.

> Tessa and Eve are back. They're in London. Tessa says she doesn't know how the poor people stick the new kind of bombs. First they had to put up with the V Ones. They called them doodle-bugs or buzz-bombs. She said it was terrible when they came over and the engine stopped and everyone held their breath until they heard the explosion. Now it's even worse because they have rocket bombs and they don't hear them until they make a kind of tearing sound – like an express train, she said – just before they land. They go faster than sound. Imagine that! Those poor people having to suffer so much.
>
> Some good news, though. Eve's had her baby, a boy, and everything went well. She leaves it with a nurse in the country while she sings. It's a real sacrifice because she adores him, but entertaining people is just as much a part of war-work as anything else.

Sid read part of the letter to Robert who said, 'I don't approve of mothers leaving their babies.'

'But if lots of them weren't prepared to put them in one of the factory crèches or engage help, we'd be short of labour. A couple of the women here go to work and the others care for their children.'

'Eve needn't have gone back to her singing. I've heard the Kissing Cousins many times, and Tessa Ware could have carried on alone if needs be.'

'People want them as a duo, and Eve intends to make sure that's what they get.'

Robert said no more about Eve. He had no wish to antagonise Sidonia.

Sid wondered whether he would be shocked if ever he learned the truth of Amy's birth. She wondered what Tom would have said. He lived so much in her mind. She could not be sure that he would have been tolerant either. He came from the same kind of background as Robert, the landed gentry. According to gossip columns, many of them seemed to take irregularities of behaviour in their stride. But not all.

She was veering towards the idea of marrying Robert and telling him later about Amy. It went against the grain to consider such a blatant deception, such an abuse of his trust, but she was driven. She vowed she would do all in her power to make him happy. He needed her as much as she needed him to protect Amy with a cloak of respectability.

Tom Barton lay shaking with fever. If he could have raised his head to look down at himself, he could have counted every one of his ribs. His legs were reduced almost to skin and bone, ulcerated and covered in sores. No matter how hard the imprisoned doctors and medics tried, they were unable to get the Japanese commandant to release supplies of quinine or any other healing drug or ointment, or to supply sufficient food. Men died by the hundred as they worked on the railway, which was being pushed at cruel speed through the jungle by emaciated workers of many nationalities. Tom was lucky to be still alive, though for how long, no man could tell. There were so many unpleasant ways to die out here. A particularly nasty one was cerebral malaria, which sent men to screaming madness before they succumbed. There was cholera or dysentery, the probability of which was compounded by lack of drinking water. There was simple vitamin deficiency, including beri-beri, in which a man drowned in his own juices, and which could have been cured by eating unwashed rice or by an issue of Vitamin B. Men could die from beatings after some minor misdemeanour, or be shot for something their guards considered fatally serious, such as an escape attempt. There had been very few of those because there was nowhere to go but into miles of jungle, where escapees could not survive.

Tom's fever came on alternate days. Tomorrow he would be back working on the railway, undertaking tasks which would have floored a healthy man. He wondered why he, like the other living skeletons, clung to a life which had become nightmarish. His lifeline was the memory of the girl in Greystone House. He concentrated so hard on that pleasant old manor in a quiet part of Bristol that sometimes he was actually able to forget he lay in a jungle clearing on a lice-ridden sleeping platform and imagined he was walking in the garden with her. Perhaps the fever induced some of his best dreams, when he held her in his arms and she kissed him and told him she loved him. In actual fact the state of his body had destroyed all sexual impulses, but for a few supreme moments he felt happy until something – pain, or yells and screams from some tormented man, or the return of his exhausted comrades – pulled him back to consciousness and the horrendous present.

Every night Tom prayed that Sidonia wouldn't forget him. That she'd wait for him until he could tell her just how much he cared. He had been a fool for not pursuing her harder when he had the chance, while his body could thrill to his aching need to possess her. If he could have the time over again he was sure she'd be married to him by now. She was the kind of woman who would always be faithful. She might even have borne him a child, a stake in a future which looked increasingly remote as men died here in their hundreds. If it were not for the memory of Sidonia, he believed he might have joined them long ago, and be buried in the jungle in a grave which would soon be obliterated by the rampant foliage. He'd had no letters from anyone for nearly three years and, although he had written, there was no guarantee that his letters were ever sent. Even the Red Cross had been thwarted in their attempts to relieve the lot of the prisoners of the Japanese. 'Don't forget me, Sidonia, my love,' he said aloud.

'What?' asked the man in the next bed.

'Just talking to myself,' said Tom.

'Best be careful. That's the first sign, they say.'

Tom managed to laugh.

Chapter Eighteen

Robert begged Sid over and over again to visit his home. He was very persuasive. 'I won't give up. You need a rest and you can get one at my place.'

'But,' she argued, 'what will your parents think if you turn up with a girl?'

'What should they think? We have always brought our friends to meet them.'

The work at the factory was hard and unrelenting and the problems of dealing with so many women and children, even with Daisy's help, often frustrated her. A weekend in the country. It sounded wonderful. In the end she agreed.

Robert's face was lit with a brilliant smile. 'I'll arrange it immediately. You'll love our place, Sidonia, I know you will, it's so beautiful. And I know my parents will just adore you.'

'Have you mentioned me to them?'

'Yes, of course. They know how you have helped me.'

'Do they know who I am?'

'What do you mean?'

'Robert! You know well what I mean. Do your parents know that I'm your landlady?'

'They know you took me in when I needed somewhere to stay and did so in spite of the large number of bombed-out refugees you were sheltering.'

They travelled by train. On the way Robert remarked casually that someone Sid knew had joined his office at the BBC. 'Celia Prosser. She was a relative of your late employer. She says she knows you well. "Very well", were her words. She laughed when she said it, though I cannot imagine why she should find that amusing, can you?'

Sid mumbled something. She could easily imagine why. She pictured Celia's 'accidentally' letting drop the fact that among the children in Greystone House was a girl who was exceptionally special. She and Amy were being threatened from all sides, and Sid was tormented by doubts which increased with every turn of the wheels. Why did she go on keeping up the charade? Babies were being born every day to unmarried women; fiancées and girlfriends of serving men, of men who had been killed, of fighting men from overseas who had no intention of marrying their lovers. Amy would not be alone in her illegitimacy. But Sid found it impossible to cope with. She supposed her upbringing had something to do with it. Mum, the aunties and

Grandma were so straight-laced. They dubbed such mothers 'fallen' women, 'sinners', and unjustly included the children in their disapproval. Her beautiful, bright-eyed, open-hearted child would suffer.

Sid had expected to be awed by Robert's family, but close association with Mrs Cardell and her successful management of an ancient house had endowed her with qualities of resilience and adaptability which surprised her. The driveway was long and Felgate Manor imposing. The front door opened straight on to an enormous hall in which a large log fire was smouldering, taking the edge off the chilly, damp day. It was furnished with antiques from many ages, including a number of chairs and couches, each one of which was occupied by a dog. They were of various breeds and varying size, but all sat firmly on the beautiful furniture as if by right.

The butler welcomed Robert and said he would inform Mrs Felgate that they had arrived. Robert turfed a couple of dogs from a Regency sofa and motioned Sid to it, ignoring the hairs and grime left by the animals which had apparently been rolling in mud. She sat down gingerly in her best costume. Robert joined her, then jumped up when his mother came down the uncarpeted stairs which led into the enormous hall, two more dogs at her heels, their claws clicking on the oak boards. Sid stood to greet her and found she towered over her. Mrs Felgate was quite short and a little stout. Her husband, summoned also, was tall, thin and silent. He shook hands with Sid, giving her a close scrutiny. After greeting Sid heartily, Mrs Felgate talked almost exclusively to her son, the conversation ranging over topics which Sid had never considered: hunting, shooting, fishing, all the more necessary nowadays, it was agreed, when food was rationed.

'That's enough of that,' said Mr Felgate suddenly. 'Miss Penrose doesn't look terribly interested.'

'I am, really,' said Sid, 'we eat quite a lot of rabbit at home.'

'Rabbit?' Mr Felgate sounded as if he had never heard of such a creature.

'So do we,' said Mrs Felgate. 'Pay no attention to him, Sidonia, he never knows what he's eating.'

'Oh, yes I do,' said Mr Felgate.

Mrs Felgate laughed. 'Robert has always enjoyed country pursuits,' she said. 'Has your family estate got good shooting? Any fishing? You have excellent rivers near you.'

Sid realised then that Robert must have emphasised her new status without going into her true background. She felt annoyed with him. Such deception could make her position here awkward. She was shown to her bedroom. It contained a four-poster bed with a very hard mattress, and several easy chairs clawed and chewed by, she supposed, the inevitable dogs. She enjoyed a bath in the wartime regulation five inches of water and put on a dress Aunt Jess had considered the correct evening attire in wartime. It was short and plain because fancy clothes didn't suit her. The regulations regarding the amount of material had been slightly eased and the dark blue dress had a fashionable peplum and had been altered in the shop to fit her perfectly. She had learned skills with make-up and hair-styling and she studied her reflection in the long cheval glass. I'm not pretty, she had to admit, but I have learned something about presenting myself.

'How distinguished you look,' said Robert when he arrived to escort her.

She felt under-dressed when guests arrived, some of the women in quite elaborate evening gowns, the men in dinner jackets. The expensive gowns had been made before the war and were very pretty; two young women, home on leave from the WRENS, Robert said, looked decidedly attractive in floating chiffon. But she knew that her dress had been expertly designed, and Mrs Cardell's real pearls, which she hadn't been able to bring herself to sell, gleamed sensuously against her throat. Several of the women looked her up and down approvingly, or enviously.

'That's a really splendid frock!' one of the WRENS exclaimed before she shimmered across to the drawing-room fire, around which as many of the female guests as possible were clustered.

'Why do they wear such skimpy clothes when it's so chilly?' Sid asked Robert. The room was so large that it was perfectly possible to hold a conversation at one end without the fire-lovers hearing.

'What? Oh, they always have. This house doesn't get really warm even in summer. Neither do theirs. Stately homes never do. It's their hardiness which breeds the British bulldog and his mate. Tomorrow, for the shoot, they'll put on thick tweeds, waterproof socks and boots and tramp round the grounds.'

'Fancy! Do the women shoot?'

'Some of them. Stout girls, aren't they?' He smiled and so did Sid. He was not often light-hearted. 'Of course,' Robert went on, 'Father's not been able to stock the place very well this year. The gamekeepers were called up and only one of their very ancient grandfathers is doing the best he can with a crippled boy to help. But there's enough to amuse them for a day or two.'

Robert's sisters greeted her with alarming heartiness; her hand was also shaken by two brothers-in-law, one invalided out of the army after losing his leg, the other on sick leave and eager to return to the battle. She watched them as they greeted Robert. Outwardly they were affable, but their questions to him about his job at the BBC were condescending. She knew they were well on the way to despising him. It made her feel protective.

Mrs Felgate took Sid to see the horses in their stables, which were, in their way, as luxurious as the house and slightly warmer. They rolled their large brown eyes at her, betraying their high temper, and stretched their slender, silken necks. She was reluctant to touch them though her hostess fed them carrots from her hand.

Mrs Felgate marked her reluctance. 'Don't you hunt?'

'Er, no.'

'Why not?'

Sid was silent for a moment as she contemplated the utter impossibility of answering the question.

'Family not a sporting one?' asked Mrs Felgate.

Sid thought of Raymond and Dad and their interest in football, and one of her uncles who liked dog racing. 'No, not very.'

'Don't hunt,' said Mrs Felgate half to herself. When it was discovered that Sid had no interest in outdoor sports, the others left her alone without a qualm, and she sat and looked through copies of *Tatler* and *Vogue* with one of Robert's sisters who was very pregnant and very bored. The guns sounded all day from a distance.

'I suppose they are shooting to help fill the larder,' said Sid to the sister, more for something to say than anything.

'It helps. They need more shoots these days to keep the vermin down. Bloody rats and foxes eat young birds.'

The language of these country aristocrats was outspoken. After living with Daisy and the others Sid was unshockable, but it came as a surprise to learn that the expletives used at Greystone Lodge with abandon were just as liberally employed in Felgate Manor.

'I thought the hunting kept down foxes,' she said tentatively.

'Oh, yes, it does in normal times, but the hunt has suffered like everything else, most of the more active men have gone to fight, and so we have to kill them with guns. You don't care to shoot, I hear.'

'No.'

'How odd. It's necessary, you know. We can get an allowance of ammunition because of the vermin and surely guns are better than traps, though we have to employ those, too.'

Robert had accompanied the party reluctantly. Sid knew that his wartime experiences had left him with an abhorrence of guns, but his family seemed not to understand this at all, taking it for granted that he would be delighted with the sport. She sympathised with him. It was difficult to resist his domineering family, and by going out with the guns, he had hoped he'd regain their respect. He wanted desperately to get back to what was in his family considered normal, but he returned before lunch, looking white and strained. After they had eaten he walked with her in a direction away from the shoot, wandering in extensive woodlands, strolling by a river, crossing green meadows kept cropped by sheep. Everything they saw was owned by the Felgates.

'You didn't enjoy the shoot?' she asked.

'I hated it,' he burst out. 'When I aimed the gun at animals, I didn't see them as four-legged creatures, but as people! They changed into people, with faces of men as fearful as I was! Some seem to enjoy killing men as much as my lot do animals and birds. Or maybe their yelling and swaggering in battle was assumed to disguise their true feelings. Sometimes I think I shall go crazy. I only know that this morning I had to beg off. My father is furious with me.'

'He'll get over it.'

'No, he won't. He says little, but he's master here and can make his anger felt more by his silence than others by any amount of harsh words. I don't think I shall ever be able to return here to live.'

Sid looked around her at all the beauty of a well-loved private estate. 'I do hope you're wrong.' How Amy would love it here, she thought.

Her adventurous spirit could have full play.

'What are you thinking of?' asked Robert.

For a crazy moment she thought of telling him now about Amy. She remembered what Daisy had said the night before. 'He's sweet on you, ducks. I'd make the most of it. I should encourage him. Get him into bed and then tell him about Amy. I bet he'd propose.'

'That's not how I want to get a husband,' Sid had protested. 'And in any case I don't care for him except as a friend.'

'Marriages have survived on less.'

She answered Robert's question. 'I was thinking how sad it would make you feel if you couldn't live here again. It's all so lovely.'

'I know, though it's a big ragged at present. All but the oldest of the gardeners and foresters have been called up. We're lucky we still have the gamekeeper and the boy. His busted leg doesn't seem to hold him back.'

'What happened to him?'

'An accident with a gun – when he was beating as a boy, a guest shot him in the leg.'

'Shot him in the leg? Does that kind of thing happen often?'

'Not really. No one takes much notice. Occasionally my father and his friends shoot each other, but there are no hard feelings and the local vet binds their wounds. There's never been a fatality on our land, not within living memory anyway.'

Sid was astonished. 'Robert, if you're so used to such things, why did the war upset you so?'

Abruptly, he stopped walking and leaned against the bole of a tree. When she looked into his pale face, she wished the ground would open and swallow her.

'I'm so sorry, my dear,' she said. 'That was horribly clumsy of me.'

'You didn't mean to hurt me,' he gasped. Pain was sweeping over him in waves, not physical pain but an agony far more difficult to contain: emotional, mental pain. He heard again the whine of shells, felt the ground shake as they landed nearby, remembered the sight of the bodies of his men, his friends, dead, or bleeding and dying slowly in agony. No matter how hard the medics worked, they could only deal with so many casualties at a time; it was their duty to tend first the men who still had a hope of life.

Sid put her arms round him, 'Please, forgive me. I never ever want to hurt you.'

He clung to her. 'I know that. But when I remember my friends who are still fighting I feel such a fraud, a coward, a man to be despised.'

'No, oh, don't say that. It's not true.'

'It is. I've seen the way those women of yours look at me sometimes. Their men are fighting. Daisy's husband was killed. And here at home, my parents are trying to accommodate my feelings, but they can't hide what they really think. None of them can.'

'They're genuinely sorry about your illness, aren't they?'

'They would have been genuinely sorry about my death in heroic circumstances. They could have taken pride in that. They could have erected a memorial stone to go alongside the men of the family who died in the Crimea, the Boer War, the Great War. As it is, all they've got left is a shell of a son who couldn't even stick it out like the commonest of his men, and had to leave a shoot because it made him feel sick.'

Sid hugged him tighter and from the depth of her pity she kissed his cheek. It was wet, and she realised with overpowering compassion that he was weeping silently.

'Oh, Robert, don't, I beg of you. No one who really knows you could go on thinking badly of you.'

'You understand, Sidonia, don't you? You are the only one who really seems to understand.'

His arms tightened round her, holding her so close she could feel his racing heart. 'I need you so much. You give me strength. Sidonia, I need you.'

'I know, Robert,' she said, keeping her voice low and even, 'and you have my friendship.'

'Thank you, darling. I cling to that.'

She might have flinched at the endearment if she had not heard his family and friends using it to men, women and dogs alike.

On Sunday afternoon Sid said goodbye to the Felgates and she and Robert caught a train back to Bristol. Sid was glad to leave. She detested the oppressive atmosphere centred around Robert. She even had a feeling that as matters stood they would not raise objections to her taking him off their hands.

Angie wrote to say that Philip Prosser was married. 'She's an officer in the WRENS, very rich and older than him. She visited him here once and I thought she looked quite nice, though not at all pretty. They say he's terrified of going out with the bomber crews. I can't say I blame him. I suppose they're all terrified, but he tries to get out of it when he can and someone else has to step in. He's not generally respected by the men, and some of the girls hate him. He's taken a few of them out on dates, then dropped them when he's met someone he fancies more. And much worse, twice one of the men who had to take his place on a strike didn't come back.'

Sid recalled the time when marriage with Philip was the whole extent of her dream of happiness. She wondered if his wife would be able to cope with him.

Sid often heard Robert's voice on the wireless, and he visited nearly every day. He had become quite friendly with Celia Prosser, though he said he didn't think she was to be trusted. 'There's something about her which makes me uneasy, Sidonia,' he said. 'She always asks after you which is understandable as you know each other, but once she asked me my opinion of you. Rather an odd thing to do, I thought. I believe she might have considered me over-enthusiastic in my description of how well you coped because she looked angry and walked off. But the next time we spoke she was as friendly as ever, asking lots of questions about you and the house. I suggested that she paid you a visit – ' – Sid thought her heart would stop beating – 'but she said not at present, though the time would come. She said it in an odd, significant way. I can't understand her at all.'

'Do you want to?'

'No, thanks. She's the kind of woman I avoid like the plague.'

Robert's nerves were improving and he smiled more. Daisy and the others were more comfortable with him and he with them although they could never meet on terms of true friendship. The barriers on both sides were too high to be breached.

'He's not so bad when you get to know him,' said Daisy. 'We all thought he was a proper pansy but he's not, is he? When you read of what those men go through it makes you wonder if you'd be brave. I'm sure now he's got a crush on you. You could do worse.'

Sid shook her head and said lightly, 'He's not my type.'

'Blow that! He's well off and good-looking. He'd take Amy in his stride if you gave him the chance.'

'I don't want someone who'll take Amy in his stride. She needs love.'

Daisy was still a constant source of support. It was such a relief to have someone in whom to confide her hopes and fears. 'Take any good husband you can get,' was still her advice. She and Sid were in the small sitting room together, a tiny fire toasting their toes. Autumn was cool and damp this year. Life in Britain was often dreary and frustrating, but the battle news was encouraging.

Paris had been liberated. General de Gaulle – who had spent years in England, from where he had heartened his people by broadcasting messages to them which they had risked death to listen to – had returned in triumph to his country. He was cheered with every step he took.

The Channel Islands were being vacated by the enemy, who were also retreating from Belgium. Russia had recaptured Bucharest, and the residents of Warsaw had risen to fight gallantly as they waited for relief.

It was learned that a second attempt had been made on Hitler's life by his own officers. It had failed, and the men had been hanged slowly from meat hooks, piano wire around their throats.

In November, Franklin Delano Roosevelt, the friend of Britain, was elected for a fourth term and the Allies were pushing into Germany itself. Hitler was forming a People's Guard, but the British Home Guard was said to be no longer needed and 'stood down'. Brindle, Keith and Patrick returned to Greystone House after their final drill, feeling bereft.

Keith in particular fretted. 'I never did get to do any real fighting.'

'You protected people,' said Daisy, 'puttin' out incendiaries and helpin' the ones who got bombed.'

Keith hadn't been satisfied with this, then Brindle announced that he'd had enough and wished to retire and Keith took his place and, in his new position of chief general factotum, his good humour and self-respect returned. They were all sorry to see Brindle go but, in accordance with Mrs Cardell's wishes, Sid made sure he had enough money to live in comfort in a little cottage nearby. The money earned by Sid, and the contributions from the women, plus the income from Mrs Cardell's estate meant that Greystone House could be run economically. The garden kept them well supplied with fruit and vegetables. Women who had never had much didn't demand luxury.

As Londoners suffered beneath the hail of rocket bombs, they had to take what solace they could from promises for a better future, and from the fact that the Germans were suffering much more from saturation bombing by the Allies.

Robert still worked at the BBC. He had made other friends and his doctor was hopeful that in time he would recover completely. He had no such faith. He still visited regularly and talked to Sid about his hopes and fears. She was pleased to learn that he was finding pleasure in the company of women of his own sort. He had not asked her to visit his home again and she was thankful.

It was getting dark as Philip Prosser left the Mess. There was a perfect sunset, but he had to turn up his collar against a cold wind. He was glad he could blame the trembling of his limbs on cold. He was deadly afraid. Fear stalked him when he was awake and invaded his dreams when he slept. Deep, unremitting fear. Fear that sometimes paralysed thought and movement, so that the skipper had to yell at him to wake up and get on with his task of navigation. They were off on yet another strike, and as always he cursed himself for the vanity which led him to apply for air crew. He hadn't even managed to rise to the most glamorous job of pilot.

'Weather seems all right,' said a junior officer. He had been reading and put the book aside, still open, page down, ready to resume reading when he returned. Philip knew this was a kind of talisman towards a safe homecoming. Men did this kind of thing. They left letters half written, cigarette packs open, chocolate saved to be eaten as a celebration of another successful strike.

In the locker room, Philip dressed. Sheepskin-lined knee-boots, flying suit, two pairs of silk gloves, helmet with earphones and microphone, a couple of flashlamps in his pocket, and his parachute. The fitters were standing by the plane giving instructions. 'Contact starboard', and the plane stuttered and leapt into life. Philip climbed in and sat at the navigator's table.

'Pilot calling navigator.'

'OK, Skipper.' He heard himself giving the course.

The pilot repeated his words. 'Thank you. Wireless operator?'

'OK, sir.'

When the gunners had answered, they checked their time, lights were turned out, chocks were removed from the wheels, and the pilot guided his machine between the flare path. Philip had heard the voice of the rear gunner with his usual disbelief at his calm. They knew how vulnerable they were in their cramped, exposed positions. Sometimes, if they received a direct hit, they had to be scooped out of the plane with a shovel or – even worse horror – hosed out. Philip gagged. Oh,

God, don't let me be sick, he prayed. Not now. Not yet. Let me wait until afterwards. Men did vomit, though no one admitted knowing about it. Philip ate and drank nothing for hours before a strike in case his bladder or bowels let him down. He was bad enough on the flight out, but over Germany when the flak was bursting around them in a deadly fusillade, he had to use all his muscle power to control himself.

Now they were fifteen thousand feet above the English Channel, and the captain was signalling to the navigator to take over the controls. Somehow this steadied Philip, as if by holding the controls he held his own safety. When the skipper had checked on each of his men he returned, and Philip went back to his maps and instruments. He was a good navigator. He knew he was disliked by many of the men, but they respected his skill. He guided then cleanly over their target, at which point they released their bombs on to a town where people died simply because they were there. They had been seduced by Adolf Hitler, a man whose fine flow of rhetoric had not been matched by his perspicacity in conducting a war.

The plane was hit. It had happened before and the skipper had got them back safely, but each time Philip had to fight to control his hysteria. It veered before being brought under control. 'We're flying on one engine,' said the skipper, his voice laconic. They were hit again, and damage to the undercarriage was recorded. 'It's going to be a bumpy landing,' said the skipper.

The men were mainly silent as they flew back to base. A bumpy landing, thought Philip. He had seen the results of a few bumpy landings. Machinery half drifting from the sky, hurtling tons of metal and what was left of the fuel along the airstrip, spinning crazily, ending up nose first, tongues of fire licking greedily before bursting into a holocaust of flames. He had heard the screams of men in agony beyond endurance. He was numb with terror. If he got out of this he'd never fly again. They could court-martial him, they could imprison him for ever, but never again would he go out on a bombing strike. Never.

They were waiting for them below. Ambulances, fire tenders, fitters, officers, looking up with the hope that their comrades would get down safely. If they didn't they would raise their glasses later in the Mess in a silent toast. How many of those had he partaken of? Far too many. The lights of the airfield were rushing up to meet them. He felt the tremendous, spine-jarring jolt as they bounced on the runway, knew the metal would be striking sparks which could so easily set off the flames that would consume them.

They hit again and again; then the plane's nose struck the concrete, there was noise, metal smashing, metal crushing bones, yells and screams, the smell of blood, there was fearful pain, then there was darkness.

Sid read Angie's letter. 'Philip Prosser is in hospital. He's the only survivor of a crash landing. He's terribly badly injured. They say he isn't expected to live.'

'It's horrible,' Sid said to Daisy.

'Do you mind that much? After all, he was a real stinker to you.'

'I know, but . . . And the other poor men. All dead. No one deserves to die in such a brutal way.'

'They bomb us, we bomb them,' said Daisy. 'Their men die and so do ours. It's war.' Sid said no more. Daisy's bleak look belied the casual quality of her words.

Christmas 1944 was made as joyful as possible for the children in Greystone House. Susan called with small gifts for them all, including the mothers who exclaimed delightedly over the packets of cigarettes she had somehow got hold of.

'How is your mother?' asked Sid when they had a few quiet moments together.

'Managing as best she can. Daisy's a great comfort to her and she can dig like a man. The garden will be kept as it always was.'

'How about Tessa and Eve?'

'Both well. They haven't seen their husbands for ages but, at present, touch wood, they're all right. Of course, they're very unhappy about Dad.' Her voice broke, then she took a deep breath and continued. 'The band is getting ready to go to Germany. Have you heard anything about Tom Barton? You haven't mentioned him for ages.'

'No. Nothing.'

'I'm sorry. You were fond of him, weren't you?'

'Yes, I was,' admitted Sid. 'We shouldn't speak of him in the past tense. He may be alive still.' It was her turn to get choked up. 'Will it ever end? How many men will come home? What will they be like?'

'Try to be optimistic,' said Susan. 'The Japanese are being pushed back now, and soon the Allies are bound to reach the prisoner-of-war camps.'

'Just as long as they don't turn out to be as bad as the German death camps they've found.'

Susan shuddered. 'They're inhuman. So many good people destroyed. You can't say killed or even murdered, really. They were destroyed as if they were vermin. It's all so horrible.'

Angie came home soon after Christmas. After the usual ecstatic greetings she told Sid, 'Philip Prosser is still hanging on. He's amazed the doctors. He's gradually improving, but they say he'll never walk again. Apparently he's paralysed from the waist down.'

Sid felt a pang of pity as she recalled the nights of their passionate love-making. Did one feel anything when paralysed? Would he ever know the ecstasy of love again?

Early in 1945 came the news for which the world had waited. Hitler was dead. He had shot himself in his bunker in Berlin before the Russians could get to him.

Sad news arrived with the death of President Roosevelt just before the final victory over Germany. He had worked unceasingly for the war effort, and the strain, severe enough to weaken a healthy man, was far too much for a constitution already attacked by the persistent illness which had finally killed him.

'At least he knew we'd won,' said Susan. She had come to say goodbye. She was being sent overseas to assist in the rescue and nursing of the many wounded among fighting men and women and civilians.

'We shall look after anyone who needs help,' she said.

'Will you mind dealing with the enemy?' asked Daisy.

'They're not the enemy any more, are they? They're the conquered. And wounded people are the same anywhere. Of course, Mum is upset about my going. Joseph's still abroad and his letters are so odd these days. He never writes about his faith and doesn't even answer the questions Mum sends him about prayers or anything. Mum wonders if he's become a bit unhinged. He writes to Angie, doesn't he? What does she think?'

'She says little about him,' said Sid. 'She's just waiting for him to come home. Whatever happens she'll go on caring for him.'

'Could I tell Mum that?'

'If you think it will make her feel better. Does she know what Angie's mother does?'

'Yes, but she's so worried about Joseph I think she'd accept any help. Anyway, she likes Angie. She said after she'd met her that she was surprised such a nice girl could come from such a dreadful background. Mum's mellowed a lot since the war, and Dad . . .' She swallowed hard.

In May, victory for the Allies was declared and parties were held everywhere: in hotels and in great London houses, reopened by their relieved owners; in the streets for the less privileged, where neighbours rejoiced together. The mood was one of jubilation, and for a while people forgot that there was another war still going on in the East, and that the Japanese were by no means conquered.

In May, a general election swept the Labour Party into power, and Churchill, as dignified in defeat as he had been courageous in war, went to the king and resigned, tendering his profound gratitude to the people of Britain for their unflinching support throughout the years of war.

When Sid visited her parents she was surprised to find Grandma Lacey installed in the most comfortable easy chair in the best room. They were discussing politics, though Grandma had an excited look in her eyes, as if she held a secret.

'Fancy people voting those dreadful socialists in!' Mum was highly indignant.

'Shameful, I call it,' said Grandma Lacey. 'After all Mr Churchill did for us. A fine way to show gratitude, I *don't* think!'

'If it weren't for him we might have given up the fight,' said Dad.

'Oh, no,' cried Sid. 'We never would.'

'She's right,' said Grandma Lacey, scowling at having to agree with her least favoured grandchild. 'How's that household of women these days? I hear tales from everywhere of their bad language and terrible manners.'

'Gossip,' said Sid.

'You mean it's not true?'

'Well, their language is a bit fruity...'

'Fruity! I suppose you mean *disgraceful*.' Grandma Lacey drew back her chin and her brooch quivered on her bosom.

'I suppose I do,' said Sid, controlling her laughter, realising that the old matriarch who had scared her half to death as a child had no power over her any more.

Her grandmother gave her a suspicious glare from beneath her heavy eyebrows, but for an instant Sid thought she saw a gleam of humour and remembered that Grandma had quite taken to Mattie's husband, even though he refused to allow her to order Mattie's life as she did the others'.

'It's a surprise to find you here,' Sid remarked.

'Is is really?' snapped the old lady, aware that she had given away some ground. 'I suppose I'm entitled to visit my daughter if I want to.'

'Put the cloth on for tea,' said Mrs Penrose nervously.

Sid opened the drawer beside the fireplace. She pulled out a blue and white checked cloth, so heavily starched that it crackled, and placed it on the table. She went back and forth with crockery and dishes and they sat down to tea.

'Irene and Audrey are still at work,' said Mum, 'but they'll be back soon. The factory manager is very good to them. He lets them work on the same shift after Audrey said they were nervous about travelling in the raids without each other.'

'He sounds a good sort,' said Grandma.

'He is. As a matter of fact,' she lowered her voice though there was no one to overhear, 'I think he's got his eye on Audrey.'

'And he's the manager, you say,' said Grandma. 'I suppose he earns a good wage.'

'He must do. And she likes him.'

'What does Irene say?' asked Sid.

'Nothing,' said Mum. 'What should she say?'

'I mean is she pleased that Audrey and the manager are getting fond of each other?'

'Of course she is,' said Mum. 'The dear girls are so close. In age, too. Lots of people think they're twins.'

'Have you heard from Raymond?' asked Sid.

'He's in Germany,' said Dad. 'He says the people are in a bad way, but it's their own faults for starting the war.'

'Susan Morland's there, too,' said Sid. 'She doesn't seem to mind that she'll be nursing the wounded of any nationality.'

'Including the Hun?' demanded Grandma.

'They call them Jerries now,' said Dad.

'They'll always be Huns to me. Does she nurse *them*?'

'She says people are people when they're hurt,' said Sid.

'She comes from a religious family,' said Mum, explaining away such eccentricity. 'Her brother used to go everywhere telling people to mend their ways or they wouldn't go to heaven.'

Grandma bit into a potted meat sandwich. 'I'll be glad when we can get some decent food again. Salmon sandwiches are what I miss most.'

'Tinned salmon's like gold,' said Mum.

'Did you walk here?' asked Sid.

'Of course,' said Grandma indignantly. 'I've got two good legs, thank God. I really came to give your parents a bit of news.'

'Good, I hope.'

'It depends what you mean by good,' said Grandma. She snorted. 'I don't know what people are going to say.' The excitement in her eyes deepened. 'Your Aunt Mattie's going to have a baby! At her age!'

'What?' exclaimed Mum.

'A baby!' said Dad as if he had never heard of such a thing.

'I knew it!' declared Mum. 'We were afraid of that when she got married. Remember?'

Sid was smiling delightedly. 'How wonderful.'

'You would say that!' said Mum. 'It could be dangerous in an older woman and don't tell me that the women in Greystone House give birth like rabbits. It'll be Mattie's first. At over *forty*.'

'So she is,' said Sid. 'The war's been on so long I forget we've all been getting older. Will she really be in danger?'

Mum softened her tone. 'We must hope not. She's lived a good life and she'll be well looked after. Wilfred can afford to employ a married couple to work in the house and he worships the ground she walks on.'

Grandma had not finished. 'She's about six months gone! And never a word of it to me!'

'Six months!' Mum was amazed. 'Fancy not telling us, her own mother and sisters.'

'You couldn't tell to look at her,' said Sid. 'I thought she'd just put on weight.'

'So did I,' said Grandma. 'I thought marriage was making her fat. It takes some women like that.'

'Why is that?' asked Sid, innocently, already knowing what the answer would be. She felt like testing her indignant relatives.

'Because they're happy with a man,' snapped Grandma. 'She'll soon find out what having a baby means. No sleep and no time to herself.'

'Well, at least Wilfred knows about that,' said Sid. 'Maybe he can afford a nursemaid for the child.'

'A nursemaid!' Grandma spluttered her indignation. 'I brought up all mine and worked in the shop when your grandpa was ill so often.'

'You did, Mum,' said Mrs Penrose placatingly. She gave Sid a cross look.

'We must just hope her stepsons feel pleased when they come marching home,' said Grandma who clearly hoped nothing of the kind. 'I wonder how those grown men will feel with a baby brother or sister.'

'If they love their father I imagine they'd be glad for him,' said Sid. 'They accepted little Elsie.'

'That's different,' said Grandma, unwilling to relinquish the drama. 'Elsie was their own mother's child.'

After Victory in Europe, the war in the East seemed almost an anticlimax, except for those who had loved ones still fighting there, or relatives who might or might not be alive in some prisoner-of-war camp. Fighting raged fiercely – some of the bloodiest battles of the war were being fought there – and the Allies had to face the fact that the conflict could continue a great deal longer, and that more and more men must be sent out to gain victory over the Japanese. Stories were told and retold of their obscene cruelties towards the Chinese, whose country they had invaded early in the 1930s. Many shivered to think of their sons and loved ones falling into their power.

In Sid's family there was a sensation when the factory manager who had been marked down for Audrey proposed marriage to Irene. It transpired that he had always preferred the gentler of the sisters, and only Audrey's vanity had made her believe, and led the others to believe, that it was she he wanted. When Sid visited her family, the house was in uproar.

'Sneaky little cat,' Audrey screeched at Irene. 'He wanted me until you went behind my back and took him.'

'I didn't,' protested Irene. 'He said he'd always liked me best but you were always there and . . .'

'Always there!' cried Audrey. 'Sorry, I'm sure. I didn't mean to play gooseberry.'

'You didn't. I was glad for you to be with us.'

'How kind and condescending of you.' Audrey's pretty face was suffused with rage, while Irene was pale. 'Just how did he decide he wanted you, by the way? I'm at a loss to understand because we always went out together, the three of us.'

'Girls, girls . . .' pleaded Mum in distress.

Audrey ignored her, though Irene looked despairingly at her. But Audrey was more than Mrs Penrose could handle.

'We didn't always go out together,' said Irene, almost in a whisper.

'What? Do you mean to say you had dates with him on your own?'

'It's natural they should if they were falling in love,' remarked Sid, not sorry that Audrey was getting a come-uppance.

'You shut up!' yelled Audrey, and Sid shrugged. For a moment it looked as if her sister would turn on her, but Audrey returned to the attack on Irene.

'You must have told lies to me and Mum,' accused Audrey. 'How did you get the chance . . .?' Memory returned. 'I know. You said you wanted to learn shorthand-typing and instead you were meeting him. You horrible, lying, sneaky bitch.'

'Audrey!' Mum was really angry. 'I won't have such language.'

'I can't help it. She is a liar. She never learned shorthand-typing at all. All that stuff about wanting a different job was lies.'

'No, it wasn't,' said Irene. 'I did go to classes and I learned a bit, but Mr Mapleton, I mean Jim, met me afterwards and walked me home.'

Audrey turned to the others. 'She knew I liked him and she deliberately went behind my back . . .' She dissolved into tears. This was so rare a sight that the others were silenced. Then Irene also burst into tears and put her arms round her weeping sister. 'I'm sorry, really I am. I'll give him up. I can't marry anyone unless you're pleased about it. I didn't know you cared for him.'

'I don't,' sobbed Audrey. 'I just thought he would ask me . . .'

They clung to each other and Mum heaved a great sigh. She jerked her head towards the scullery and she and Sid tiptoed away.

'They'll be all right now,' said Mum.

'Will Irene really break her engagement?'

'Of course not. And Audrey's come to her senses. It's about time those two were parted anyway.'

'I never thought to hear you say that.'

'No. But I've always known Irene was the weaker. Audrey will be free to find her own kind of man. He'll need to be tough to control her.'

Sid had begun work at six and arrived home twelve hours later, running from the tram through a thunderstorm, soaked because she had forgotten her umbrella. She was tired and looking forward to her supper. She could hear raised voices before she reached the kitchen, and almost succumbed to a longing to escape to her room, but she needed a cup of tea. Mrs Dawson and Mrs Partridge were quarrelling again. They still shared the nursery quarters and, as their children were growing, their arguments grew longer and louder.

When Daisy saw Sid she yelled, 'Shut up, the pair of you. Sid looks exhausted. If you must have a row go upstairs and have it.'

The two women left, muttering, and Sid sank into a chair.

'Come on, now,' said Daisy, 'take off those wet things.' Sid obeyed, handing over her mackintosh and dripping beret. 'And your shoes and stockings,' ordered Daisy.

There was a circle of curious children watching, and Sid smiled faintly. 'Not in front of this lot. Here, you can have my shoes.'

'Amy, run upstairs and bring Aunty Sid's slippers,' commanded Daisy in a tone which even the independent Amy wouldn't dare argue with. 'And you others, go and run about outside. It's stopped raining but it may start again soon. Get some fresh air while you can. Aunty Sid wants a bit of peace and quiet.'

Sid raised her hand in protest at their banishment. 'They'll get cold out there.'

'Nonsense! Now for a pot of tea. And I've made some biscuits. I got a bit of rice flour today and the shortbread's just how you like it.'

Amy came back with the slippers, then ran to join the other children. She returned a few moments later. 'There's three ladies out there and a man in a big pram and another man pushing him. They saw me and one of the ladies held on to my arm but I bit her.'

'Bit a lady? A big pram . . .?' Daisy was mystified.

Sid jumped to her feet. 'She means a wheelchair. I'm sure she does.'

'What? Oh, my God, it'll be him!' said Daisy.

There was no time for more. The kitchen door opened again and in walked Celia Prosser. 'My grandmother is upstairs in the library with my brother, Philip, and his wife. They wish to see Amy.'

Sid stood and had to hold on to the back of her chair for support. 'Will you and your family never stop pestering me?'

'We are not pestering,' said Celia calmly. 'Surely my poor injured brother can have a look at his child.'

Chapter Nineteen

Sid stared at Celia, whose pretty mouth was curved in a small, mocking smile, her eyes reflecting a sardonic gleam.

'I haven't the faintest idea what you mean,' she said, glad that she could keep her voice firm. 'There is no child here belonging to your brother.' That wasn't a lie, thought Sid; Amy was hers and hers alone. She had borne her and kept her and loved her while Philip had denied her.

'Liar,' said Celia calmly. 'If we hadn't been sure before – which actually we were – the sight of her just now verified it. Grandmother has brought a photograph of me as a child of just about that child's age and, except for our eyes, we could have been twins.'

When she had heard Celia's approach, Daisy had sunk into a high-backed chair by the fire, but she was so tall her head showed over the top. Celia noticed her and walked swiftly to the fire. Daisy's hostility to this toffee-nosed woman radiated from her. Celia said furiously, 'She doesn't have to be here. This is family business.'

'Daisy is family.'

Celia looked horrified. 'Don't tell me she's a relative of mine!'

'We are all sisters here,' said Daisy.

'I see. A sisterhood. How quaint. Well, you can take yourself off.'

'She may stay,' said Sid, needing Daisy's powerful presence beside her.

'I see. If this is a sisterhood, I dare say Amy looks upon this woman as an aunty.'

'And a good friend,' said Sid. 'I'll see your family. Where are they?'

'In the library.' Celia turned without another word and Sid followed her.

Daisy jumped up and gave her a quick hug. 'Don't let them beat you,' she said.

Sid entered the library ready to repulse Philip and his family, but then she saw him and for the first time understood what a horror of an accident he must have had. She would never have recognised him. He was extremely thin, there were burn scars which twisted his face grotesquely, he had lost fingers and his hands were as bony as an old man's. His scalp was imperfectly covered by patches of hair which had been allowed to grow long and were combed over the scarred areas. A rug covered his useless legs. Only his eyes seemed alive in that ravaged face. They burned at her with a fire which threatened to engulf her.

'I want my child,' he said in a voice which rasped with bitter emotion.

Sid stood still and silent, pitying him, confused by an impulse to help him if she could, yet hating him.

'Did you hear what I said? I want my child. The child I gave you!'

His brazen claim momentarily took her breath from her. She looked round at the other members of his family. Mrs Prosser sat upright on a straight-backed chair, Celia sprawled in a deep leather sofa, lighting a cigarette, impervious to her grandmother's frown. There was another woman present who Sid assumed was Philip's wife. She wore a severely cut dress and a small hat, which sat rather oddly on her large head. Her nondescript-coloured hair was scraped back unattractively. Sid remembered she was an officer in one of the women's services; she certainly looked officious. Not one of them appeared to find Philip's demand astonishing. His wife actually gave him a fond look and patted his head, as one might a favourite dog. She held out a big hand, 'I'm Dolores, Philip's wife.'

Anyone less like a Dolores, Sid could not have imagined. Dolores should be slender, dark-haired, sloe-eyed. This woman was big with muscle, her face ruddy and plain, but she looked kind and Sid was sure would be tender with her husband. Indeed, the fact that she was here at all argued that. In his weakness he could lean on her, cling to her strength, and she would pamper him like a pet.

'There are a number of children here,' said Sid. 'Which one did you have in mind?'

'Don't pretend to be stupid,' said Celia laconically. 'It's the brat who met us outside. She tried to kick Dolores, then bit me. She also called me a bloody old cow. Does she usually use such language?'

'She picks it up from the others. She'll soon forget it as she grows older and learns better manners.'

'Not if she stays here,' said Philip.

'I'm sorry she tried to kick you,' said Sid to Dolores.

'It doesn't matter. I like a kid with a bit of spirit. I must say, though, I was astonished by her resemblance to Celia.'

Sid tried to think clearly, but images whirled in her brain. Images of saying goodbye to Amy, of being forced to relinquish her to these people. This was her home, here were her friends with whom she had romped and squabbled and whose company she had enjoyed for years; just up the road was her school where she knew and liked the teachers. How could anyone expect a mother to tear her child from everything she knew and hand her over like a stray kitten? Hand her to Mrs Prosser with her cold dignity? To the selfish Celia who referred to her as a brat? To Philip with his virulent fury at his fate? She looked at Dolores. She would probably never mean to be unkind, but she looked like a woman who would prefer a career or a horse or dog to a child. Could she, or any of them, be relied upon to show love, tenderness, forbearance to a child with Amy's high spirits?

'We'll get a lawyer,' snarled Philip.

Sid looked again at Dolores, who seemed to be the only member of the party who possessed any decent feelings. She had laughed at Amy's kick, and she was gentle to her wounded husband. It occurred to Sid that, if Philip couldn't father a child, Dolores too would be childless. Did she mind? Is that why she was backing Philip. Was Amy to be a substitute for her own baby? These thoughts and speculations flitted through Sid's mind in an instant, while she felt as if she was in a trap, a terrified creature surrounded by hostility.

'What makes you think you fathered a child on me?' she asked Philip as calm as she could.

'You told me I had. You came to London for that express purpose.'

'Did I?'

'You know you did,' yelled Philip.

Dolores put her hand on his thin shoulder. 'You must not excite yourself, darling. Remember, you are still not entirely well.'

'Entirely well!' cried Philip. 'I'll never be entirely well. Sidonia, tell them the truth. Tell them how we met in London and you said you were expecting my child.'

'I shall do no such thing.'

'All right, said Celia. 'Tell them how you went to Scotland with Cousin Louisa and had your baby and left it there until you were ready to take responsibility for it. Tell them how Cousin Louisa cherished the child and why she left you this house and everything in it.'

Sid felt the iron of the trap closing in on her. 'I admit nothing,' she said, her voice half strangled.

Dolores said, in the kindly way which so belied her appearance, 'We hired an agent who discovered the truth, Miss Penrose – Sidonia, we know how you and Mrs Cardell stayed with the McGregors and you bore a child.'

'I see. So I bore a child.'

'My child,' said Philip.

'No.'

'I'll find witnesses. The McGregors will testify to the truth.'

'They can say I gave birth to a child. That's all.'

'I'll find other witnesses.'

'Witnesses to what?'

'To our affair in this very house. To the fact that you came to London and told me what had happened.'

'What witnesses?'

Philip's face became suffused with colour which made the white scars stand out, giving her another pang of pity. But pity must not weaken her. She wasn't going to hand over her beloved daughter. 'There are no witnesses.'

'Cousin Louisa knew the truth!'

'She is dead,' rasped Mrs Prosser.

'I can't have another child,' said Philip, the words wrung from him in an access of wretched misery. 'Give me the one who is mine.'

'You have no child!' gasped Sid.

'I want my daughter, Sidonia. Please, please, give her to me.'

Every merciful instinct was imploring Sid to help his agony of frustration. She pitied him, she might even forgive him, but to hand over Amy . . .

Philip sensed her weakness. 'I admit I didn't play fair with you,

Sidonia, but think of me. I am condemned to spend what's left of my life in a wheelchair. Can you imagine what that means? You knew me as I was. I need something to keep me going. Amy looks a nice little thing, she would amuse me, help look after me. Admit she is mine and give her to me. You could see her sometimes. And later perhaps the three of us could travel.'

See her sometimes? Amuse him? She was to be used as a live toy. Philip wanted her as a slave to serve him. What would happen to Amy beneath such a regime? It would be like imprisoning her. Suffering had not refined him. It had coarsened him; he was even more self-centred and selfish than before.

'No!'

Philip stared at her with hatred. If he had shown one vestige of caring, one trace of a need to love his daughter, if he had been a different kind of man, she might have given way, at least enough to share Amy; but the idea of permitting her lovely child to come close to a man whose resentment was burning him up was terrifying.

'Is that all you have to say?' asked Mrs Prosser. Her voice was not quite steady, and Sid looked from her to Philip and back again. Both of them had been almost destroyed by his terrible plight. 'Have you nothing more to say?'

Sid had no appropriate answer. She remained silent.

'Sullen,' said Mrs Prosser. 'Sullen and sulky. Are you the proper woman to bring up Philip's daughter?'

'I have not said he has a daughter.'

'You don't need to,' said Celia. 'It's obvious. Honestly, Grandmother, I can't see what all the fuss is about. Offer the woman enough money and she'll give in. She's only sticking out for that.'

'I say, that's laying it on a bit thick,' said Dolores. 'Hardly sporting.'

'Is that what you want?' asked Mrs Prosser. 'If I pay you enough will you relinquish her?'

Sid sat down quickly before she passed out. The room was going round and the ground seemed to be heaving beneath her. She was incapable of speech.

'So that's it,' said Mrs Prosser, mistaking her silence. 'You're after money. I hadn't thought of that.'

'She doesn't look too well,' said Dolores. She glanced about her. 'Is there any brandy here?'

Sid motioned towards the cupboard where Mr Cardell had stored his spirits, and where a couple of bottles had always been kept since his death. Dolores poured her a measure and she sipped it slowly, beginning to feel better. 'I don't want money. I just want you to go.'

Mrs Prosser rose and Philip cried, 'You aren't giving up, are you, Grandmother? You can't give up.'

Sid stood up and looked down at him. 'I am sorry for you.'

'I told you I don't want pity,' he snarled.

'Nevertheless, you have it. I hope you regain more health and strength as time passes. I'll say goodbye. You know your way out.' She had to leave this room. She didn't think she could ever again enter the library without feeling sick and giddy.

Mrs Prosser stood up and walked swiftly to the door where she confronted Sid. 'This matter is by no means finished. I shall see my lawyer later this week. If necessary, if you persist in your stubbornness, we shall take you to court.'

Sid's heart was pounding with fear, but she said, 'I see. I can't think what you hope to gain by it, or by dragging Amy's name through the dirt, but that's for you to decide.'

'You'll be the one whose name is dragged in the dirt. You'll be the one who will be exposed as a loose woman, a woman who had a child in secret, then abandoned it until you were ready to give it your attention. You will be shown to be a liar who denied the truth to my grandson, a war hero, who almost gave his life for his country; who has, in fact, given more than his life, has given his chance to father the children he wants. And he can offer Amy a home such as should be hers. You have her existing here among a pack of women and children who are totally unsuited to her background. Whom do you think the court will favour?'

Sid's fear grew greater. She had no doubt as to who would come out on top. They would hire experts who would paint word pictures of Philip's plight, while he would sit brooding, going over the past, and sooner or later he would remember Angie. He would remember that she had shared the nursery suite with Sid. If she were to be put into a witness box under oath she would have to admit that she knew of Sid's affair with Philip and its consequences. Daisy might have lied and to hell with the oath, but Angie would feel compelled to be truthful.

Mrs Prosser moved away from the door. Sid went upstairs and sat on the edge of her bed. She heard the commotion as the wheelchair was pushed, surrounded by children, to the waiting car. She sprang up in sudden fear, remembering that Amy was there. She wouldn't put it past the Prossers to pick her up there and then and take her away. But at that moment Daisy arrived holding Amy's hand. 'Here's Aunty Sid. Tell her how you kicked that nasty woman.'

'She wasn't really nasty,' said Sid gently.

'She held my arm and wouldn't let go when that old lady told her to take me with them to see you.'

'So you bit Celia?'

'Is she the one with a very red mouth? I hate her.'

Joseph Morland tried to sleep. But every time he closed his eyes he saw their faces, their bodies reduced to skin-covered skeletons in striped suits which were a travesty of a pair of pyjamas. That camp. A death camp it was called. There were others like it. Camps where human beings had been systematically gassed, then burned. When the Allies had drawn nearer and it was obvious that they would soon discover the atrocities, the guards had been detailed to kill as many prisoners as possible; many of the bodies had been pierced by thrusting bayonets. There hadn't been time to kill everyone and there were still many hundreds of beings, semi-human they looked, impossible to tell even their sex, unless they were naked as some were, shuffling about, leaning on one another for support, crawling through mud and filth, holding out their hands for food, their voices high and bird-like, resonating on the nasal bones because there was no supporting tissue; others, whose lives they were too late to save, lying in their own dirt. He smelled the stench, he saw their eyes, eyes that shocked him because they were so huge and staring because all the surrounding muscle and flesh had been lost through starvation and disease.

Some, a few, hadn't been in the camps for so long. They had been used as labour to keep the ovens alight, to shovel in the pitiful bodies, knowing that at some point they too would succumb and be cremated. But they still had some strength and had gained more in their fury and laid hands on some of the guards and torn them to pieces.

Joseph would once have been sickened by such revenge. Now he understood. He would have done the same. That frightened him. Since he had lost his faith, his emotions had swung wildly out of control. If there had been a need for him now to fight as a soldier, he could do it. He could even take pleasure in it. A shudder ran through his body. That was wrong. The men who fought battles did so because that was their job. Most of the others disliked killing, and the ones who enjoyed it were not respected by their mates. He wondered if he would ever be whole again. The people in the camp were mainly Jews. True, they had never recognised Christ as the Messiah, but they believed in God, the same God from the Old Testament used by Christians. And He had let this happen to them. No, the devil had let it happen. But if there was no God, there was no devil. Man had done these things. Man at his most vile. And if there was no God he would never see his father again. The news of his death had struck him a terrible blow. There had been a time when prayer would have helped him to bear it, but he hadn't uttered a prayer since the day he had killed.

He fell asleep, only to dream he was back in the camp, tending the sick as best he could, watching the men and women who had been guards gathering bodies and throwing them carelessly into the ground for mass burial. These bodies, which would have been unrecognisable to even their closest relatives, had once been members of families who loved and laughed and had children and celebrated family events, just like his own. In his dreadful dreams he saw the guards' eyes, too, as hard as granite, no sorrow or pity in them, working sullenly under the command of the men from the Graves Registration Units. The eyes suddenly grew and filled his mind, and he awoke with a gasp and sat up, wiping the sweat from his face. He hoped the camp guards would be tried, condemned and sent to hell. If there was a hell. Could any hell be worse than the camps?

He sank back to his pillow again. Beneath it he had placed the latest letter from Angie. It had been waiting for him, but he hadn't been able to bring himself to open it, any more than he had been able to open the others, because he couldn't endure anything emotional. And he couldn't face food. He wasn't the only one. Americans, British, Russian, no matter which nationality, would never be quite the same again after what they had found. They had worked mainly in silence, avoiding one another's eyes, sick with shame to be part of a species which could sink to such depths of cruelty.

He lit a cigarette and the man on his right asked, 'Can't you sleep either?'

'I slept a while, but I dreamt.'

'I hate to sleep. I always dream. I can't stand it. Have you got a fag to spare, mate?'

Joseph handed over the packet of cigarettes to the man. What was his name? Tony. They were crowded into a gasthaus, temporary quarters. Other men spoke up. It seemed that very few could sleep. Joseph told Tony to pass the cigarettes round and the men lay smoking. A voice broke through the darkness. 'Bastards! Sodding bastards!'

Another said, 'I volunteered for medical duties because I couldn't face the thought of killing, but now . . .'

The men fell quiet again and after a while there was an occasional snore. From a bed near the end came the sound of quiet weeping from a young Jewish soldier.

Joseph got up and went to him, standing by his bed, helplessly, as the boy continued to weep.

'I'm sorry,' Joseph said. 'Benny, isn't it? Benny, I'm sorry.' The sobs went on.

'We've managed to save some,' said Joseph. There was no response. He touched the boy's shaking shoulder. 'I'm sorry,' he said again. He returned to his bed, reaching for another cigarette, then remembered he had let his packet go. He thought of Sammy Jacobs, the pianist in Josh Raven's band. Sammy had visited Joseph's parents a few times and Mum had tried to convert him. He wondered if Sammy's relatives had ended in a camp like the one he had seen that day. He lay in the darkness listening to the young soldier's weeping.

When he arrived in Berlin, he looked at the ruins of that once beautiful city, he watched the people, ill-clad and hungry, sifting through the bombed buildings, searching endlessly for food, and he couldn't find it in his heart to be sorry for them. Even the plight of the children failed to move him. There were terrible stories of camps where horrible medical experiments had been conducted on children, of twins being found especially useful by the Nazis as guinea-pigs, because one could be used as a control while the other suffered. Joseph looked at the desolation around him without emotion, the barrier between himself and the awfulness of life set like concrete. He added Angie's latest letter to the pile which was growing daily, because now she wrote to him more and more often. She would be wondering why she was not getting answers. So would his mother. Her letters were unopened, too. They would have to wonder. He wasn't capable of writing to anyone.

Mrs Prosser had not made an empty threat, and Sid received a letter from a solicitor. The official writing paper, the printed heading, the list of partners was daunting in itself, but the words horrified her.

The position was set out clearly in legal terms. The evidence of the private investigator had been sworn in an affidavit; it was known for certain that Miss Sidonia Penrose had borne a child out of wedlock. It gave the address and full names of the McGregors. That was all anyone would learn from them, Sid was sure, but the letter went on to say that the evidence of Philip's stay in Greystone House, coupled with the photographs showing a vivid resemblance between his client's sister and the child, Amy Brown, would prove to all, beyond doubt, that Amy was Philip's daughter. There was clear evidence also of her wild behaviour, the lack of training suitable for such a child, proved by her use of bad language. 'Obviously,' the letter read, 'my client feels that her present environment is exceedingly damaging. My client intends to deal with the matter of her behaviour and later she will have the advantage of attending a decent boarding school where she will meet with others from her own sphere.'

Sid almost sank into despair. How could she fight, how could she win her fight? Was there anyone to whom she could turn for help? She supposed she would have to engage a lawyer. The last of Mrs Cardell's jewellery must be sacrificed, the pearls, too, but it would be a small price to pay for victory. Then she would pick up the letter and find new meanings, new threats in every word. She had never been inside a courtroom. Would it be like the ones in films? A terrifying judge in a wig staring down at her, the shameless hussy who had borne an illegitimate child, then lied to keep it from people who could bring it up with dignity, in the midst of wealth? She showed the letter to Daisy who read it twice.

'That Mrs Prosser will do anything for him. She's a bitch. I don't suppose that wife of his minds which way it goes. She won't look after Amy, anyway, there'll be a nanny. And as for that little madam, Celia . . .'

Her sympathy helped for a few moments. The worry never left her, whether she was travelling to and from work, or at her machine which she had operated for so long, or at home. In the end, she went to Mr Mapleton, who had been so kind to her when Mrs Cardell died. She began by showing him the letter which he read intently. 'I see. Is what they say the truth? Is Philip Prosser the child's father?'

'Yes.'

'There was no other man?'

'No.'

'Forgive me, Miss Penrose, but has there been another man since?' She was startled. 'Of course not. I loved him. Well, I did at the time.'

'And now?'

'No.'

'I heard about his dreadful injuries.'

'Yes. I'm sorry for him, for all the people who have been hurt in this ghastly war, but if anything his nature is worse.'

'I heard he was married. Did you meet his wife?'

'Yes. She seems quite nice. She's not the type I would have expected him to choose.'

'She is very wealthy.'

Sid was encouraged. He understood without too many words spoken.

'I guessed as much. Will you act for me?'

'I can do so as a solicitor, but if this goes to court you will need a barrister.'

'Would that be expensive?'

'I'm afraid so.' He knew how much money Sid was getting from the estate, and had admired her managing skills. He knew about the women and children who crowded the old house. He knew she worked long shifts and that she had kept the old place in reasonable repair, that the gardens were still productive in spite of Brindle's retirement. Sidonia Penrose had courage and far more strength than she realised.

'If you need a barrister I will find one for you,' he said.

'I suppose there are young ones with their way to make in the world,' she said eagerly. 'They would fight hard and not expect such a big fee.'

He looked at her gravely. How she had changed. She was thin and not pretty, but her high cheekbones gave her face character, her eyes were beautiful and she had acquired elegance and a natural dignity which seemed only enhanced by her dreadful problems.

'Many of the young ones are away fighting,' he said gently, 'but I'll find someone for you, never fear.'

He would, too. For this brave young woman he would pay part of a barrister's fee himself, damned if he wouldn't. He'd like anyway to see the abominable Prossers brought down.

After Sidonia had left he was thoughtful as he faced the facts. She was going to have a hard fight on her hands. She had loved and cared for her child as far as she was able, but a judge would examine the prospects offered by her mother, one moreover who had lied relentlessly, and those available to a good family with money and power to protect Amy and care for her as only a rich family could.

Sid had seen the doubt which the elderly man had unwittingly revealed, and she went back to Greystone House feeling unutterably depressed. Amy ran to greet her, arms outstretched, her face held up for a kiss. 'Aunty Sid, Aunty Sid, we've made a treehouse and Daisy's given us lots of teeny little cakes and sandwiches and we're going to have a christening party. That's what she calls it. She says babies are christened. Was I christened, Aunty Sid?'

'Of course you were.' I christened you myself, she thought. There had been no ceremony held. She had the birth certificate locked in a special box she had bought; she had never looked at it since she had put it there, unable to bear the absence of a father's name on it.

Joseph got through the days as best he could, obeying orders, eating because the body demanded food even in these sickening circumstances, though his healthy appetite had all but gone. He had met Susan, who had greeted him with an enormous hug and a kiss. 'Joey,' she said, reverting to his childhood name. 'It's you. I'm so glad to see you. Isn't Germany an awful place? The wounds we are treating are truly dreadful.'

'They are indeed.'

'And the children! The poor little children! Some of them have lost their parents and are wandering round, begging for help, trying to find something to eat in refuse dumps. Poor little souls.'

When Joseph realised that his sister's sympathy was directed towards Germans, he withdrew into his protective shell.

She stared at him shrewdly. 'What's happened to you? And why aren't you answering Mum and Angie's letters? Angie telephones Mum all the time. They're terribly worried about you.'

'If you've been through what I have, if you'd seen what I've seen!' This unexpected meeting, her love for him weakened him, and he felt tears threaten. Self-pity! He had no time for it, any more than he had time for stupid people who had helped their Führer, Adolf Hitler, plunge the world into a devastating cauldron of war.

Susan stared at her brother's ravaged face and calmed down. She asked quietly, 'Have you been to the death camps?'

'One. That was enough.'

'I haven't. They sent us straight here. Was it as bad as we've been told?'

'Worse.' He choked. 'There aren't any words.'

'Is that why you don't write home?'

'One of the reasons.'

Susan was called away and Joseph went on with his work, but her love and gentleness had weakened him and he took out the pile of letters and stared at them. He wasn't being fair to Mum and Angie. None of this was their fault, and Mum had lost Dad. Compassion for her swamped him, and he opened the latest letter from her. Its messages were only of love and hope. There were no reproaches, no trivial complaints. She seemed to know how he felt and sympathise. He didn't understand how she would know, but she did. He wanted to weep, but couldn't. But he would write to her. Just a few sentences, but enough to let her know he was all right. of course he wasn't and never would be, but he hoped she wouldn't see the truth between the lines.

Having read Mum's letter, he drew out some of Angie's. She didn't reproach him either. The first few recounted incidents from her life, amusing things mostly. Then they began to change. It seemed the longer she heard nothing, the more she cared for him. At first she spoke of her affection, of her care for his welfare. She spoke of a time after the war when they could get to know one another all over again. Then she began to speak of love and her letters grew warmer. Her love, she said, was unending and would always be so. She realised he must be having a horrible time and couldn't think of a way to tell her, but she loved him and would even if he couldn't return it. She would continue to write because it comforted her. He opened the latest letter. It was simply a declaration of her deepest feelings. She demanded nothing, expected nothing. 'If my love helps you in any way I shall be thankful,' she wrote. 'I go to chapel with your mum when I'm on leave and am beginning to understand why you care so much for religion.'

He put the letter down. 'Care for religion'? It seemed that while he had been losing his faith, Angie had been gaining hers. What a stupid, ironical, consuming waste of emotion. He read her letters again and again; gradually the love seeped from them as if it were a tangible entity eating through the shell and into his heart and soul. The tears came then. He sat on the edge of his hard camp bed and wept. He had seen other men weeping. He remembered Benny. Some of those who wept were hard men, the sort who swore vilely and drank heavily, who had gone out looking for destitute women who would give their bodies for a bar of chocolate. They paid for what they took, however ruthlessly and inadequately. There were those who took women's bodies by force, but even some of them had returned to barracks sick at heart. Joseph lay down to sleep, knowing that his tears had joined with Angie's love to destroy his protective barrier. He still couldn't pray, but he could think of love. Tomorrow he would write to Angie.

How odd, he thought fleetingly, that the daughter of a prostitute should be the means by which he might find his way back to God. If there was a God. He still wasn't sure, but there was always love. He shouldn't have forgotten that. On the following day he allowed himself to really see the people in the wreckage of the city, especially the children, to see them as victims, and the anguish of his pity hit him all the harder because it had been previously withheld. They were all victims, but he had the means to alleviate some of the distress. Now the barriers were down, and their suffering piled itself upon the agony he felt for all victims.

Chapter Twenty

Mrs Cardell's solicitor received a letter from the Prossers' solicitor asking for an early reply to his last.

Sid felt very lonely when she visited Mr Mapleton. He listened to her while she stared at a spot over his shoulder, failing to see the sympathy in his eyes. She even told him about Robert. 'I can't encourage him to think of marriage, I'm fond of him, but only as a friend. Please, what should I do?' she finished.

Mr Mapleton chose his words with care. He had never married. He had considered it once, but decided it was not for him. 'A dry old stick' was the description bestowed upon him by some of his clerks. They were too young to realise that his expertise in dealing with his many clients came from a profound compassion. He was intensely sorry for Sid's situation.

He had seen her selfless care of Mrs Cardell who had rewarded her quite unexpectedly, and knew of her kindness to the rough women and children she had taken in.

'From what I saw of the Prossers,' he said carefully, 'I do not think that Amy would be happy with them. It is unfortunate that they have learned that you are Amy's mother and that she resembles Miss Prosser so strongly. And of course your being single is against you. Forgive my plain speaking, my dear, but only truth will serve us.' He paused. 'You are absolutely certain that encouraging Robert Felgate would be a mistake? I have met Mr and Mrs Felgate. They believe themselves far too much above the crowd to care about possible tittle-tattle. As for Robert, his own suffering might make him all the more understanding of yours.'

'No, I can't do it,' said Sid. 'I believe that in the end it would make matters worse for us all.'

'I dare say you know best, my dear. I will answer the letter and we must see what happens.'

Constant worry made Sid even more tired than usual and the factory was as busy as ever. While the war continued in the Far East there was still a need for weapons and planes. But the black-out had ended, and lights blazed out from street-lamps and houses. Many towns had been rendered desolate, their fine old buildings and many of their houses in ruins. But people had begun to return, relieved that their ordeal was over, determined to rebuild their interrupted lives. Prefabricated houses were waiting to receive many of the homeless. They were small, but had been well designed to give maximum efficiency with comfort. Women who had never before had a decent kitchen or bathroom were delighted with them. Others wanted to resettle into their former communities, and were sad to discover that it wasn't possible. But wherever they could manage it, neighbours were reunited. And their children returned from evacuation, most of them happy to be home again in Bristol.

The women began to move out of Greystone House. As rooms were vacated Amy lost her friends until only Daisy and her family remained.

'I'd like to stay on a bit, if that's all right, Sid?' Daisy said.

'All right? I was hoping you wouldn't go. You'll be welcome here always. And Amy loves her "brothers and sisters." '

'My young 'uns will be comin' back,' said Daisy. 'Not all of them, of course.' Her voice broke. One of her sons had died at Arnhem, and a daughter in the ATS had drowned when the ship in which she had been on her way overseas had been torpedoed.

'Anyone belonging to you will always be welcome here,'

Daisy bent and kissed Sid. 'You're an angel.'

'Not exactly.'

'Well, perhaps not exactly, but who wants angels?'

Sid went to visit her family to discover that Mum, the aunts and Grandma Lacey were visiting an expensive private nursing home where Mattie had been taken with a threatened miscarriage.

'Is she very ill?' Sid asked her father anxiously.

'I suppose she must be if she's in a nursing home, though that Wilfred fusses over her too much.' Dad could never quite overcome the irritation caused by Mattie's husband being richer than him.

Sid hurried to the nursing home. In spite of the seriousness of the situation, she could have laughed when she entered the luxurious waiting room. There they all were, the group headed by Grandma Lacey in black. She sat squarely in her chair, back straight, hands folded in her capacious lap, surrounded by her daughters who tended to her every need, like a spider in the centre of her web.

'How is Aunty Mattie?' Sid asked.

'Well might you ask!' said Grandma Lacey.

'I do ask. How is she?'

'How do you think?' demanded Ella. She lowered her voice. 'As well as can be expected for a woman of her age having a first baby!'

'I knew no good would come of this marriage,' said Mum, who was in her allotted place in this small army of middle-aged, indignant women.

'Where is Wilfred?'

'With her,' said Grandma, 'and I think it's disgraceful. No man was ever allowed near me when I had my children. My husband was turned right out of the house.'

'So were our husbands,' agreed the others.

'A woman needs other women around her when she's got that sort of thing going on,' continued Grandma. 'I wanted to sit by her and

I'm sure I should do her no harm. We were all asked to leave her alone! Her mother and sisters, if you please! I remember the time when—' she dropped her voice, glaring suspiciously at other visitors in the waiting room '—your Aunty Joan had a *full* miscarriage.' She said the last word so quietly that one had to guess exactly what it was – 'I never left her side.'

'You didn't, Mum,' said Joan.

'I stayed with her and her sisters came and went and did all the necessary things just as I told them. Nursing homes! Bossy nurses! Huh!'

Sid left them expressing their indignation, thinking how wonderful it must be to have a husband who dared stay in the room while his wife was suffering from such a distressing female disorder. She found a sister who informed her that Mrs Chandler was by no means very ill.

'A slight blood loss, but quite rightly her doctor decided that she should receive the best of care. With rest I'm sure she'll be fine and probably at home again soon. I know she'll be well looked after there.'

'Yes. Her husband takes great care of her.'

'He is with her now. Such a nice man. He was entirely on my side when I insisted his wife should be left alone with him. Her relatives mean to be kind, but there are just too many of them, and they did tend to make rather a fuss. However, you look the sensible type. Just for a minute then.'

Mattie was in a bed with its foot raised, her fruitful stomach swelling beneath the sheets. Wilfred was holding her hand, seated as near as he could get without actually being in bed with her.

Mattie smiled. 'How nice to see you, Sid. And how good of you to come when you're so busy.'

'Not too busy for you. Besides, life isn't so hectic now. Everyone but Daisy and her children has left. But I came to ask after you.'

'I'm well, thank you. My darling Wilfred here got alarmed over nothing and sent for a doctor.'

'Quite right,' said Sid.

Wilfred beamed. 'That's what I thought, and the doctor agreed with me. If he hadn't, he'd hardly have sent you here, my dear.'

Mattie smiled at him. 'Are Keith and Patrick leaving, too, Sid?'

'Not Patrick. Keith may look for a better job now he's older.'

'You must miss them all.'

'I do. We were together a long time, and I got very fond of them, even the quarrelsome ones.'

'You've plenty to do, though. Daisy still has children under fourteen, hasn't she? And there's your job.'

'If Daisy had a dozen children I should still want her to stay. She's a true friend.'

'I'm so glad. You deserve true friends.'

Wilfred smiled down at his wife, his love clear in his eyes, and Sid felt a pang of envy. Would any man ever sit at her side in this way? Would Tom? She thought of bearing Tom's children and knew she would have revelled in the joy of it. For the thousandth time she cursed herself for her timidity in not accepting the love he'd offered.

'What are you thinking about, dear?' asked Mattie in her gentle voice. 'You look so far away.'

'Oh,' said Sid unguardedly, 'I was just wondering what it must be like to be waiting for a baby by a man you—' She stopped.

'Go on,' encouraged Wilfred, 'finish it. A man you love. Wasn't that what you were going to say?'

'Yes.'

Wilfred smiled. 'Your aunt tells me it feels wonderful. I wouldn't know. I'm a mere man.'

'Not any old mere man,' smiled Mattie. She squeezed her husband's hand, then put out her other hand to Sid who grasped it. 'You will know one day.'

Having ascertained that Mattie was in no danger of losing her much-wanted child, Sid said goodbye and made her way home.

Daisy had prepared the midday meal and the children were seated ready to eat. The WVS had removed the furniture no longer needed but the old kitchen table was more than big enough for those that were left. Amy was among them, of course, looking her usual serene self. The thought of plunging her into a vindictive struggle, possible scandal and perhaps even then losing her, destroyed Sid's appetite, and she refused when Daisy wanted to add a second spoonful of mashed potatoes to her plate.

'Bangers and mash,' said Amy. 'That's the stuff to feed the troops.'

Daisy grinned. 'Right you are, Miss Brown. Have some chutney.'

'Is it tomato or onion?'

'Tomato, made just the way you like it.'

'You spoil her,' said Sid.

'Nonsense. I don't spoil any of the kids.'

Her own sturdy brood was shovelling away food as fast as possible, and Amy followed their example. If a judge sent someone to inspect her living conditions, surely he would favour the Prossers, who could make her over into a little lady. The thought took away the rest of Sid's appetite, and she couldn't face even a morsel of the suet pudding served with jam and custard that the others were enjoying.

The weather was fine, enabling the children to tumble around outside in the garden. Keith was repairing damaged furniture and Patrick was chopping wood, enjoying the sun and keeping an eye on the young ones.

Daisy had smilingly assured Sid that even if Keith did get another job he wouldn't go far away. 'For now, anyway. He's got his eye on my Peggy.'

'But she's a child!'

'She's nearly fourteen and likes Keith a lot. I'll be takin' her for an interview next week to Fry's Chocolate Factory. If she gets a job there, it won't be too far for her to cycle. I've been savin' for a bike for her.'

'Fancy little Peggy looking for work and being courted.'

'Little Peggy has grown up,' said Daisy.

316

'I suppose so. You tend to forget how long the war's been on.'
'Thank God it's over.'
'Not quite,' said Sid. 'There's still Japan.'
'Yes, I was forgetting.'
'I can't forget.'

Daisy was annoyed with herself. She glanced at Sid, opened her mouth, then when she saw the expression on her face closed it.

'I'm sure Peggy will get the job,' said Sid. 'You've brought the children up so well under such difficult circumstances, but wouldn't you rather she stayed on at school? I know you approve of higher education for girls.'

'It isn't what I want that counts, Sid, it's what she wants. She's not got a lot of brains, but she's a good girl and likes workin' about the house. She'd make Keith a decent wife. My two boys in the forces are goin' to go to evenin' classes and try for university. They've had their eyes opened an' seen what education can do.' She sighed. 'Of course, all the learnin' in the world can't seem to stop the wars an' the killin'.' She jumped up and began to clear the table. 'I won't let myself think sad thoughts. I'm lucky to have so many kids alive and well. I've heard terrible stories of widows losin' their only sons or daughters, an' more than one family losin' all their kids. The government should have left some of them behind.'

'I don't suppose they could have kept them at home if they'd tried. It was all so patriotic at the beginning of the war. They wanted to get at the enemy. Even some of the men who fought in the Great War were keen. They're calling this the war to end all wars. I hope they're right.'

Later, to Sid's surprise, Audrey called. She had always been envious of her sister's luck in inheriting a large property, even if it was run down; and Irene's engagement to the factory manager had given her a jolt from which she hadn't easily recovered. She held out her left hand on the third finger of which sparkled a very large solitaire diamond ring.

If she had expected envy from Sid she was disappointed. Sid was unequivocally delighted. 'That's beautiful, Audrey. Who is he?'

'A captain in the American Forces stationed in Bristol. He's going to Germany soon and we'll be getting married as soon as possible so that we can be together. Here – she delved into a capacious bag – 'I brought you a few odd things, nothing much. A couple of pairs of nylon stockings each for you and Daisy, a carton of cigarettes – Lucky Strike, they're called – a few candy bars. I can get as many as I want from him. And he's promised me some perfume from Paris. Irene's green with envy,' she added in tones of deep satisfaction.

Joseph left the bus. He had written to say he had leave and now he strode up the familiar stony lane to the cottage, carrying his kit. Mum was waiting for him and threw open the front door. She held out her arms and he walked into them. But her hands were too clinging, her hugs too smothering, and he released himself quickly and bent to fuss over the dog. He felt brutal, especially when he saw the tears raining down her face. He knew they expressed more than her joy at seeing him. They were tears of sorrow, too, for her beloved husband, for all the cruelties of war. They hadn't met since Dad's death, and her son's long silence had added to her burdens.

'Come in, Joseph, come in. Tea's ready. I've made all your favourite things. You're quite thin. Haven't the army been feeding you?'

'The grub's not bad. I hadn't the appetite for it.'

Mrs Morland calmed down. This was not the same Joseph who had gone away filled with zeal for the work of compassion he was about to do. He wouldn't fight, he would never kill – he couldn't, not with his deep religious beliefs – but he had been eager to help men with wounded bodies and tormented souls. His eyes had been alight with fervour, now they were lack-lustre.

She talked softly as he washed his hands at the kitchen sink, giving him news of his sisters and his cousin Eve. 'The band's been doing some concerts for the wounded here, but now it's on its way to Germany. From all accounts the forces out there need something to lighten things.'

'Lighten things!' She was startled by his vehemence. 'Oh, Mum, how can a band and two girls singing lighten what's over there?'

She poured tea for them. 'Tell me,' she said.

'No, I can't. I can't talk about it. Perhaps Susan will.'

'Her letters are full of her usual fun, though she does mention the wounded. She says our doctors make no difference between our wounded and the enemies'.' Mum sounded proud.

'There's a big difference. When the Germans recover they go out to a wilderness of bombed buildings and not enough food, while our boys get taken care of.'

'It's sad, I understand that, but after all we didn't begin the war. We didn't want it. And the enemy did some terrible things. I went to the art gallery to see the pictures from those dreadful concentration camps. The poor people. How they suffered. What wickedness!'

Joseph thrust the memories away. 'I wonder who did want war?' he said harshly. 'A few maniacs in power?'

'Hitler was voted in legally. Dad told me so.'

'People voted without knowing the consequences.'

'We all do that. We do it here. You know Labour's got in. Fancy throwing that dear Mr Churchill out after all he's done for us.' Joseph said nothing. 'I got some meat paste for sandwiches and we've some of our own greenhouse tomatoes, there's scones and your favourite jam. And fruit cake – I saved points for the fruit – and fairy cakes. No icing, but I sprinkled a bit of sugar over the top.'

For the first time Joseph looked at the food. She had gone to so much trouble. He felt angry with himself. Poor Mum. She had stayed behind, done her best to serve and suffered so much. He missed his father's presence desperately. Even when Dad had been out of the cottage his courageous spirit had remained. He thought of Mum, day after day, still waiting to hear those familiar footsteps, to see him come in, hang his coat and cap behind the kitchen door and wash his hands after a hard day's work; then remembering he never would again.

'I feel quite hungry,' he lied. 'What a wonderful spread. No one bakes like you, Mum.'

She smiled her relief and he ate as best he could. 'Have you heard from Angie lately?' he asked.

'I have. She says you didn't write for a long time. I told her that you hadn't written to me either and we decided that you were too busy looking after other people. That's your way. But then she got a very nice letter. Thank you for mine. It was a great relief to me to get it.'

'Sorry about the gap. I had a lot on my mind.'

They finished their tea and Mum said, 'You'll be wanting to see Dad's grave. Shall we go now?'

'Why not? I suppose it's as good a time as any.'

Mum was anxious again. Something was very clearly wrong. He was reluctant to go to the churchyard with her. There had been a time when he had accepted death as a natural and even glorious end.

Joseph stood and read the tombstone several times. Its inscription was plain, as became a plain man. 'He did his best to serve in the sight of God.'

'Do you like it, Joseph? It's right for him isn't it?'

'Absolutely.'

'Shall we go in the chapel and say a prayer.'

'No!'

Mrs Morland jumped. 'But—' She stopped. She didn't know how to handle this different Joseph. 'Come along, then, we'll go home.'

Angie had wangled a few days leave. Mrs Morland was thankful to see her. After their first greeting, Joseph left Angie and Mum together while he walked in the garden. He heard the rise and fall of their voices through an open window. August this year was warm and dry, but there had been a lot of rain previously and the soil was dark. The garden had been well tended and the vegetable patches were as abundant as always. He remembered that some of Sid Penrose's women had been helping. Sid was a good sort. He was glad Angie had found such a friend.

He strolled with her back to Greystone House as darkness was falling. For a while they said little. Angie spoke first. 'I was terribly worried when you didn't write.'

'But you understood after I'd explained.'

'I think so. I know you've been tormented by this damned war. Oh, sorry, I shouldn't swear.'

'Swear if you want to. It relieves the feelings. I've been doing a lot of it lately.'

'I'm not surprised after what you must have seen.'

He stopped abruptly. 'I lost my faith,' he said.

The words were so surprising that Angie was nonplussed. 'Lost it?' she stammered.

'It's gone completely. Angie, I killed a man.' In the fading light his face was a pale blur, but all the anguish of war was in his voice.

'No, you didn't. People died, but it wasn't your fault. You couldn't help it if patients died. I know you always did your best.'

'No! I killed! Listen, Angie, I've got to tell you or I'll go mad.' The words poured out of him in a monotone, as if it were a lesson he had learnt by heart. Maybe it was. How many times, she wondered, had he rehearsed this? As she listened Angie felt his desolation, lived with him through the horror of the moment he had plunged a scalpel into a man and taken his life. The fact that he had done it to save another was of no moment to him.

He stopped speaking and she said, 'Thank you for telling me.' She knew instinctively that he wanted no more from her at present.

They walked on and he slid his arm through hers. When he returned home, his mother was relieved to see that the strain in his face had lessened, and she wanted to thank God for Angie.

The evening after Angie had to return to duty, Mum said, 'It's prayer meeting. Do you want to come?'

'No, thank you.'

'Aren't you feeling well?'

'I'm feeling well enough. I shan't be returning to the ministry.'

Mrs Morland didn't argue. He was hurt and bewildered. He'd get over it, just as Walter had got over the Great War. He had been angry with God for a while, but it had passed.

'I'll go on my way then.'

Joseph sat in the kitchen. The house was silent except for the dog who stirred in his sleep and yelped once as he chased dream rabbits. The evangelical life was not for him. Never again. He would probably still go to chapel somewhere, Whitefield Tabernacle maybe, or Zion Methodist, where religion was more austere and never fanatical. He would search for his lost faith whose strength he missed, but he would never have time again for anything which spoke of fanaticism. He and Angie would get married and together they would build a life for themselves and their children, a decent life with everything in moderation, everything ordered in a tranquil pattern, which would keep the horrendous images from invading his mind.

One of Daisy's children developed German measles and it ran through the others.

Daisy's comments on the illness bearing the name of the enemy were many and varied. It wasn't serious but both women were kept busy dealing with the itchy rashes and trying to keep children with only slightly raised temperatures who weren't feeling particularly unwell from escaping into the garden. Amy took the illness a little worse than the others, perhaps because she was such a volatile, emotional child. She called repeatedly for Aunty Sid who realised that Amy loved her above the others. The knowledge was sweet, yet terrifying. The cloud that hung over them grew blacker.

Then she received a letter from Mr Mapleton. It was couched in as gentle terms as he could manage but made it clear that the Prossers were pressing even harder. The letter from their side said, 'If a satisfactory reply is not received within one week from this date, my clients will have no course other than to institute proceedings to gain care and control of the child, Amy Penrose Prosser.' It gave Sid a sickening jolt to see Amy's name coupled with that of Philip.

Daisy's opinion of the Prossers was forthright. 'Bloody toffee-nosed pigs. Think they own the world, they do.'

Robert arrived at Greystone House unexpectedly. He looked depressed and said, gloomily, 'Some women are utterly ghastly.'

'What's happened?' asked Sid.

He frowned. 'You don't sound really interested.'

'I am,' she lied. Robert had been seeing a succession of girls none of whom apparently possessed whatever it was he wanted in a woman. Sid was patient with him, knowing that she was his only confidante. He seldom went home. He said that his family still showed their dissatisfaction with his war record.

He dropped into a chair. They were in the kitchen which was empty for once. 'I've been seeing a girl for weeks. It's the longest friendship I've had since I joined the BBC. Do you recall I mentioned her to you a couple of times? I thought she liked me, but she's let me down badly. I discovered that she's been on dates with another chap. Girls often let one down. Except you, Sidonia. You're always the same.'

'Am I?' She wondered if this was a compliment. 'You'll meet the right girl one day.'

'I've been doing a lot of thinking. I believe I already have met the right girl. At first I didn't know it. Then I wasn't ready to admit it.'

'Oh? So you have some good news for me?'

'I hope so. The truth is, I've fallen for you.'

'What?'

Robert stood up and came to her. He looked down at her, his eyes soft, his manner confident. 'I love you. I've known it really for some time, but I've tried to fight it.'

Sid was flustered. 'Have you? Why?'

'Maybe because I was afraid you would reject me. After all, I'm not much of a catch. My nerves are still pretty ragged. It can't be easy to cope with me. But you know me inside out and I'm sure I can always depend on you.'

Always depend on her? She wondered how deep his love went. Was he looking for a wife? A nurse? Or a kind mother-figure?

But he'd be a father for Amy. The thought flashed through her mind. If she encouraged Robert, Amy would have a home where she could grow up in safety and respectability. Her security had become desperately urgent. Pictures were crowding into her mind of Amy protected by marriage, of access to money to fight the Prossers, of being able to relinquish the lonely struggle against adverse circumstances.

Robert watched her. He must have seen something in her face to encourage him. He pulled her to her feet and held her close. 'You care for me, don't you, Sidonia?'

'I'm fond of you,' she admitted.

'You love me, I know you do, though you're too shy to say so. You are so modest and hard working. You've been too busy to think seriously about men, haven't you?'

His words were a shock. Was that how he saw her? As a labouring, bashful virgin?

Robert held her tighter. 'I wish you'd marry me. Do say that you will. I am sure we'd be good for each other.' She was gagged by conflicting emotions. He gave her a little shake. 'Say something, darling.'

'I need time to think,' she managed.

'Surely you've had time. We've known one another long enough.'

'As friends,' she protested.

'And I hope our friendship will continue. It will make our marriage so much happier.'

She sat down again and he pulled a chair close and faced her, holding her hands tightly. 'We need each other, you and I. Sometimes you have such a lost look. You seem to be searching for something. Is it love you want? I have plenty to give. Marry me, darling. I'll make you as happy as you'll make me.'

'Robert, this is so new to me. I *must* have time to think.'

He was disappointed. He was like a child who wanted everything as soon as he asked for it. 'I'll give you time. How much? Not long, I hope.'

'Stay away from me for a week at least.'

'I promise. I know what your answer will be. Don't worry if you don't think you love me yet. I've enough for us both for now.'

After he had left, Sid went about her work in a dream. At one moment she veered towards the idea of marrying Robert; at another she knew she wanted more than a husband who was pleasant, but weak. She wanted a man she could love with all her heart. But for Amy's sake perhaps she should encourage him. Of course, she would have to tell him about Amy. How would he take it?

Robert broke his promise and visited after three days. 'I couldn't stay away from you, Sidonia.' She was annoyed with him, yet his tenacity, his repeated assurances that he couldn't live without her, his certainty that she would be happy with him, couldn't fail to affect her. He kissed her on greeting and parting, and every day as he left he asked, 'Will you know by tomorrow?'

Daisy watched his coming and going. 'He's definitely gone on you,' she informed Sid.

'He wants to marry me.'

'Well, of all the—! That's marvellous, ducks. When's the weddin'?'

'There will be no wedding.' The words escaped Sid though she hadn't realised they had formed in her mind.

'Are you crazy? Think of Amy.'

'I am.' She was thinking of a child growing up in a home where there was no real love between her parents. Where the atmosphere might have soured over the years. 'Robert's a decent enough man, but I just can't do it.'

'Have you thought about this properly? What about the horrible Prossers? Robert has money.'

'I've thought of little else lately.'
'A week isn't long. Ask for more time.'
'No, I can't marry him.'
'Oh, Sid! Don't throw away such a wonderful chance.'

Daisy's arguments were familiar. They were the ones Sid had put to herself during long, sleepless nights.

Then Daisy said, 'It's Tom Barton, isn't it? You still think of him, don't you? But the odds are against his being alive.'

Sid looked stonily at her friend. 'He could be. Human beings often survive against the odds.'

'But you've said yourself he's probably dead. And even if he was alive you've no guarantee he'd still be in love with you. Or if he was, that's not to say he'd want Amy. Some men aren't all that keen on bringing up other men's children. Especially when they're born out of wedlock. You don't know how Tom feels about it.'

Sid knew that Daisy was being deliberately cruel in an attempt to shock her into accepting Robert. Daisy had her welfare and Amy's at heart.

Robert took her refusal badly. He stormed and argued and sulked. Sid knew for certain then that she was right. He would, no doubt, have agreed to rear Amy and fight for her in court simply because he would not have faced the implications. She would always be fond of him, and she was sorry for him, but she could never marry him.

He left, vowing he'd be back. She thought of the other men she had been close to. Philip. She had loved him passionately once, or believed she did, but now he was her enemy. Poor Roy, who was dead. And Tom. Her breathing became restricted when she thought of Tom. She had to admit to herself that he was probably dead, too. Once, crazy with longing, she had telephoned his parents, explaining that she was a friend and asking for news of him.

His mother's answer had been courteous and kind. They knew he had been critically ill when captured and feared there was no real hope. They had had to accept that, but his mother hadn't sounded altogether sure. She was probably hoping against logic, as were many women, that their particular beloved would return.

Sid pushed her hands through her hair in a gesture of despair. Now the Allies were punishing the Japanese in battles, pushing them back, but slowly. So many of them fought until they died, seeing only shame in being taken prisoner. Some British and Australians had been freed from prisoner-of-war and forced-labour camps and fearful atrocities were being discovered. They terrified the families of the men who had not been heard of for years.

Chapter Twenty-one

On a day which would live on in history for ever, the world learned that the first atomic bomb to be used against human beings had been dropped on a Japanese city called Hiroshima. Three days later, before people understood the full, overpowering horror of its effects, a second bomb was launched on Nagasaki and, soon afterwards, Japan surrendered. The war in the East was over. Statistics about a single bomb which could destroy a city and its inhabitants were printed alongside the accounts of rejoicing that the war was truly ended.

'It says in the paper that a mushroom-shaped cloud rose five miles into the air,' said Daisy. 'They say "it brought instantaneous death to over fifty-five thousand people". The figure could rise. Some people have just *disappeared*! More are dyin' every day.'

'It's fearful,' said Sid. 'Terrible!'

'I know. But we had to do it, didn't we? How many more would have been killed before the Japs gave in? That special bomb has ended everything.'

'Maybe this really will be the war to end wars,' said Sid. 'Who can think of fighting when they can destroy whole cities like that?'

'There's somethin' in the paper about radiation,' said Daisy. 'It burns people. Makes them sick. I wonder what it is? It sounds awful.'

A few days later Sid learned that the Prossers were moving mercilessly ahead with their claim.

Mr Mapleton said, 'They have been warned that their case is not straightforward. If you continue to deny that Philip is Amy's father—'

She sat opposite him in a wooden chair with a polished round seat and arms. 'Will I be under oath?'

'They are pressing for the case to be heard by a judge.'

'What other ways are there?'

'Magistrates are empowered to deal with family disputes and adoptions, but the Prossers have elected to appear before a judge.'

'Adoption!' she cried. 'How cruel!'

'I'm sorry to hurt you, Miss Penrose. I am only answering your question.'

'Yes, I know. I'm sorry.'

'In court you will be required to take the oath.'

'Take the oath? On a Bible? Lying doesn't come easily to me at any time. I certainly couldn't do it under oath. I'd have to tell them the truth.'

'Then we have a fight on our hands.'

Sid visited Mrs Cardell's jeweller. His eyes gleamed when she spoke of the pearls. 'One of the finest strands I've seen. I shall be glad to purchase them.' Then, obviously regretting his display of enthusiasm, he sucked in his breath through his teeth. 'Of course, there are many people trying to sell jewellery nowadays. Money is desperately needed to restock gardens, repair houses, so many things. I can't offer you as much as I would like to.'

'How much?'

He named a sum that took her breath away and reminded her of the difference in outlook and expectations between the rich and the others.

On an unexpectedly balmy evening in late October, Sid and Daisy sat together in the kitchen. Like so many others they were still trying to come to terms with the years of war and its aftermath. Fifty-five million men, women and children had died because of it. Others had lost all contact with their loved ones, not knowing if they were alive or dead.

Keith had taken Patrick to the pictures to see *Blithe Spirit*, a comedy by Noël Coward. The young children were asleep, the older ones had gone out pursuing various activities.

The two women could never keep their minds from the approaching legal struggle for long.

'I know you think I'm a fool to turn Robert away,' Sid said.

'No, I'd never think that about you, but you have tossed away an easy chance of keeping Amy. You could have been married to him by now. That would have taken the wind out of the Prossers' sails.'

'Maybe.'

'I'm sure of it. Mind you, I don't think he'd be much good as a husband for you. You need a strong man. Someone,' she smiled, 'who can control you.'

'So I need control?'

'You do, and you need love. Like the rest of us.'

She sounded bleak and Sid was contrite. 'Sorry, Daisy. I've been so wrapped up in my problems I've forgotten yours. You must miss your husband so much more now that the men have begun returning.'

'Yes, I miss him.'

The telephone extension bell shrilled in the kitchen and Daisy jumped up. 'Sit still, ducks, I'll answer it.'

She returned. 'It's for you.' There was an odd, excited look in her eyes.

'Who is it?'

'Go and see.'

Sid frowned and ran lightly up the steps to the hall.

'Hello?' she said.

'Sidonia, is it really you?'

She thought she might faint. Her mouth went dry. 'Tom?' she croaked.

'Yes, I'm home at last.'

'Home?'

'With my family. I'm not far away.'

'Tom! Oh, Tom.'

'Can't you say more than that?' There was a touch of humour in his voice and it brought her memories flooding back. She had known she wanted him, but she had not allowed herself to realise until this moment just how much. How she loved him! 'What happened? Are you well? We all thought you were – Tom, thank God you are home.'

'Amen to that. I've been stuck in hospital in Singapore.'

Sid waited. Surely he would say he was coming to see her. Or ask her to visit him. She ached to touch him, to make sure that he really was alive. But it had been years! She had no guarantee that he still cared for her.

'I'm looking forward to seeing you,' he said. His first excitement no longer infected his voice and she felt cold.

'I want to see you, too. When can we meet?' Her words sounded stilted in her own ears.

'Not for a while. I'm really a shocking sight at the moment. All sorts of things are wrong with me. I'm lucky to be allowed home.'

'When were you released?'

'About two months ago. But I've been rather ill and when I got stronger there was the debriefing.'

'Debriefing?'

'Telling the officers what we remembered about the camps. Names of chaps who died. How they died.' His voice became grim. 'The names of guards who were sadistic. And those who murdered.'

'Of course. Their people need to know.'

But two months! And he had not told her.

'I managed to telephone my parents from Singapore, though it was devilish hard to get a line. And I wasn't able to write.'

'Why not?'

'My hands, bandages, you know. The work they gave us was terrible. I never seemed to toughen up enough for my skin to cope.'

'I see.' But she didn't. Surely he could have asked a nurse to write for him. Or asked someone to phone her. During the passing years she had mourned him and now he was home, talking to her as he might to any friend.

'Sidonia, are you still there?'

'Yes. Will you be going into hospital here?'

'No need, thank goodness. Father can employ nurses for me.'

'Nurses? How badly wounded are you?'

'I'm not wounded. I'm suffering from various kinds of this and that. Skin problems and illnesses caused by lack of food. I'm terribly weak. Most of the chaps coming out of the camps are like me. Sidonia, are you well?'

'Perfectly, thank you.'

'I'm so glad. And have you settled down? Boyfriend? Husband?'

'No, I'm still fancy free.' She failed to sound casually jocular.

'We must meet. When I'm more fit to be seen.'

'Yes, we must,' she said coolly. She had no intention of flinging herself at him. 'I look forward to it.'

'So do I.'

'I hope it won't be too long. I mean, I hope you will soon be well.'

'Thank you. Goodbye for now.'

'Goodbye.'

There was a click and the phone went dead. She returned to the kitchen with slow steps.

Daisy looked up. 'It was *your* Tom, wasn't it?'

'My Tom? Yes.' Sid sank back into her chair by the fire.

Daisy made a couple of attempts to speak, but seeing the unhappiness in Sid's face she remained silent.

Sid said abruptly, 'He sounded glad to hear my voice, then he seemed to get tired of talking to me.'

'Don't worry, ducks. I dare say he's in a bit of a state. I've read about the poor men coming out of those awful camps.'

'So have I. I've seen pictures on the newsreels too. They look like skeletons.'

'He'll get well. He'll come to see you soon, I know he will.'

The war was really over at last. Factories were turned over to their original use. They had much to make up for. Metal goods were in great demand; women had had to make do with battered pots and pans, railings needed replacing, and dilapidations rectifying. Cars were wanted too. People were warned not to expect normal conditions to apply for some time and rationing would have to continue. They complained, but half-heartedly. Their relief was intense.

Men and women looked in their mirrors and saw the ageing wrought by their years of anguish and self-denial. Sid noticed lines on her face. She touched them, wondering what Tom would see when he looked at her. If he ever did look at her. Nevertheless she began to take more pride in her appearance. She rubbed in some precious face cream that Daisy had found in a small chemist's. She cossetted her rough hands with the Vaseline and glove treatment. She wore gloves for housework. Having no outside occupation, she began to restore Greystone House. She had a reasonable income and Daisy paid her way. She could afford basic repairs, though they were a big item; between them she and Daisy could manage the rest and they chose paints and wallpaper together. They shared the housework and Daisy still worked long hours in the garden. They preserved the autumn fruits and vegetables.

Patrick's mother had visited and Sid assured her that Patrick would be kept on. 'I don't mind if you only pay him pocket money,' said his mother. 'He's never been so happy as he is here.'

Keith, with the confidence gained during the war, found himself a well-paid job.

Angie returned to Greystone House. She helped with the work while busy preparing for her marriage to Joseph. He visited most evenings. Thanks to Angie, he was gradually losing his look of despair, though

Angie said he'd never be the man he was.

'He's suffered horribly,' she told Sid. 'Mrs Morland says he has awful nightmares, shouting and screaming. When we are married I hope I can stop them.'

Daisy looked forward to seeing her children home at last.

Sid lived from day to day, afraid to look into the future.

There was a bright spot when Mattie had her baby. A boy, born prematurely, but strong and vigorous. Grandma, who had not hesitated to show her disapproval of the whole affair, suddenly veered and became enamoured of the small boy. She was as proud of him as if she had given birth herself. Mattie's sisters grumbled at this show of favouritism but they could never stay alienated from their mother and they loved Mattie too well not to be glad for her. Wilfred's sons were happy for their father and Elsie, his young daughter, was delighted to have a brother younger than her.

Mattie lay in comfort in the expensive nursing home. Her room was filled with flowers and boxes of chocolates lay untouched on her bedside table. 'People have been so kind,' said Mattie, 'giving up their sweet points. Take some home for the children. I sent Elsie a box. But leave the Fry's Milk for your grandma. They're her favourites. She'll be in later.' She gave a little giggle. 'Do you know, she's visited every day, even though she has to take a bus.'

'I'm so glad for you,' said Sid fervently. 'How wonderfully everything has turned out.'

Mattie gave her a keen look. 'You don't look happy, Sid. What's up? Tell your Aunty Mattie.'

'I'm fine,' lied Sid. 'Just suffering from the after-effects of the war, like most people.'

Mattie sighed. 'If you need me I'm always ready to help. I'm so lucky.'

'You deserve to be.' Sid kissed her aunt and hurried out. She was afraid if Mattie showed her too much sympathy she would weep. She had told no one of the court case which loomed over her. They didn't even know that Amy was her child. That was another hurdle which must be jumped. Mr Mapleton said that he could ensure absolute secrecy if she would just let Amy go. But Sid could not. And she wasn't thinking only of herself.

Last time she had seen Mr Mapleton he had told her that the Prossers had already entered Amy's name for a leading girls' public school. Sid felt sick at the idea of her spirited child suffering any sort of confinement. And she would lose all that she had grown up with. How bewildered she would be. Sometimes Sid was tormented by the idea that Amy, with her brave, sunny disposition would quickly accept the Prossers' way of life. Amy loved animals and had long wanted to ride. The Prossers could afford a pony for her. How long would it take for her to forget her mother in the midst of such indulgencies? She began to doubt her motives. Was she depriving her child of a brilliant future? Did Amy truly need her mother, no matter what the circumstances?

Tom telephoned occasionally, but their conversation was stilted and unnatural. And what if he did care for her? How would she explain Amy? Especially after she had refused to make love to him.

January 1946 was cold and wet. Sid sat in the kitchen alone. She could not keep her mind on the housekeeper's book. Angie and Joseph had been quietly married at Christmas, enjoyed a short honeymoon, then returned to their respective camps, looking forward to demobilisation. Sid had been happy for them, but their joy and obvious love for one another had made her feel even more isolated. Daisy had been to London visiting relatives and was due home. Sid wondered if she'd decide to live in London again. After all, she was a true cockney. She had taken the younger children with her and the elder were at work. Amy was at school. She had wept on the first night the other children were not there to share bedtime. It was the first time she had been in the house without her playmates. The fire burned low but Sid lacked the impetus to refill the scuttle from the cellar and to stoke it. She waited for Patrick who was upstairs. He left his cellar for quite long periods nowadays and he was polishing the newly-varnished doors, an occupation he enjoyed almost as much as stoking. She could hear him moving about above her. The fire burned lower and still her lethargy held her captive. There was a step on the stairs. Good, Patrick was coming. He would heap in the wood and some of their precious coal.

She only had time to realise that the step was too light to be Patrick's when the door opened.

She turned. The figure who stood in the doorway looked extra tall because he was so gaunt, little more than skin and bone, his eyes unnaturally large as he stared at her.

Then she knew.

All coherent thought departed. She flew into his waiting arms. 'Tom. Oh, Tom! My love!'

'What did you call me?'

'My love,' she said, her defences down, tears in her eyes.

'That's what I thought. I'm truly your love?'

'Yes, oh, yes.'

He hugged her. 'Thank heaven. You sounded so distant on the phone I was afraid to tell you how I felt. I had no idea how you felt about me after so long a time. And I was in a ghastly mess, you can't imagine. I was endlessly, everlastingly tired. I can't begin to explain how deeply I was affected by exhaustion. Starvation does terrible things to you. I didn't want to burden you—'

She stopped his mouth with a long kiss. 'Darling, darling,' she murmured as they broke away. 'Come and sit by the fire. I'm afraid I've let it go low.' She picked up a few sticks and pushed them into the range, then knelt by his chair, unwilling to put space between them.

'I can't believe you are actually here.'

'It's true. At last. Oh, darling, they are in such chaos out East! It's unbelievable. Prisoners who have been freed from all kinds of conditions in every conceivable state of sickness. Mopping-up operations against the Japanese holding out in pockets in the jungle. Civilians milling around, poor devils, trying to find loved ones.'

He stopped and lifted her ringless hand. 'Thank heaven you are still free. It's been so long. I thought perhaps, Roy Hendy—?'

'He was killed.'

'Oh, I'm sorry.'

'So am I. He was a good friend.'

'No more than that?'

'No more.'

'I'm sorry the poor chap died, but glad that he was only a friend.' Then, as if the images buried in his mind were too strong to resist his eyes went dark as he lost himself in thought. He said slowly, 'I couldn't come to you before I knew I would recover. I didn't want to burden you with a useless lover.'

'Useless?'

'Prolonged hunger and disease take away everything but desperation for food and the relief of pain.'

'Oh, Tom!' She hugged him. 'I was so afraid you must have died. And here you are. My love, my love,' she murmured against his lips. Her tongue traced the curve of his mouth. 'I knew I should never want anyone else. I never stopped missing you.'

He gently kissed the tip of her nose, then her mouth. But part of him was lingering in the past. 'We became less than men,' he said. 'I couldn't come to you until I knew I was restored to health. They've got some marvellous new drugs these days. Penicillin, for one. I'm much better but I've still a way to go. Some poor devils never will be as they were, but the doctors are sure that in time I shall be fit enough to live a normal life.'

She stopped the speech with a long kiss. 'Darling, darling,' she murmured as they broke away. 'How could you think I should love you less because you were broken by the war?' She held his hands. 'Heavens, you're so cold.' She poked the fire, sending up a few bright sparks.

'I've still not got over the heat in that bloody jungle. England feels chilly, but I'm jolly glad to be back. I feel I'll never go abroad again.'

She got up and went to sit on his knee but he pushed her gently away, smiling ruefully, 'Sorry, dearest, but I'm still so thin my bones are like knife blades. I wouldn't want to injure you in so vital a part.'

She laughed and seated herself as close to him as she could get.

He said seriously, 'Once I got home, I couldn't contemplate being with you in the state I was in. I couldn't even make love over the phone until I knew I was restored to manly strength.' He had tried to sound facetious, but his voice broke a little. 'And that damned weariness. I thought my body would never be the same again. And, to put it bluntly, love without sex would have driven us both crazy.'

The kitchen clock struck three-thirty and automatically Sidonia pushed the kettle over the hob. 'Tea-time soon. They'll all be back.'

'The women and children? Are they still here?'

'Only Daisy and some of her children. They've been to London but I expect them back quite soon now. And Amy's at school.'

'Oh, I remember Amy. A lively, pretty child. Intelligent, too. No one's claimed her yet?'

Sid felt cold for a moment. 'Not yet,' she said quietly.

Tom sensed something. He stood up and pulled her to her feet. He wanted to banish whatever devil was bothering her. His arms tightened round her. She responded fiercely. Their bodies were so close she was easily made conscious that his fear of impotence was groundless.

'After you were freed, you didn't get in touch,' she breathed. 'And you stayed away from me for so long.'

'Because I love you so much—'

'I'm sure I could have restored you.'

Tom sighed. Civilians, even the most sensitive and willing of them would never quite comprehend the horrors of the past years. But he kept his tone light. 'If we prisoners had seen a chorus of dancing girls from the Windmill we should only have asked them if they had any food on them.'

'Oh, poor you. Poor you.'

'In hospital in Singapore, back at home, I had to wait. I had no idea if I would ever be normal again. So much had happened to me. When I did get home I knew I wanted you, but my body refused to respond. I had nothing to offer you in that department.'

'Just having you here and alive would have been enough,' she murmured.

'Not for me,' he said firmly. 'I would never have stopped loving you, but I wanted to make love to you!'

He shivered. 'Oh, you're so cold,' she cried. 'You've no flesh on you to keep you warm. I'll fetch some coal.'

'I was thinking of a better way to keep warm,' said Tom.

She turned to search his face. There was no mistaking his meaning. 'You want to make love to me?' Her need for him left no room for being coy.

'Yes,' he said simply. 'Now. At once. The thought of you, of making love to you, was all that kept me alive. I had to get home, get well enough to tell you how very much I loved you.'

The words were hauntingly sweet to her. 'I refused you once,' she said softly. 'I've regretted it hundreds of times. I can't refuse again.'

He held her tight against him. 'Is there somewhere we can be alone?'

'In my room.'

They climbed the stairs arm in arm and she led him to her room, locking the door. The winter sun had already set and the shadowy room was so overfull of the excess furniture which could not be moved until the decorating was finished, that it was like being in a dim, rock-strewn cave. The soft, claustrophobic darkness added to Sid's aching desire. 'If I'd known you'd be here I would have lit a fire,' she said, half humorously. 'I'll put a match to it.'

The paper and sticks blazed but long before the coal caught Tom had led her to the bed. She sat on the edge while Tom watched her.

Had she felt this way before? With Philip? This was not the same. She loved Tom, really loved him.

He was taking stock of her. He saw that war had exacted its toll on her as well. She was far too thin; she had suffered.

He tipped her face up with gentle fingers and kissed her mouth softly, then with increasing hunger. She put her arms around him, murmuring his name. 'Lie beside me,' she begged. 'Let me feel you beside me.'

They lay side by side, each content for a moment to sense the nearness of the other. 'The times I've dreamed of this!' he said.

'In the prison camp?'

'Yes.' A shudder ran through the length of his body and she wished she hadn't mentioned the camp again.

But Tom seemed to want to refer to it. 'My dreams led me into pictures of what we could be to each other, what we could do. Then I'd wake and find myself still a prisoner and incapable anyway. As the years passed my dreams were all of food. God, the torment!'

'It's over now, my darling.'

'Over. And we really are together.'

He touched her cheek with gentle fingers. 'When I began to dream of making love to you again I knew the worst was over. I knew then that I could give you proof of the love I have for you.'

His hand moved over her body with infinite care. It lingered on her breasts which strained against the bodice of her dress towards his touch. He stroked her, arousing dormant fires which blazed into life for him. She grasped his hand, longing for his touch to continue, yet shrinking from such a wild arousal of unfulfilled desire.

'Don't torture me,' she gasped. 'Please—'

She undid the buttons of her dress and Tom's hand slid inside, cupping her breasts tenderly.

Following an instinct she hadn't known she possessed, she began to explore him. He had been right about his bones. They really were blade-like. But as her hand travelled over him she could have no doubt that his amatory instincts had returned in force.

He gasped at her touch, then sat up and, with her willing assistance, tugged her dress over her head, following it with her petticoat. He swiftly removed her bra and she kicked off her panties and lay there, naked except for a slim suspender belt and stockings. She was hot with need as she struggled with the belt.

'Leave it,' Tom said. 'You look like an adorable hussy.'

'How much do you know of hussies?'

'Not much.' He smiled. 'But I read a lot.'

He rested his hand on her stomach and gazed at her until she felt she would go insane with longing.

'How beautiful you are, Sidonia.'

Through her painful need she felt a rush of happiness at being told she was beautiful. He really believed it.

But her craving for him was too urgent for further delay. 'Don't you want me?' she breathed. 'Don't you want me?'

'Do you want me?'

'You know I do. You must be able to tell.'

He smiled, a slow smile which transformed his gaunt face. 'I can tell. But I have to be certain. I won't push you into anything you aren't sure about.'

She raised herself on her elbow. 'Are you positive you've recovered? It's all right, darling, if you haven't. If you need time, I'll wait. I shall understand.'

'Will you? And you on fire with love? What a heroine you are.'

'Are you mocking me?'

'As if I would! I really do believe you'd take me whatever way I am.'

'You can believe it,' she murmured. 'So for God's sake stop tormenting me.'

Her fingers dealt with the buttons and he tore off his clothes. When he was naked they turned to one another and revelled in the sensation of skin against skin. Gently their hands began once more to explore, piling on the sweet agony, each recognising the powerful sexuality of the other. When he entered her it was entirely natural, an act of grace for which both had waited a long time. She moved beneath him in an irresistible rhythm. He deepened his strokes until there was nothing in the world but flesh within flesh, soaring escape from the deep-rooted loneliness they had suffered until in a burst of ecstasy they arrived at their fulfilment.

Afterwards they lay beneath the bedclothes, basking in the afterglow of love. And Sid knew finally that making love with Tom was worlds away from what she had known with Philip.

Tom reached his arm out for his cigarettes. 'Where's my jacket?' he asked.

Somewhere in that heap of clothes.'

He laughed, and leaned over the side of the bed while she switched on the bedside lamp.

She gasped when she saw his back. It was a mass of criss-crossing scars. He turned at the sound. 'Oh, sorry, I should have told you.'

'How did it happen?'

'Beatings.'

She touched the puckered flesh. 'Why? What did you do to get such wicked punishments?'

'I intervened when one of the Imperial Emperor's soldiers was kicking a youth who was no more than eighteen. Just a boy. He forgot to be humble and answered back. The guard was one of the most vicious. A bastard!' His voice had taken on a quality which scared her. There would always be an aspect of him she couldn't reach. 'The boy died.'

'How horrible.'

'Everything about being a prisoner of Nippon was horrible. Everything! Some of the men went mad. Literally mad. Sometimes I thought I would go that way myself.'

It would take years for him to recover properly, if he ever did, thought Sid. But she would be there to help him.

'Did they often treat you that way? Beat you, I mean?'

'Yes. But you counted it lucky to have just a beating. Men were killed for trivial disobedience.'

'Couldn't you have lain low and just obeyed them?'

'Not if we wanted to keep our sanity. It became a point of honour to bait the enemy. Not that he needed baiting. Sometimes a man was tortured, even killed, at the whim of a sadistic guard.' He lit two cigarettes and gave her one. 'Don't let me burden you with these things. I must forget them.'

'You can't expect to shove such horrors from your mind as if they hadn't existed. Talk to me, Tom. Tell me anything you wish. I want to share everything with you.'

Tom knew he would never be able to explain the abysmal depths to which he and his fellow-prisoners had fallen, but he could tell her some things, skim some facts from the top. It might even help him.

He spoke rapidly. 'We were first in Changi jail. A terrible place with almost no facilities. Then we were shunted around from camp to camp, labouring like slaves. That's what we were. Slave labour. There's a railway line built in the Burmese jungle that's been annointed by the blood of thousands of men. One day, after an eternity, without warning we were returned to Changi. We had illicit radios and knew the Allies were winning. When the gates were opened to let us free we were ready. God, I've never been so glad of anything in my life as I was when those gates opened.' He was silent for a moment, then said slowly, 'So many of my friends have gone, buried in some hole in the jungle.' He stopped again, striving to cope with deadly recollection. 'I wanted to see you above everyone, Sidonia, but suddenly, after years of waiting and hoping, I was afraid. I didn't even know if you cared for me and God, the mess I was in! Stinking ulcers on my legs, my feet with ghastly wounds, abscesses that wouldn't heal, everything was wrong with me. And then I collapsed with another dose of malaria.'

'Oh, Tom. My poor love.'

'Sidonia, I've many scars on my body and worse, some on my – my soul, I suppose you could say. It must sound melodramatic to you.'

'No,' she murmured. 'It doesn't. You must tell me everything.'

'You mean it, don't you? Thank you, my darling. But now I want to talk about us. Dearest Sidonia, will you marry me?'

The answer to her dreams came upon her with such swift simplicity! She wanted, craved the delight of saying yes. But she could not. She had so much to explain to him.

He sat up. He was puzzled. 'What's troubling you? I'm not a fool. I know I was not the first with you. Why shouldn't you have taken a lover? You needed love through the long war years. I want to marry you. That's all that matters. To me, anyway.'

'To me, too.' Her mind leap-frogged around. It was almost four o'clock and in less than ten minutes Amy would return, followed soon after by the others. She couldn't afford to be interrupted during an explanation which needed to be undertaken with immense care. Even if Amy didn't come looking for her, banging on the bedroom door indignantly, she couldn't keep her mind steady. She would be waiting for her knock, or Daisy's. And she needed time to talk, time for him to assimilate her news and deal with it.

'Will your parents accept me as your wife?' she asked.

'You bet! They'll be thankful to see me settle with a nice, respectable girl like you. There were times when I was younger when they didn't know which way I'd jump. Neither did I. Do you remember how I chauffered for the deadly Prossers? What a family! The old lady behaving like a bad-tempered queen, Celia hot after the men, and as for Philip, he's a real stinker.'

Sid felt ill. 'You obviously dislike him. He's thought to be a hero now. Wounded terribly in the service of his country.'

'Yes. I sympathise with that. But there are tales of men who died because he made excuses not to fly on bombing missions.'

Every word Tom uttered drove Sid further into depression. 'Tom, before I give you my answer, I have to explain—'

'It's all right, my love,' he said gently. 'You don't have to answer at once. But don't keep me in suspense for too long, will you?'

'No. Tom, Daisy and her children – they'll be here soon – and school's almost over.'

'I see.' He grinned. 'Hadn't we better dress?'

'My God, yes!' She leapt up and dragged on her clothes. He dressed more leisurely. As they were ready to go downstairs they both heard the shrieks of excited pleasure rising from below as Amy, released from the bondage of school, discovered Daisy and her playmates turning into the gates.

'I see what you mean,' smiled Tom.

Sid ran lightly down the stairs and into the kitchen. Tom followed at a more sedate pace.

'Look who's here,' Sid cried, when Tom entered the kitchen. 'Mr Barton.'

Daisy jumped up. 'Tom! It's good to see you.'

Daisy's children gave him a cursory glance then returned to their bread and jam.

Amy stared at him then said, 'I remember you. You're my Uncle Tom. You came to my garden and my house.'

'So I did and I remember you, too. But you've grown into quite a young lady.'

'No, I haven't! I'm still a girl. Daisy says that when I'm a young lady I can't climb trees any more or play football with the boys so I don't want to be a young lady. I was a bridesmaid once. I had a velvet dress. I suppose I was a young lady that day.'

'I am sure you were beautiful.' Tom smiled. 'She's as engaging as ever,' he said quietly to Sid.

'Sit down,' said Daisy. 'We've only got the nasty wartime loaf but the jam's home-made and I've got a bit of butter you can have.'

'I won't deprive the children of their butter.'

'Do they look deprived?' demanded Daisy.

Tom smiled at the pink-cheeked, bright-eyed children who were gobbling food as fast as possible so that they could go to play in the nursery which had been turned over for their use. 'They look wonderful.'

Patrick had been down and made up the fire and its cheerful blaze warmed the kitchen. Daisy motioned Tom to a chair next to Sid's and they sat together, though they had both lost their appetites.

'Blimey!' said Daisy. 'You two'll never put on weight if you don't get some food down you.'

When the children had gone Daisy washed up and Sid wiped, while Tom watched them. Then Daisy tactfully left.

'What a jolly houseful,' said Tom. 'Amy is even prettier than I remember. You'd think she'd have some family who'd claim her.'

Sid said, 'We have something stronger than tea. What can I get you? Port? Brandy?'

'I understood the civilian population went short of such necessary items.'

'Mrs Cardell's man looked after her cellar very well.'

'Brindle? Where is he?'

'Retired.'

'Is the old boy well?'

'Hardy, but growing older.'

'As we all are. The minutes are passing. So why are we not talking of us? Forget the drink. Are you still working at the factory?'

'No. They've stopped making munitions.'

Late that night Sid sat in the kitchen with Daisy. Tom, tired out, had gone to bed in one of the vacated guest rooms which they had recently renovated.

'He's suffered, hasn't he?' said Daisy. 'I like him, Sid. And it's plain to see the way you two feel about each other.'

'He loves me,' said Sid.

'That's obvious. You looked as if you were joined by an invisible rope. When one moved so did the other. I wonder you're not with him now. Oh, sorry ducks, me an' my big mouth.'

Sid went red and Daisy grinned. 'He was here when we got home. Upstairs, weren't you? When you came down you both looked happy and, er, satisfied.'

Sid's blush grew deeper. 'He's asked me to marry him.'

'Oh I'm ever so glad for you. That's the best thing that could happen. You deserve it, too. It's about time you thought about yourself.'

'But I have to tell him about Amy.'

'Yes, he'll have to know. And of course being you you'll feel obliged to tell him before you make any plans.'

'Of course.'

'I bet he'll understand. He seems a very understanding bloke to me. And you'll not be the first to have got caught, not by a long chalk. It's all over the newspapers. Men coming home to a little stranger, when they haven't seen their wives for years. Some are getting divorced, but others are doing their best to take the odd baby in their stride.'

'I've read about it,' said Sid quietly.

'Women have things to forgive, too. Some of the men have brought back some diseases that weren't exactly brought about by the war. Well, only in a roundabout way.'

'I know. It's better now penicillin can cure them. But it's not so simple for me. Have you forgotten the Prossers?'

'Damn! I had for the minute. The court case.'

'Tom knows the family and dislikes them all, Philip most of all. And Amy is his daughter.'

'It's going to be tricky, I grant you. But I reckon he's so gone on you, he'll take it in his stride.'

'I wish I'd never hidden the truth. It's made things impossible for me.'

'You did it for Amy's sake.'

'I believed so at the time. But she's growing up and knows nothing of her background. One day she's bound to ask. It might have been much better for her if I had been honest from the start.'

'You did what you thought best at the time. Mrs Cardell loved Amy, didn't she? She wasn't ashamed of her.'

'No, but she kept her identity a secret. She took it for granted that we would. How will I tell him? I can't find the words.'

'Just start at the beginning. The words will come.'

Tom stayed at Greystone House. 'I'll have to go back for a medical appointment,' he explained, 'but until then I want to be near you.'

They had made love again and their pleasure deepened each time.

'We're made for each other, Sidonia,' said Tom, after a bout of frantic love-making. 'Surely you can give me an answer now.'

She had shaken her head and he had got a little angry. 'You say you love me, you say you want to be with me always, yet you refuse to give me the assurance I need. I don't understand.'

A letter arrived from Mr Mapleton asking her to call. He had engaged a King's Counsel who needed to talk to her. He would be in Mr Mapleton's office on the following Monday.

On Saturday Daisy decided to take the children to the zoo. 'It'll give you a clear field,' she said significantly. 'If you don't get it off your chest soon you'll go crazy and so will Tom.'

They made love and it seemed infinitely sweeter to Sid because she feared it might be their last time. Afterwards, as they smoked, Sid said, 'Tom, I can give you an answer now, but first I have to tell you something.'

'Not necessary, darling. I told you that I want you as you are.'

'I'm afraid it is necessary. You despise Philip Prosser. I hate him!'

'Hate? A strong word. Why?'

'He's a womaniser. Or he was. He's married now and helpless in a wheelchair.'

'I know that.'

'He was very active before. He was Mrs Cardell's great-nephew. That's why she helped me.'

'You're talking in riddles.'

'It will make sense when you know everything.'

She fell silent and Tom again lit cigarettes for them. She accepted hers, wondering if he would ever make this sweet gesture for her again.

'Go on,' he said.

'Philip Prosser stayed here before the war. I was housekeeper, cook, companion to Mrs Cardell. Philip said he loved me.'

'Keep talking,' said Tom quietly.

'I thought I loved him.'

'And?'

'He persuaded me— No, I can't blame him, I was an adult and knew what I was doing. For a week I went to his room.' Sid told Tom the story and he listened without another word. As she finished and was about to explain the complications her folly had led to he said, 'Amy was the result?'

'Did you guess? I mean, before now?'

'No, but she's so different from the others. And you love her deeply, don't you? I'm sorry, my darling, for what you've suffered. Surely you know I would not condemn you.'

'No, I didn't think that. I just wonder – it's Amy, you see. I couldn't let her go. I want to acknowledge her, tell her who I am.'

'Of course you must. You owe it to her.'

'That's how I feel.'

'And rightly so. A child should know its own mother.'

Sid's relief brought her close to tears. 'What about Philip? He has rights.'

'He threw them away.'

Sid felt she would drown in the sweetness of Tom's words. 'Thank you, my love. But I'm afraid there's more.' As briefly as possible she outlined the approaching case.

Tom lit a cigarette from his lighted stub.

'You're smoking too much,' said Sid automatically.

'I know. I'll cut down. At present it steadies my nerves.'

'I'm not helping.'

'You're helping more than anything. I love you.'

'But the Prossers!'

'We'll see it through together.'

'What about your family!'

'They are the most compassionate people in the world. You'll find out when you know them better.'

Sid wept now, tears of relief pouring down her cheeks.

'Hey, what's this?' demanded Tom. He wiped away her tears with a corner of the sheet. But more rained down.

Tom held her in his arms and let her cry away the frustrations and anguish of the years.

Tom postponed his medical appointment to extend his time with Sid. He accompanied her to Mr Mapleton's office and shook hands with the solicitor and the KC, a portly man with a fatherly air about him.

'Am I to understand?' he asked in the rich voice which reached to the far corners of any courtroom, 'that you, Miss Penrose, and Mr Barton are to marry?'

They assured him that they were.

'Then this case may prove much simpler than I had expected. I suppose it wouldn't be possible to marry soon? Before the case is heard?'

'Definitely,' said Tom before Sid could speak. 'Sidonia and I have waited long enough.'

'Good,' said the KC. 'We shall be heard in a closed court. It involves matters far too delicate to be aired in public. We are trying for a hearing at the first possible opportunity.' He rubbed his hands together in apparent glee. 'I have every hope of winning this one.'

It's like a game to him, thought Sid. Well, what matter so long as his side won the game and Amy was not damaged?

A visit to Tom's parents was of course inevitable. They were as unlike the Prossers as it was possible to be; nor did they resemble Robert's family.

Sid had told Robert that she was going to marry Tom. It seemed that he had still held on to a hope that she would change her mind about him and he pointed out all the disadvantages of taking an ex-prisoner-of-war for a husband. 'He might pass on any number of diseases to you or his offspring. He can't have much real love for you or he'd never risk it.'

Sid had listened without saying much, but she was glad she had never yielded to her fear for Amy and married Robert. He was weaker than she had understood. When she had refused to be influenced by him Robert sulked. He had finally accepted her decision. 'But we must stay friends for ever, Sidonia,' he said.

The Barton place had been built as a small manor, but had been added to over the centuries until it now sprawled extensively in various styles. It was set in the midst of meadows and woods.

Mrs Barton was as gentle and kindly as her voice had sounded on the telephone. Mr Barton clearly adored his wife. The house had a genuinely serene atmosphere. They were elderly and Sid remembered that Tom had been a late baby. They welcomed Sid as Tom's chosen partner and when his brothers and sisters visited to inspect his choice they too were kind. Sid insisted on Tom telling his parents about Amy and the court case as soon as possible. There was an opportunity on the first evening after the others had gone to their own homes. She stayed by his side as he informed them succinctly and they listened without comment.

As Tom finished speaking Sid waited, her heart racing.

Mrs Barton said, 'I like to be charitable, but I've always detested the Prossers. Naturally, I am sorry that Philip was so dreadfully wounded – who could not be? We know Dolores's family quite well. Decent people. However, I cannot see Philip Prosser making a decent father. Tom will make an excellent one.'

By her simple response Sid learned all she needed to know. She loved Tom's mother from that moment.

'I don't understand why Dolores took Philip,' said Tom.

'All she could get perhaps,' said Mr Barton. 'Nice girl, but dismal looks.'

'Uncharitable,' reproved Mrs Barton. 'Though I must admit you are right. However, her strong, pleasing personality will be important to a man who is wheelchair bound.'

There was no reason to delay the wedding. Daisy was thrilled and worked hard to be ready for the small reception which was to be held in Greystone House. Amy danced about in delight when told she was to be a bridesmaid for a second time. 'Auntie Sid is marrying Uncle Tom,' she sang.

Tom and Sid had discussed Amy at length.

'I think we should tell her at once that you are her mother,' said Tom.

Sid was not so sure. 'She may be too upset to enjoy herself. Shouldn't we wait until afterwards.'

'I think not, darling. Imagine how she'll feel when we present her with such a momentous fact. She's quick and clever, but volatile. She could be very upset that we withheld the deeper meaning of our marriage from her.'

Tom had no objection to Daisy joining the discussion. He admired and respected her.

Daisy said, 'I think Tom's right. Right now, Amy can think of nothin' but dressin' up and bein' a bridesmaid. She'll not have time to worry about your news until later and by then she'll be used to it.'

'Very shrewd,' approved Tom.

'But slightly dishonest?' said Sid. 'It sounds as if we are tricking her.'

Tom said, 'We have to be clever about this for her sake.'

'What if she asks about her father?' said Sid.

'She may not think about that straight away. It'll be something we can face later. Together.'

So one day when the house was quiet, Sid took Amy to her little sitting room. The fire was blazing and Daisy brought them tea and the tiny sweet cakes Amy loved.

Amy was suspicious. She was not yet eight, but her instincts were well developed; she could sense when something was afoot.

Sid gave her some of Daisy's home-made raspberry cordial and told her to help herself to cakes. Amy obeyed, but the wary look never left her eyes.

'Darling, I have something to tell you,' Sid began.

Amy put down her half-eaten cake. 'You're going to send me away!' she cried. 'Someone's coming to fetch me.'

Sid was horrified. 'Whyever should you think such a thing?'

'I've thought about it for ages, ever since I was six at least. You're not really my aunty, are you? And all the others haven't really been aunties and uncles.'

'No,' admitted Sid, 'but it's quite usual for people to adopt aunties and uncles. It's not a new thing.'

'Someone is coming to take me, aren't they?' Amy flung herself at Sid, clinging to her, her arms locked round her waist. 'Please don't let them take me. It's that nasty woman who came here – Celia, I know it is – and her horrid grandma and that other lady. And the man in the wheelchair. It's them isn't it? Oh, please don't make me go away with them.'

'No! my darling, no!' Sid heard herself saying the words, praying that they might be true. Her happiness had driven the devils underground for a while, but now they came to torment her even more cruelly. What if she lost the court case?

She managed to disengage Amy's clinging arms and pull her on to her lap. 'Listen, my pet, stop crying and listen.'

But Amy couldn't control herself and in the end Sid almost shouted her message. 'I am your mother!'

For an instant it made no difference, then Amy stopped crying abruptly. 'What?'

'Darling, you are my little girl. I am your mother.'

Amy held her drenched face up to Sid's. 'No, you're not. You're just trying to cheer me up.'

'I'm telling you the truth, my darling. I am your mother.'

Amy stared at Sid for a long time. 'Really and truly?' she whispered. 'My mother? I am your little girl?'

'Really, truly.'

Amy gazed up into Sid's face. 'My mother. My very own mother.'

It was Sid's turn to weep and Amy brushed her tears aside with her small, hot hand.

'Why did you say I was someone else's girl?' she asked.

'I can't explain it all to you now. I will some day.'

'And you'll never make me leave you, not ever. You'll never let those horrid people take me away.'

Sid hugged her child and kissed her. It was a promise she dared not make. 'I'll always be your mother,' she said. Seeing Amy about to ask more questions, she reminded her, 'You are to be my bridesmaid.'

But the child was not so easily deflected. 'My mother,' she breathed. 'I thought I didn't have one.'

'Are you glad it's me?' asked Sid a little wistfully.

'Glad! Glad! Glad!' declared Amy. 'And Uncle Tom won't be my uncle any more, will he? He'll be my father. My dad. My dad and mum. Can I call you Mum?'

Sid realised she faced another problem. Naturally her relatives had been invited to the wedding. She had not wanted to break the news about Amy to them until after her marriage. But she could do nothing more which might hurt her daughter. 'Call me what you like,' she said firmly. If anyone asked questions they would be fobbed off. A muttered word about adoption should do it. More potential lies. Sid sighed.

Sid's wedding day was blessed with sunshine, even if it was a little watery. She would not have noticed if there had been a tropical downpour. She was almost unbearably happy.

Tom's relatives turned up in force as did hers. Each side viewed the other curiously but there was no friction. Mum and the aunties had even spared some rations and Daisy and Sid had baked for hours for the reception. When they weren't baking they were cleaning the big drawing room, putting a lick of paint here and there and, with the aid of Patrick's wood collection, keeping a fire going day and night.

After the brief wedding with a special licence in a register office all the relatives came to Greystone House. Grandma Lacey looked at home in the imposing drawing room. She was seated in a wing-backed chair near the fire, rather like a queen viewing her subjects. Mr and Mrs Barton clearly enjoyed her.

They liked Mattie and her husband and exclaimed over little Elsie who behaved perfectly and admired the new baby. Aunt Jess and Uncle William already knew the Bartons; Grandma Lacey was indignant about that.

Amy skipped about in her lace-trimmed dress (made from a find of turquoise velvet in Mrs Cardell's wardrobe). Her joy shone, her eyes sparkled and everyone, even Grandma Lacey, made a fuss of her.

Mum watched her. 'She's a lovely child, Sid,' she admitted. 'What will become of her?'

'I shall keep her,' said Sid.

'Does Tom want to?'

'Yes.'

Sid's mother was gazing at her in some puzzlement. Her ugly duckling hadn't turned into a swan; but she was certainly different. Not pretty like Audrey or Irene, yet she had an air about her. She owned a grand house, and she had landed a treasure of a husband from a family of real life gentry.

Soon after the wedding Tom had to undergo a strict regime of treatment. He was admitted to a Bristol hospital and Sid was able to visit him every day. Amy was indignant when informed that they didn't allow children into the wards.

'He's my dad!' she exclaimed. 'I'm not allowed to see my dad!' Then with her usual adaptability to any situation she sat down and concentrated hard on drawing pictures for him, colouring them with crayon and writing short, loving messages. Sid watched her, her own love swelling inside her. If the Prossers succeeded in court she could only pray that Amy would be able to take it as bravely as she met everything in her life.

Patrick, who had mostly stayed in hiding on the wedding day, was indignant for her. 'Can't see her dad,' he said. 'It's not right.'

When Sid returned from a hospital visit one afternoon she found a visitor waiting for her.

Daisy met her at the front door. 'Celia Prosser's here.'

Sid was astonished. She had been advised that during the period leading up to the court case the two sides should keep apart.

She went to the sitting room which was hazy with the smoke from Celia's cigarettes. 'What an age you've been,' Celia said without preamble.

'What do you want?'

'Is that the way to treat the bearer of good tidings? Good for you and me, anyway. I never wanted a brat in the house, especially one likely to cause complications, but Grandmother is seething. She hates to be thwarted; she's furious about the money she's wasted on lawyers. And Philip is fit to be tied.'

A small flame of hope flickered in Sid's breast.

'Grandmother has been persuaded that in the present circumstances we would probably lose the case. Courts are reluctant to take children from their mothers and now you have a respectable background to offer her they would probably come down in your favour. The Bartons are a far older family than the Prossers and have an impeccable record of respectability. Your damned KC has been delving and come up with a few peccadilloes committed by Philip and me. Nosy swine!'

Sid sat down hard. 'You're giving up? You are not claiming Amy?'

'You said a mouthful, kid,' said Celia who enjoyed Hollywood gangster films. 'I thought I'd give you the news myself. The whole thing has been such a shocking bore.'

'A bore?' Sid thought of the nights she had lain sleepless with worry. 'What about Philip? What does he say?'

'Don't tell me you care about my dear brother! After the way he behaved to you?'

'You sound as if *you* don't care about him, even after what he's suffered,' said Sid.

'I can't pretend what I don't feel. Oh, I'm sorry for him, but I have never been able to put up with illness. Philip and I have never got on. We had to show some semblance of friendliness or Grandmother might have punished us. The old martinet threatens to reduce our allowances, or even withhold them if she's cross with us.'

Celia's cynicism took Sid's breath away.

'Don't look so shocked. One can't force one's feelings.'

'Is Philip prepared to let Amy go?'

'He has to. Between you and me he only wanted the child as a diversion. And I think he had it in for you and wanted to punish you, though I can't think why. The fact is, my dear brother has always had a grudge against everybody, against life itself. I don't know how Dolores puts up with him. Of course, she's out a lot of the time and his manservant has to bear the brunt. But Dolores takes things calmly. I think she actually cares for him. It's certain that he'll never find a better wife. Not in his condition.'

Celia sounded as bored by her brother's shackled life as she had over Amy. She stubbed out her latest cigarette. 'I'll be going then. I'll see myself out.' Sid remained seated, feeling weak at the knees with relief.

At the door Celia turned. 'I needn't have come in person. There's a solicitor's letter on its way to you. But do you know what? I'm glad you've won. Not only because I didn't want the ordeal of a fight over the brat, with all the aggravation it would have caused, but because you've got guts.'

She was gone before Sid recovered from the shock.

The next hurdle to be tackled was Sid's family. She went first to her mother and explained as calmly as she could about Amy.

'She's yours? *Yours*? I can't believe it! It's shocking! How long ago? Nearly eight years. How did you manage it? Did Mrs Cardell know?'

'She knew and looked after us.'

'Well! Fancy! Thank God you kept it quiet. I can just hear what Grandma and your aunties would have said!'

Her reception of the news was no surprise. 'Have you told Tom?'

'Of course. What a question.'

'Well, I'm not to know, am I? What's he going to do?'

'Adopt Amy.'

'So you won't need to tell people the truth.'

'Not directly, but I won't lie about my daughter any longer.'

Mum sighed and reached for the teapot and poured two cups. 'Your daughter! And that old woman plotted with you. You're full of surprises, aren't you? Well, I shan't say a thing. You must do whatever you think best. You will, anyway, no matter what I say. You always have.'

'Not quite always,' murmured Sid.

'Maybe not, but you're making up for it now.'

Tom gave as much love to Amy as if she had been his own. The child adored him.

Sid seemed to float above solid ground whenever he was near. They had decided to make their home in the old house and Daisy had asked if she might remain as housekeeper with two of her daughters to train as maids. She had taken Sid's place in the kitchen and now it was her turn to pore over the housekeeper's books to learn all she could.

'Won't it be awkward having Daisy there?' asked Mum. 'She calls you by your name.'

'We'll manage,' said Sid.

Mum had begun to make regular visits and she watched the assimilation of Amy into the family. She saw how efficiently Sid ran Greystone House and began to view her daughter with awed respect.

Daisy served a special dinner on the night of Tom's final release from hospital medication. They lingered over coffee and brandy in the small sitting room, revelling in one another's company, looking forward confidently to their future.

Tom raised his glass. 'To Sidonia and Amy Barton.'

'And to Tom Barton,' said Sid, raising her glass.

'To us,' said Tom.

He got up and pulled Sid to her feet. 'Come on, sweetheart. I think it's bedtime.'

'It's only nine-thirty!'

'Time has nothing to do with love,' he said firmly.

Sid found this a most satisfactory statement. Arm in arm, they went upstairs.

A2 27 MAR 1997

10 APR 1997 A2